SHE FELL FOR
THE ONE
VAMPIRE WHO
MAY NOT
HAVE LONG
TO LIVE....

Santa Clara County
LIBRARY

Renewals:
(800) 471-0991
<u>www.sccl.org</u>

Praise for Katie MacAlister's
Dark Ones Novels

Much Ado About Vampires

"A humorous take on the dark and demonic.... Her world building is excellent.... A plot full of surprises.... If you enjoy a fast-paced paranormal romance laced with witty prose and dialogue, you might like to give *Much Ado About Vampires* a try." —*USA Today*

"Once again this author has done a wonderful job. I was sucked into the world of [the] Dark Ones right from the start and was taken on a fantastic ride. This book is full of witty dialogue and great romance, making it one that should not be missed." —Fresh Fiction

In the Company of Vampires

"Katie MacAlister is an excellent writer and never ceases to amaze us with her quick aka wicked wit and amazing romantic tales ... a funny but masterfully written romantic tale with all the paranormal types you could want and more." —Night Owl Romance

"Zany [and] clever." —*Midwest Book Review*

"An excellent read.... Hysterical and surprisingly realistic, considering it includes witches, deities, vampires, and Viking ghosts, *In the Company of Vampires* delivers a great story and excellent characterization." —Fresh Fiction

continued ...

Also by Katie MacAlister

A TALE OF TWO VAMPIRES

A Dark Ones Novel

Katie MacAlister

A SIGNET BOOK

SIGNET
Published by New American Library, a division of
Penguin Group (USA) Inc., 375 Hudson Street,
New York, New York 10014, USA

Penguin Group (Canada), 90 Eglinton Avenue East, Suite 700, Toronto,
Ontario M4P 2Y3, Canada (a division of Pearson Penguin Canada Inc.)
Penguin Books Ltd., 80 Strand, London WC2R 0RL, England
Penguin Ireland, 25 St. Stephen's Green, Dublin 2,
Ireland (a division of Penguin Books Ltd.)
Penguin Group (Australia), 250 Camberwell Road, Camberwell, Victoria 3124,
Australia (a division of Pearson Australia Group Pty. Ltd.)
Penguin Books India Pvt. Ltd., 11 Community Centre, Panchsheel Park,
New Delhi - 110 017, India
Penguin Group (NZ), 67 Apollo Drive, Rosedale, Auckland 0632,
New Zealand (a division of Pearson New Zealand Ltd.)
Penguin Books (South Africa) (Pty.) Ltd., 24 Sturdee Avenue,
Rosebank, Johannesburg 2196, South Africa

Penguin Books Ltd., Registered Offices:
80 Strand, London WC2R 0RL, England

First published by Signet, an imprint of New American Library,
a division of Penguin Group (USA) Inc.

First Printing, September 2012
10 9 8 7 6 5 4 3 2 1

Copyright © Katie MacAlister, 2012

PUBLISHER'S NOTE
This is a work of fiction. Names, characters, places, and incidents either are the product of the author's imagination or are used fictitiously, and any resemblance to actual persons, living or dead, business establishments, events, or locales is entirely coincidental. The publisher does not have any control over and does not assume any responsibility for author or third-party Web sites or their content.

ALWAYS LEARNING   PEARSON

Sometimes in life, you are blessed to find people who make you laugh until you cry (or wheeze until you need your asthma inhaler, whichever comes first). I'm lucky to have Sara Thome and Danny Bates to keep me wheezing and crying with hilarity. And since they will be married a few weeks after this book is published, I'm dedicating it to them in hopes they have long, happy, and dog-hair-riddled lives full of joy.

The Incredible Adventures of Iolanthe Tennyson

July 10

"Nipple tattoo, madame?"

That's how it started, really. It didn't start at the airport, or at Gretl's house, or even the few days I spent sightseeing around St. Andras, the little town in Austria where my cousin Gretl lived. No, it started with an inquiry about nipples, and since I'm determined to set this all down for posterity, I will do my best to record exactly what happened.

It's certainly the oddest thing I've ever lived through, but I probably shouldn't mention that, because according to the creative writing class I took seven years ago, that's considered foreshadowing, and it's a grave sin when trying to explain how events came about. I'll stick to just what happened without the benefit of hindsight from here on out, I promise.

Shoot, now I've forgotten where . . . Oh, the nipple tattoos.

"Er . . ." I blinked in surprise at the polite inquiry

made by a spiky-haired woman in a short Lolita skirt
and a red and white striped vinyl PVC corset that I was
willing to bet made her sweat like crazy. "I don't
think . . . On the nipple? That has to be impossible, not
to mention beyond painful and into the land of down-
right insane."

The woman shrugged, dusting off a black leather
barber's chair with a small cloth. "It's a personal statement that cannot be denied by all who see it. I thought
perhaps since Madame was staring at the photos, Madame might be interested in one for herself." The woman's light gray eyes cast an assessing glance toward my
chest. "Since perhaps Madame feels a need to empha-
size what she has."

"Yes, well, Madame may not have big boobs, but she
isn't into pain at all, especially on her nipples. I wasn't
staring at the photos of your past customers," I added,
avoiding looking at the various shots of newly pierced
and tattooed customers that bedecked one wall of the
small stall. "I was intrigued by that bust you have in the
back. It's a phrenologist's head, isn't it? The kind used
in the last century to illustrate the meaning of the
bumps on people's heads?"

"Yes. It belongs to Justinia, my partner. She is in Salz-
burg tonight, but will return tomorrow if you wish to
have her read your head."

"Actually, I'm a photographer." I held up my small
Nikon. "Amateur, but I hope to take enough photos
while I'm spending the summer here in Austria to start
a new career, and I just love the setting of that phrenologist's head. Would you mind if I took a few pictures
of it?"

She shrugged again, gesturing with a lazy hand at the back of the booth. "As Madame desires."

"Are you guys going to be here for long? The ... uh ... sideshow, I mean?" I asked, taking a few preliminary shots before digging out one of my filters to add a more stark look to the image.

"The GothFaire is not a sideshow. It is a traveling fair featuring feats of magic as well as vendors purveying many curiosities and fantastical services that you will not find anywhere else in the world," the woman answered in a faintly singsong Scandinavian accent. "We are not freaks or desperate attention seekers. We are learned in lore that has long been hidden from common knowledge. We are artisans, dealers in magic, granters of the most unlikely fantasies."

"Wow, all that in one little traveling fair," I murmured as I moved to the side to get another series of shots with a second filter.

"We are unique. Madame will find nothing like us anywhere else in the world. Here are mystics and philosophers, magicians and conjurers of the ethereal."

I had doubts that a tattoo and piercing artist could be described as ethereal, especially when viewed in relation to one's nipples, but kept that thought to myself, instead murmuring inconsequential comments as I satisfied my need to capture on film the fascinating old bust.

"Io? You're not thinking of getting something pierced, are you?"

I turned to smile at the middle-aged woman who stood clutching a plastic carrier bag, her eyes wide and wary. "No, this kind lady was letting me photograph her phrenologist's head."

The spiky-haired vendor eyed first Gretl, my second cousin, whom I'd known since I was a small child, then me. "I can offer a discounted price for more than one tattoo, if Madame's friend would care to join her. I am happy to do a tattoo of a more intimate nature, if that is desired. I am told that my work on labias is unparalleled."

Gretl's eyes widened even more. I took her by the arm and steered her away from the tattoo artist, saying as we left, "I appreciate the offer, but I never jump into something without thinking it through, and that includes tattoos on my naughty parts. Thanks again for letting me have pictures of your partner's head."

"Did you know that woman?" Gretl asked as we moved down the center aisle of the fair. She cast a glance over her shoulder, as if she was worried the tattooist was going to chase us down and force us to get vagina tats.

"Not at all. But she was interesting, don't you think? Well, this whole place is interesting. How did you hear about it?"

"An old friend of mine works here. I went to see if she was here, but her booth was closed. The Wiccan lady next to her told me that she was off shopping, though, and she should be back any time. What would you like to do while we wait for her?" Gretl stopped and looked around.

I looked with her. The GothFaire itself consisted of two rows of booths set up in a U shape and a large main tent standing at the bottom. Flyers rippling in the breeze proclaimed that two bands would be playing later in the evening, but a couple of magic shows were scheduled earlier. I glanced at my watch. "I'd love to see the magic acts, but those don't start for an hour. How about we check out the palm reader? Or they have some sort of aura-photography thing. That might be fun. I wonder what sort of camera tricks they use to give people auras? Maybe I could examine their setup and figure it out."

Gretl laughed and nudged my hand, which was still holding my camera. "Trust you to want to see the photography booth."

"That's why I'm here, after all," I said lightly, gesturing down the length of the fair to where a booth with a giant eyeball was painted on a wooden sign.

"You are here to recover from recent events in your life, nothing more," Gretl said firmly, stopping me when I began to protest. "I would never be able to look myself in the face if I made you work while you were staying with me. You relax. You rest. You get your feet under you again, and then you will return to the States and find yourself a new job—a better one, one that will not have an employer who tries to grope you."

"I could have handled Barry's octopus hands if it had just been that, but when he found out I filed a sexual harassment charge, he cooked a few accounts to make it look like I messed up. Lying, despicable, boob-grabbing bastard." I took a deep breath, reminding myself that I had two and a half long months to get over losing my job and my apartment in the same week. A new home shouldn't be too hard to find, although this time I'd make sure the owner of the building didn't plan on selling it out from underneath all his tenants. "And photography is relaxing to me, Gretl. This is going to be the best summer I've had since . . . well, since the last time I spent the summer with you."

She laughed. "You were sixteen then. Much has changed in St. Andras in that time."

"It still seems to be the same cute little Austrian town to me." I nodded over her head to where a ruined castle perched on a hill. "Picturesque as hell, and so charming I probably won't want to go back home at the end of the summer, just like I didn't when I was sixteen. Have I told you that you're the best cousin ever for inviting me to stay with you?"

"Yes, and I have an ulterior motive, you know," she answered, pushing me along the line of booths. "Now that Anna is married, I have the empty tree."

"Empty nest? Yes, I suppose you do. But it's not like you don't have a lot going on in your life, what with your yoga classes and that program for encouraging new artists that you were telling me about on the way here."

"*Pfft.* I am never too busy for family. Oh, look! Imogen is back. That is my old friend. I have known her for, oh, over thirty years. You will like her—she has a way about her that makes everyone very comfortable. Imogen!"

Gretl hurried forward to where a tall, elegant woman with long curly blond hair was arranging bowls of small polished rocks on a black velvet tablecloth. I followed slowly in order to give Gretl time to greet her friend. The woman turned and Gretl checked for a moment.

"Gretl? Can it be you?" The blonde started toward Gretl with a surprised but welcoming smile.

"Yes, it is me," my cousin answered, her voice sounding

odd. "But you! You have not changed since the last time I saw you more than twelve years ago. How is this? What magical face cream are you using to look so young?"

Imogen laughed, but the lines around her eyes were stark rather than happy. Her complexion was pale, normal for blondes, but it struck me that she was a little too pale, as if she was under a great strain. "It is nothing but genetics, I'm afraid. You, however, look as wonderful as you did when we last met! And you are a grandmother! It must be all those yoga classes about which you wrote to me."

The two ladies hugged, and I was pleased for Gretl's sake to see genuine affection in her friend's blue eyes.

"I do not look even close to wonderful, but I am content as I am," Gretl said as she released Imogen. "Now I must introduce to you my cousin from the States. Iolanthe, this is Imogen Slovik. Iolanthe is staying with me for the summer."

We murmured pleasantries and shook hands. "You are being a tourist?" Imogen asked a few minutes later when she and Gretl had caught up on the most immediate of news. "Are you traveling around Austria, or staying in St. Andras?"

"A little of each. I'm using this break as kind of a working holiday," I said, holding up my camera. "I'm trying to make a start in the photography world, so right now I'm poking around St. Andras looking for interesting locations. Luckily, there's a lot to choose from here."

"There are many lovely sites in this region," Imogen agreed.

I eyed her. There was an air of fragility about her

that intrigued me, and I wondered if there was any way I could capture that on film. She was certainly lovely enough to model, but a sense of tension seemed to wind around her, as if she were only just being kept from fracturing into a million pieces. It prompted me to ask, "Would you . . . This is going to sound awfully presumptuous, but would you be willing to let me take a few pictures of you? I can't pay you, I'm afraid, but I'd be happy to give you copies of any of the prints you want."

Imogen looked startled for a moment before smiling. "How very sweet of you. It's been . . . oh, so long I can't even remember when someone has asked to take my photo. I would be delighted to, although we are only in St. Andras for five days. We are taking a bit of a holiday, you see, and keeping only short hours for the fair until we move on."

"Well . . ." I glanced at the skyline. It was dusk, and a dark purple had started to creep across the sky from the inky black silhouette of the mountains. "I know you're busy tonight with your pretty stone things—"

"Rune stones," she interrupted, touching with reverence a deep purple stone bearing an etched symbol on one side. "I have an affinity for them, although I do occasionally read palms, as well."

"Ah. Rune stones. Interesting."

She flipped a long curl over her shoulder. "Right now Fran is doing palm reading because she and Benedikt are . . . er . . . helping here at the fair. Benedikt is my brother," she added, turning to Gretl. "Do you remember meeting him in Vienna that time in the 1990s?"

Gretl's round face lit up, a faint blush pinkening her

cheeks. "Who could forget him? He was absolutely gorgeous. And he's here?"

"Yes, with Francesca. They were married a few months ago. You'll like Fran—she's very sweet, and she absolutely adores Benedikt, although she teases him mercilessly about the fact that women are prone to swooning over him."

"Wow. He must still be quite the looker. You guys must have some really great genes," I commented before steering the conversation back to where I wanted it. "I know you're busy tonight, but perhaps I could shoot you tomorrow, if you are free."

"Benedikt is very handsome, yes," Imogen answered, ignoring my attempts to steer her. "He resembles our father in that way."

The sense of tension in her increased, and I noticed she glanced over my shoulder, a flicker of pain passing across her face.

"Your father must have been a very handsome man, then," Gretl said with a dreamy look in her eyes that made me want to giggle. "I don't believe you've ever mentioned him before."

"He died when I was twenty-two," Imogen said swiftly, her gaze now on the stones that she stroked with long, sensitive fingers. "He was destroyed by his two half brothers."

"Oh, how horrible!" both Gretl and I said.

"It was very tragic. He inherited our family home, and they obviously coveted that, so they lured him into a forest one summer night and destroyed him." She stopped, obviously hesitant to go on. "It is why I am here, as a matter of fact. The anniversary of his . . .

death . . . is a few days from now. I try to make a pilgrimage to this area whenever I can, to remember happier times."

"I'm so sorry," I said as Gretl murmured sympathetic platitudes. "I should never have brought up the subject of genes."

She sniffed back a few unshed tears. "No, no, I don't mind talking about Papa. Before that horrible night, he was a good man, an excellent father, and I loved him very dearly."

"You must miss him terribly. I assume they caught his killers?"

"They disappeared before they could be tried, unfortunately."

"That's so sad. But I'm sure that wherever your father is, he knows how much you loved him."

She looked up at me, her eyes wide with surprise. "*Wherever* he is?"

I gestured toward the sky. "You know, looking down on you." I had no idea what religion, if any, she subscribed to, so I didn't want to be too specific in my attempt to provide her with a little comfort.

Imogen gave a delicate little shrug, returning her gaze to the stones. "Ah. Yes, I'm sure he does. At one time I had hope that Ben and I would find Nikola's brothers, but we were unable to do so."

"Nikola is your father?" I couldn't help but ask. I didn't want to be nosy, but my curiosity got the better of me, and she honestly didn't seem to mind talking about him, so long as we kept off the subject of his manner of death.

"Yes." She set down a stone she was stroking and

looked up again at us, a little smile lighting her pure blue eyes. "Nikola Czerny, the fifth Baron von Shey."

I blinked at her. "Your dad was a baron? A real baron? Does that make you anything?"

She laughed aloud, patting my arm for a second. "Yes, it makes me a woman."

"Oh, I'm sorry," I apologized again, blushing a little at the stupidity that had emerged from my mouth. "You have to excuse me—I'm an idiot. But I've never met someone who was from the aristocracy before."

"Most of the nobility lost their power in Austria almost a hundred years ago," Gretl said gently, giving me a little squeeze on my arm. "Although I, too, did not know that Imogen's father was a baron. The title passed to Ben?"

"No, it didn't," Imogen said, her expression darkening for a moment before she gave us both a bright smile. "It was all a long time ago, and we have much more pleasant things to speak of, yes?"

It was a not very subtle hint that she was through talking about the subject.

"Of course," Gretl said soothingly, and made a date for the next afternoon to have tea and pastries.

"I hate to bother you if you're busy," I said, not sure whether she had responded to my request for a photo session because she was polite or because she really wanted me to take some pictures of her. "If so, then I will totally understand. But if not, I'm sure we can find somewhere locally that would make a good backdrop."

Imogen looked up with a genuine smile. "No, I am not too busy. I would love to be your model."

"Oh, you must go to Andras Castle!" Gretl said, clasping my arm. "It would make a lovely setting—"

"No," Imogen said quickly, her expression as brittle as ice. I blinked at the change in her demeanor. She suddenly relaxed and gave a forced little laugh. "I'm sorry. You must think me very odd, but Andras Castle holds . . . bad memories for me. I would prefer not to go there again."

"Of course we won't use it," I reassured her, curious at such a strong reaction to a ruined castle. Perhaps she'd been frightened there—when Gretl had told me about the ruins, she said that it had a bad reputation by the locals as being unpleasant to visit. "There are lots of other places around here we could use."

"The rose gardens?" Gretl suggested. "The town hall? The church? It is quite old."

"Mmm . . ." I scrunched up my nose as I thought. "To be honest, I'd like to try something a little different as a backdrop for Imogen. Something to contrast with all that fair delicacy."

Imogen laughed, her expression once again changing like quicksilver. "I'm sure you meant that as a compliment, but I assure you, I am anything but delicate. Fair, yes—I got that from my mother. But delicate? No."

"Appearances are often deceiving," I agreed. "I think I'd like to see you set against somewhere dark and gritty. That would make for some wonderful depth to the picture."

"As you like. You're the expert," Imogen said with another of her little shrugs.

"I'm far from that, but I see you . . ." I narrowed my

eyes and thought about an image of Imogen against the ruined castle. That would have been ideal, but there were other places that I could use. "Oh! Gretl told me about this haunted forest near here—"

"No!" Imogen all but squawked, drawing attention from the people moving past us. She shot them a reassuring smile before turning it on me. "I'm so sorry. You must think me terribly emotional, but if you are talking about the Zauberwald, the woods near Andras Castle, then I must again say no. It is not a good place, that forest. I will not step foot in it again."

"I didn't mean to suggest somewhere that would make you feel uncomfortable." I thought for a moment. "I don't really know many places around here, but surely there must be some other location we can use that would give the same sense of—oh, I don't know—something otherworldly."

"Otherworldly? Yes, of course I can do that." She shot me a startled glance that quickly turned speculative, then amused, as if we shared a secret, something that struck me as hugely odd. I had only just met her— how could we share a secret? When Gretl turned to greet an acquaintance who had called her name, Imogen leaned over to me, saying with a little nod at Gretl's back, "I had no idea you were not mundane."

"Er . . ." Mundane? Was she making a dig at Gretl? I bristled righteously in defense of a much-loved cousin. "I've always thought of myself as something . . . different, but just because Gretl chose a more traditional path in life doesn't mean she's not a wonderful person."

"Of course she's wonderful. She's been my friend for

many years." Imogen smiled and squeezed my arm briefly. "And we all feel *different* at some time or other, don't we? At least until we settle in with our own kind. But who exactly are you? I realize it is rude to just come right out and ask you, but I'm sure you do not wish to speak of your true nature in front of dear Gretl."

I blinked at her, once again taken aback and unsure of how to respond, but luckily Gretl finished her chat and turned back to us, so I was content to simply smile in answer to Imogen's wink, and made a mental note to ask Gretl or her eldest daughter, Erica, to accompany me on the photo shoot. It was becoming clear that Imogen was a few apples shy of spiced cider.

"Oh, there are Benedikt and Fran. Come. I must introduce you both to them. Benedikt will be delighted to see you again, Gretl."

I followed as Imogen bustled off with Gretl in tow over to where a tall man with shoulder-length black hair stood with a woman who was almost as tall as he was. The woman, who faced me, looked to be in her early twenties.

"Well, now, that's interesting," I murmured, eyeing the woman named Fran. No matter how good Imogen looked, she had to be nearing fifty for Gretl to have known her for thirty years. Which meant her brother was probably in his forties or fifties, too, or he was a whole lot younger than Imogen. "Even if there is a big age difference," I said as I strolled toward them, "he would be close to my age."

And yet his wife was probably twenty-two or twenty-three. I glanced at Gretl as the couple stepped forward to greet her. A puzzled frown pulled her brows together for an instant before she smiled, quickly returning to her usual charming self. When the man turned to greet me, I saw why Gretl had frowned. I stared at him for a moment, unable to believe what I was seeing. He was in his mid- to late twenties, at least ten years younger than me, which meant Imogen was old enough to be his mother. Not an unknown situation, but not a common one, either. I realized that everyone was staring at me as I gawked so obviously at Imogen's handsome, much, much younger brother, and I pulled my wits together.

"Sorry," I murmured, shaking first his hand, then Fran's. She gave me an amused glance before leaning into her husband, her arm around his waist in a possessive move that I'd have had to be blind to miss.

I chuckled to myself, wanting to assure her that I might be single and not averse to finding a man, but I wasn't about to stoop to husband stealing and cradle robbing. "It's a pleasure to meet you both," I murmured.

"Iolanthe wishes to take my picture tomorrow," Imogen told her brother. "She is a photographer. She wishes to take me somewhere *otherworldly*."

The emphasis Imogen put on the word seemed to have some meaning for them, because they both raised their eyebrows for a few seconds. Ben slid a gaze to Gretl before returning it to me, saying in a low voice that couldn't have been heard by anyone but his wife, "Are you with the Court of Divine Blood? I don't recognize what you are, but I'm not very familiar with members of the Court."

"I'm a woman," I answered, ironically echoing Imogen's words as I moved a few steps away from him. Clearly there was some sort of mental instability in Imogen's family.

"Yes, of course you are," Fran said with a comforting smile that I didn't for one minute buy. Ben turned to answer a question Gretl asked him, leaving Fran chatting with me in a low voice. "What Ben meant was what *are* you? You're not a therion or a Guardian or a Summoner. I've seen those, and you don't look like them."

"I used to be an accountant," I told her, feeling that diplomacy was going to be my best bet if I wanted to get pictures of Imogen. It wouldn't do to offend any of Imogen's family by calling them crackpots. "But Barry, my boss, kept hitting on me, and when I tried to turn him in, he got me fired. Illegal and reprehensible, but true."

"No, I meant—" Fran stopped talking when Gretl turned back to us.

"Io, you don't mind that Imogen has asked me to sit with her for an hour or so while she reads the rune stones, do you?"

"Not at all. I'll just wander around the fair and see the sights."

"We'll take care of your cousin," Fran told Gretl as we moved off. I couldn't help but notice that Fran wore a pair of long black lace gloves that disappeared into her shirt cuffs. "We'll show you around and introduce you to all the people who work here. You might find someone you'd like to photograph in addition to Imogen, you know. There are lots of interesting folks. My mother is— Ratsbane! What's he doing here?"

Fran had been steering me down the center aisle

when she suddenly froze and glared to the side, where a blond man with a short goatee was strolling toward us. The man also froze when he caught sight of us, an expression of joy on his face as he waved an arm in the air and bellowed, "Goddess Fran! We have returned!"

"I thought you said they'd gone back to Valhalla?" Ben asked in a tight, low voice.

"They had. Dammit, they promised me they wouldn't come back until I asked for their help again. . . . Excuse me a minute, Io. I have to deal with an old . . . *friend*. . . ."

She hurried off to the blond man, who was joined by a second man, who also enveloped Fran in a bear hug.

"Oh, Christ, not both of them," Ben said, rubbing a hand over his eyes.

"You don't have to escort me around the fair, you know. I'm quite capable of trotting around by myself."

"I'd much rather show you around than deal with those two lunatics," he said, nodding toward the nearest booth. "What would you like to see first? I can't vouch for the tattooing, but the demonologist is a friend of mine and can be quite interesting if he's holding a private group session."

"I'm fine just people watching, if truth be told," I said politely, the hairs on the back of my neck standing on end. The words "demonologist" and "private session" just seemed like an incredibly bad juxtaposition. "People are so fascinating if you have the time to really study them."

"True words. I won't ask you any more about yourself, since I'm sure Imogen will pump you for all the information you're willing to divulge," he said, laughter rich in his voice as we moved on at a slow amble. "My sister appreciates people watching, as well. Some might call her nosy, but in reality she just likes mortals."

Keep in the open, I told myself. *Stay around other people. Do not, under any circumstances, go off anywhere alone with this bizarre man.* "I really am not all that interesting, I assure you. I do feel bad about my horrible foot-in-mouth disease with Imogen, though."

He paused in front of a booth dedicated to personal time travel, shooting me a curious look. "Pardon?"

I made a little face. "I said I wanted to take photos of Imogen at the place your father met his end."

"My father?" Ben blinked. "My father is in South America."

"Oh, I'm sorry." A blush warmed my face as I realized that once again I'd verbally embarrassed myself. "I thought you and Imogen had the same father."

"We do. He's in Brazil, I believe. Or Argentina. Somewhere with lots of nearly naked young women and a high level of debauchery."

I stared at him in incomprehension. "He's not dead?"

"No." He leaned in close and said in a low voice, "My father is a Dark One. He can't die unless someone goes to quite a bit of trouble, and I can assure you that no one has done that in several centuries."

"Several centuries," I repeated, just as if that weren't the least bit startling, although, of course, my brain was screaming at me to run far, far away from the crazy man.

And then the thought hit me—what if Imogen and her brother were having me on? What if they were teasing me, the ignorant little American tourist? What if they were waiting to see me freak out, whereupon they'd all have a good giggle at my expense?

The bastards. I wouldn't give them the pleasure!

"Well . . . three hundred? That seems about right. I think it was in 1708 that he flipped out. So three hundred and a bit."

I may not have had a lot of pride left that wasn't in tatters after the smear campaign by Barry of the Many Hands, but what I did have I gathered around me. "Oh, *that* kind of Dark One. I thought you meant the . . . um . . . non-three-hundred-year type."

He looked at me as if potatoes had started a cabaret act on my head. "The what?"

"You know, the kind that aren't around for three hundred years."

I think the potatoes may have begun a trapeze act, because the look he gave me was one of utter incredulity. That killed my idea of his pulling my leg—people who were teasing you seldom bore that sort of expression when you sussed out what it was they were doing.

"You did say three hundred years, didn't you?" I asked, suddenly worried that I misheard him. Maybe he had every right to look at me as if I was the odd one.

"Yes." He continued to eye me. "My father is actually older than three hundred years. He's . . . let me see. I'm three hundred and nineteen, which means he must be around three hundred and sixty. Or seventy. Somewhere around that age."

What do you say to a man who claims he's over three hundred years old? I don't know what you would say, but I decided that the best thing to do was to agree with him and try to get rid of him.

"Just so. Those are my favorite kind of Black Ones."

"Dark Ones."

"Sorry." I cleared my throat and tried to sidle away. "I think I'll just—"

Ben evidently wasn't having any of it. He followed after me, giving me a curious look. "There are only two types of Dark Ones, Io—redeemed and unredeemed. My father is the latter, naturally."

"Naturally." I wondered whether if I dashed into the big main tent, he would come after me, or whether I could lose him in the crowd that was starting to gather.

"Although he did love my mother. In his own fashion. It was only afterward that he lost the ability to feel any such emotions."

"Well, you know how it is with Dark Dudes—that happens."

He stopped me by taking hold of my arm, swinging me around to face him, his eyes narrowed on my face. "You *do* know what a Dark One is, don't you?"

"Of course," I lied, giving him what I hoped was a serene smile. "They're . . . um . . . They live a long time, and they . . . uh . . . hang out at fairs, and . . . er . . . do other stuff like . . . urm . . ."

"Being vampires," a female voice said behind me.

Eyes wide with disbelief, I spun around to find Fran smiling over my shoulder at Ben.

"Sexy, sexy vampires," she added with a little sigh of pleasure.

Panic hit me then, hard and hot in my gut. I looked around wildly for an escape, throwing to the wind my desire to photograph Imogen. There was no way on this green earth I was going to spend any more time with people who thought they were three-hundred-year-old vampires!

"Io, let me introduce you to my ghosts. They're Vikings, and although they're supposed to be in Valhalla, they claim they were sent back to help Ben and me with a little project—"

I didn't wait for Fran to finish her sentence. I bolted, wanting nothing more than to escape the insanity that seemed to surround me.

The Incredible Adventures of Iolanthe Tennyson

July 11

"**A**re you sure you're all right on your own, Io?" Gretl watched me for a few seconds, her brow furrowed. "You're not feeling ill, are you?"

I set my small camera bag on a smooth boulder just off the shoulder of the road, giving her a reassuring smile. "I'm not sick, and I'll be fine. I was just tired last night at the GothFaire, nothing more, but I'm right as rain this morning."

She bit her lower lip, still eyeing me. "You were so distraught last night, insisting on returning home early. . . . If Imogen's brother said something to upset you—"

Like he was a three-hundred-year-old vampire? Oh yeah, that would do the job, but I would never admit to Gretl that her friends were wack jobs, since they obviously acted perfectly normal around her. I rubbed my bare arms against the chill of the memory of the previous evening. "I told you that he didn't do anything. I was just having low biorhythms or something. I needed some rest, and as you can see, I'm peachy keen today."

"Mmm." She glanced over my shoulder to the woods beyond, shivering a little at the sight. "Why you wish to come here to photograph when you know the area is said to be haunted . . . and it is where Imogen said her father was killed. I think maybe you should find somewhere else to take your photos."

"Imogen may not want to be here—not that I blame her if it has such a bad connotation for her family—but there's no reason I can't take some pictures of the woods."

I turned to consider the dense growth of trees. I knew from perusing Gretl's map of the area that the forest was fairly small, probably under ten acres, and shaped roughly like an oval, lying between the town of St. Andras to the south, the castle to the north, and, to the east, a mountainous rise that curved to the neighboring town. To the west, the trees petered out, the land sloping down into the valley where the GothFaire was currently camped.

"I suppose not," Gretl said slowly, doubt evident on her face. "Although it's so spooky. I would never go in there."

I had to admit, there was something about the woods that raised the fine hairs on the back of my neck, a sense of a place that wasn't quite in sync with the rest of the world. "I think it's beautiful. I love fir and pine trees so densely packed together that you can see the sunlight streaming through their branches. That's an awesome look. See over there, just past that boulder shaped like a sleeping cat—see how the sunlight pours through the tree like honey? And those vines, whatever they are, are like streamers of green and brown tangled through the lower branches of the trees, wafting down to the ground where they gently wave." I took a couple of steps forward, intrigued by the woods, studying the scene with a critical eye for composition, and finding nothing at fault. "It's the breeze that moves the vines, but honestly, Gretl, can't you imagine them as some form of sentient life, beckoning the unwary traveler into their midst, pulling you deeper and deeper into the cool, dark, mysterious heart of the woods until you find—"

"Find what?" Gretl's voice was at the same time hushed and high-pitched, but it was enough to break the spell that had gripped me.

A little shiver ran down my back at the thought of what lay in the heart of the forest. Then with a mental shake of my head at such fanciful thoughts I turned back to my cousin with an apologetic smile. "More woods, no doubt. I'm sorry if I spooked you. I'm normally a very feet-on-the-ground sort of person, but there's just something about those woods that makes me go emo."

"Emo?" She shivered and rubbed her arms again. "Emotional?"

"Yes."

"I don't blame you. I don't like the woods, Io. They are bad, and I do not like you spending the day there. It is unnatural."

"Ah, but don't you see, Gretl—it's just that unnatural sense of an otherworld that I'm seeking for my photos. Can't you envision a shot of Imogen set against it as a background? A little Photoshop magic, and voilà, I'll have a killer series of pictures that I just bet I can sell. Or at the very least, add to my portfolio."

"But you'll be all alone in there." Her brows were pulled together in worry as I collected my bag from the rock, removing from it my camera, which I slung around my neck on its strap. "Aren't you afraid?"

"Me? No, I'm a curious little kitty. I like to poke around mysterious sorts of places. Besides . . ." I pulled from the bag a small canister the size of the palm of my hand. "I have your pepper spray, so should there be any weirdos camping out in the forest who feel like attacking me, I'll be set. OK?"

"I don't like it," she repeated, shaking her head.

"I know, but just wait until you see the pictures. They'll knock your socks off." I glanced at my watch. "How about you pick me up at six? Will your book group be done by then?"

"Yes, six will be fine. Io, be careful."

"Promise! Nothing will happen except I'll spend the day in the spooky woods getting bit by mosquitoes and taking tons of fabulously moody shots."

"I hope that is *all* you are bitten by," she said darkly, but, to my relief, got into her compact—but expensive— car and started it up.

I waved, straightened my navy and white print sundress, hoisted the camera bag, and with a deep breath started for the woods, musing on her words. "She hopes that's all I'm bitten by?" I shook my head as I left the warm sunshine and entered the coolness of the shade cast by the dense growth of trees, the pines filling the air with scent, while the sound of discarded needles crunched underfoot. "Like what else would bite me? A vampire? Ha! I laugh at that."

I did laugh, but it came out strained and curiously flat, as if I was trying to convince myself.

"I am so not afraid of trees and vines and the weird trick of light that makes it look like there are little sparkles of things floating in the air around here. It's just a small wood, nothing more."

The words were brave, but the sensation of closeness seemed to wrap around me, almost like an embrace, leaving the everyday sounds—the noise of cars traveling on the road, the occasional airplane droning high overhead—muffled and distant.

"It's just muffled by the trees," I told myself as I pushed aside a long tendril of vine to march resolutely toward a particularly bright spot where light streamed through the branches. "Trees do that to things. Even the normal stuff like birds and insects get damped down by the—" I stopped as I listened intently for a few seconds.

There was no birdsong, no whine of insects. There was no noise whatsoever except the muted rustle of the vines as they rubbed on the branches.

Just like they were alive and reaching for me.

"It's all that talk of vampires and Viking ghosts and haunted forests. That's what's making you scare the bejeepers out of yourself," I said with a nervous laugh, trying hard to shake off the feeling that everything around me was aware that I was in its midst. "You're not in a Tolkien book, Io, and there are no Ents around here to scare the snot out of you, so just mellow out and get down to business, or you'll have to explain to Gretl why you spent the entire day sitting on the rock next to the road because you scared yourself."

That little pep talk did the trick—mostly—and with a squaring of my shoulders, I walked resolutely toward the spot I wanted, and spent the next few hours snapping photos of it, and various other locations. There was a particularly magnificent outcropping of rock that rose some twelve feet in the air, almost like it was part of the ruined castle to the north, all covered in ferns and creepers, surrounded by budding little pine trees. I shot it from all angles, imagining in my head the composition of a series of pictures with Imogen set against it.

"This is going to be great," I said quietly to myself as I pushed deeper into the woods. The sunshine was less plentiful here, since the trees fought for space, their branches tangled and twisted together, making an effective fir canopy. The air was cooler, as well, and sharp with the scent of the trees and earth, enough that it made me shiver a little as I skirted another large boulder. Although I continued to speak aloud, more to bolster my own spirits than because I was of the habit of doing so, my voice had taken on a hushed quality normally confined to places such as churches or graveyards. "I can't wait to get back to my laptop and see how they turned—whoa. What the heck is that?"

I plucked from my arm a vine that had somehow snagged me, and I slid between it and a massive pine tree to stop and squint at the object in the center of a small clearing about thirty feet in width. The ground rose slightly to the center, where a sort of cloud seemed to hang, slowly twisting and turning upon itself.

"Well, that's not something you see every day," I

said slowly, and shuffled forward a few feet to get a better look at it. It still looked like a cloud, faintly bluish black in color, just lingering over the spot at the top of the little rise. "How on earth . . . ? Is there, like, a hot spring or something beneath here?"

There didn't seem to be anything dangerous about the cloud, so with a glance around the clearing, I took a few shots of it from three different angles before approaching it, holding out my hand to feel any steam that might be leaking through a crack above a hot spring. My fingers brushed the edge of the cloud, making them tingle.

"That is just the strangest thing. . . ." I held the camera to my eye and focused on one section of the cloud. It wasn't completely opaque, but the way it gently moved around on itself was not quite . . . well, normal. I reached out to touch it again. It wasn't hot at all, and studying the ground, I found no signs of disturbance, which let out my spring theory. I waved a hand through the cloud, swishing it around vigorously to see if it would dissipate.

Tendrils of the cloud broke off and evaporated into nothing, but the rest seemed to fill in the part that had been removed.

"*National Geographic*, here I come," I said, moving in a complete circle around it, photographing as I did so. "They're guaranteed to want these pictures, and even if it's just some sort of swamp gas—on the side of a mountain, which is really weird if you ask me—the results will be completely spectacular."

A thought struck me then—perhaps this was why the locals considered the area haunted? I lowered my camera and eyed the cloud with speculation.

"It certainly is a strange phenomenon, and I suppose if one was superstitious or the least bit prone to being weirded out by things, it would be possible to imagine that you are a ghost. But you're not a ghost. You're nothing but a cloud," I told the strange anomaly, moving closer to it in order to stick my arm entirely through it. "I wonder if I can get a picture of just my arm coming through the other side?" I adjusted the focus and leaned to the side to do just that, but at that moment, the ground beneath my feet seemed to shift, toppling me forward.

I shrieked and threw out my hands to catch myself before hitting the ground, swearing even as I did so when my camera flew out of my hands, leaving me to be completely swallowed up by an inky abyss.

Nothing surrounded me. At least, that's what it seemed like when I regained consciousness. I sat up, aware of throbbing in my head and mouth.

"Ow," I mumbled, sitting on my heels as I felt my mouth, pulling away my fingers to see if it was bleeding.

I couldn't see them to tell if I had drawn blood. At that moment I realized that the visual fuzziness had nothing to do with me waking up, and everything to do with the fact that night had suddenly fallen. Right smack-dab in the middle of the day. I looked up to where stars glittered overhead with a cold silver blue light. "Holy bizarre-o-rama, Batman," I said slowly, letting my gaze drop back down to the trees surrounding the little clearing.

The wind rustled through them, raising goose bumps along my bare arms, and sending a shiver skittering down my back. Ebony fingers stretched toward me, seeming to shimmer in the moonlight. I stood up slowly, feeling as if I'd stepped through the looking glass into another world. "Only this isn't another world," I said aloud, my voice piercing the velvety quiet of the night. "Everything is the same, except it's night. I must have hit my head and passed out. Oh, Gretl will be insane with worry. . . ." I spun around to find my camera bag, which held my cell phone and wallet, but the move was a bit too much for my still-dizzy brain. I staggered backward and tripped over a small rock, landing on my behind.

"Whoa. OK. Slowly this time." I waited until the world stopped spinning and got to my feet again, brushing off my dress before carefully surveying what I could of the immediate area.

There was nothing but grass, dirt, pine needles, and the swirly bit of cloud that was now almost invisible in the darkness. "It has to be here. I set it down right before I started taking pictures." I tentatively felt around the ground. There was enough light from the moon to make out basic shapes, but nothing in the immediate area even remotely resembled a camera bag, or my camera.

"Of all the . . . someone must have stolen it while I was passed out!" Indignation filled me at such a thought, and gave me the spurt of adrenaline I needed to get moving. I was through the forest and heading for the road before I had the bulk of rude things I wanted to say worked out of my system. "And so help me, if I ever catch the person who left me unconscious in the middle of the woods, they'll be one sad little panda. Hey. What happened to the road?"

The pale silvery blue light of the moon made the grass verge appear sooty. I glared at the road. "I don't remember you being a dirt road. I remember you being a normal paved road. What the hell is going on?"

Gingerly, I felt my head, braced for some sort of wound that would indicate I had hit it when I had fallen, but there was nothing there but normal, undamaged head. I took a deep, deep breath and, with only a few minor muttered imprecations, turned to the left and started walking down the (now dirt) road that wound down the hill and led to the town in the valley below.

I was on a flattish stretch that curved through some forest—not the haunted one—when I heard the dull rumble of thunder. "Oh, great, this is just what I need—rain while I have to walk the three miles into town. Someone really does not like me today."

I increased my pace, hoping against hope that I'd make it at least into town before the rain hit, muttering to myself about my spate of bad luck of late, and why that needed to change immediately. The sound of the thunder increased.

"Screw this," I snarled, and sprinted down the road, bits of dirt worming their way into my sandals, grinding painfully against my soles. Despite the slight decline of the road, I ran like crazy, my eyes on the lights of the town just visible in the valley below. The road hairpinned back and forth up the side of the mountain, however, and just as I was contemplating taking a straight route across a rocky bit of land that dropped down to the stretch of road below, the devil rose up out of the darkness, and ran me over.

12 July 1703

"You're sure you do not wish to spend the night, Gnädiger Herr?"

The woman's voice was as smooth as the pearly white skin that he had moments ago been caressing with his mouth and tongue. Nikola gave the invitation serious consideration for a few seconds, aware that this particular pigeon could be his with just a nod of his head, but despite the rather insistent urges of his body, he declined.

"Another time, my sweet." He dropped a few coins onto the table next to where the innkeeper's wife sat in boneless grace, and he worried for a little moment that he had taken too much of her blood. But one look at the sultry eyes with their obvious invitation reassured him that the woman was under the influence of the peculiar form of bloodlust common to his donors, rather than the loss of blood itself.

With a little bow, he strolled out of the inn, giving his

waiting coachman orders to return home. His daughter would be home awaiting him, no doubt, and as his journey from Heidelberg had been delayed by bad weather, she would be worrying. Imogen was a worrier, he mused as the carriage lurched forward in the cooling night air. She got that from her mother.

Pain spiked through him at the memory of Margaret, pain and guilt that he hadn't loved her as she had deserved, and certainly not to the depth with which she had worshipped him. And that irritated him, for Margaret had been a gentle, loving woman who had spent the last twenty-three years of her life attending to his every need.

"Women," he muttered to himself, staring blindly out into the night as the carriage left the town and began the long, winding climb to Andras Castle. "They insist on being loving and kind and caring, and why do they do that? To make a man feel guilty, that's why. And then they lure innocent men who are busy with important scientific research into impregnating them, and then said busy men end up caring about said spawn. And these ladies smell good, too. Deliberately. The wenches."

Nikola nursed his sense of injustice as long as he could—about ten minutes—but even he knew it was a foolish attempt to avoid the truth: He had honored Margaret as best he could, but it wasn't what she was due. And now she had been dead seven years, and their youngest child, his son, his Benedikt, was off to university in Heidelberg. Margaret would be pleased by that. She had been the daughter of a cobbler, and had never imagined herself catching the local baron's eye, let alone being his wife and bearing him children.

"And the truth is that I would never have married her except for the curse." Saying the words aloud seemed to make the guilt ease a little, as if acknowledging it took away some of its power. "I could not love her, but I gave her my name, position, and wealth."

But not your heart, a tiny little voice pointed out. *You gave her everything but your heart.*

"I did the best I could," he argued with the voice, shifting uncomfortably. Why the hell did he always end up having these arguments with himself? Did other people do such? Or was it something particular to his nature? He made a mental note to ask Imogen if she regularly held mental debates with herself, or if it was something that came with the curse. "I gave her all I had."

That lie stung him even as the words passed his lips, and he slumped back against the cushioned seat, wondering why his conscience had chosen this moment to flagellate him. "It's not as if I can change anything. It's not as if I could go back in time and—"

A flash of white caught his peripheral vision just a scant second before the carriage rocked, and the coachman shouted angrily.

"What the devil is going on?" Nikola was out of the carriage when it lurched to a stop, his gaze, always good at night, immediately catching sight of a body lying to the side of the road.

"'Tis a woman, Master Nicky. She was suddenly right out in front of me, and ran right into Heinrich."

Old Ted, the coachman, slid down out of his seat with an audible grunt of pain, hobbling over to where Nikola crouched over the body of the woman. "Be she dead, do ye think?"

Nikola placed a hand on her neck. Her pulse was a bit fast, but present. "No. Just stunned. Let's roll her over to see if she's injured."

"I'll get the lantern," Ted said, limping heavily to the carriage to lift off a hook one of the lamps that illuminated the road before them. The light bobbed and jerked as he returned, but Nikola didn't need its yellow glow to see that there were no signs of blood or obvious injury on the woman who had run so heedlessly into his horse.

"It's just like women," he said with a glower at the form lying before him. "Always doing things like running headlong into a man's carriage without the least thought of the damage they could do to a valuable horse."

"Aye, that they are," Old Ted agreed, spitting to the side as he considered the body of the woman. "Looks like a proper hoor, she does, too."

"Hoor?" Nikola was momentarily distracted from the fresh injustice that had been brought into his life by this heedless woman. He cast his mind around his knowledge of the English language, which was excellent given that he had spent several years of his youth in England. It was in that country that he had first encountered Ted.

"Aye, Master Nicky, a hoor. Doxy. Woman who ain't no better than she should be."

Nikola looked over the woman with a critical eye. "She doesn't appear to be a prostitute."

"She's runnin' around in naught but her underbits. That's the sign of a right hoor, that is. No proper woman'd be scamperin' down the road in her chemise, now, would she?"

"An excellent point, and one I can't dispute. She is no doubt a whore, and best left to her own."

Carefully, he gathered her up in his arms and stood, surprised to find that not only did the woman feel exceptionally good pressed against him, but she smelled wonderful, as well. He closed his eyes for a moment, breathing deeply to capture the scent. It danced elusively on the edge of his awareness, something that was vaguely floral, but not at all like the scents used by the women with whom he'd been familiar. It was earthy, and yet delicate, intriguing and mysterious.

"I don't like mystery," he told the unconscious female.

"That's right, ye don't. And don't ye be having nothin' to do with the hoor, now, Master Nick. I'll just move her to the side of the road and we'll be on our way home."

"It's certainly what she deserves, scaring poor Heinrich like that." Nikola wondered who the woman was, and what she was doing running down the road clad in a flimsy garment.

The bay, one of the two horses harnessed to the carriage, tossed his head up and down, and whinnied his agreement, pawing the ground to add a further comment on the travesty that had been done to him. His nearly hairless stump of a tail twitched in aggravation. Lucy, the one-eared mare next to him, leaned over and tried to bite him. Heinrich bared his teeth in return.

"Madame. I would have your name so that I might know who to send the bill to should Heinrich prove to be injured." Nikola gave the limp body in his arms a little shake to wake her up, but she simply lolled there, warm and soft and smelling of things that made him feel too warm for his wool coat, not to mention the fact that his breeches had suddenly grown two sizes too small. His gaze traced down the soft swell of her bare arms up to lightly freckled rounded shoulders, and even more rounded breasts that were just barely visible at the square neckline of her chemise. He wondered what it would feel like to touch her arms, to sweep his hands along the delicate lines of her shoulders and neck, to dip his head down into the valley between her breasts and taste—

"Just you leave her on the grass." Ted's voice interrupted his thoughts. Nikola tore his gaze from the woman to see his coachman hobble over to the edge of the road, gesturing at a spot suitable for the removal of whores from the road. "Her people will find her sooner or later."

"I certainly have no need for a stray woman, let alone one of such dubious background," Nikola agreed, and strode over to the carriage, gently placing her on the seat. He pulled down a small footstool and placed it next to the coachman's box. "Let us go home quickly, Ted, before Heinrich is forced to suffer any more indignities."

Ted sighed as he limped over to the carriage, but said nothing when Nikola held out an arm, instead grasping the carriage rail with one hand while stepping up onto the footstool, then more or less pulling himself into the coachman's seat.

Nikola tucked the footstool away again, and swung himself lightly into the carriage. As he closed the door, he heard a muttered, "So it's going to be like that, is it?"

"I can do without the jaded comments. I'm quite likely to find myself no longer in need of your services should they continue," Nikola called loudly, tucking the carriage blanket around the still-unconscious woman.

"And just what will the young lady say about you bringin' home a hoor? That's what I'd like to know," Ted yelled back, clucking to the horses to get them started.

Nikola was careful to brace the woman as the carriage lurched forward again, finally leaning back against the cushions when he was sure she would not roll off the seat. "I am master in my own house, and none would dare gainsay me. Imogen does what I tell her."

He could have sworn that a disbelieving snort was the answer to that statement, but it could well have been Heinrich, so he let it pass without comment. Instead, he spent the rest of the ride home alternately fighting the need to slide down the blanket so he could stroke that luminous, soft skin, and worrying about just how he was going to explain the strange woman to his daughter.

"Papa!"

Imogen was at the entrance to the large dwelling he called home when the carriage finally rolled to a stop outside the massive oak double doors. It might be a run-down, ramshackle sort of castle, but it was still his, and he loved every crumbling stone, every rotted board, every grimy window of it. Wrapped in a large woolen shawl, Imogen stood alongside a small group of servants, several of whom held torches. The smile on his daughter's face warmed something cold and tight inside him. His little Imogen, now a woman grown, but still his, and in the very likeness of her mother with soft blue eyes, and golden hair so bright it all but glowed.

Odd how he used to think that blondes were the epitome of beauty in a woman. He realized with a start that now he had a preference for brunettes, ones with freckled skin that seemed to beckon to him.

"I was worried that you had an accident," Imogen said, coming forward when the footman opened the carriage door with powdery flourish. "I thought you would be home three days ago."

Nikola held out his arms for her, suffering her to hug him, giving her a squeeze and kiss on the forehead in return. Like her mother, Imogen was an emotional sort of woman, not at all the clearheaded, logical beings that he and Benedikt were. Odd how families worked that way. "I was delayed by the rains. You look peaked. Are you unwell? Have you been eating enough? Frau Leiven! Why is my daughter as pale as the moon?"

Imogen laughed as he bellowed at the short woman who was as round as she was tall, her spherical self topped with a huge mound of fat sausage curls. The woman toddled forward, her hands twisting around themselves. She made a bobbing gesture that passed for a curtsy. "The Fräulein is very well, Baron, very well indeed. I have seen to it that she has eaten plentiful meals, and she has slept without interruption, and has indeed been most studious during your absence."

"She is as pale as a ghost!" he said sternly, waving a hand toward Imogen, now giggling in a most inane fashion. "I did not employ you to ignore my daughter when I am away from home, madame. If you wish to keep your position, you will see to it that my orders are carried out to the fullest extent."

"You would not . . . you could not be so cruel as to cast me from your very fireside?" Frau Leiven clutched at her throat, her eyes huge with horror. "Please, my lord, I am but a poor widow with no family who will take me in!"

Imogen rolled her eyes and put an arm around the rotund woman. "Papa, you're scaring poor Anna. Pay him no heed, my dear."

"I shall perish in the cold!" the woman wailed.

Nikola sighed to himself.

"I am too old to start again with a young child! Oh, please, please, Fräulein Imogen, do not let your father do this terrible thing and cast me out to the wolves!"

"He's not going to do anything of the sort, Anna. He doesn't mean a word of it. You know as well as I do that Papa is never so happy as when he is stomping around pretending he's a tyrant."

"I am a tyrant, woman, and I will thank you to remember that," Nikola growled, setting the footstool in place before turning back to the carriage interior. "Be so good as to have a fire lit in the Chinese room."

"Why?" Imogen asked, releasing her former governess, and now companion, to peer over Nikola's shoulder. "Are we having a guest? Papa! Who is that woman?"

"Sainted Mary," the round little Anna gasped, crossing herself as Nikola turned with the unknown woman of obviously ill repute in his arms. "She's dead! And that is exactly what will happen to me should the baron order me from your side, my dearest Fräulein Imogen!"

"She is *not* dead," Nikola corrected. "She merely knocked herself insensible by running into Heinrich on the road below. Imogen, see to the room. You, Robbie—"

"But who *is* she, Papa?"

"Rob*EHR*, monseigneur," the slim young footman said in a heavy French accent. He wore a powdered pale salmon wig, white satin breeches that Nikola felt were entirely too tight for viewing by innocent damsels like Imogen, and a navy blue jacket, part of the livery of his former employer. Copious rings bearing large jewels of dubious authenticity glittered on his fingers, while in one hand he held a lacy handkerchief that waggled when he spoke, leaving faint clouds of powder that drifted gently to the ground with each gesture. "My name, she is Robert, not the so mundane Robbie of the English."

Imogen tugged at Nikola's arm. "Is she a friend of yours? How did she run into Heinrich? Have you known her long?"

"My father, he was named Robert, as well," Robert said with a haughty sniff and a curl of his lip as he eyed the unconscious woman. "It is a family name, monseigneur. A *French* family name."

"I shall die, die, I tell you, if you make me leave Andras Castle! It will be nothing short of murder!" Frau Leiven danced around him, her hands clutched together.

"I don't care if your name is Louis XIV, remove my trunk and things to my bedchamber. Imogen, cease fussing this instant and do as I ordered. Frau Leiven, if you continue to drivel in that annoying fashion, I really will cast you from the house."

"Aaargh!" The governess clutched her sausage rolls and wailed. Imogen fluttered around her, offering reassurances that no harm would befall her.

Nikola hoisted the unknown woman higher up on his chest, annoyed that no one did as he commanded. He was lord and master of his home, by the saints, as he had long been telling his servants and children. The fact that they all disregarded that point was more than any sane man could bear. Not that his actions the last half hour had been particularly fraught with sanity, he thought as he looked down at the warm body that pressed so solidly against him. Men of intellect did not, as a rule, bring home stray women who insisted on flinging themselves on horses.

Then again, perhaps they did, and he just hadn't been in such a situation before. He was in the middle of wondering whom of his acquaintance he could consult upon the matter when it struck him that he was once again arguing with himself.

"Imogen!" he said loudly as he strode up the stairs and into the great hall.

"Yes, Papa?"

"Do you debate various subjects with yourself?"

"Debate?"

"Yes, debate. Argue. Discuss."

"With . . . *myself*?"

"Yes, with yourself."

"Do you mean actually speak out loud?"

"Sometimes. Sometimes it's just an argument carried on in your head."

Imogen appeared at his side as he headed for the

staircase in the center of the hall, her brows pulled together in puzzlement. "No, Papa, I don't."

"Ah." Perhaps it was something that came down the male line of the family. Or it could be the curse after all. That would imply Benedikt was stricken with it, as well, then. "I will write to Benedikt and ask him," he said, nodding his head as he mounted the stairs, all five members of his household on his heels.

"Gone barmy the master 'as," Young Ted the stable-boy said in a voice filled with dark portent.

A smacking sound answered that statement, immediately followed by a howl of pain.

"Mind yer tongue, lad. Master Nick isn't barmy; he's just eccentric. All them lords are," Old Ted said, then turned back to the door, shoving his son in front of him. "Ye come help me get the harness off of Heinrich. Ye know how testy he gets when he's not groomed right away...."

Their voices trailed off when Nikola marched up two flights of stairs and turned down the wing that housed the family rooms. He passed first the lord's bed-chamber, then the one belonging to his late wife, pausing at the door just beyond it.

"Open it," he commanded.

A small figure with red hair straggling out of her mobcap dashed toward the door, only to be stopped and pushed to the side. "I am the footman most extraordinaire. You are only the maidservant," Robert told the redheaded maid, scowling at her as he wiped off the hand he had used to stop her. "It is *my* duty to open doors. Begone you and your so bent arm."

"I can open a door if I wish to," the maid named Elizabet answered, squaring her thin shoulders, one arm, smaller and more emaciated than the other, clutched just under her nearly nonexistent bosom. "The master said I can do anything anyone else can do. He said my arm is nothing to be ashamed of, and that in some foreign places I'd be revered as a god because I'm different."

"You're just a woman," Robert said with another of his superior sniffs. "You cannot be the god. Only a man like me can be a god."

"That's not what Master says. He says I could be a footman if I really wanted to be one."

"You would not be a footman, then," Robert argued. "You would be a footwoman. And no one wishes to have a footwoman. It is not done. Let go of the doorknob!"

"I will not! Master says—"

"Master says that if you think it's easy hauling a deadweight upstairs and all around the house," Nikola interrupted loudly, "you're bloody wrong. I don't care which of you opens the damned door just so it's opened before my arms break off from the strain, leaving me with the need to learn how to feed myself with my feet. And given the fact that I have never been able to do so much as pick up a quill with my toes, learning to eat with them is not going to end well. Open. The. Door."

"Papa, I still want to know who this woman is—"

Luckily for Nikola's sanity Robert managed to wrest Elizabet's hand away from the door, and flung it open with a glower at the little maid, saying as he did so, "The monseigneur rescued *me* from the so lecherous

Count d'Orville when he attempted to do wicked things to me with parts of his person that I will not mention in front of Mademoiselle Imogen. Me, and not you. Therefore, it is *I* who will open his doors when he has upon his hands the dead women."

Nikola, for what seemed like the hundredth time, wondered why he put up with the odd group of servants that seemed always to find him. "I could have normal servants, you know, ones who knew their places and acted accordingly. At one point in my life, I did have normal servants. I wonder what happened to them, and whether they'd be willing to return."

"But they would be so boring," Imogen said, following him into the room.

He laid the woman gently on the bed, staring down at her for a few moments. In the lamplight, she seemed to be sleeping, nothing more, and the logical jump in thoughts from a sleeping woman to a woman in his bed giving him more pleasure than he could humanly conceive had him aware that his breeches were growing tighter by the second.

His gaze played along the length of her, lingering on the highlights of her attractions—small but perfectly shaped breasts, rounded hips, and supple-looking legs. Just the thought of those legs wrapped around his hips while he buried himself in her left him in a state that might have been best described as "full to bursting."

It was not a pleasant experience.

"Wake up," he told the woman, tired of her just lying there demanding that he ogle her. He hated being bossed around, and if this woman of ill repute thought she was going to twist him around her long, sensitive fingers—fingers that he suddenly could imagine doing so many things to him—she should start thinking again.

To his surprise, her eyelashes fluttered a few times, then squeezed tightly shut for the count of three before they parted to reveal eyes the color of the stormy North Sea.

"Hrn?" she asked, her gaze on him, her expression filled with confusion. "What . . . uh . . . who are you?"

She spoke English with an accent that he couldn't place for a moment before realizing it was one that he had heard from a colonist. How on earth had a colonial prostitute traveled to Austria? And why would she go to all that trouble? Were there no customers in the colonies with whom she could ply her wares? He allowed his gaze to wander over her again. If he were at all the sort of man who had to resort to a courtesan, she would most definitely fit his needs.

"Hello? Eyes up here, buster."

Nikola straightened up when the woman snapped at him, giving him an annoyed look. No one had ever snapped at him before. He did not care for the experience, and said with frosty dignity, "I beg your pardon?"

"You were staring at my boobs," the woman answered, a defiant tilt to her chin that seemed to warm him despite his irritation with all the untoward snapping. "That's seriously over the line, and even if I didn't just turn in my boss for sexual harassment, and thus have become very familiar with what does and does not constitute inappropriate ogling, then I still would have an issue with you eyeing me like I'm a slab of meat and you're a hungry wolf."

"Sexual harassment?" Was she mad as well as heedless? "I am not a wolf. I am a Moravian."

"What you are is a damned ogler."

Imogen and the others in the room gasped in surprise at her use of profanity.

He flared his nostrils at her in a manner that had, in the past, never failed to intimidate those who had the audacity to irritate him, although now that he thought about it, there weren't very many people who deliberately attempted to try his temper in the manner of this annoying, delectable woman. "Madame—"

"Io."

He stared at her for a few seconds. "What did you say?"

"Io. My name is Io." She pronounced the name "eye-oh," as if that were perfectly ordinary. Which was ridiculous, because no one he knew bore a name with only vowels. It had to be something indigenous to the colonies. "It's actually Iolanthe, but no one calls me that but my tax accountant. Who are you?"

He took a deep breath, determined to take charge of the situation. "My name is Nikola Czerny."

"Nicole? I thought that was a girl's name."

Imogen gasped again. Frau Leiven clutched her throat and staggered over to a chair. Robert studied himself in a mirror that hung on a wall, and adjusted his wig to a rakish angle.

"It's Nikola, and it is *not* a female name," Nikola answered in an even tone, despite the sudden and almost overwhelming urge to throttle the woman. Or kiss her. He wouldn't mind doing both, to be honest. "It is my name, and I am a man. It is nothing uncommon, not like a name that contains nary a single consonant."

"My name has consonants!"

"I-O," he said with much portent.

"Well, that part is just vowels." She looked grumpy now, as if she did not like having the flaws in her reasoning pointed out. "But there's more to my full name than that. Just don't call me Yolanda. I hate that."

"Very well, Iolanthe."

"Dammit, I just said don't call me that!" She sat up, frowning and rubbing her head.

"No, you said not to call you Yolanda. I called you Iolanthe, which is a name that has proper syllables and consonants."

She punched his arm. "It sounds the same!"

"It's not. The 'the' at the end sounds rather like a 'da' when pronounced in German, but—"

"Oh, for the love of the five and forty virgins, just give it up! Call me Io. Yes, just the vowels, I know, you don't need to point it out again. Nikola, you said?" Her nose wrinkled slightly as she thought. "Oh, with a *k* in the middle, like Tesla? That's actually a pretty cool name."

"Thank you," he said gravely, making her a little bow. "Were my parents alive, I would pass along to them your appreciation of it. I do not know this Tesla, but I have not met all the people in the valley. Now, if you would be so good to tell me what you were doing running into Heinrich. Were you fleeing your proprietress? Or a customer?"

"A what, now?" Io winced as she continued to rub her forehead. "Man, I have the headache to end all headaches. What happened? Do I know you? You sound Austrian—are you one of Gretl's friends?"

Nikola refused to notice what an endearing picture she made when she blinked up at him with those smoky, mysterious eyes.

He did not like mysterious people. They were often annoying. "I was born in Moravia, not Austria, although I have lived here from the time I reached my majority. For whom do you work?"

"No one, not anymore." She swung her legs over the edge of the bed, gripping the blankets and wobbling just enough that Nikola put his hands on her shoulders to keep her from toppling over.

The feel of that tanned, freckled silken skin under his fingers made his blood tingle with desire. He told both his blood and his desire to cease acting inappropriately. He had better things to do with his time than stand here and touch this woman, his fingertips positively burning with the need to stroke that flesh, to lick it, to bite and drink his fill in the warmth that he was suddenly certain only she could bring him.

What the deuce was he thinking? He did not want to lick or bite or drink from this prostitute. He did not want to lay her in his bed and sate himself on her over and over and over again. He did not want to watch her eyes go dark with passion, or to feel her body tighten around him. . . .

"Hey, are you all right? You look funny, like you've got a painful gas bubble or something."

"Hrn?" With an effort, Nikola dragged his attention from the erotic mental images that gripped him, and blinked down at the woman. "Painful gas bubble?"

"My mother used to get them a lot. She said they were a real bitch when she was around others."

He was aware of more horrified gasping from the servants and his daughter, but the amusement in the woman's eyes seemed to hold him in thrall. Who was she? And, more important, why did she affect him so strongly?

"Mind you, she also had a tipped uterus, but I really don't think that has anything to do with the matter."

Had she cast some spell over him?

"And of course, that's not a situation that would affect you, either."

It had to be a spell. He'd never before reacted in such a manner to a woman.

"My mom used to say that drinking water helped a lot. The painful gas bubbles, that is, not the thing with her uterus."

He would simply demand that she remove the spell. Once she knew that he was aware of her trickery, she would be ashamed and would take her desirable, tempting person away from him.

"You don't talk much, do you?"

And then life would return to normal, and he could continue to be a martyr to his servants. He nodded to himself. That was what he'd do. He'd demand she remove the spell.

"Nikola?"

Io was asking him something. He rummaged around in his memory to find whatever it was she'd been babbling about. "No," he finally said. "I am not afflicted by painful wind in bubble or any other form."

"That's always good to know," she said pleasantly, a

little smile curling the edges of her mouth. "So, anyway, I got fired from my last job by a boss who was Mr. Grabby Hands. Thanks, you can let go of me, I'm OK now. I was just a bit dizzy for a few seconds. Is Gretl here? I assume I had some sort of an accident, but I'll be damned if I remember just what happened to me."

He released his hold on her shoulders, stepping back a foot in order to better pin her with a look. "I wish for you to remove the spell you have cast upon me," he told her with a firmness that he felt brooked no opposition.

"You want me to what?" Her forehead scrunched up, her nose wrinkling in such an adorable manner, it almost brought him to his knees.

More gasps sounded around the edges of the room, but this time they were less shocked and more fearful.

"She's a witch!" he heard Frau Leiven cry. "She's cast a spell on the baron! Where's the witch finder? Someone get the witch finder!"

"Oh for the love of Mike," Io said, peering around him to where the servants stood against the wall. "A witch? I'm not even remotely Wiccan."

"Mike?" Nikola pounced on the word. "Who is this Mike? Is he your lover?" A sudden surge of hatred for this lover made his heart pound. He hated Mike. He had no idea who the man was, but he hated him with every morsel of his being. He had to curl his fingers into fists in order to keep from grabbing her and demanding to know where this wastrel, this Mike, was located.

Io was back to looking at him, as she should be, but he could have sworn there was real confusion in her eyes as she answered. "No. My last boyfriend's name was Thomas, but he was a real dick, so I dumped him."

"Dick?" How many lovers did she have? There must be limits, even for prostitutes. If nothing else, time must be a factor. If she serviced customers on average ten hours a day, at one hour per customer, with four days off per month, then that would make a yearly maximum of . . . He did the calculations in his head, didn't like the answer, and decided his equation was faulty.

"Oh, sorry, it's slang for—" She waved a hand toward the front of his breeches. "Penis."

Instantly, he was hard.

More gasping ensued from the woodwork. "The witch speaks words of the devil!" Frau Leiven declared, her reedy voice ringing with righteousness. "She will bespell us all if she is not tortured to reveal the truth about her dark master, beheaded, and burned, her ashes scattered to the four quarters so she cannot resume life and bespell us all again."

"Really? All that just for saying 'penis'?" Io shook her head at the emotional woman. "I'd heard there were some uptight folks in this part of the world, but I thought it was all just a bunch of bullshi—er—hooey."

"You will cease speaking of your many lovers in front of my daughter," he said sternly.

"Many lovers? I've had exactly three boyfriends—"

"She is a gentle and unlearned maiden, and does not know the ways of men."

Behind Io, Imogen snorted, then instantly schooled her expression into one of innocence.

"Look, I know you guys are more conservative here—although really, beheading? Scattering ashes?

And I'm sorry about saying the D-word if you have a kid, but really, you're overreacting. And it was you who asked about my last boyfriend, not that I see mentioning him is going to corrupt your snow-white daughter, but still, you mentioned him first."

"Papa—"

"Silence." He narrowed his gaze on Io, picturing her beheaded. The thought gave him no pleasure. Quite the contrary, such an idea greatly disturbed him. "Do you deny that you have put a spell on me?"

"What is with you people? Yes, I deny it!" Io slapped her hands on her thighs, a thought that sent his brain on a little mental trip that ended up with him clearing his throat and hoping the witch prostitute would not look toward his groin. "And you can just stop that right now, too," she added.

"Stop what?" He wanted nothing more than to pounce on her, he really did, but he was never one to allow his sexual needs to drive his actions, and he'd be damned if he started now.

He smiled at the irony at the fact that he was already damned. What could a little more damnation hurt?

"That." Io pointed at his crotch. "You're getting all bulgy, and I resent your penis's implication that I'm doing something to arouse you. Unless you're some sort of weirdo who gets off by women saying the word 'penis,' which is frankly kinda sad."

"Baron, you must stop her from speaking! It is the devil's words that come out of her mouth!" Frau Leiven hurried around the bed to stand behind it, clapping her hands over Imogen's ears. "She will bespell us all!"

"Baron?" Io stopped glaring at his admittedly bulgy

breeches and glanced up at him. "I thought you said your name was Nikola."

"It is. I am also a baron. Frau Leiven, if you do not cease squawking, I will have you put out of the castle. Imogen, go to your room. This conversation is not suitable for you."

"Wow, a real baron? Not one of those mall kinds that you become when you buy a square foot of land—*Imogen*?"

"But, Papa—"

"Leave!" he commanded, feeling that if there were fewer people in the room, he could get about to seducing the woman properly.

His mind did a double take. *Chastising her,* he corrected to himself, despite the nagging suspicion that the first would be infinitely more enjoyable.

Io got to her feet and turned around, gawking in surprise. "Imogen, it *is* you. Nice to see you again. What happened to me? I seem to be a bit wonky in the brain. I remember doing . . . something . . . but just can't pin down exactly what."

"You know my daughter?" he asked, frowning first at Imogen, then at Frau Leiven. "You allowed Imogen to consort with whores?"

"No, Papa—" Imogen started to say, but Io interrupted her.

"Whore?" she bellowed, then immediately slapped both hands to her head, weaving with pain. "Oh my god, someone get me some ibuprofen. I think my head is going to explode."

He helped her to sit back down on the bed, his body warring with his mind. "I do not know who Ibuprofen is, but if he is another of your lovers, I will have to adjust my equation."

"What equation? No, wait, it doesn't matter. I don't care if you're the king or emperor or whatever they have here in Austria now—you do not get to call me rude names." Io stood up again, weaving only slightly before she squared her shoulders and shot him a look that should have enraged him, but simply went straight to his groin.

He really was getting a little tired of everything about her making his rod stiff with need and desire and wanting that all but left his tongue cleaving to the roof of his mouth.

She must be the best prostitute in the world if she could do all that without so much as touching him.

"If you don't mind," she said, trying to brush past him, "I'm going home. Or rather, I'm going to go to my cousin's home. You guys can just continue on with your oddball ways without me. Imogen . . . hell, I don't know what to say to you. I guess I'll just keep mum to Gretl about the fact that you evidently have some . . . did you say daughter? Imogen is your daughter?" Io looked startled when she turned to face Imogen again. "You told me your dad was dead. Although your brother said he wasn't, but I kind of figured he was a little light in the noggin since he also said he was some sort of a vampire."

Everyone in the room froze, including Nikola. The odd side of his mind noticed that Io's declaration had, at least, had the benefit of killing his erection, but that wasn't really important.

"Who are you, how did you meet my children, and

how do you know about—" He stopped, unwilling to speak in front of the superstitious servants. He'd carried his secret close to his breast, not even allowing his valet to know the truth about Benedikt and Imogen, or how the curse had come to be. Other than his children, only two others knew the truth. He eyed the woman again. Had one of his half brothers spoken to her about him?

It was all very much a puzzle, and along with mysterious women, he disliked puzzles intensely.

The Incredible Adventures of Iolanthe Tennyson

July 12

If someone finds this journal someday and says to herself, "Holy jumping cats, whoever wrote this seriously needed to have some penmanship lessons," please note that I'm writing with a quill. A *quill*. One from a bird. Goose, I think, or something big like that. Regardless, it's really, really hard to write with a quill without leaving big ole blotches of ink everywhere, not to mention ripping up the paper, and just trying to get letters formed so they're actually readable.

Man, things have gotten so weird, I'm actually ranting about a feather.

But I promised I was going to do this properly, and I am.

Right after I woke up in some strange dude's place (and when I say "strange dude," I don't just mean someone I didn't know—Nikola was a very odd man, what with his demands that I tell him about my boyfriends, and then getting bent out of shape when I did so, and some strange equation that he kept yammering on about), I knew immediately something seriously wrong was going on.

For one, I couldn't remember a damned thing about how I had ended up in the room.

For another, and I'm totally at a loss how this could even be, I seemed to have woken up in some ultraconservative cult, kind of like Amish people who insisted on living just as if they were three hundred years in the past.

And lastly, the strange dude appeared to be under the impression that I was a hooker. Me! And Imogen was a part of it. "Look," I said to Imogen's father, who more closely resembled an older brother than a father, but it was clear there was some sort of weird genetic thing going on with that family.

You could say that.

"Look, I'm not a ho." I stopped, frowning at the voice in my head. I've never been one to talk to myself, and I didn't want to start. "And I'm not exactly sure what I'm doing here, but I really do think it's time I go back to town. Does someone have a phone I could use? I seem to have lost mine."

Everyone, every single person from the effeminate guy in some sort of Georgian costume with a big pink wig to the mega-conservative short, round lady who kept calling for the others to do heinous things to me, stared just as if I'd said something exceptional.

"What, you guys don't have any technology here?" I glanced around the room. There was a fire in a fireplace set in the wall opposite the bed, and lots and lots of candles all over the room. It was a bit of a fire hazard, to be honest, and I wondered what sort of sprinkler system they had in place just in case one of those candles tipped over. "None whatsoever? Even the Amish folks can have cell phones if they keep them in a special place."

"She's speaking in tongues!" the crazy round lady exclaimed, pointing at me with one hand while clutching the tall, willowy Imogen with the other. "She is the devil's plaything and must be destroyed!"

"I am *no one's* plaything, and nice manners abroad or not, you're really starting to work my nerves, lady," I told her, giving her a gimlet eye. "I wouldn't dream of telling you people how to run your cult or religion or whatever it is that you're doing here, but I am *not* a doormat, and I will not let you walk all over me. So you can do the rest of us a big ole fat favor and just get over yourself already."

I might have yelled that last sentence at the crazy lady, but that's no excuse for the handsome Nikola to suddenly snap into action, clearing the room of everyone in a matter of seconds.

"Leave us!" he bellowed, waving one imperious hand.

To my surprise, everyone did as he ordered. Imogen slid me a long, long look as she left, as well. That surprised me a bit, but I realized I had no claim on her friendship with Gretl.

Still, it would have been nice of her to offer me the use of her cell phone.

"Now you will explain to me what game you are playing," Nikola demanded.

It was his eyes, I decided, that made a little shiver

run down my back. He had the eyes of a white wolf: pale, icy blue, with a black ring around the outer edge of the iris. Set against that black hair, and a face that could have graced any fashion magazine, his eyes packed a wallop that I was steadfastly determined to resist.

I was not in the market for a man, even an older one who probably had worked out all his issues. *Especially* one who looked like Nikola did—I knew from experience how men who felt they were god's gift to the world acted, and I wanted nothing to do with another one of that ilk.

"I do not play games, not the sort you're referring to," I said with much dignity. "I'm sure you're busy with your party or cosplay or religious cult or whatever it is you folks are doing, so I'll just get out of your hair. I'd prefer to call my cousin, but if you don't have a phone, then I guess I'll just have to walk to the nearest one."

"Who told you I was a Dark One?"

"No one told me . . . wait, you mean Dark One like vampire?" I gawked at him for a minute. Had I gone completely insane? "You think you're a vampire, too? Like Benedikt?"

"You will tell me what you know of my son!" he said as he stalked slowly toward me. "You will tell me how you have learned about the curse."

"I will?" He really was a handsome devil, once he stood where the candlelight could play all over his face. He was dressed in a costume, as well—*costume!* He was wearing a costume! I slumped in relief on the bed, my anxiety level dropping when I realized that everyone must be attending a costume party. That or they were part of a local theater troupe. "What curse would that be?"

The one that has made my life a living hell.

I sat up straight at the voice in my head. Since when did my brain play tricks like that on me? I must have hit my head harder than I thought. Great, now I'd have to go see a doctor to find out why voices were suddenly talking in my brain.

"Do not play coy with me, madame. I neither desire nor seek such an attitude. Was it Rolf? Arnulf? Did they tell you what happened to me?"

"I don't know an Arnold or a Ralph, so the answer to that is a rock-solid no." I eyed him as he moved toward me, all sorts of warning bells going off in my head, and not just because the man moved like a panther about to pounce on some unwary prey.

He wasn't a whole lot taller than me, but he was broad across the chest and shoulders; that much I could see even through the fancy outfit he wore. His hair was black, curly, and worn longish in the back, not—thank god—in a mullet, but still long enough that it was caught up in a little ponytail. He had an interesting face with a long, straight nose, a chin that made me a bit weak in the knees, and those eyes . . . oh, those eyes. He certainly didn't look like a man in his sixties, which he must be if Imogen was in her forties. I shook my head at my confused thoughts. There was just something different about Nikola that went beyond the obvious sex appeal.

Warmth flooded me at that acknowledgment, a sexual sort of warmth, one that startled me with its intensity. "Oh, lovely, I probably have some sort of serious brain injury as a result of ... of ..." I screwed up my eyes and tried to force myself to remember what I had been doing before I woke up here.

"You did not hit Heinrich hard enough to injure your brain," Nikola said, his voice, a lovely rich baritone, doing something wonderful to my insides. "You will look at me when I am speaking to you!"

Nothing breaks the spell of a yummy male voice like an obnoxious demand. I popped open one eye to glare at him. "OK, one, you are so not the boss of me, and two, I do not respond well to orders. If you had asked politely, I would have told you that I've closed my eyes so that I can try to remember what happened to me before I woke up here."

I closed my eye again, and concentrated.

"I can tell you what you did to end up here."

"Really?" I opened my eyes once more. "What?"

"You ran into Heinrich."

I frowned, not recognizing the name. Was it one of Gretl's friends? "I don't think I've met a Heinrich."

"You were running down the road in your underthings, and you ran directly into Heinrich, knocking yourself senseless."

I looked down at myself, shocked at the idea of running anywhere in my undies. "I was running around in my underwear? What the hell was I doing that for? Who's Heinrich? And who dressed me again?"

"Yes, I have no idea, one of my carriage horses, and we did not find your gown, let alone put it on you. Now, you will cease—"

"Wait a minute, I think we're talking at cross-purposes," I interrupted, holding up a hand to stop him.

He looked thoroughly outraged that I'd do such a thing. "You will *not* interrupt me!"

"I just did, didn't I? Thus, I will. Er ... did. And someone must have put my dress back on, assuming that I was, in fact, running around in my undies, because I'm wearing it now. My dress, that is." I waved toward my torso. "This is really a bizarre conversation, you know that? Like, on the level of reality TV sort of bizarre."

He glanced down at my dress, his eyes lingering on my breasts in a way that had me tightening my fingers into fists. "*That* is your gown?"

"Yes, and I've asked you once to stop staring at my boobs. Keep it up and I'll make you one very sorry little cowpoke."

His gaze shifted up to mine, genuine confusion visible in his pale eyes. "You speak words that I do not know, and yet my grasp of English is excellent. What is a cowpoke?"

"It's someone who's going to be sorry if he doesn't stop staring at my breasts."

His gaze flickered straight back to my boobs. "Why? You present them for male appreciation, do you not?"

I looked down, found the first button on my sundress had slipped open, and hastily rebuttoned it. "No, I wore this dress because it was hot and I wanted to stay cool while I ... I ..." I frowned again as I tried to concentrate. Vague images seemed to flicker just out of the range of my vision, dark, fleeting images. "I can almost see it."

"Your breasts? You will if you undo those buttons again." His gaze was frankly appreciative, but I had learned my lesson. I crossed my arms over my boobs, giving him a quick glare.

"No." I turned my attention inward again. "It's just . . . there. I can almost see it. I was doing something important, something . . . profound."

Trees flashed passed my unseeing eyes, trees that were first richly green, then inky black in the night, the tips of their pine needles kissed by sunlight and moonlight alike. And something else hovered just beyond my awareness, something big, something important that I could almost reach out and touch. . . .

"The swirly thing!" I exclaimed, seeing it again when it came into mental focus, the blue-white light twisting and turning back upon itself in that strange fashion. "I was taking pictures of it, and of the creepy forest, and I put my hand through the swirly thing. . . ."

I remembered again the feeling of static in the air when I leaned forward into the twisting light. I swayed, suddenly as light-headed as when I had fallen through the strange smoky object, but this time when I pitched forward, I fell right onto a warm, hard, very solid shape.

One who smelled faintly of lemon, leather, and something slightly earthy that had me turning my head into his neck in an attempt to capture more of it. A sudden urge flared to life in me, one that swept through my blood, making it impossible to resist. Before I could even weigh the consequences of my action, I opened my mouth and gently bit the tendon in Nikola's neck.

It was as if I'd lit a match to a bonfire. He froze for a moment, and I knew I'd shocked him, knew I was guilty of a far greater form of harassment than merely ogling my breasts, but before I could do so much as to pull away from him, I was on my back on the bed, Nikola covering my front, his eyes darkening even as I stared in complete astonishment. He didn't say anything, just dipped his head down until his lips burned a brand on my neck.

I was so shocked by what I'd done, I didn't think to push him off me so I could apologize. On the contrary, I slid my hands up his arms, my legs moving restlessly as his weight made me sink into the soft mattress of the bed. All sorts of wickedly naughty erotic images danced in my head as his teeth scraped on my neck. I knew he was going to give me a love bite in return, knew I should stop it by apologizing for biting him, knew I should get far, far away from him, but apparently my brain had ceased to function, because the second his teeth bit my flesh, I arched back against him, writhing in ecstasy.

"Oh my god, do you know how to do this," I moaned, clutching his hair and squirming at the sensation of his mouth on my neck. My entire body seemed to be made of fire. "But really, I suppose . . . oh, lord, yes . . . I suppose we should stop because this really is way over the line, not that I'm blameless since I bit you first, and dear god, you're not going to stop, are you?"

He pulled back from me, his eyes now a pure sapphire blue, his lips suddenly holding an unholy fascination for me. They were red, as if he'd been kissing me, all gently curved lines, and so enticing I almost pulled him back down onto me.

A morsel of common sense remained to me, however, and I'm proud to say that even in the full onset of a massive lust, I managed to keep from kissing the breath out of him.

"I must stop, or you would die," he said in answer to my question, giving me an odd look before sliding off me.

For a few seconds I lay in a boneless, quivering mass of want and need and too many other emotions to untangle. "Well, that was probably the best hickey I've ever had, but I don't think it would have killed me."

He frowned as I sat up, rebuttoning the top button of my dress, which had popped open yet again. "I do not know this word 'hickey,' either."

"It means a love bite. Kind of a passionate one. Look, I'm sorry I bit you. I don't know what possessed me. I'm not at all a bitey sort of woman, and especially not with strangers. I'm mortified that I was just yelling at you about ogling me and then I went and bit you—"

"I enjoyed it. No one has ever bitten me before, not even my wife. She was always afraid to. She was afraid she would become like me."

A blush unlike any other washed up from my chest, burning my face with shame. "I am so sorry. I didn't know you were married. There's no excuse for my behavior—"

"I am widowed. My wife died several years ago." He eyed me as I put my hands on my blazing cheeks. "If you are not a whore, as you claim you are not, then who are you?"

"I'm just me," I said with a little frustrated gesture. "I'm a former secretary. I like photography and traveling, although I haven't done much of either. I'm spending the summer in St. Andras with my cousin Gretl. And I don't normally bite men, especially strange men, and really especially not men who are as handsome as you are. So no, I'm not a whore, although I admit that after what I did to you, you'd be justified in questioning that statement." I couldn't stop reliving the feel of his mouth on my neck. It was the most sensual thing I'd ever felt.

It will only get better.

I froze, a dull feeling of worry filling my gut. What had I done to myself that I was hearing voices?

"I told you that I enjoyed it. You will cease blushing over it. Who were you running from?"

"No one. At least, I don't think I was." I stopped worrying about having to go to the hospital for CAT scans and the like, and tried to remember what happened after I had fallen near the twisty light.

"Not near it . . . through it," I said aloud, my eyes widening as the memory came flooding back to me of the daytime that had turned to night, of a dirt road where a paved one should have been, and of a carriage and horses looming up out of the night as I raced toward the town and safety.

A horrible, horrible idea started to dawn in the dim recesses of my brain, something so fantastic that I didn't even want to consider it.

"Through what?" Nikola held out a hand for me, and without thinking, I took it, allowing him to pull me to my feet. I stared at him, my brain seizing up and refusing to process the idea.

"It was . . . I don't know what it was. A big swirly thing in the middle of the woods. Made up of light. I know this is going to sound really odd, but what's today's date?"

"Woods? What wooded area? Near here?"

"I don't know where here is, so I couldn't say. It's the place that all the people in St. Andras say is haunted. It's like halfway up the hill to the ruined castle. You didn't answer me about the date."

"Andras Castle is not a ruin," he said, his fingers still holding mine. "The east wing needs some repairs, but I will attend to them now that I have returned from settling my son at university in Heidelberg."

The horrible idea my brain refused to cope with grew even stronger. "What's the date?" I asked again, holding my breath against the answer.

He frowned. "Today? It is the twelfth of July."

"And the year?"

His beautiful eyes, now back to pale, glacier blue, narrowed on me. "You do not know what year it is?"

"I thought I did, but I have a magnificently horrible feeling I'm going to be wrong. What year is it?"

"It is 1703."

I closed my eyes for a second, my stomach lurching when the room spun. Nikola's fingers tightened, pulling me toward him.

"Are you swooning?"

"No, just . . . oh, boy. You're kidding, aren't you? You're playacting that it's 1703? Or . . . or you're with some reenactment group or living-history place, right?"

"I am not jesting, no," he said, still frowning, and I could feel the truth of what he said.

"No. This is just . . . no. Impossible," I said softly, slumping against him when my brain fought to find sanity in this madness. "Houston, we have a problem."

"Nikola, not Houston. As for the problem you

pose—" He eyed me again. "I foresee much inconvenience in my future until you leave, not the least of which is the fact that despite just feeding from you, I wish to do so again. I will not be dictated to in this fashion, do you understand? I am not at all pliant, nor will I allow you to twine me about your fingers! I will feed when I wish to feed, and nothing you can do will change that!"

I straightened up and stared at him, a beautiful, angry man, and wondered what the hell I'd gotten myself into now. Whatever it was, he'd have an aneurysm if he didn't calm down, and although his lack of anger management skills wasn't my problem, I kind of liked him. I felt some sort of a need to help him, although heaven knew why when he was being as unhelpful as possible.

The temptation is too great. Distance is protection.

"OK, Mr. Brain, you can just stop doing that because I'm not taking you to a hospital right this second," I said sternly to myself.

Nikola's left eyebrow rose.

"Sorry. I don't normally talk out loud to my brain, but it's been doing weird things the last few minutes. What were we talking about? Oh, yes, I'm sorry if you think I'm twisting you around my little finger. I promise I'll stop doing that, OK? I don't know about feeding you, though. I'm not a very good cook, although I've been told my chicken spaghetti is pretty good. Feel better? Excellent. I think I need to go into town, though, because otherwise, I really am going to worry that I've gone insane, what with you telling me it's 1703, and my brain thinking that maybe it could be if that swirly thing was some sort of *Doctor Who* TARDIS thingie, and if it is, I can tell you that this isn't going to end well." I smiled brightly at him and headed for the door.

He didn't stop me, as I half expected him to. Instead he just followed me as I opened the door and stepped out into a narrow hallway dimly lit by a stand of candles at the far end. "You guys really take your reenactment seriously, huh?" I said as I strolled down the hall, determined to be as calm as I could. There would be all the time in the world to panic later if I found out I really had gone insane. "I had a friend who used to be into the Civil War stuff, but she got tired of wearing the big hoop skirts. Said it was impossible to go to the bathroom without having to disrobe first."

"Why do you not believe that I am speaking the truth?" Nikola asked. "I feel obligated to point out that if you were a man, I would challenge you for such an insult. But as you are a woman, and a strange one at that, I will merely make a mental note to punish you later for such insolence."

To Nikola's (and my own) surprise, I laughed at such an outrageous statement. "Punish me?" I asked, smiling over my shoulder at him before descending the long, curving staircase to the floor below. "Like what, a spanking? Or are you going to send me to my room for a time-out?"

I could send you to my room. That would be far more interesting.

I paused, and blinked, my fingers tightening around the banister, a little spurt of fear making my stomach hurt. Why was my brain doing this to me? What the hell was wrong with me?

"I am simply stating a fact. I am literally the lord and

master here, madame, and as you have placed yourself
in my protection—"

I continued down the stairs, distracted from my wor-
ries about my impending mental breakdown by Nikola's ridiculous attitude. "I did nothing of the sort. I
simply ran into some guy named Heinrich."

"Horse. Heinrich is my horse, as I have stated already. Do not make me repeat myself."

I paused again, watching with disbelief as he
marched steadfastly down the stairs, stopping at the
bottom to glance up at me. "You really are a piece of
work, you know that? Even if this was 1703, and honestly, I'm not so far gone into derangement that I'm
willing to believe that, but even if it was the truth, then
still that attitude must have been pretty much unbearable."

"No more so than your insistence that I'm lying
about the date," he said, making an irritated gesture
toward me. "As for your other claims, they are just as
ridiculous. I am not unbearable. I am generosity per-
sonified. I must be, or else I would be demanding rec-
ompense for the damage you've done to Heinrich, not
to mention the indisposition you've put to my house by
forcing me to give you shelter when you knocked yourself witless. A lesser man, an unbearable man, would
have tossed you on the verge as Old Ted suggested.
That you are here now, lambasting me with the vilest of
slurs, is proof to the contrary."

"I like how you talk," I said, slowly continuing down
the stairs until I stood next to him. "I don't quite understand why you have an English accent rather than an
Austrian one, but I like it nonetheless."

"I spent many years in England," he said, frowning. "My mother was English. My father is from Moravia. I mentioned that, too, although you apparently wish to ignore it. Why, I have no idea. I will consider it one of your many peccadilloes, and move past it to more important things, such as who told you about the curse, how you know my children, and just what you were doing out on the road where you might ambush my carriage." He squinted at me slightly. "I begin to suspect you are misleading me with regards to your acquaintanceship with Rolf."

I shook my head and walked past him, taking in the entryway hall. It, too, was lit by clumps of candles, and a fire crackling away in a huge fireplace across the room. I headed for the double doors that must surely lead outside. "I don't think I've ever met a Ralph—"

"Rolf—"

"Him, too. Let alone know one well enough to mislead you about him. I'm going to town. How far is it?"

"Slightly under four miles via the road. Less as the crow flies."

I opened the nearest door, rubbing my arms and shivering a little when the night air swirled around me. Outside, the darkness was broken up here and there by a gentle glow from a handful of windows. Gravel crunched under my feet as I took a few steps away from the house before turning to look back at it.

It wasn't a house. It was a castle. A big ole stone castle, right there in front of me. I tipped my head back as far as it would go, allowing my gaze to wander along crumbling bits of stonework, and the tall, pointy spire that rose closest to me. It was a castle with a tower. Of course it was. Where else would I be but a who-knew-how-many-hundreds-of-years-old castle.

"This looks like the painting of Andras Castle that Gretl has hanging on her dining room wall," I commented, still rubbing my arms.

Nikola *tsk*ed impatiently, pulling off his long-tailed coat jacket, and slung it around me. "That is because it *is* Andras Castle."

I gave him a long look.

He gave it right back to me.

"I'm going into town," I said. "Which way is it?"

He pointed over my shoulder. I turned and started walking, somewhat disappointed when he didn't join me.

"You don't need him," I told myself a minute later when it was clear he was just going to let me walk off wearing his fancy costume coat. I glanced back, but he stood at the doors, watching me. He didn't even wave good-bye, the rat. "Just because he's the world's best hickey-giver doesn't mean you want anything more to do with him. Besides, he's bossy and arrogant and clearly thinks he's above the rules the rest of us have to follow, and if you haven't learned by now what trouble that sort of man can be, then you really are insane."

Lecturing myself didn't help much. Especially once I got beyond the boundaries of the landscaped lawns, somewhat seedy topiaries, and an avenue of arched, leafy trees. Three minutes after I had walked away from Nikola, I was beginning to regret my actions. The darkness seemed to close in around me, while the soft thud of my footsteps on the now-dirt road echoed the beat of my heart. Overhead, fleeting shapes of obsidian danced across the night sky, the moon too obscured for me to make out if they were night birds, or bats.

"I really hope they're owls or something," I muttered to myself, rubbing my arms again, this time in reaction to the thought of creepy little bats flying around me. The darkness was beginning to get to me, making me twitchy at the slightest of sounds, and just the possibility that they were bats made me want to run straight back into Nikola's arms.

Castle! His *castle*, not his arms. What on earth was I thinking? "And if wanting to throw myself into his arms isn't a sign I've done myself some sort of head injury, I just don't know what—argh!"

A large shape loomed up out of nowhere, making me shriek and stumble backward into a small shrub.

"I suppose I should be thankful that this time you sprang away from my horse rather than into him," a male voice said with calm indifference.

I pushed my way out of the shrub and glared up at Nikola where he sat mounted on a white horse.

"What the hell! You run me down and have the nerve to complain about the fact that I flung myself out of the way of that monster's pounding hooves?"

He sighed and dismounted, leading the white horse toward me, and a second that I hadn't noticed until that moment. "You did so unnecessarily. Demeter hasn't trampled a lady underfoot in months."

"What are you doing?" I asked when he held out his hand for me, and split my suspicious look between him and the horses.

"You wish to go to town. Old Ted has retired for the evening. Since it is not a pleasant walk, we will ride."

He took my hand and pulled me over to the second horse, a long-faced bay who snuffled me curiously when Nikola led me to his side. "Oh. Well, that was thoughtful of you. Hey, wait just a minute. You don't expect me to get up there, do you?"

"It would be difficult to ride him any other way, although I admit that I would enjoy watching your attempt to do so. Are you afraid of horses?"

"Not particularly." I eyed the animal. It didn't look overly pleased to see me. I seconded its sentiments. "I just haven't done much riding."

"Thor is Imogen's mount. He has very nice manners. Gather up your gown."

"Huh?" I stopped tentatively patting the neck of the horse in order to give it the (wholly false) impression that I was a competent horsewoman, and turned to ask Nikola what he meant, but before anything more could come out of my mouth, he grasped me by my waist and heaved me upward, plopping me down sideways on the saddle.

That was when I realized there was something wrong with it. Or rather with me. "This is—I've never ridden in a sidesaddle. Am I supposed to sit sideways? It's kind of uncomfortable if I am."

"You haven't ridden at all?" Incredulity fairly dripped off his words.

"No, and you can stop with the superior attitude. I'm a San Francisco girl, born and raised. I haven't been on a horse since I went to fat girls' camp when I was eleven, and they had proper saddles. This one is seriously funky."

"Hook your leg over the pommel," Nikola explained, gesturing toward a curved piece that poked up off the front of the saddle. "Your other foot goes in the stirrup."

I leaned back a little and pulled my knee toward myself in preparation to doing as he said, but ended up just continuing on backward, promptly falling off the horse.

"Ow," I muttered, spitting out a mouthful of dirt and glaring up at the horse's legs. "You did that on purpose, didn't you?"

"Are you addressing Thor or me?"

"Both of you." I took the hand offered and allowed Nikola to assist me to my feet, brushing off the front of my sundress, and covertly trying to dig out dirt from where it had gotten into my bra. "You know, I think I'll walk to town. I'm less likely to end up with a broken nose."

"Don't be so weak," he said, and hoisted me up onto the dratted horse again. "I can't imagine how you never learned to ride properly, but now is not the time to give in to your fears. Hook your leg thusly."

It took a good five minutes of coaching, but at last I had my legs arranged to Nikola's satisfaction. I wobbled a bit precariously while he walked the horse in a circle and explained how to adjust my balance for the movement of the horse, but in the end, I decided to stick it out rather than walk the three miles into town.

Mostly because some unknown romantic part of me wanted a moonlit ride with a handsome man, even if there was the possibility that one of us had gone over the deep end.

"This isn't so bad," I said a short while later, after having released the death grip I held on a clump of the horse's mane. "I think I've gotten the hang of this whole move-along-with-the-horse thing. Can we go faster? Without me falling off, that is? I could walk as fast as the horses, and I'd really like to get to town to see if it's you or me who's deranged."

"If you like," was all he said, and the next thing I knew, he clicked his tongue and the white monster he was riding took off like a rocket. One with four legs and a tail.

Here's the thing about horses—evidently if they hang out together a lot, they buy into this whole "best friends forever" thing, and when one of them suddenly bolts, the other feels obligated to join in the fun and frolics.

"I believe the answer to your question is no," a voice said to me when I groaned and rolled over onto my back to stare up at the night sky.

"Huh?" Gingerly, I moved my arms and legs to make sure everything was in working order. It was, although parts of me were slightly bruised. I was also somewhat dazed from the unexpected impact with the ground. "What?"

"You asked if you could go faster without falling off. The answer to that is no, you cannot. Are you injured?"

"I dunno." I groaned again, just because I felt like I was due a bit of pity. I looked at Nikola to see if he was likely to feel sympathetic toward me, but caught him ogling my legs, which were exposed up to midthigh since my dress had gotten twisted around. "Hey, what did I say about eyes up here?"

"You objected to me enjoying your breasts. You said nothing about your legs."

"It applies to everywhere." I sat up and pulled down the skirt of my dress, giving him a really quality glare that I suspected he couldn't see, even though he seemed to have no problem seeing my legs.

They would be a shame to miss.

"Whoa!" I scrambled to my feet before Nikola could even get out of my way. "Help me onto this horse. I have to get to town to get some serious medical attention."

"You *are* injured, then?" Nikola asked, boosting me onto the horse.

"Not in the way you mean, but I keep—" I bit off the words, not wanting to tell him that I had suffered some sort of weird brain thing when I blacked out earlier, and was now experiencing delusions of the highest caliber.

You seem anything but delusional to me.

"Oh, god," I sobbed, swinging my leg around the pommel, and using both hands to clutch the reins along with Thor's mane. "We have to get into town fast. Does this horse have a turbo mode, or third gear, or whatever you do to make them go really fast?"

"What's wrong? Why are you shaking? If you tighten those reins any more, Thor will assume you wish for him to rear, and you'll end up on the ground again."

"I'm going insane. I keep hearing voices in my head," I said without realizing it until the words left my lips. I loosened up my death grip on the reins to clap one hand over my mouth, my eyes on Nikola to see how he'd react to my admission of insanity.

He simply raised one of his glossy black eyebrows.

And for some reason, that seemed to make me feel much better.

It's true that is odd, but there could well be a reasonable explanation.

"Ack!" I screeched. "There it goes again! Quick, I have to get to doctor before my brain erodes any further."

12 July 1703

Nikola wasn't sure what instinct warned him that the oddly named woman was close to losing control of her wits, but some innate sense given to men regarding women had come through when he needed it, and rather than point out to Io that her insistence that the nearest doctor could help her over her derangement was not at all reasonable (given that Herr Doktor Huebe had four-footed patients as well as those of merely two), he did as she demanded, and rode with her into town.

"You are not in the least bit good at riding, and in saying that, I use the broadest definition of the word 'good,'" he said conversationally some ten minutes later when he managed to catch her as she almost slid out of the saddle. He set her aright again, wincing in sympathy with Thor when she dropped the reins and clutched the horse's mane in a fierce grip. "You're not even tolerably mediocre."

"Well, that's no thanks to this stupid saddle," she snapped back in a wholly undeserved manner. "It's got to be the most ridiculous, most sexist thing ever invented. I just bet that whatever man thought up this monstrosity of a saddle was bent on keeping women subservient and dependent on others."

"Women are subservient and dependent on others," he pointed out, catching her again as she skewed around to glare at him. "It is the way of things, and if you cease flinging yourself about in the saddle, you might stay atop Thor rather than repeatedly sliding off him."

"Look, you may think you're all Mr. Seventeen Hundreds Nobility and whatnot, but until I find out that I've really gone to la-la land, and not having a mental breakdown like I think I'm having because of the voices in my head, I'm not going to play your little game of how things used to be. So you can just stop trying to work my nerves, and tell me instead how to make this horse go faster. We've been riding forever and I still don't even see the town."

"If we went faster, you'd fall off again," he pointed out, ignoring the gibberish part of her conversation despite finding it more than a little amusing.

He realized with a shock that he found her amusing, as well. How long had it been since he'd been entertained merely by conversing with a woman?

Chauvinist pig.

He frowned, wondering where that thought had come from. He wasn't entirely sure where Chauvin was, or why their pigs would occur to him at that moment, but he assumed that something Io had said had triggered a long-lost memory.

"Oh, man, I'm so going insane. Distract my wonky brain, Nikola!" Io demanded.

He thought of pointing out that he was not accustomed to people making demands of him, let alone fulfilling them, but admitted that he did not find conversation with her tiresome, as he did so many other women.

Dawg!

"Well?" she asked, impatience quite audible in the single word.

"Hmm?"

"You're supposed to distract me so I don't sit here and freak out any more about going insane while we slowly amble our way down the side of this mountain, like a couple of slugs out for a leisurely stroll. So get on with the distracting. What are you thinking about right now?"

"I was thinking about dogs."

"What sort of a dog?"

"I don't know." Absently, he reached out and grabbed her arm to keep her from slipping off the side of Thor.

The look on her face was priceless. "You're thinking about a dog, but you don't know which one? Maybe I'm not the only one who should be seeing the doctor."

Nikola considered this. "He is certainly fairly conversant with their ailments."

She blinked at him a couple of times. When she spoke, her voice was fairly strained. "Who is fairly conversant with dogs' ailments?"

"Yes," he agreed, turning his mind to the issue of what he was going to do with her. Oh, it was true she hadn't begged him for help in escaping her local protector, whoever that should be—and he wasn't entirely certain he didn't believe her claim that she wasn't a light-skirt, since she hadn't once made an attempt to touch him, not in a sexual way, at least. Well, there was that little bite she had given him, but surely that wasn't an overture. It hadn't felt like a blatant sexual hint, and it had been his experience that women of loose morals made bold with their hands, something Io had most definitely not done. No, she most likely was not a doxy, and that meant he couldn't just give her over to the local horse doctor and be on his way.

For whatever the reason, he felt the need to protect her. He had a suspicion, however, that she wouldn't enjoy that sentiment.

Io took a deep breath. "OK, we're going to do this again, because if nothing else, it's keeping me from worrying about the state of my brain. I said you're thinking about a dog, and you said—"

"I believe I said that I was thinking about a dog, not you," he interrupted, considering the fracas that would follow if he should attempt to install her in his house. The temptation she posed him would surely disturb his peace of mind, if nothing else.

The noise of more air being sucked in registered on his ears.

"And you said that some dude would be familiar with dogs' illnesses, and I said who, and you said yes."

"I did." Perhaps he could house her somewhere in town where she wouldn't distract him with that silken flesh, and those long legs, and the small, but pert, breasts that looked like they were made just for his hands. And mouth. And possibly other parts of him.

"Who is the dude?"

"He is, yes."

"So help me god," Io said, breathing heavily through her nose, "if you say 'Who's on first?' I'm going to deck you good and proper."

"First what?" he asked, confused now.

"I don't know! Wait, he's on third base! Hahaha-hah!" Io sounded the slightest bit hysterical.

He cast her a wary glance, wondering if she might not be as deranged as she kept claiming. "If you don't know Huebe, why are you convinced he's first at any-thing?"

"Aaaargh!" Io screamed, her arms flailing wildly, causing Thor to take exception to such behavior, and before he could say "hasenpfeffer," once again she was on the ground spitting out dirt and grass.

By the time he had dusted her off, and worked out that she was saying the English word "who" instead of Huebe, he decided that she would be one mass of bruises if he allowed her to continue to ride on her own. With-out further ado, he mounted Demeter, reached down with one hand, and told her to swing herself up in front of him.

To his surprise (and no little pleasure) she did so without any objection, settling sideways across his thighs, one arm wrapped around his waist while the other clutched his jacket front.

"All right, but only because your horse doesn't like me at all," she said, her breath skittering across his cheek in a way that left his groin heavy and in bad need of a woman's attention. "Can we shift into third now, please?"

"I've shifted as much as I can," he replied, trying to

squeeze a little extra room for her between his body and the pommel, which he knew had to be pressed uncomfortably against her thigh.

Her long, luscious thigh.

"That's not what I meant. Can we go fast?"

He tied the reins of Thor to his saddle, and pressed his heels to Demeter. She didn't care to have two people on her back, and did a little dance of annoyance that he quelled with a muttered imprecation about females.

"Who, now?" Io asked.

"Huebe, not who."

The look she gave him by rights should have dropped him dead on the spot, but of course, he couldn't die. Not anymore.

"Take a look at my face. Do you see my expression? Does it scare you? It should, because this is the expression of a woman who's fallen off a horse too many times to put up with more shenanigans of the verbal variety. Got that? Good. What female, exactly, were you muttering those bad things about?"

"Demeter. Although I was also close to speaking my thoughts about your thighs, but I felt that, given the present circumstances, you would not care to hear them."

She blinked again at him. "Hear my thighs?"

"My thoughts. You can't hear thighs. Not unless they were wrapped around one's head rubbing against the ears." And just the thought of that was enough to almost bring him to his knees. Metaphorically speaking.

Io froze for a moment, her fingers tight on his jacket

front. "Why, oh, why did I leave my pink penguin at home?"

Nikola wasn't sure how to best answer that question, but being in a somewhat benevolent mood despite the insistent throb of his personal parts, he made an attempt at answering it. "Perhaps penguins were not allowed on the ship that you sailed on to Europe. However, I will admit that I have never seen a pink penguin, and I take quite an interest in natural history. The only descriptions I've read all state that they are in shades of white, black, and gray, some of which have slight touches of color around the head."

"No, it's not ... er ... it's not a real penguin." For some reason, Io seemed flustered by this turn in conversation. He was more than intrigued by that phenomenon. "It's my Tingleator. It's shaped like a penguin, you see."

He frowned, but not because they were approaching a shaded section of the road into the valley below. He had no difficulty seeing the road even in the darkest of nights. No, his was a frown of incomprehension, and that was something he disliked intensely. He hated feeling left out of knowledge. "I am unfamiliar with a Tingleator. You will describe it to me."

"Sorry, that may have been too regional. It's my hoe, you know?"

His frown deepened.

"My hoe for the ladygarden."

Perhaps she was mad. Her conversation certainly didn't make too much sense. "You wish to discuss gardening?"

"No, it's not *that* kind of garden. Oh, god, you're going to make me spell it out, aren't you?" Her breath teased his cheek again as she sighed. "Because my life couldn't be any more embarrassing than sitting on some strange man's lap talking about vibrators."

"Woman! You are doing this deliberately!" Nikola had reached the end of his patience. He stopped the horse, shifting Io slightly so as to be able to reach into one of his coat pockets.

"Huh? What have I done? Eek! Stop moving like that or I'll fall again, and I've reached my limit of daily falls from a horse!" She wrapped both arms around him, her eyes huge as he struggled to extract his hand from his pocket. "Oh my god you're going to shoot me!"

"I'm not, but I will admit that it is a tempting thought. Cease struggling or Demeter will object. If you release my arm, I can move it."

Her eyes narrowed on his. "You're just going to pull out a gun or Mace or something and get revenge on me because ... because ... well, hell, I don't know why you'd want revenge on me. I'm the one who's been dumped on the ground all night long."

By sheer dint of superb horsemanship, Nikola managed to keep control not only of his mount and the interested Thor, who kept bumping his back in hopes of treats, but the wildcat in his arms. "I am simply tired of you flaunting your knowledge at me," he snapped, pulling his hand from his pocket. In it was a small memorandum journal.

"I'm what? What knowledge?" Io stopped struggling and watched with curiosity as he flipped open the journal, and wrote with a small pencil that had seen better days.

"Your words. You are using them deliberately to show me that I am inferior to you, and that I will not have. Is 'ladygarden' one word or two? And this 'vibrator'—is it a proper noun?"

She started to laugh, causing Demeter to lay back her ears in warning. Nikola, with one eye on his annoyed horse, tucked away his journal after making a few notes, and sent Demeter into a fast trot.

Io stopped laughing, *eep*ed, and clung to him in a highly gratifying manner for a few minutes before evidently realizing he wasn't going to allow her to fall.

She loosened her hold on his arms and gave him a long look from those lovely eyes. "You seriously think I'm using words you're not familiar with on purpose?"

"I have told you that I have an excellent grasp on the English language. I have not been to the colonies, but I understand that English is spoken there. You seem to have no difficulty in understanding my speech; therefore, you are deliberately attempting to confuse and belittle me linguistically."

"I can assure you, Nikola," she said with a telltale twitch of her lips, "that I am not trying to do either. I don't play the superior game with people, and even if I did, I certainly wouldn't with someone for whom English isn't a first language. I'm horrible at languages, so honestly, I'm impressed with anyone who can speak more than one."

"I will accept your apology for making me feel inferior," he said magnanimously.

"I didn't apologize—"

"But only because you will now proceed to explain the phrases I do not understand. Let us commence with 'ladygarden.'"

She started laughing again, but after a few false starts, and quite a number of blushes, he was finally able to store the words 'ladygarden,' 'vibrator,' and 'love rocket' away in his mental dictionary.

"Do women from the colonies use phalluses frequently?" he was driven to ask as they neared the outskirts of town.

"It's no longer a colony. . . . Oh, skip it. Yes, women in the U.S. use lots of vibrators. And . . . er . . . other things. Nonvibratory ones."

"Why?"

She blinked at him again. He was beginning to find it a wholly endearing gesture. "Why do they use a vibrator?"

"Yes, why? Are there not enough men in the colonies?"

She took a deep breath. He enjoyed the effect that action had on her chest, one breast of which was pressed against him. He began sorting through conversational gambits to pick out the ones that would continue to make her take deep breaths. "Some women," she said with obvious emphasis, "don't need a man in their life. Some of us are quite happy as we are, and like to be in control of our sexual needs and gratification, rather than leaving it to a man who may or may not get his jollies in two minutes flat and leave us lying there unfulfilled and so frustrated we could scream." She took another deep breath, and his penis commended the action. "Not that I'm speaking from experience, you understand."

"You are a virgin?" He found that difficult to believe, not because he had first assumed she was a prostitute, but because she was so clearly meant for male delight, he didn't believe any man would be so foolish as to leave her alone.

She sat bolt upright in his lap, her eyes spitting annoyance. "That, sir, is none of your business."

"You *are* a virgin?"

"No, of course not! I'm in my thirties, for heaven's sake. What do you think I am, some sort of nun or something? Sheesh."

"Ah. Good. I dislike virgins. They tend to weep, and wring their hands, and recoil in horror from the sight of an erect penis, and nothing disturbs a man's peace of mind more than a weeping, hand-wringing virgin shrieking about his penis up and down the house." A thought occurred to him at that moment, an unpleasant thought. If she wasn't a virgin, then she must have been with a man. He gritted his teeth at the thought of some man, probably one of those rough, unkempt colonials, sating his manly lust upon her.

"I think a wee chink in your research armor is showing, Nikola," she said softly, turning her back to him.

He wanted to demand she tell him the name of the lusty colonial who took pleasure in her tempting body. He also wanted to tell himself he didn't care one infinitesimally small jot about how many men had touched her body, but he knew that thought wouldn't even complete itself satisfactorily before it was dismissed as irrelevant and untrue.

"In the history books I've read," she continued, just as if he weren't suffering untold torment envisioning the dirty, slovenly, no doubt ale-addled wastrel as he touched her with his filthy paws, "men were always super big on virginity for their women."

His fingers itched for the rapier he'd left at home. He'd teach that odious, woman-defiling colonial a thing or two about sullying innocent, silky-thighed maidens!

"I hate to say it, but your Google-fu must not be very strong if you missed turning up that fact." She glanced over her shoulder at him and smiled.

He bared his teeth in return. "This monster who de-flowered you—he isn't on the continent, is he?" Oh, how he hoped for an answer in the affirmative.

Her eyes widened in surprise, then narrowed as she thought through what he had asked. "My first boy-friend? You mean Tony? A monster? You know, I'd point out yet again that you're way over the line as far as what's politically correct by asking about him—"

"First?" He pounced on the word. "Good god, woman, how many defilers have there been?"

Her jaw dropped a little. "I can't believe you just asked—no. You didn't. In the interests of U.S.-Austrian relations, I'm going to pretend you didn't ask me how many men I've slept with. In fact, I think I'm just going to pretend I don't know you."

She turned her back on him again, sitting rigidly upright, careful not to touch him any more than she had to.

He didn't like that at all. He liked the idea of her having multiple lovers even less. And most of all, he didn't like just how much it mattered to him to find

each and every man who had touched her, so he could
lesson them within a hairsbreadth of their lives.

"Google ... fu ..." he growled, pulling out the journal and making another note. Then he added the name
Tony, and a reminder to investigate the nearest ship
sailing for the colonies.

He could have sworn she giggled, but she kept her
back turned to him, and said nothing when they entered the outskirts of town. The silence lasted until she
got a good look at buildings they were passing, and
then all hell broke loose.

"What the—no!" she wailed, pushing herself off his
thighs, almost pulling him off the horse as she struggled to the ground. "No, no, no! This can't be! It just
can't!"

"The day I understand women is the day that I turn
back into a normal man," he told Demeter, watching as
Io ran first to one side of the road, then the other, yelling at the top of her lungs at the small houses that staggered in a drunken line toward the town square. "I
suppose I should stop her before she wakes up everyone."

With a martyred sigh, he dismounted. Io was spinning around the square, her hands clutching her hair,
her eyes huge with genuine fear, visible to him even in
what remained of the moonlight.

Something in him stirred at the sight of the fear. She
didn't strike him as the type of woman who backed
down from any challenge, and yet there she was, looking every inch the madwoman she claimed she was on
the verge of becoming.

"Cease this noise," he said sternly, striding toward

her, the horses following him. He stopped and spun around to face them. "Stay there," he said, pointing to the ground.

Demeter lipped his finger and nickered at him. Thor bit her flank, and received a swift rear hoof to the chest in response.

"Stay," he repeated before turning back to Io. The horses followed him, just as he knew they would. He sighed yet another martyred sigh. When had anyone, his horses included, ever done as he ordered? "What is the matter now, woman?"

"The town is the matter!" Io wailed, her lower lip quivering. "It's not right! It's not the way it's supposed to be, and even if you guys were some weirdo reenactment group, you couldn't duplicate an entire town, could you? I mean, I can see that it's right where it's supposed to be, but it's not right, not right at all!"

He put his hands on his hips and considered the town. "I don't see anything amiss. It is not a large town, but it does have three inns, and four wells. I do not know of another of this size that has those amenities."

She quivered for a few seconds before wrapping her arms around herself. "It's . . . it's . . . oh my god, it's true, isn't it? It really *is* 1703. You're not pretending to be an Austrian duke."

"Baron," he corrected.

"I haven't lost my mind. Well, except for the voices talking to me, but maybe that had something to do with the swirly thing, too, because that's what did this to me, Nikola." She took him by the edge of his lapel and shook him with a fervor that boded ill for his coat. "It was that swirly thing in the haunted woods. It sent me back in time. Me! Perfectly normal me! And *now* what the hell am I going to do?"

"What do you wish to do?" he asked.

"Go home!" she answered quickly. "Back to my own time, that is. Not *home* home, because there's nothing waiting for me there but unemployment and all sorts of stress and crap that I really don't need right now. But back to 2012."

He was silent for a few seconds, assessing her behavior. He hadn't ever run across anyone who'd believed they lived in another time, especially not more than three hundred years in the future, but despite all her talk of losing her mind, and the abuse to his coat, she didn't strike him as mad.

Quite the contrary, she was reacting just as he thought he might should he be in her shoes. He ignored the memory of just how lovely her feet and ankles and legs and thighs were as she lay splayed on the ground, and instead asked, "Where is this phenomenon that you believe is responsible for you being here?"

She started to answer, then stopped, releasing his coat and giving him a curious look. "Wait just one second. . . . You aren't telling me I'm nutso-cuckoo."

He stared at her for a moment, then pulled out his journal. "Nutso-cuckoo."

She smiled. "It's a flip way of saying deranged. How come you don't think I'm crazy, Nikola? Why haven't you even said it's impossible for me to have traveled back in time?"

He shrugged. "I have ample proof that the impossible is often all too possible."

"You mean because your son thinks he's a vampire?"

He glanced around the square, taking her arm and pulling her toward the road that led back up the side of the mountain, the horses trailing behind them. "The term is Dark One, as I've told you, and if you do not mind, I prefer to keep that news from the townspeople. Benedikt is young, and I have tried to shield him as best I can from the prejudice that arises from the unenlightened."

"Wait a minute." Io frowned down at the road for the time it took them to walk past three cottages. "I saw Benedikt and Imogen in my time—whoa, I can't believe I just said that. Don't you think I'm handling this whole impossible situation really well? I do. I think I should get some sort of commendation, or award, or at least a 'Didn't Go Insane When Others Would Have' tiara. Where was I? Oh, I saw both Benedikt and Imogen yesterday. That's my yesterday, not yours. Anyway, I just saw them, and they look a bit older than they do here, but not a lot older, not, you know, three hundred years older. Imogen looks like she's in her early thirties, and Benedikt a few years younger than that. How can that be?"

"I was told that the children of unredeemed Dark Ones carry the stain of their father's curse; hence Benedikt is as immortal as Imogen."

"Imogen is a vampire, too? Wow. So, that stuff about vampires being immortal isn't just folklore? It's really true?" She was silent for a moment or two while she thought about that. "That's kind of scary, and yet at the same time, really intriguing. I mean, all that stuff Imogen must have seen firsthand! It kind of boggles the mind. And it would also explain why she looks so much younger than Gretl."

"Your cousin?"

"Yeah. I just can't wrap my mind around the idea that Imogen is a vampire, too. She seems so normal. Does she drink bloo—whoa Nellie!" She stopped, spinning around to face him. Demeter bumped into his back when he, too, stopped. "The *children* of a Dark One? You mean *you're* a vampire?"

"We established that fact earlier," he answered, pulling her forward again so Demeter would stop nibbling on the back of his head. He'd gone out without a hat, a fact he now regretted considering the horse's propensity to graze on his hair.

"We did? When did we do that? You mean—" She gasped, sucking in a huge quantity of air. "Oh my god you bit me! You're a vampire and you bit me! You drank my blood! I'm going to turn into a vampire now!"

"It doesn't work like that, I've found," he said, steering her forward once more. Honestly, if she shouted any louder, the neighboring towns could hear, as well. "I believe you have to be cursed to this state, as I was. I've fed off of many women over the past twenty-five years, and none of them have ever turned into a Dark One."

"You bit me!" she repeated, her voice warming slightly as she obviously remembered the experience. It would certainly remain high on his list of memories. Just the thought of her warm, silky softness beneath him had him hard and aching, the hunger deep inside him rising to claim his mind, leaving him extremely aware that she was just a few inches away from him.

He wanted her, wanted her in more ways than just to satisfy his hunger. He wanted to touch and caress and stroke every inch of her. He wanted to feast on her with all his senses, tasting and touching and licking. He wanted to join with her in the most fundamental way a man can with a woman, and he wanted it all right that very instant.

"Holy shit," she said, her eyes huge as she looked at him two seconds before she suddenly lunged, her arms and legs wrapping around him, sending him rocking backward into Demeter.

The horse sidestepped him, dammit. He hit the ground with a loud whump, but even Io's head impacting his chin didn't stop her. She tugged at his neckcloth until it was freed, baring his throat. He had just enough presence of mind to say in what he hoped was an outraged tone of voice, "Madame! Unhand me! I do not find seduction on the road within view of town in the least bit arousing."

It was a lie, of course, since he didn't believe he could possibly be more aroused than he was at that moment, but a man had to have some standards, and making love to this delectable, enticing woman in the road was not one of them.

Now, if they moved onto the grass, that would be an entirely different situation.

Io froze, her eyes growing large as she looked down at him. "Oh my god, I did it again! I attacked you! I can't believe I attacked you a second time!"

"It wasn't quite what I think of as an attack, although

I would have appreciated a softer fall." He got to his feet when she rolled off him, her face suffused with color.

"I'm so sorry! I can't believe I just jumped you like that. I have no excuse at all, except all of a sudden I was so . . . and I wanted to . . . and it was like I was hungry of all things, which I guess now that I think about it, I am, but this was a different kind of hunger. It was red, and pulsing, and so overwhelming that I just wanted to touch and taste and lick you—" She stopped speaking, snapping her teeth together before adding, "I'm sorry again. I shouldn't have said that. It's like I've suddenly become Ms. Wholly Inappropriate Sexual Harassment."

He finished brushing himself off, looking at her and wondering. "It was red?"

"My face? Oh, yes." She marched off, her hands briefly rising to her cheeks, which he had to admit were a dusky rose. "I can't tell you how embarrassed I am. I just seem to lose all control around you."

"No, the hunger you felt. It was red, you said?"

"I'm never going to be able to live this down, absolutely will never be able to live—what? Oh, yes, red and hot and . . . and . . ." She stopped and slid him a curious look. "I'm not going to continue or I'll end up shaming myself again, and really, I think I've about reached the limit of things I can cope with in one night. Between unexpected time traveling and sexual moves on a man I don't know, who just happens to be a vampire who drank my blood . . . hey, do you think that could be why I want to jump you so bad? Maybe it's your fault. I think it is. I think you did something to me to make me want to do wholly inappropriate sexual things to you.

Anyway, between that and the whole going-back-in-time thing, I think my brain is pretty much going to explode if I do anything else out of the ordinary, so I'm just going to walk quietly and meditate to calm myself down. Om."

"I wish to try an experiment," Nikola said after a few minutes' thought. He glanced around, making sure they were out of view of the town. Dawn was less than an hour away, and he knew the townspeople would be stirring with the coming light.

"What sort of an experiment?" Io asked suspiciously.

He pulled her off the road and into a field that had been left fallow, tall grasses skirting the edges of it. He leaned into her, not touching her, but allowing her scent to sink deep into his pores, the hunger immediately responding with urgent demands that he claim her.

She growled low in her throat, and flung herself on him again. This time he was ready for her, and braced himself, rocking back only a little as her body slammed into his. He thought for a moment or two that he might just die of pleasure when she bit his earlobe, his neck, and his chin, all the while scattering kisses, and murmuring words that didn't make any sense, but he felt such an extreme act on his part might be interpreted as being unappreciative, not to mention rude, so he held his ground and allowed her to have her way with him.

Until one of her hands snaked its way into his shirt and touched his bare chest. Then the hunger that he'd been keeping so carefully leashed slipped his control.

"Woman! You push me too far!" He lowered her onto the soft grass, shredding her gown from where it hid her body from his eyes. She shrieked a little shriek that turned into a moan of pleasure when he bent over her, nuzzling his face in two delectable mounds of breasts where they were contained in some sort of abbreviated stays.

"Oh my god, yes!" she cried, then suddenly began to struggle, shoving him over onto his back.

He stared at her in surprise. Did she not want him the way he wanted her? "You say yes, but you thrust me away from your breasts and belly and those thighs that are begging for my mouth? I begin to believe your claim that you are deranged!"

She stared at him for a moment in utter disbelief, then pounced on him, just as if she were a cat and he something hard and manly and about to spontaneously combust with the need to bite and taste and claim her once and for all. She bit and licked and murmured some more, all the while tugging and pulling at his coat and shirt until she had his upper parts bare. He thought of protesting such liberties, but in fairness, he had shredded her gown first, so he felt it was only right that she should have equal time with his garments.

"Not the breeches, though," he told her when her hands wandered down to the buttons that kept him from bursting out into the open. "My daughter made them for me for my last birthday, and she would not like it if you, in your wild and unfettered female lust, ripped them off my body."

"Too much talking!" Io snarled, and, straddling him,

leaned over his chest to take one of his nipples in her mouth.

He arched up, unable to articulate the sensation of her mouth, hot and sweet and so wonderfully wicked, on a purely mundane piece of his personal equipment. *Yes, yes, there is entirely too much talking! Cease it immediately and do the other one!*

She moved along his chest, her mouth burning a path over to where his second nipple was waiting impatiently for its turn. *You taste so hot. Spicy hot, like the fire that burns inside of me. I want to bite you and taste you and ride you like you're a bucking bronco.*

His eyes, which had rolled back in his head at the touch of her mouth on his nipples, promptly rolled forward again so as to enable him to stare down at the top of her head in surprise. What the devil? There was a voice in his head, a foreign voice, one that hadn't been there before. What was going on? Had Io somehow infected him with her voice-in-head derangement? Was that even possible?

She froze, slowly pushing herself upright. *I've infected you? That's . . . you? Nikola? You're talking in my head?*

Goose bumps rolled along his body at the touch of her mind to his. This was extraordinary! He must, at once, take notes on the phenomenon, detailed and lengthy notes about exactly what was happening to him. Only by keeping the strictest scientific control over the situation could he learn from it. He would write a paper about it, and submit it to the best of the scientific journals. He would no doubt become the world's most preeminent expert on mind-talking.

How the hell are you doing that? Io asked, shifting backward.

All thoughts of the acceptance speech he would make when granted an award by whatever university first recognized his brilliance faded to nothing when Io's ass, her round, warm, so incredibly tempting ass, pressed his extremely erect penis, making him see stars for a few seconds. Her eyes opened wide a scant second or two before she rocked backward again, nearly causing him to spill his seed right then and there.

I don't know how I'm doing it, but if you do not cease tormenting me with your derriere, I will do all those things you are thinking about, including the one where you are on all fours. And that one, as well, although I can't imagine being upside down like that would be very comfortable for you.

Aiee! she shrieked into his head. *You can read my smutty thoughts! Oh my god! I'm sexually harassing you* and *I'm insane! Wait . . . if I'm insane, then you are, as well, and you're thinking just as many naughty thoughts about me as I am about you. Oooh! Especially that one, Mr. Likes the Cowgirl Position. And for the record, don't knock the Kama Sutra, because that wheelbarrow position is made of all sorts of awesome. Er . . . so I'm told.*

"The what?" he managed to gasp out as his mind was filled with the most erotic images he'd ever in his life entertained. That they had their source in Io just made them all that much more irresistible.

"Kama Sutra. Old Indian sex guide. Not that I'm going to have sex with you, because I don't do that with men I just met, even if my mind has coped with a lot of crap in the last few hours, and thus I'd be excused to give in and jump you as you obviously wish to be jumped."

Despite his demands to the contrary (and her odious statement that she didn't intend to give in to the urges she was projecting to him), she slid backward down his body, her nimble fingers unbuttoning the fall front of his breeches. "Sweet mother of seriously fabulous penises! You're really ... *statuesque.*"

She didn't wait for an invitation—which was a good thing, since at that moment he fully believed that the power of speech and cognitive thought had abandoned him—she simply reached out and took him into both hands.

And I thought the thing with the nipples was good, he moaned into her head shortly before falling back on the grass, his hands twitching spasmodically as she stroked him.

Oh my god, you're so very hot. And hard. Your dick is like steel or something. That has to hurt.

It does, it does. A glorious hurt, he moaned again, his hips moving in time to her hands.

I can't believe you're talking to me. Right inside my head, you're talking to me. Thank god I'm not insane. Although maybe I am after all because, Nikola, I really, really want to bite you.

His hips froze for a moment while he opened one eyelid and looked down at where she straddled his thighs, his extremely happy penis twitching slightly in her hands. "Rough bedsport is not enticing to me, Io. Although I did enjoy you biting me on the neck. If you insist on biting me—and rest assured that I will reciprocate—then you may do so there, but nowhere else."

She looked down at where he overflowed her hands. She looked up to his neck. Her gaze wandered back and forth between the two spots for a few seconds while the hunger in him surged and demanded to be sated upon her.

"Deal," she said at last, releasing his arousal and crawling up his body, her mouth hot on his neck before once again, she gently bit the corded tendon found therein.

He thought he might pass out from the pleasure her touch gave him.

You really like that, don't you? she asked, wiggling provocatively against him, her breasts still confined in their satin stays, some sort of matching undergarment clad about her loins. He wanted to object to that garment, but as the warm satin fabric covering her crotch pressed against his penis, he knew he was once again perilously close to emptying his stones.

I do, but not as much as I like this. He wrapped his hands around her delectable ass, moving her back and forth against him as at last he gave in to the hunger, biting the soft, silky flesh of her shoulder.

She moaned aloud while he drank, moving against him now with soft little urgent cries. His fingers slid beneath the material, around the soft globes of her ass to her warm, welcoming depths. She cried again, her body shaking as she shifted against him, pushing him past a point of all bearing. His fingers brushed against sensitive flesh, and sent her spiraling into an orgasm that triggered his own, his cry mingling with hers as it floated up into the predawn sky.

"Great." Io's voice interrupted his blissful sense of

sexually sated oblivion. He opened his eyes and looked down to where she had pushed herself off his chest, her knees still clasping his hips. "Now I can add dry-humping a stranger to my list of sexual harassment sins. Thank you, Nikola, thank you so very much."

"You're welcome," he said, sensing that for some reason she didn't mean the words literally. She seemed slightly annoyed, as a matter of fact. He wondered why that would be when she had enjoyed herself as much as he had. Could it be because he had spilled his seed on her undergarment, thereby staining it? He frowned at the undergarment in question.

"What the hell are you doing frowning at my lady parts?"

Io sounded outraged.

"I'm not frowning at them."

"You are. Your eyebrows are all pulled down be-tween your gorgeous eyes, making me want to run my fingers along them to smooth them out. That, sir, is a frown, and it's directed at my nether bits. There's noth-ing there to frown at, I assure you. I pruned before I came to Austria, not that I expected to get it on with anyone, and especially not that we're going to hook up." She paused. "Other than what we've already done, obviously. But that's not really going gung ho forward, is it? It was just kind of quasi there."

He had absolutely no idea what she was going on about, so he focused on the one thing that did make sense. "My eyes are sufficiently smooth, thank you," he corrected her, still frowning at that part of her that was so tantalizingly close. It was true that the entire front of the pale peach undergarment was wet with his seed, but that wasn't what bothered him.

"You know what I mean. Why are you frowning at my crotch?"

"I am frowning at that ridiculous garment you are wearing to hide it from my view."

She looked startled for a moment before looking down to where his penis—now succumbing to a restful state—lay against her pubic mound. "My...underwear?"

"Whatever it is called, I dislike it."

"It's Victoria's Secret, you boob! It's very expensive! I got it for myself last Christmas, before I was fired by my asshat of a boss. Besides, it matches the bra."

"I don't care what it matches, or whose secret it is, I dislike it because it keeps your flesh from meeting mine as is right and proper. Remove it immediately."

"Look, I may have done things with you that I never do with a man I've just met, but that doesn't give you the right to demand I remove my undies even if they are a bit ooky now because you got all excited on them. Not that I'm holding you entirely to blame for that, since your vamp-biting thing made me crazy wild with lust. But still, it's not going to happen, so just get over it already." She got to her feet and stalked over to where the remains of her gown lay on the ground.

Nikola stared up at the lightening sky and considered and discarded a number of scenarios in which he showed Io that he was not the type of man who cared what others thought or felt, and decided, in the end, to be magnanimous. He would allow her to continue believing that she had every right to speak to him in that wholly irreverent manner, but only so long as it took to write his brilliant paper and receive his award. In the meantime, he would sate himself on her, giving in to the siren lure of her delicious person, and take his fill, then simply walk away from her and continue on with his life.

The Incredible Adventures of Iolanthe Tennyson

July 13

I'm a bit embarrassed to write what happened early this morning. Oh, it was totally Nikola's fault, because it's obvious that he did something to my brain when he sucked my blood and all, but even with the vampire compulsion or thrall or whatever it is that vamps do to ensnare innocent women's minds and make them their love slaves, it was still me that jumped his bones. Repeatedly.

And enjoyed every damned second of it.

"You are wholly to blame for this," I pointed out to Nikola a short while after the scene on the side of the road.

"A fact which I have admitted, and reassured you that I will replace your gown," he said in that yummy British accent he had. That voice seemed to do something to me, make all of my innards vibrate with happiness every time he spoke. I told my innards to cool it, that we'd shamed ourselves enough for one day.

"I was actually talking about the fact that you enslaved my mind with your lustful thoughts rather than the fact that you ripped my brand-new sundress to shreds," I corrected him, glancing down at myself. With my dress in tatters, I wore his shirt and coat, the former of which reached down to my knees since it was exceptionally long.

"I didn't enslave your mind." Nikola rode next to me, the rosy fingers of dawn managing to caress his bare chest and arms in a way that made my breath stop in my lungs. "I cannot enslave anyone's mind."

I cleared my throat and dragged my eyes off him.

"Then you enthralled me or did something to make me your love slave."

He sighed. "I've just told you that I cannot do that. That's not to say I wouldn't if I could, because the idea of being surrounded by love slaves appeals to me, and being a man, I am naturally in need of many women to attend to my varied sexual needs, but unfortunately, I have not yet discovered that a Dark One can enslave minds."

"You'd love a herd of love-struck women swooning over you," I said with a glare at him. The dawg!

"It is the way of things," he agreed.

I was about to tell him what I thought of that sentiment when a thought occurred to me. "You said your wife has been dead for a bit?"

"Seven years, yes." He shot me a curious look.

"How long were you married?"

The look got significantly more pointed. "Sixteen years."

"And what did your wife think of you messing around

with this great big herd of women that your manful lusts demanded?"

He stiffened in the saddle, making his horse do a little side step that he quickly got under control. "Madame, I can assure you that my wife never had complaints about me in that regard."

For some reason, his outrage made me want to giggle. Oh, I had his number all right—he was all bark and little bite.

So to speak.

"However, I have been without a wife for many years, and it is a well-known fact that men have sexual needs greater than those of women."

My amusement faded. "You are so—that is utter and complete bullshit! It is *not* a well-known fact! It's a well-known fallacy put around by a bunch of horny men who want to justify having sex with every woman they can sweet-talk into bed, that's all. For your information, women have the same amount of sexual needs as men. Boy, you guys really did have some messed-up ideas about things."

"I have read many scientific papers on the subject, and they all agree that men's needs are more prevalent and varied than women's."

"You can stuff your scientific papers where the sun don't shine as far as I'm concerned."

"Doesn't."

I gawked at him for a few seconds.

"The correct grammar is 'where the sun doesn't shine.'" He frowned as he thought. "Although that is an odd thing to say. If you meant night, why did you not simply say 'at night'?"

"I know what the correct grammar is, you ignoramus! It's a saying. It means you can shove your outdated, woman-stifling, chauvinistic ideas up your butt."

His eyebrows rose a quarter of an inch. "I do not at all enjoy that sort of thing, either. And if you do, I regret to inform you—"

"No!" Thor, Imogen's horse, tossed his head around at my shriek. I lowered my voice and gritted my teeth. "I don't like that, either, not that I've tried it, but it's not something I intend to experiment with, so let's move past that, shall we?"

"You're the one who brought it up," he pointed out.

"I didn't mean to literally stick something up your—" I took a deep breath, struggling to get a good, solid grip on my temper, which was not an easy task when Nikola seemed determined to drive me bonkers. "I don't even remember how we got onto the subject of your ridiculous ideas about women and sex."

"You accused me of making you my love slave, which is lamentably incorrect, because if you were my love slave, you would even now be impaled on my penis."

The image of that so filled my mind, I had to take a minute or two to get past it. "Er ... while we were on the horse?" I eventually managed to ask, unable to keep myself from glancing at his lap.

His eyebrows rose again. "If you desire. I've heard it can be stimulating, assuming both persons have good seats."

That thought kept us both quiet for a short bit. After realizing that I was considering just where my arms and legs would go with regards to his saddle, I gave myself another mental scold, and returned to the matter at hand. "I was simply pointing out that someone is responsible for my state of mind. How else do you explain the fact that I've jumped you three times now?"

He glanced at me with those wickedly gorgeous pale blue eyes, a little smile dancing on his lips. "Perhaps you simply desire me as much as I desire you."

"We just met, and I'm the sort of a woman who likes men for their minds, not their bodies. It's a well-known fact among my friends that I have to know a man for some time before I get sexually interested. Gretl says I'm too picky that way, but it's just the way I am. So clearly, this whole situation with me wanting to do things to you is your fault, and not mine."

"Indeed." That was all he said, but when he did so, he brushed a bug off his chest. Instantly, my gaze went to his bare chest, my hands tingling with the desire to stroke the lovely muscles that made up some really spectacular viewing.

Oh, dear lord, I was doing it again! Honestly, I wasn't such a ninny that I couldn't be near the man without wanting him to do all sorts of erotic things to me.

But I want to do those erotic things. Especially that one where you spread oil on us both and slither around on top of me.

"And you can stop egging on my poor, deluded brain! Besides, that's eavesdropping pure and simple, and I'm not going to stand for it. Now, what we need here is to get organized."

"I am completely organized," Nikola said blandly. "Every aspect of my life is orderly and well-thought-out. I run my house with a firm hand. My children and servants know that should they disorder that to which I have brought order, they will suffer the most grievous of penalties. Dedicated study to the unknown, order, and a calm clarity of mind are all my bywords. In short, madame, I am the personification of the word organized."

I murmured a word to myself that was not at all polite, and gave some thought to the situation. "It's clear that somehow that swirly thing in the woods was responsible for me being zapped back here. Therefore, I need to find it again, and let it send me back where I belong."

"You have not fully explained this swirly thing, as you call it. What, exactly, is it?"

"It's kind of hard to describe." I spent a few seconds summoning my memories, and explained to Nikola the happenings in the woods.

"I do not understand this photograph that you keep referring to," he said after a long pause. He had pulled out his notebook from a pocket in his breeches, and made a brief note or two. "Nor why a cloud of smoke had the ability to alter time."

"The swirly thing wasn't really smoke—it just kind of looked smoky. It was more like—I don't know—light, I guess. Swirls of light twisting around on itself. And a photograph is like a painting, only more realistic. It's a two-dimensional representation of an object or scene."

"Indeed." He made a few more notes. I smiled to myself. I'd never thought that I was an overly curious person, but the fact that Nikola's interest in the world around him was clearly far more developed than mine tickled me.

It also made me feel profoundly stupid about those things that people in my time took for granted.

"And why were you in the woods to begin with?"

"Hmm? Oh, I was looking for a setting to take some pictures of Imogen, but she—" The words stopped as a memory of Imogen's face rose with horrible clarity in my mind.

Imogen refused to go to the woods because she said that's where her uncles had killed her father. Slowly, I turned to look at Nikola. He rode beside me, one hand holding the reins against his thigh while the other hand flipped through the pages of his notebook.

I was confused pure and simple—Imogen said her father was killed in the woods one fateful night, while her brother had claimed he was alive and well and living in South America, enjoying the scantily clad women that abounded there.

My eyes narrowed at Nikola. I had no difficulty imagining him being in seventh heaven in such a surrounding.

But which of the siblings was right? Had Benedikt lied to me about his father being alive? Or had Imogen? And if Imogen was telling the truth—a cold wave swept over me despite the warmth of Nikola's coat. "The anniversary of his death is in a couple of days," I said softly, repeating the words Imogen had spoken to me.

"Whose death?" Nikola asked, looking up from his notebook.

"Er . . . no one's."

A chill swept over me. It was clear now that Imogen had been speaking the truth. No doubt she had told her

younger brother a lie to keep him from being traumatized by the true events of that dreadful day.

None of that altered the horrible realization that
Nikola could be in deadly peril. Possibly we were a few
hours away from the day when, in some unknown year,
Nikola would die.

What if it *was* this year?

That thought held me in its terrible grip the remainder of the trip back to Nikola's castle. By the time we
got there, I'd come to two conclusions—one, that I
needed to waste no time finding the swirly light thing,
and returning to my own reality, and two, if it was at all
possible to warn Nikola about his brothers' murderous
intent without messing up the time-space continuum,
or whatever it is that the people in *Star Trek* were always worried about whenever they time traveled, then
I would do so.

"I'm not going to sleep with you," I told the empty
room into which Nikola deposited me once we arrived
at his castle on the mountaintop. "But Imogen is Gretl's
friend—will be Gretl's friend—and for that reason, and
because you were nice enough to let me wear your
shirt, not to mention the fact that your chest holds an
unholy fascination for me, because of all that, I will
warn you about the evil plot your brothers are hatch-
ing. But that's it. Nothing more. No sex, no more nooky,
nothing."

The fire crackling in the fireplace across from the
bed was the only response to my bold statement. I
sighed and sat down on the bed, wondering how on
earth I was going to manage to keep myself from jumping Nikola the next time I saw him.

"You're doing this on purpose," I said three minutes later when the door opened and Nikola strolled in, clad once again in a white shirt, long waistcoat of blue and gold, and midnight blue coat that reached almost to his knees.

"Yes, I am. I frequently have a purpose when I enter a room. I find that if I don't, I just wander around the castle bumping into things. Why aren't you in bed?"

I gasped and clutched a beautifully embroidered pillow to my chest. "I knew it! You just want to get into my pants! Well, I meant what I said, Buster Brown, so you can just put that in your pipe and smoke it."

Nikola frowned. "I do not smoke a pipe. Tobacco bothers my daughter. You are supposed to be in bed. I instructed you to retire since you have fallen off a horse four times—"

"That last time was totally your fault! I told you to catch me and you didn't."

"I wasn't aware you were going to dismount on the incorrect side. If you had done it properly—"

"Oh, I like that! I'm the newbie at riding, so you should have made your dismounting instructions more comprehensive. And as for your instructions—"

"In addition to which you ran headlong into Heinrich with such force as to make yourself insensible—"

"That was probably also your fault, too," I said darkly. Although most of my memory had returned, I didn't remember running into Nikola's carriage, as he said I had.

"And finally, the exertion of attempting to seduce me on three separate occasions must all have taken its toll on your constitution, and thus you need rest." He finished with a little bow to me, hands making an elegant gesture that was heightened by the pretty lace at his wrists. Oddly enough, the lace didn't make him look effeminate—quite the opposite, it enhanced the raw masculinity that he seemed to exude.

I was about to point out to him that I was a big girl, and perfectly able to determine when I needed sleep, but the truth was, I felt as if I were two inches away from shattering into a billion pieces of exhaustion.

The door opened before I could inform Nikola of my intention to get some rest. Imogen bustled into the room with her arms full of white linen.

"Papa?" she asked, giving him a curious look before sliding it toward me. "What are you doing here?"

"This is my castle. I own it. I inherited it from my father, your grandfather for whom you are named." Nikola frowned at his daughter. "Thus the answer to your question is that I am here because I have every right to be here."

"Your father's name was Imogen?" I asked Nikola.

He moved the frown over to me. "Of course it wasn't. Imogen is a female name. My father's name was Fidele."

"But you said—"

"Papa, you should not be here. Miss Iolanthe is an unmarried woman in an advanced state of undress, and I will not allow you to take advantage of her," Imogen interrupted, setting down the stack of clothing on the corner of the bed. "You may leave, and I will attend to her."

"Woman!" He fairly yelled the word. "I will not be gainsaid in my own home! If I wish to be here, in this room of the castle of which I am the lord and master, so that Io might seduce me again, then here is where I will stand, and there is naught you can say to me to remove me from the premises. Now begone, so that the lady might begin her seduction without an audience."

Imogen slowly turned to look at me, a speculative glint in her eyes. "You seduced my father?"

"No! I would never! I just happened to jump him once or twice—"

"Three times."

"Once or three times, not that anyone should be counting." I shot Nikola a potent glare. "But there was no seduction. It was just ... er ... how old are you?"

Imogen's lips pursed for a moment. "Does my age matter?"

"It does if you don't know about the birds and bees."

She frowned. "What birds and bees?"

"It's a euphemism for ... eh ... men and women. Being together. Intimately."

"Sexual congress, you mean?" She nodded. "Of course I know about that."

"You do not!" Nikola roared, pinning her back with a glare that should have ripped her hair right off her head. "You are a young and thoroughly innocent maiden!"

"Yes, of course I am, Papa, but I have eyes. I've seen the animals, and the people in town, and that really handsome stableboy with the very large ... muscles." Her gaze dropped demurely, but I didn't believe for one second that Imogen was as innocent as Nikola believed.

It wasn't any of my business, however. "The fact is

that I did *not* try to seduce your father, or rather, I did, but I was under the compulsion of the thing he did to brainwash me into thinking I wanted him right at that very second. And I don't. So it was all a mistake."

She pursed her lips again. "I see. You find my father handsome."

Oh, handsome wasn't the word for what Nikola was. He went far beyond that and hovered over the "devastatingly gorgeous" range. "I don't see what my opinion of Nikola's looks matters, but as it happens, yes, I think he's pretty easy on the eyes."

Nikola looked pleased.

You're also arrogant, pushy, and you have so many wrong ideas.

You want me nonetheless. You want me naked on that bed behind you, covered in some form of lemon oil that I've not seen before. You want to rub yourself on me.

Dammit, stop reading my smutty thoughts!

They're about me. I would be remiss in my hostly duties if I did not offer the common courtesy of being interested in what devilish things you wish to do to my man's body. Next time you wish to have sexual fantasies about me, however, please let me know in advance so that I might enjoy them, too.

"How old are you?"

Imogen's question took me a bit by surprise. "Er ... thirty-something." I glanced at Nikola. "As long as we're playing twenty questions, how old are you? Not that I care in any way, shape, or form, because we are *not* going to have a relationship, despite you offering yourself for seduction, but it will make me feel a lot better about the way you made me jump you if I know you're not young enough to be emotionally scarred by the circumstances."

"I was two score when Imogen was born, and that was a little more than a score ago," he said, his frown growing darker. "Imogen, I have ordered you to leave this chamber. Why have you not done as I have commanded?"

"Miss Iolanthe—I'm sorry, but I don't know your surname—is obviously in need of assistance since you managed to remove almost all of her garments before bringing her home," Imogen said mildly. "I know my duty, and that is to ensure her safety while she is under our protection."

"I will see to any protecting that needs to be done," Nikola said firmly.

"You're the one I need protecting from," I said, throwing grammar to the wind. "I'm not afraid to be alone with anyone else, least of all Imogen."

"There, you see?" Imogen shooed her father toward the door. To my surprise, Nikola allowed himself to be shooed, casting belligerent looks over his shoulder toward me. "I will take care of her, Papa."

"Unhand me, daughter! I will not be treated in this manner!"

"No, of course you won't," Imogen said soothingly, and then more or less shoved Nikola through the door, ignoring his sputters of protest. She closed the door behind him and turned around to face me, a faint smile on her lips fading away to nothing.

"I really don't need help, but I appreciate the offer," I said, wondering at the odd look she was giving me. "I hate to give your father the satisfaction of being correct, but I am very tired, and wouldn't mind a little nap."

"I have brought you some night things," she said, moving to the stack of linen on the bed. "And also a gown, because yours was destroyed by Papa. Although I'm not sure I understand why that is so, since he's normally a very circumspect man. Perhaps you would care to enlighten me?"

I clamped my lips closed on the truth. Although Imogen was certainly old enough to know her father had a sexuality that was normal and natural, I had no idea if eighteenth-century women were copacetic discussing such things, especially when it concerned a parent. So instead I smiled and thanked her when she held out a lacy, frilly nightgown.

"Is it true that you ran into Papa's carriage horse?" Imogen asked as she puttered around the room, picking up Nikola's shirt from where I tossed it in order to slip into the nightgown.

"That's what he says. I don't remember anything about it. Imogen—" I bit my lip, not sure how to ask her the question I wanted most to ask. "About your father—he has two brothers, doesn't he?"

"Why do you wish to know that?" Imogen countered, a small frown pulling her brows together.

I took a deep breath and gave up trying to tie all the little ties on the front of the nightgown. "This is going to sound completely crazy, and I don't blame you one bit if you think I've gone insane, but I'm from the future. Your future, that is."

She just looked at me for a few seconds, then pulled

a wide, armless chair over, and sat in it. "I don't see what that has to do with my family."

"You're not going to even question the idea that I am from the future?" I asked, completely surprised by her apparent nonchalance in accepting such a bizarre idea. "If the situation was reversed, I'd totally be calling the local loony bin for you."

Imogen's frown increased for a few seconds. "I do not know this loony bin. As for what you claim . . ." She made a delicate shrug. "I do not believe or discount what you say. I merely am inquiring what that has to do with my father's family."

"It matters because we've met. Or we will meet. In my time, I met you two days ago, and one of the things you told me was that your father had been killed by his brothers. I just want to know if that's true."

"It can hardly be true if my father is alive, which he is." Imogen's voice may have been light—and slightly tinged with a mocking tone that I could have done without—but her expression was grave.

"I meant, does he have two brothers?"

"No," she answered.

I sat on the edge of the bed, wondering what the present-day Imogen had been up to, since she had obviously been lying to me.

"He has two half brothers, younger sons of my grandmother when she married a second time."

A chill swept over me despite the warmth from the big fire. I shivered and clutched a puffy eiderdown around me. "Half brothers. That's right, you said half brothers. Those are the dudes."

She shook her head. "They are not here. They live in

a small town to the north. They've never gotten along with Papa, so he gave them a small property he owned, where they could be their own masters and not be beholden to him."

I racked my brain, trying to remember what Imogen had told me about her father's death. Was there something about the brothers being jealous of him? "Whereabouts do they live, exactly?"

She named a town that I didn't recognize, adding, "We see them twice a year, once on Papa's birthday, and the second at the anniversary of my grandmother's death, but neither event is for some time. Why would my uncles want Papa dead?"

I just looked at her, unsure how to answer. I didn't want to cause her more pain by admitting her uncles were jealous of Nikola's luck in being born first, and thereby being the heir to a castle and title, but on the other hand, she deserved to know the truth. Assuming it was the truth. "I'm afraid I don't know all the details, because when we met—in 2012—you didn't say much other than the anniversary of your father's death was coming up, and that he'd been killed in some woods by his two half brothers. I think you said something about them being jealous, but I can't really remember for sure. So much has happened since then."

"You said he was killed in a woods? What woods?"

"I'm afraid I don't know. You just said woods, and from what I could tell in the dark coming back here from the town, this whole region is covered in woods. Then there's the weird woods that held the swirly thing that brought me back in time—Gretl said it was haunted, and that people in the area had avoided it for a long time. But that reputation is understandable given what happened to me there. I don't know where that is, either, since my memory seems to be incomplete, but I plan on searching for it as soon as I've had a little nap. Does your father have a favorite spot in the woods he likes to visit?"

"Not that I know of. He likes to go hunting, but he does that in a number of places." Pain flickered across her face as she clasped her hands together. "I can't thank you enough for coming back through the centuries to make sure this tragedy will not happen. Truly, it is a miracle that you are here with us now. Fate has indeed been kind to us in that you have been sent to save Papa."

"I don't really believe in fate that way," I said slowly, more than a little uncomfortable by the fervent light in her eyes. "I believe people make their own futures, rather than being a bit of flotsam that gets picked up by some random happenstance. But back to the subject at hand—I guess if your uncles aren't around, then this wasn't the year your father was killed, which frankly makes me very happy because I don't want to see anyone killed, let alone someone as lickable as Nikola. Likable! I meant likable! Not lickable at all."

She shrugged again. "I do not mind that you find my father sexually attractive. He *is* attractive, and my mother has been dead for many years. He is lonely. He desires women, but does not take them when they are offered to him. It is most perplexing. My brother says— but you are not interested in that. I must consider how best to approach the subject of my uncles with my father. Needless to say, I am grateful that you have traveled so far to save him."

"About that . . ." I said with obvious hesitation. "See, the thing is, I didn't come back in time to save Nikola. That is, I would if it was feasible, although your dad is kind of bossy and has some seriously antiquated ideas. He seems very nice once you get past those points, even if he is a vampire, but there's more to saving him than showing up and warning him that at some point in the future his brothers are going to off him. For one, we don't know when that is going to happen. . . . Wait a sec." A faint memory returned to me. "Your dad said he was more than three score, right? A score is twenty years, isn't it?"

"Yes."

"So he's over sixty?" I shook my head. "He doesn't look older than maybe thirty or thirty-two at a stretch."

"He is a Dark One. They do not appear to age unless they desire to do so."

"Gotcha." I let go the idea that I was turned on by a sixty-plus-year-old vampire, and focused on what was important. According to Nikola, Imogen was just twenty, and the faint memory I had of her saying she was twenty-two when her dad died told me exactly when the event was going to happen: two years in the future.

I closed my mouth on that knowledge, though. If saving Nikola had the potential to mess up the future, the thought of how things might change if either Imogen or he was in possession of the date of his death was even worse. "If only we could get around this stupid paradox," I murmured more to myself than to Imogen.

"Paradox?" She was back to frowning again. "What paradox?"

"The one that happens if you change the past. OK,

it's been a moot point up to now, but there's been a lot of speculation about what would happen if you changed something minor in the past. The most popular conclusion is that even something so simple as stepping on a bug could have major ramifications down the line. So imagine how something as big as stopping a man being murdered could affect the future."

Imogen crossed her arms. "Are you saying that you will allow Papa to be killed?"

"No, not at all. At least . . ." I bit my lip. "At least not until I can figure out a way to do that without upsetting the future."

"Is your future life so important that you would allow my father's life to be taken from him?" Imogen demanded, suddenly reminding me of Nikola at his most outraged.

"My life is no great shakes, no, but that's just my situation. There are millions of people out there who probably have perfectly wonderful lives, and saving Nikola might change that."

"I don't see why," Imogen said scornfully, getting to her feet. "He is but one man. I shall consider best how to deal with this situation. Until then, you must get some sleep, or you will not be recovered enough to feed my father."

I glanced at her in surprise. "How did you know that Nikola had knocked back a pint or two of my blood?"

She shrugged a third time. "There is something about you that tells me you have allowed him to feed from you. That is good. I believe it will do much for him to have someone he admires be the source of his nourishment. Now, if you will excuse me, I must think upon

all that you have told me. I must warn him, Miss Iolanthe."

"Io, please. Iolanthe is such a mouthful."

"You must call me Imogen, then. Io, hear me — I cannot let my father be harmed, even if we have no proof
that my uncles would do anything so heinous."

"I know, I know, but there's the whole messing-up-
time thing to consider. . . ." I gnawed on my lip again.
"We don't have to act rashly by rushing the situation.
It's not like your dad is in danger right now." And
wouldn't be for another two years.

"Perhaps not, but I will not risk his life for anything."

"Think, but don't act. At least not yet," I warned her.
"I really don't want to go back to a future where lizards
are ruling the world because we warned Nikola about
his future trip out into the woods with his brothers."

"While I, on the other hand, would prefer anything
to seeing my father destroyed." She gave me a look
that said I should be thoroughly ashamed of myself,
which I admitted I was. The door closed softly behind
her, leaving me in a warm, silent room.

"Now what am I going to do?" I asked the room.

No one answered.

"Thanks a lot, life!" I climbed into bed, and gave in
to the exhaustion that had been pulling at me with
leaden fingers.

Nine hours and a handful of minutes later, I sat at a
table and stared down at the plate before me. "You're
kidding, right?" I leaned forward and sniffed. My nose
wrinkled in response. "Would you mind if I asked if this
meat is fresh? Because it's seriously green on that edge,

and brown on the rest, and I don't think meat is supposed to smell like that."

The thin young woman who had gravely informed
me her name was Elizabet adjusted her ruffled head-
wear—some sort of cap with a bit of dirty ribbon tied
around it—while holding an obviously stunted arm
against her midsection. She said with a sniff, "Master
loves pheasant like this. Cook made it especially for
him a week ago Sunday."

I flinched and pushed the plate away from me. "You
know, I think I'll just save this for Nikola, then. I'd hate
to deprive him of his rancid pheasant. You wouldn't
happen to have some fruit, would you? Apples?
Peaches? Something like that? Maybe with a piece of
bread? Fresh bread," I added hastily, not wanting to
appear like a demanding guest, but at the same time
not willing to risk my intestinal happiness.

"Aye, if you like, although Master says no one does
pheasant like Cook."

I said nothing more, just smiled as she took the plate
and a tankard of murky-looking water back to the
kitchen.

I wandered out of the small sunny breakfast room a
short time later in possession of two apples, and a cup of
goat's milk. I drank the latter, and was munching on one
of the former while considering what I needed to do.

Obviously, locating the woods and returning to my
own time was the top priority. Second to that, but much
less important, was the opportunity to examine what
life was like in the eighteenth century. If only I had my
camera, I could document my amazing experiences.

"Hmm. That's not a bad idea, actually. Hey, you, foot-man . . ."

The flaming servant with the salmon-colored wig sa-shayed into the room, pausing to admire himself in the surface of a highly polished silver urn that sat on a small table in the main hall, his lip curling at me in an "I smell dog poop" sort of expression. "My name is Robert, not footman."

"Sorry, Robert. Do you happen to know if there is some paper and something to write with that I could use?"

The footman, with another expressive curl of his lip, allowed that there was writing paper in the ladies' sit-ting room. I toddled off to a small room at the back of the house, pausing at the entrance when Imogen looked up from where she sat at a beautiful oak writing desk.

"Oh, my apologies. I didn't know anyone was here. Robert said there was some paper here. I thought I might just make a few quick notes about what I've seen and done for historical purposes. I didn't mean to inter-rupt you. I can come back another time."

"No, do not leave." Imogen rose from the desk, fold-ing a piece of paper and tucking it up her sleeve. "There are many household tasks for me to perform now that Papa is home. You are welcome to use my desk and stationery to make your notes." She smiled, and paused at the door. "Papa loves to take notes about things. Benedikt—that is my brother—Benedikt is forever teasing Papa that he should be an alchemist, but Papa says he's already discovered the secret of perpetual life, and does not wish to discover anymore."

"Huh? Oh, because he's a—" I made bitey motions with my fingers.

Imogen nodded.

"This is really personal, but do you drink blood like your father? You never said anything about that when I met you in my time, not that I suppose you would announce to a total stranger that you were a vampire and all, but still, you don't look at all how I imagine vamps look."

"I am a Moravian, not a vampire," she said primly, then gave a negligent one-shouldered shrug. "I can drink blood if I desire, but I much prefer wine. I will leave you to your notes. If you have need of more paper or quills, ring the bell."

It took me a bit to get used to the quill and ink method of writing, and I managed to spill ink all over one sleeve of the pretty dress that Imogen had loaned me (she had wanted to give me one of gold brocade and old rose watered silk, but I managed to talk her down to something she called a work dress, which was a flowers-and-birds-patterned cotton dress that opened in the front to reveal a pale green underskirt), but soon I mastered the quill and was happily scratching away on some hand-laid paper.

I fully intended to make only brief notes, but once I got started, it seemed important to get down every bit of what I had seen and done, lest I forget about this amazing trip to the past.

I shook my head at myself as I wrote, murmuring, "I still can't believe how well I'm coping with both time travel and a hunky vampire. I seriously need an award or something."

What seemed like a few minutes later, the footman Robert came into the room to deliver a tray with a beautiful teapot and accompanying accoutrements.

"The lady Imogen, she says you will take the tea," Robert said, setting it down rather carelessly. I grimaced, my eyes on the delicate teapot.

"That sounds lovely, and be careful! That's an antique!"

Robert's perfectly plucked eyebrows rose almost to the hairline of his wig as he glanced at the teapot. "It is not. The monseigneur, he had it brought back with him from Paris a few years ago."

"Well, in my view it's an antique, and a very nice one, so be a bit more careful of it."

Robert rolled his eyes dramatically and, with a spin that would do a model on a catwalk proud, sauntered to the door.

"What time is it, do you know?" I asked, stretching. I was surprised to find I was slightly stiff from sitting at the writing desk.

"It is half after five of the clock. Lady Imogen desires to know if you will be taking supper with her."

"Five thirty? Holy time sink, Batman! I've spent four hours in here?" I looked down at the stack of papers splotched and smeared with ink, and admitted that I'd done just that. "Boy, time gets away with you when you're writing. Um ... Imogen wanted to know about dinner? No, I don't have time for that. I have to go search the woods for my swirly thing. But first, I need a potty break. Please tell me there's a contraption downstairs like the one in that tiny room upstairs?"

I gave a little shudder at the memory of my time at

the toilet upstairs. . . . It was more like a camping toilet than a real one, with some sort of a wooden cabinet built around a chamber pot—complete with lid—but evidently flush toilets hadn't yet been invented. I wondered what else hadn't been invented yet. Indoor plumbing and electricity, obviously. But what about important things like health care? Did they even have real doctors at this time? The one I'd been going to see when I thought I was deranged had turned out to be a vet. What if they still used leeches to cure people?

I shuddered again at just how perilously close I had been to being leeched. That was just one more reason to find the swirly time-travel portal.

"Contraption?" Robert asked in a wholly uninterested voice. "I do not know this contraption."

"The toilet. Or . . . um . . . chamber pot. Is there one downstairs?"

"*Oui.* There is the privy next to the kitchen garden. There is also the chambre du convenience in the rear of the stairs. Lady Imogen prefers that to the privy, since she says Master Benedikt has the aim most terrible."

"Now, there's some TMI fodder. Thanks, I'll find it." I tidied up the papers as best I could, hoping Imogen wouldn't notice the ink splashed all over the leather top of her writing desk. "And now, I should go find the swirly thing."

I'll gloss over my experience with the convenience (you may thank me now). When I was done, and had the one-handed maid Elizabet help me readjust all those skirts—and make me incredibly thankful that I had turned down Imogen's offer of a corset, preferring to stick with my own bra instead—another half hour had passed, and I was fast running out of time to search the woods.

"Right," I told myself as I marched with determination down the hall. "Time to get to business. First, I'll get a horse. Then I'll start with the woods near the spot that Nikola said I ran into his carriage. Then, I'll make sure the swirly thing is there, and after that . . ."

My words trailed away, my feet stopping at the same time, leaving me standing in the middle of the hall. What would I do if I found the woods and the swirly portal? Would I just pop through it to my time without so much as a good-bye to Nikola?

That didn't seem right. I might not want to sleep with him—my mind skittered over that lie without so much as pointing it out—but that didn't mean I was happy to leave him at the mercy of his brothers. What if Imogen didn't tell him about their intention to kill him? What if she did tell him, but he, being a man and thus prone to the stubborn belief that he knew best, either didn't believe her or didn't take action in time?

What if he died and it was my fault?

Robert swished his way into the hall in a swirl of dirty lace, a faint halo of pinky orange powder around his giant wig.

"Just the person I wanted to see. Do you know where Nikola is?" I asked, hurrying toward him.

He backed away from me with one hand daintily clutching a scrap of linen to his nose.

"*Mais oui*, of course I know. The monseigneur is where the monseigneur always is at this time of the day—in his study with the tools *astronomiques*, and the bodies of the things most dead, and the little cow maid whose cream he favors."

"Cow maid whose cream ..." I squared my shoulders, outrage inexplicably filling me. Dammit, I would *not* allow myself to care if he was scarfing down the cow maid *or* her cream. Nikola might be Mr. Historical Sexy Pants, but that did not mean I had to give in to those urges that had already led me astray three times with him. "I refuse to give him that satisfaction! Not again, anyway. I have standards, and it's about time I start standing by them. Just where is this den of iniquity?"

"Study, not den. It is directly above us," Robert answered, dismissing me with a disinterested wave of his hankie before he continued his way through the room.

"Seriously, the world would be better off without such a dawg," I growled to myself, firmly intending to march out to the stables to ask for a horse.

Which would explain why I was so surprised when I found myself not only upstairs but standing in front of a door that I assumed led to Nikola's study.

"Fine," I told the door. "I'll just tell him what I think of him dining at Café Io when he has a cow maid on tap. So to speak. Then it's back on track, and to the stable for a horse before going off to the woods to find my way back home to sanity."

The door opened just as I was reaching out to knock at it. Nikola leaned against the doorway, his arms crossed over his chest. "Do you always talk to people through doors?"

"I was talking to myself, thank you very much," I told him with a scowl, looking past him into a dimly lit room. "Where's your cowgirl?"

"Ah. I, on the other hand, find it much more efficient to speak to someone while she is in the same room as me. No doubt you, having been raised in the colonies, will view that as an odd method of conversing, but I can assure you that it is a standard practice in civilized countries."

"What part of 'talking to myself' didn't you understand?" I asked him, a bit annoyed at his attitude. "And for the record, in my time the U.S. is a major world power, so you can just knock off the condescending tone, buster."

"My name is Nikola, not Buster. You seem to have difficulty remembering that." He tipped his head to the side in a way that made my knees melt. Once again I was overwhelmed with the urge to fling myself on him and kiss the living daylights out of him. "I wonder if that is due to a personality flaw, or if it's something that you've picked up from living with savages?"

I took a deep, deep breath, and was preparing to blast him when he gave a little wave of his hand. "It is of no matter. Since you are busy conversing with yourself, I will return to my studies. Good day."

He shut the door in my face. I gawked at it for a moment, unable to believe he'd done that. A little titter from down the hallway had me glaring at Elizabet, who held a coal scuttle with her good arm.

"He's crazy as a loon, you know that, right?" I asked the maid.

She grinned. "We're all a bit daft here, Mistress Io. Even my own da says I'm not right in my head for leaving England and coming to a foreign country to work for the baron, but I say it's how you're treated that matters, and the baron treats us like people, not animals what don't have no feelings."

"I didn't say he wasn't a good employer, just that he's not going to be awarded a Sane Person of the Year award." I took another deep breath—just because I felt I needed one—and, without knocking, opened the door and entered Nikola's study.

Instantly, I felt as if I'd stepped into another world. Which I had, given the whole time-travel thing, but this . . . "This is amazing," I said on a long breath, gazing in wonder around the room. It was L-shaped, with the short end to my left, while to the right ran the long side, sunlight pouring through the tall windows, illuminating intricate Middle Eastern carpets that dotted the floor. There were numerous tables of all sizes, from petite round ones to long, solid-looking desks bearing stacks and stacks of papers, books, and odd bits of equipment. A mechanical bird perched in a black iron cage sang as I stumbled forward, too intent on seeing everything to watch where I was walking. A marble mortar and pestle nestled up against a sphere depicting the constellations, which in turn sat on top of mechanical sketches that looked very familiar somehow. I headed toward them, my eyes widening even further when I extracted the top sheet of sketches, and recognized it.

"This is a da Vinci drawing of an airplane," I said, showing the sheet to Nikola, who sat behind a monstrously large ebony desk crowded with even more books. "A real da Vinci!"

Nikola looked up from where he was tinkering with a three-foot-tall mechanical statue of an African, complete with turban and spear. "Oh, it's you, is it?"

I walked over to him, weaving my way around stacks of books piled on the floor, a tray with tea things, and two ginger-colored cats who were curled up together in front of a fire. "It's a da Vinci, Nikola."

He looked at the paper. "So it is. Not a very practical design, though. But I liked some elements of it, particularly the wings. Stretching skins over the wooden frame to mimic a bird's anatomy is very intriguing, very intriguing indeed."

"You don't understand. This—" I found myself shaking the paper at him, and forced myself to gently set it down. "This is a da Vinci. An original. It should be in a museum! It's priceless."

"I don't think it is," he answered, returning his attention to the mechanical statue. "I bought several notebooks full of those sorts of drawings, but didn't see much that seemed very reasonable. Creative, but not terribly useful."

"Not useful . . ." I murmured to myself, staggering over to a tall armchair before falling into it. I lifted a wan hand and gestured toward Nikola. "What is it you're doing there?"

"Working on my automaton. It freezes up after just a few turns." He glanced over at me again. "Did you want something in particular, or did you just come to tempt me with your breasts and thighs and all the bits in between?"

At the mention of breasts, I sat up, leveling a glare at him. "I'd have thought you had enough of that with this cow maid person that everyone says you're hot on."

"Hot?" He blinked a couple of times, then extracted

his notebook from a stack of papers. "Used in this context, what is the meaning of the word?"

"Don't you dare be all endearingly adorable by asking things like that!" I stood up and pointed a finger at him. "I'm onto you now, buster! You're deliberately being cute so I'll forget about the cowgirl and let you dine at Ristorante Io. Well, it won't work, do you hear me? I will not be charmed!"

He set down a small tool, and leaned back in his chair, considering me. "Then I will stop my unceasing and yet obviously futile attempts to sway you with my considerable erudition. Are you here because you believe I need feeding, and that only you can perform that function? If so, I will take this moment to reassure you that I will not trespass on your good nature by doing so again. There are ample numbers of men and women in the village who have provided me with sustenance for the last thirty-nine years, and will continue to do so for at least another thirty-nine more. Assumedly more, since I am now immortal, but I don't like to presume. You may take your blood and begone, woman. I have no need or desire for either you or it."

By the time he finished that little speech, he had gotten up and moved around to where I stood, pulling me to my feet until I was pressed against him, the hard lines of his body making all my soft, squishy bits cheer with happiness.

"Stop touching me," I told him, and leaned in to nip his lower lip.

"I have no desire to—"

His words stopped when his mouth descended upon

mine, his tongue instantly barging into my mouth in a manner just as arrogant as its owner.

Oh, you have desire, I said, feeling the passion flaring to life in him like a burst of electricity. *You have oodles of desire. Oh, dear lord, right there, do that again!*

His hands had slid down to my breasts, cupping them and teasing them mercilessly, all the while his mouth was driving me insane with want and need until I felt just as electrified with desire as he did.

I may have misspoken, he admitted, his tongue mapping out my mouth before retreating back into his own. *I find myself wanting you more than I've wanted anything I can think of.*

The feeling's mutual, I started to say, then remembered my good intentions of keeping my distance from him.

Slowly, with more strength of mind than I thought I had, I managed to push myself back from the warm, solid, so very alluring man, and stepped back, one hand on my mouth. My lips felt sensitized, like they, too, had been touched with electricity.

"Why did you come here?" he asked, his eyes a smoky navy color. Evidently when he became aroused, his eyes grew darker. It was a bizarre phenomenon, and yet at the same time one that intrigued me to no end. I wondered if there was a way I could control how his irises shifted in color.

"Here as in your study, or here as in 1703?"

"Either. Both."

"I've told you how I came to this year. As for being in your study right now, I wanted to ask you to help me find the swirly thing that brought me here," I heard myself saying. I was a bit surprised at that last bit, since I didn't remember even thinking such a thing, but once the words were spoken, it seemed to make sense. Who better to hunt for the exact place I'd popped into this world than the man who lived here?

Nikola glanced over my shoulder to the row of windows. "It's early evening."

"So?"

"The sun still has an hour to set, and one of the things I've learned over the last thirty years is that sunlight does not agree with me."

"Oh, right, you're a vampire." I gave him a weak smile. "I keep forgetting that. Well, I can go hunt for the spot by myself, but I don't remember anything about where I emerged, so I kind of hoped you'd come with me."

He toyed with a metal file that he had been holding before he had kissed me. "I might be persuaded to spend my evening in such a search, should the company interest me enough."

I stiffened. "Is that some sort of a slur? Because if it is—"

"It was an invitation for you to use your feminine wiles upon me, and tempt me with promises of much pleasure to come should I accede to your wishes." I swear his eyes glittered with humor.

"Oh, that's what that was. And here I thought you were just making a dig at me. Well, since you want pleasure . . ." I dropped my eyelids and gave him a smoldering look. "How about we do something really fun?"

His eyes started to go dark again. "What would that be?"

I smiled at the fact that his voice was a bit rough around the edges, but before he could grab me, I snatched up the da Vinci page and held it up. "What do you say we go put this in the eighteenth-century equivalent of an archival protective frame?"

Nikola was silent for a moment before saying in a conversational tone, "If, in the time it takes me to count to four, you do not put down that drawing which for some inexplicable reason you value so highly, you will regret it."

I glanced from the drawing to his face, wondering if he was pissed.

His eyes were midnight blue.

"Oh," I said on a breath, and had just barely placed the paper back on the desk before I found myself on my back before the fire, the two ginger cats scooting over with disgusted looks at us. "Nikola, I don't want to make love to you."

That's not what your body tells me.

"I am not responsible for my body's actions," I said, my breath coming fast and hard as Nikola paused in the act of removing the cloth around his neck, and his jacket. I flinched at the look he gave me. "I didn't just say that, did I?"

"You did." He continued to remove his clothing until he was clad in nothing but his breeches and stockings. "But I find the unique twist of your mind quite entertaining. You are unlike any other woman of my acquaintance."

"I'm going to take that as praise, because . . . well, because it feels like praise."

"It was. Since your body desires me physically, would

you mind if I indulged it in some acts that I will personally guarantee to bring it exquisite pleasure?"

"Yes, I mind. I really don't want to make love to you, Nikola."

He did that head-tipping thing that was so damned adorable, I just wanted to punch him in the face. "Why?"

It took a few minutes to find the words, a situation that was not made any easier by the fact that his bare chest and arms were distracting me almost to the point where I just tossed all my good intentions to the wind and flung myself on him. "I've told you—I don't become involved with men until after I've known them for a long time."

"That's not how you feel toward me, however," he pointed out, damn his delectable hide. "You desire me. I can feel the strength of that desire, one that is more than matched by my own for you. What is wrong with allowing those desires to merge?"

I was still on my back, a little fire warming one side (the castle was, I had discovered, slightly chilly even in the summer, probably due to all that thick stone). Above me was an even warmer man, one who I could feel meant every word he said—he found me very desirable, and was prone to thinking some of the most erotic thoughts I'd ever entertained. I was in a century that was not my own, and might in a few hours be back where I belonged, leaving any physical relationship in which I might wish to indulge myself wholly uncomplicated or fraught with emotional entanglements.

In short, I could have my cake and eat it, too.

"I can't, because I'm afraid that once might not be enough," I admitted, hesitant to bare the truth.

"Who says it has to just be once?" He trailed a fingertip down the exposed flesh of my collarbone, making me arch up to his hand.

"I can't stay here, Nikola. Who knows what horrible repercussions I'm already having on the future? To stay longer is to risk all sorts of trouble."

He leaned over me, his hands on either side of my head. His eyes, that handy-dandy barometer to his emotions, were the color of the summer sky. "And if I asked you to remain with me? Would you stay? Would you give up your own time for mine?"

Luckily for my peace of mind, I wasn't forced to answer that question—not that I had the slightest idea what I'd say, because to be wholly honest, just having him so close to me made common sense seem like the most ridiculous attribute ever—but because at that moment, the door was flung open and an agitated Imogen burst into the room, scattering words behind her.

"—and I don't know what they're doing here when they never come here before December, and it's all going to be just like Io said, and I'm afraid of lizards and don't want them ruling the earth, but only Io knows when and where, so really, it's up to—oh!"

Imogen looked from her half-naked father leaning over me, to where I lay prone on the ground, my hands somehow having found their way onto his arms, where they might have been stroking his biceps in a wholly shameless manner.

"Imogen. Hi. Um . . . this isn't what it looks like," I stammered, snatching my hands back from Nikola's silky flesh.

"It looks to me like Papa is seducing you," she said with a frown at her father.

"That is exactly what was happening. If you leave us now, I will continue, although your interruption has no doubt broken the mood, which means I will have to begin all over again with Io, and it is no easy task to seduce her when she is in one of her resistant moods."

I gawked at him. "You say that like all I do is resist you!"

"You do."

"May I remind you that I was the one who seduced you first? I jumped you three times before you got around to reciprocating."

He grinned (which melted my innards) and kissed me on the tip of my nose. "Annoyed, sweetling?"

"Not in the least. I told you that I wasn't interested—" It took until that moment for Imogen's words to register in my smut-riddled brain. I shoved Nikola back and sat up, looking over to her. "Did you say lizards? You don't mean . . ."

She nodded, her gaze unreadable as she watched her father, with an exaggerated sigh, pull on his shirt and fancy embroidered waistcoat. "My uncles are here."

"Now?" I shook my head. "They shouldn't be here for two more years. Er . . . that is, I'm sure it's nothing, Imogen."

"Arnulf and Rolf are here now?" Nikola did not look happy as he pulled on his boots. I got to my feet and hiked up the neckline of my dress. It had a tendency to expose more boob than I was comfortable seeing displayed. "They should not be here for months."

Imogen sent me a look fraught with anguish.

"No," I told her. "It's got to be just a coincidence."

"One that could have dire repercussions," she argued.

"I sense that you are excluding me from this conversation, and I do not enjoy the sensation. You will both cease it immediately, and tell me of what coincidence and what repercussions you are speaking, not to mention how lizards are involved, or what it is that only Io knows."

Imogen watched me for a few seconds as I wadded up a handful of the gown I was wearing, not sure how to begin to broach the subject of Nikola's demise. I wasn't even convinced I needed to at that point, since his half brothers' arrival could be nothing more than a coincidence.

Could it?

Nikola disliked mysteries. He disliked mysterious women who ran into his horses, he disliked people having conversations around him that were deliberately intended to not be understandable to him, and most of all, he disliked the feeling that something was going on to which he was not privy.

That, along with sexual frustration, general hunger, and a desperate need for Io to admit that she wanted him as much as he wanted her, all contributed to a surliness that was evident in his greeting to his half brothers.

"What the devil are you doing here?" he demanded as he stomped into the sitting room where two men of middling years lounged with more ease than grace.

"Ever the charmer, eh, Nikola?" Rolf said with a sneer on his thick, oily lips.

Nikola considered his sibling with distaste. Both men were in their early sixties now, and time had not sat well on their countenances. Balding, with a fringe of brown and white hair, Rolf tried to disguise his enormous belly by means of stays that creaked and groaned when he walked. Arnulf was as thin as his brother was round, his body full of angles and sharp points that hurt just to look at.

Although Nikola had tried to love his half brothers as he should, he had never been close to them. Far from it, the two had always mocked him, made fun of his scientific interests, dropping sly innuendos about a range of subjects, and generally conducting themselves in a manner unpleasant to the point where he resented them intruding upon his well-ordered life. "What is it you want?"

Rolf, the elder of his two brothers, smiled, showing blackened broken teeth. "Do we have to want something to visit our dear brother?"

"You usually do, yes. If it's an increase on your allowance that you're after—"

"We shouldn't have an allowance," Arnulf said, stepping over his brother's sprawled legs to stand in front of Nikola. "We're your brothers, for the lord's sake. Our mother's estate should have been handed over to us as was right and proper!"

"If she had wanted you to have it, she wouldn't have given it to me to hold in trust," Nikola said, wearily wondering how long he could bear the company of his brothers, and whether it wouldn't save them all grief if he just had them removed from the house now.

"That's because you convinced her we were unworthy!" Arnulf snapped, and clearly would have continued the timeworn argument had not Rolf interrupted.

"We have not come for an increase on the allowance, brother," he said with another of his oily smiles. With a grunt, he hoisted himself to his feet. "We are here to discuss a matter of the gravest importance, one which, once we determined its veracity, we knew would require your immediate attention."

"What sort of a matter?" Nikola asked, despite his intention to get rid of his brothers. Damn his curiosity— he had never been able to quell it as he would like.

"A highly personal one. It seems, brother dear, that someone close to you, someone very close to you, desires to see you—"

The door behind him opened as Io and Imogen entered the room, the latter arguing quite forcibly with the former.

"—don't tell him, then I will be forced to. It's just too dangerous for him not to know."

His eyes narrowed on Io. *What is too dangerous for me not to know?*

Io looked startled for a few seconds, before glancing over to his brothers. *Er . . . I think we may need to have a talk.*

One involving lovemaking? I approve of this plan.

Er . . .

"I have no time to hear whatever it is that you believe is so important," he told his brothers, grabbing Io's arm and pulling her toward the door. "Iolanthe wishes to feed me, and as you know, I hold true to the precept that one should never discommode a lady."

"Papa!" Imogen said as they left the room.

"Don't look so shocked, sweetling—your uncles found out the truth about me years ago. Now, my little strudel," he said as he closed the door behind them. "Let us go to my bedchamber so that we might have this talk you so fervently wish for."

"Oh, no, you don't. And stop reading my smutty thoughts. Just because my mind and body want you to do all those things you're thinking about . . . Really, Nikola? Do you have a tub big enough for that? . . . Just because the rest of me says, 'Oh, lordy, yes, let's get down and boogie' doesn't mean that we're going to."

He paused at the foot of the stairs and gave her his best smoldering look.

She just thinned her lips at him and crossed her arms over those delicious mounds of breasts that he knew were created just for his satisfaction.

Right. The smolder was out. He switched it to a pathetic pleading expression. Surely she couldn't resist that. "It shall be as you wish, of course. I do need to feed, but I will find another."

Her jaw tightened, and her eyes narrowed until they were tiny slits. Damn. Perhaps he had been wrong trying to make her jealous.

He sighed, and said with as much pathos as he could muster, "Or I can just wait until such time as you see fit to feed me. It won't be easy controlling myself around you when I am so hungry, but your wishes come first."

She rolled her eyes at that, and punched him in the arm. "Oh, like I don't see through that shallow attempt at passive-aggressive manipulation? Please, my mother was the master of it. I'll be happy to let you . . . er . . . dine . . . but our discussion should probably wait until we have some time for a really long explanation."

"What if I have a quick nibble now? One that won't take much of your time."

"Like any nibble you take is going to be quick? I know exactly what you're thinking, buster, you just remember that."

"A light repast, then."

"No." She punched him in the arm again.

"A sip or two. That's all, I swear."

She considered that for a moment, but unfortunately, his gaze drifted down from her face to her breasts, and soon his mind was filled with all the things he wanted to do to them.

She crossed her arms again. "Do you seriously think I don't know what you're doing, Mr. Guilt Trip? You're not even that hungry, so don't give me those big blue puppy dog eyes. I'll feed you later, when we have time to talk. How come your half brothers are here? Imogen said they shouldn't be here until Christmas."

"They wished to impart some important message to me. They were about to do so when you burst in and distracted me with your adorable breasts, and—"

"Thighs, and all the parts in between, yes, I know," she told him with a look that made him grin. "Nikola, I meant it when I said I don't have sex with men until I've known them for some time."

"How long, in whatever measure of time you choose, does 'some time' translate?"

"I'll know when it's happened," she told him, turning to face Imogen when she emerged from the sitting room, his annoying brothers on her heels.

"Papa, I really must tell you—"

"Imogen," Io interrupted, hurrying forward to take his daughter by the arm and tug her down the short hall to where the ladies' withdrawing room was located. "I think we should continue our conversation before you say anything more."

"I don't think—"

"There's something I neglected to tell you," Io said with emphasis, and with a quick glance back at him hurried Imogen off.

Are you plotting something? he asked, mentally gnashing his teeth at the sensation of being left out of the discussion. *Are you planning on asking my daughter's permission to ravish me as I deserve? If so, please take heed when she informs you that I am lonely and need a woman in my life. She's been nagging me for the last five years to find one.*

In your dreams, bat boy.

Bat boy? What the devil did that mean? He was making a note of it in his notebook when Rolf jostled his arm, sending the tip of his pencil deep into the paper of the notebook.

"We need to speak to you about this situation," Rolf said, shooting a glance down the hallway into which the ladies had disappeared. "Privately."

"What situation?" Nikola put the notebook away, irritated by all number of things—his brothers' presence, the fact that Io was being so determined to not be seduced, and this air of mystery that clung to her and Imogen, to name just a few items. The last thing he wanted to do was to spend time closeted with his two annoying brothers.

"The one we told you about," Rolf said, struggling to hide his exasperation. "The one involving a grave threat to you."

Mostly it was Io who claimed his thoughts. Why was she being so insistent that they not give in to their mutual desire? She acknowledged that it existed, so logically it made sense for her to allow him to seduce her.

"We must speak with you, but it is too dangerous to do so here."

And yet, the sad truth was that things had progressed much further when she was seducing him, rather than vice versa. . . . Nikola froze, the whole of his attention arrested by that sudden observation.

"Aye, Rolf speaks the truth. There are some here who should not be trusted, some who are *very close* to your bosom," Arnulf added.

What if he let Io seduce him again? It would solve all the problems, since it would allow her to be in control— women always liked to feel they were in control of situations, especially those regarding lovemaking—not to mention it would take care of all her notions about having to know him for some unspecified length of time before they could proceed along natural lines of engagement.

"We must speak to you somewhere away from the castle, where we can't be overheard." Rolf leaned in close to him. Without thinking, he shied back. "Somewhere we can tell you all that we know."

Engagement. He frowned as that word echoed in his head. Was that the reason Io was so hesitant to engage in lovemaking? Was she saving herself for marriage?

"How about that woods where we found that stag a few winters back?" Arnulf suggested. "The one halfway between the town and here."

No, that couldn't be. She admitted she had lovers in the past—he spent another few seconds mentally grinding his teeth over that irksome fact—which meant her innocence was long gone.

"Aye, that would be a good spot," Rolf agreed. "Excellent suggestion, Arnulf. Do you know the place, brother?"

Perhaps, though, she was seeking a husband. Women did that. Would she expect him to make her an offer of marriage? Personally, he had been in Io's company enough to know that he wouldn't mind spending the next fifty or so years with her at his side, but he had buried one wife, and didn't know if he could go through the pain of watching another woman he cared for die.

"You know the spot we're talking about, don't you, Nikola? There's a clearing in the center of it, from what I can remember. We could meet there and tell you the truth about those closest to you. What's the name of the woods? Sauber? Sauston?"

"Zauberwald," Nikola said without thinking, his mind busy on the conundrum that was Io. The second the word was spoken, however, his attention shifted. He ought to know the spot—it was where thirty or so years ago he had run into a demon lord, and been cursed into his present state.

"Yes, that's the spot, Zauberwald. The so-called enchanted forest." Arnulf smiled before adding, "Although I've never seen what was supposed to be so enchanting about it."

Nikola frowned as he eyed the two men before him. "What about it?"

"It is the ideal place for us to have a meeting, dear brother. One that will, I'm afraid, open your eyes to the true nature of those who are around you."

"What the devil are you talking about now?" he demanded.

Rolf laid a finger on his lips, glancing over Nikola's shoulder to where the footman had just entered the hall. "Tonight. Shall we say midnight? In the Zauberwald, at the center. All then will be made clear."

It was on the tip of his tongue to refuse, since he had hopes that at that time of the evening Io would be in the middle of seducing him, but there was a slight chance that she might not yet understand that he was no longer pursuing her.

"As you like," he said, turning on his heel and heading toward his study. "I have business to attend to. You will no doubt entertain yourselves."

"Of that, you can have no fear," Arnulf called after him as he left the hall. There was a slight tone to his youngest brother's voice that rubbed him the wrong way, but now, he told himself as his boot steps echoed in the side hallway that led to his study, was not the time to worry about such mundane irritations. Now was the time to focus on alerting Io to the fact that she was free to seduce him at her convenience.

How very hungry I am, he projected to Io an hour or so later, as he worked on his automaton. He allowed the red, biting sensation of the hunger to claim him for a few seconds, knowing that she would feel that, as well. *I shall need to find sustenance soon.*

I said I would feed you later. I'm busy with Imogen right now.

Busy with what, may I inquire?

None of your beeswax, she said curtly, and closed her mind to his before he could attempt to broach it and see just what it was she was doing in such secrecy.

His steward brought work that demanded his attention then, with concerns of the estate, following which he was obliged to visit the stables and attend to Old Ted regarding one of the mares due to foal at any moment.

Have I mentioned that I dislike intensely women who adopt an air of mystery in order to captivate a man?

Have I mentioned that I dislike intensely men who barge into women's heads without at least knocking first?

Knock, knock.

Oh, very funny. There was a slight pause. *I'm not trying to captivate you, Nikola. I just want to . . .* Her voice trailed off in his head.

What? he inquired, curious.

The echo of her thoughts came to him so faintly, he wasn't absolutely certain he heard it. *Save you.*

Save me?

What? The word was spoken with a sense of Io being startled.

You said you wanted to save me.

I did not!

I heard you. "Save you," you said, and since you can speak only to me in this manner, you must have meant that it was me you wished to save.

You're imagining things, she said somewhat desperately, followed immediately by another echoed thought, this time of an oath.

And now you just swore at me. I heard that, too.

Argh! she yelled in his head. *Stop talking to me!*

Why?

Because I'm busy!

Doing what?

Argh, she yelled again.

I dislike this sense of mystery you insist on having around me, he pointed out.

I know you don't like it, and I don't really care, so just mind your own business and leave me alone.

You should care. You'll never seduce me if you don't pay attention to the little hints I have been giving you about how best to tantalize and entice me.

Seduce you? Are you insane? I just got through telling you, numerous times as a matter of fact, that I don't want to have sex with you. Why on earth would I want to seduce you?

From what do you wish to save me? he asked, congratulating himself on neatly turning the conversation back to that subject. *My own lust? If so, I must tell you that the only way to save me from that is to apply your nubile, smooth body to mine.*

That's it, it's official, you're completely bonkers. Now stop talking to me so I can figure out how to keep the future from being destroyed.

That seems an odd pastime, but since you are determined to seduce me at your own pace, I will allow you to get on with it. But you should be aware that I will be busy for the next few hours, and thus will be unavailable to perform those sexual acts about which you are even now thinking.

Silence followed that statement for the count of twenty. She hadn't been thinking of anything erotic, at least not that he was aware, but the second he mentioned it, she did.

He smiled to himself.

I'm not thinking of any sex acts! she protested, but it was a feeble protest, and they both knew it. *Dammit, all right, I am, but only because you're putting them in my head. Stop putting your smutty fantasies in my head, Nikola!*

I have done nothing of the kind. You are thinking about how you wish to touch and lick me, and to sit astride me and take me into yourself. Although I'm quite willing to allow you to do those things to me, they are not my fantasies. These are my fantasies. He let her see some of the things he wanted to do to her.

You bastard, she swore, and immediately pushed him out of her mind.

He laughed, delighted and charmed by her personality as much as the way her mind worked, and, of course, by that luscious body that by now he was convinced was created just for his enjoyment.

By the time he had attended to some overdue correspondence, taken a stroll out with the gamekeeper to discuss the current stock of wildlife on his lands, and avoided his brothers' company, dinner was upon them.

"Why, Robbie," he asked as he stood in his bedchamber, clad in only a dressing gown, "is the water not hot?"

"Is it not?" The footman pursed his lips and looked

thoughtful as he stood at the end of the squat metal bathing tub.

"I'm sure it is not sufficiently hot. You know I desire my bathwater to be very hot. I have told you that every week for the last four months, since you insisted on taking up the duty of bringing my bathwater. I have told you that I wish for it to be boiling before it leaves the kitchen, so that it will be a suitable temperature for bathing by the time the tub has been filled."

Robert shrugged. "It was hot when I checked last. Perhaps you should check again. Perhaps it is hotter than you think."

Nikola, about to remove his dressing gown and bend over the tub to do just that, paused and slid a glance over to where the footman was watching him with a hopeful expression. He sighed. He didn't mind being the subject of unrequited lust, but he preferred that the luster be of the female gender. It just made things easier that way. "Leave that can of water, and you may go."

"But, monseigneur—the water, she is not the way you desire."

"Robert—"

"I will fetch you more water, very hot water, steaming water that will make little beads of moisture appear on your chest."

Robert—"

"No, monseigneur!" Robert held up a hand to stop his protest. "It is no trouble. You must have the water most hot so that it slides across your belly just like the, how you say it, slithering of a tongue."

Nikola took a deep breath, picked up the tall metal

can of by-now-lukewarm water, and emptied it into the tub. "This is fine. You may leave."

"But—"

"You may leave!"

Robert, pouting a little at the stern command, minced on his exceptionally high heels around the screen that protected the tub from drafts, and on to the door. He sniffed, but exited the room without further incident.

Nikola divested himself of his velvet dressing gown— the castle was always chilly, especially in the evening— and got into the tub, busily washing himself while he thought of Io, and how he was going to get her to seduce him again.

A brief flurry of cold air alerted him to the fact that someone had come into the room. He sighed to himself, about to tell Robert that he had no need of any further services, especially those of an intimate nature, when a hesitant voice spoke. "Nikola?"

"Iolanthe?"

"Listen, I wanted to talk to you really quickly—" She came around the end of the screen and stopped, her eyes huge. "Oh! You're having a bath! I had one a little bit ago. You have really weird tubs, but at least the water was nice and hot. Um. Nikola, you're naked."

"Yes. I am also wet."

Her eyes widened even more as her gaze flickered between his face and his chest, and knees. "So you are. You don't fit in your tub. Your legs are all scrunched up. Why don't you get a bigger tub, one you can sit in properly?"

"That would take an inordinate amount of time and water to fill. Did you desire something in particular, or did you just wish to see me at my bath? Is this an attempt at seduction? Because if it is, you must first allow me to get out of the tub, since there isn't room in it for both of us."

"No, no, I don't want to seduce you—" She stammered a little before swallowing. "I . . . er . . . I wanted to talk."

"About what?" Casually, he rose from the tub. Nikola was not an overly modest man, but he was very aware of her gaze as it crawled across his naked flesh when he reached for the bath linen to dry himself.

She just stared at him for a few seconds, her eyes now moving from his groin to his chest and back to his face. "Um . . . what?"

He took in her flustered expression, and decided to make things easier for her. "Is it my penis?"

"Huh?" She looked at the object in question.

He gestured toward it. "You seem to be looking at it quite a bit. And yet, you've seen it before. Does it, for some reason I am unable to fathom, now startle you?"

"No!" She stared at his groin in fascination as his arousal at her inspection of his body quickly became apparent.

"Ah. Then I must assume you wish to caress it, and perhaps take it in your hands as you did earlier this morning. Dare I hope that you might wish to indulge in that most wicked of all practices, and use your mouth instead?"

"No! I don't want to touch you or give you a hand or blow job. I don't give a hoot about your penis."

"Then why are you still staring at it?"

"I'm not," she said mendaciously, her gaze locked on his nether parts. Her fingers twitched.

"Io."

"Hmm?"

"I wish to make love to you, and feed from you, and then possibly make love to you again, because the way you are staring at me makes me think I would be able to achieve a second bout of lovemaking immediately following the first, not that I've successfully done so in the past, but if there was a woman who could ensure such a thing is possible, you are that woman."

"Too many words," she said, and as he was half expecting, she lunged at him, flinging herself with wild abandon that he wholeheartedly appreciated.

He was ready for her, though, and backed up with her in his arms until he bumped into the bed. He allowed her to push him down onto his back, his hands busily divesting her of one of Imogen's gowns that had obviously been lent to her.

"I have never, ever felt this way about a man," she murmured as she swept her hands up his chest, her fingers tracing out all the muscles in his arms and upper torso. "My god, you're really ripped. Like, work-out-at-the-gym sort of ripped. I didn't think people in the past could have a six-pack, but you actually do have one. You must do a lot of physical stuff."

"I ride," he answered, pulling off the gown and her chemise, leaving her in the odd matching short stays and undergarment that hid all her warm, delectable secrets from him. "I hunt when needed. Imogen likes to go for walks, and many times, I accompany her. I taught my son swordplay, and he and I spent many months working on his technique. How do you remove the stays?"

"The what, now?" She bent down to swirl her tongue around his nipple. He saw stars for a few seconds.

"Your stays. The ones confining your breasts."

"It's called a bra, and it unhooks in the back. Nikola, this is wrong."

"No, you're right, it does unhook in the back." He pulled the stays off her, his hands immediately filled with her sublime little breasts. Just enough to fill each palm, he thought with satisfaction as he rubbed his thumbs gently over the little brown nipples.

She moaned, and arched back, thrusting her breasts into his hands. *Not that, this is wrong. Us. Together. And the fact that damn you, you're right, I do want to seduce you. Again. My god, I must be insane, but I want you more than I've ever wanted a man.*

"That's quite sane, I assure you, since I feel the same way about you." He pulled her down to a kiss that scorched his mouth, the feeling of those pert little breasts pressing against his chest enough to fill his mind with hunger—for both her blood and her body. He slid his hands over her hips to the undergarment. It had no hooks on the back of it, so he assumed it simply slid off her legs. He pulled her upward, peeling the abbreviated garment from her body, reveling in the heat of her as she grasped his hips with her knees.

"I really did intend to just talk to you," she moaned again as he pulled her forward enough to take the tip of one of those tempting breasts into his mouth, laving his tongue over it. Her fingernails stung his shoulders as she clutched him, her head thrown back, her chest heaving in time with his mouth as he paid homage to first one, then the second breast. "Just talk, that's all. I didn't intend to jump you again, but dammit, Nikola, you were naked! Wet and naked! That's more than any woman can bear! Oh dear god, do my left boob again, please."

He obliged her, ignoring the drawing sensation in his privates, aware he was perilously close to spilling his seed again, but determined to give her the time she needed to make up her mind once and for all.

"I meant what I said—I really don't do this with guys I've just met," she told him as she slid down his body, rising up and grasping his penis with a firm hand that made him twitch with anticipation. "It just doesn't happen! I'm not programmed that way. Although really, when you think about it, you're not like any other man, are you? So it makes sense that I'm reacting to you in a way that I've never done before. Because I've never met a vampire before. That makes sense, right?"

He didn't have the slightest idea what she was babbling about, but he was happy to agree with her, since it appeared that she had, at last, worked out in her mind the fact that they were meant to indulge in all the things they both had been thinking. "It makes perfect sense. I am unique. As are you. I have never met a woman from the future. Therefore, it is a sound conclusion that you should impale yourself on me at this exact moment, and I will happily lose myself in your heat."

"It sounds a bit crazy when I explain it," she continued on, "but it feels right."

"It feels *very* right." He gave a little lurch upward and moaned in happiness at the resulting sensation of her hands around him.

"This is just one of those situations where common sense doesn't apply, I think. I don't suppose you have any condoms?"

He frowned at her, automatically reaching for his notebook, but it was across the room.

"Never mind, I'm on the pill, although if I go home with some sort of weirdo eighteenth-century STD, I will personally geld you. Are you ready?"

She held him poised at the entrance to her gates of paradise. He could only nod; his penis was so hard at that point, it could probably have been used to hew stone.

"OK, but just so you realize that I don't normally do this." Her eyes closed in rapture as she sank down on him, enveloping him with warmth and heat the likes of which he'd never experienced.

A thousand velvety muscles seemed to ripple around him as she moved, easing him into her heat, allowing the invasion of him in a way that once again had him seeing stars.

"My god," she panted as she moved gingerly on him, slowly making her way down his length until her pubic bone rested against his. "This is . . . man, you're just there, aren't you? It's like . . . wow. It feels so good."

"It will feel better if you move," he advised her, amazed he could actually speak, so overwhelming was the sensation of being buried inside her.

"Yeah, I know, but this is good, too." She flashed him a grin, then leaned down to nip his lower lip, her eyes growing wide when he shifted his hips, causing him to slide a little more into her.

It was as if he'd set a torch to a keg of gunpowder.

She moved in a rhythm that seemed to leave him mind-less, his whole being focused on her, and the pleasure that she was pouring into his mind. He pulled her tighter to him, licking a spot on her shoulder, asking her wordlessly for permission.

Yes, she groaned into his mind, her hips moving in an erotic dance that he knew would drive him over the edge in just a matter of seconds. *Oh, yes, please, Nikola. Feed. Take it from me.*

Her flesh was warm and smooth against his mouth, but the moment he bit deep, and her life flowed into him, he knew that she had captured more than just his fancy.

The Incredible Adventures of Iolanthe Tennyson

July 15

The postorgasmic glow wasn't the only thing that knocked me out, but it did contribute to the effect. I'd like to blame the mouse in my room for the bulk of the reason that I was so tired after seducing Nikola that I conked right out afterward, missing dinner and, more important, missing the fact that Nikola roused himself from his own snooze, and had toddled off.

"What do you mean, you blame a mouse? What has a mouse done to you?" The vindictive round lady with the big fat gray curls stood over me as I struggled to get into all the various layers of clothing that women wore at that time. "You are trying to confuse me with talks of this mouse, but you will not do so! I can see through your ways! I know you for what you are—the devil's bed partner! I will listen not to you, and so I shall advise Fräulein Imogen, for she is of the tender heart and innocent mind, and she will not see you for what you truly are."

"The devil's bed partner, yeah, yeah—dammit, can you hook that up or whatever it does?" I asked, spinning around in a futile manner trying to see my own back. I stopped when she jerked the back of the gown closed, swiftly tying up a bunch of little cloth tapes, and connecting a series of hooks and eyes. "And just for the record, Miss Casting the First Stone, I was talking about the mouse that was in my room that kept me awake a long time this morning when I was trying to take a nap. I'm not used to sharing my room with rodents, and I was worried it would walk on me or bite me or nest in my hair or something while I was asleep. Thus, I've been operating on very little sleep these last few days, and also thus, I fell asleep after Nikola and I—" I stopped, eyeing her as she snatched up a pair of shoes and shoved them at me.

"Engaged in copulation with the baron!" she said, giving me a scathing look. "It is all over the castle that he has taken you to his bed. The Lord shall smite you for your wicked ways, and if He does not, then we, the decent people of Andras Castle, shall see to it that you do not pervert us all with such immorality!"

"Oh, for the love of—what did Imogen say she wanted me for?" I sat on the edge of Nikola's bed—which still smelled like him, and made me want to burrow back into its warmth and remember the wonderful experience of a few hours previous—and strapped the shoes onto my bare feet. "It's got to be the middle of the night. Can't it wait?"

"She is ill, and cannot rise from her bed. She made me swear I would bring you to her, for nothing would dissuade her from the idea that she must have talks with you. I do as she bids, but I will protect her! I will be at her side when you are there, so that you may not turn her into a devil's bed partner, too."

"You've got sex on the mind," I told her, getting to my feet. "You seriously need to see a shrink. And if you poke at me one more time with that, I'm going to talk to my partner the devil about you!"

She gasped, clutching a large enamel crucifix to her massive bosom, her eyes filled with horror. Even her giant curls seemed to shrink back in horror. "You would not! The devil will steal my soul and turn me into a Krampus!"

I had a vague memory of Gretl telling me about a mythical being called a Krampus, but connected it to Christmas. What on earth did that have to do with being the devil's love bunny? "Whatever. Let's just tone down all the accusations and maybe we'll get through this without anyone being Krampused, OK?"

She sucked in her breath again, but confined herself to muttering in German as I tottered down the hall toward Imogen's room. I didn't like the sound of Imogen being sick, which was pretty much the only reason I had let her crabby companion drag me out of bed.

"How are you feeling?" I asked a few minutes later when I sat on the edge of Imogen's bed and studied her face. She looked pale and fairly clammy, with two bright spots on her cheekbones. "Your nanny, or whatever she is, says you've been sick, but that you wanted to see me. Can I do anything to make you feel better?"

"I have been poisoned," Imogen said weakly, but the hand that clutched my arm had a grip that made me yelp. "My uncles put something in my wine."

"They *what*?"

Her eyelids fluttered at my shriek of horror before she nodded. "They know I have a weakness for a fine wine ... but that is not important."

"I don't know, I'd say being poisoned is pretty damned important! Oh my god, Imogen! What can I do?"

"Blasphemer!" gasped Anna. "Profaner!"

"Get a doctor, you deranged woman!" I ordered, taking Imogen's hand in mine and trying to remember what one did for poisoning. "Is it drink lots of milk, or eat bread? Or maybe barf ... man, I knew I should have signed up for that first aid course at work, but I never got around to it. Hang in there, Imogen! You'll be OK."

A little smile touched her lips. "I will not die, if that is what you are concerned about. My kind does not do so easily, and never from poison. It makes us ill for a little while only, and Anna has already purged the wine from me, so I will feel more the thing soon. I am just a bit weak, too weak to go after Papa."

"I'll go find him for you if you want to tell him what his brothers did. I bet he'll open a serious can of whoop-ass on them, and after hearing about this, I wouldn't mind helping him. Are you sure you're OK?"

"I'm fine, just weak. You must save Papa, Io. You are the only one who can stop them."

"Stop ..." Enlightenment dawned as she clutched my hand. I glanced at Anna, not knowing if I should speak in front of her. "I thought we had that out earlier, when I explained about how certain things weren't supposed to happen for another two years."

"I know that is what you said, but somehow, it has changed to now. Perhaps you misunderstood what I said in . . . in the other time."

I shook my head. "I don't think so. You said you were twenty-two at the time, and your dad said earlier today that you were only twenty—"

"No!" Imogen struggled to sit up, sweat breaking out on her forehead as she took me by the arms and shook me. "I am twenty-two! Papa is forever forgetting my age, but I am twenty-two now, Io! It is today that he is meant to die!"

Goose bumps crawled up my arms, making me shiver. "Good god. Then his brothers—"

"He is out with them right now!"

I got to my feet, unsure of what to do, but feeling a desperate need to do something. "Are you sure? Maybe Nikola is in his study playing with his robot. Did you check there?"

"He is gone to meet my uncles," she wailed, falling back on the pillows. "I know because Robert told Anna, and she came to tell me that you were seen going into Papa's room, and that you should be stoned because of your loose ways, and that if we waited until midnight, Papa would be off meeting my uncles and we could capture you, and stone you."

I stared at her in horror before turning my gaze to the woman in question. She bared her teeth at me. "You are so over the line, babe. And we're going to have a little talk about that later."

"I will stop up my ears to your unholy words! The devil will not have his way with me!"

I shook my head and leaned down to Imogen to say,

"You need to seriously consider getting someone else as your nanny before this one goes completely bonkers. I mean, sheesh, Imogen—wanting to stone people because they sleep with someone isn't right."

"We can talk about this later. You must go save Papa!"

I straightened up and took the woolen shawl she pushed at me, turning to the crazy lady. "Where exactly did Robert say Nikola was going?"

Her lips tightened as if she didn't wish to speak, but after a sharp word from Imogen, she finally said, "The Zauberwald."

"What the heck is a Zauberwhoosits?" *Nikola? You out there in brain radio land?*

Silence was the answer to my tentative question. I wasn't sure if we could do the brain talking thing if we were far apart, but I felt obligated to give it a try.

"It is the name given to a small curve of wooded area slightly more than two miles from here. It is said to be a magical place, one where enchantment is heavy in the air." She shifted slightly, pressing my fingers in a painful grip. "Io, you must go there immediately and stop my uncles. Do not let them destroy my papa."

"I don't—I don't know how to stop guys intent on murder," I stammered. "I'm not good with martial arts or anything. I suppose I could throw a rock at them, but I'm just pretty much useless about that sort of thing."

"I don't care what you do." She jerked me forward until my face was a few inches from hers, her eyes, a darker blue than Nikola's, filled with a fervent light. "I don't care how you save him, but save him you must. Swear to me you will do it."

"Even if I knew how—"

"Swear!"

I swallowed back all my protests, all my doubts, all my concern for what sort of effect I might have on the future. All those protestations would be useless—the second I gave in to the desire that had been building ever since I met Nikola, I signed away any ability to act in a dispassionate manner.

"I'll save him," I promised. "I don't know how, but I'll do it." *Nikola? Can you hear me at all? If you can, don't go with your brothers. They're going to try to kill you.*

She collapsed back on the pillows again, her skin deathly pale. Instantly, Anna was there, shoving me out of the way to *tsk* over Imogen, and offer her a sip of some pale-colored beverage.

"Go," Imogen said, her voice barely above a whisper. "And may God go with you."

Nikola?

Silence remained the only answer, so I gave up trying to contact him, and instead tried to concoct some scheme whereby I could save Nikola, and not leave the future at risk. I left Imogen's room, wondering just how I was going to pull off such a thing. Ahead of me, Elizabet was approaching with a branch of candelabra in her hand.

"Just the person I need," I told her, snatching the candles and setting them on the nearest table. "Where's the stable?"

"Outside," she answered, giving me a quizzical look.

I gave her a shove toward the stairs. "Show me!"

She looked over her shoulder at me. "But I don't—"

"Now, sister! We don't have time to stand around arguing, not while Nikola is in danger."

Her eyes widened as she hurried toward the stairs. "The baron is in danger? How so?"

"It's a long story. Come on, show me where the stable is, so I can go find him and help him beat the crap out of his brothers."

I'll give her this—she didn't stand around arguing; she simply bolted like a deer, racing down the stairs to the ground floor, a few tendrils of red hair coming loose from her elaborate, curly hairdo that all the women seemed to wear ... those who weren't wearing more elaborate wigs, that is. Imogen's maid had tried—and failed—to duplicate something similar on my own head. I had finally convinced her to simply tuck my shoulder-length hair up in a modest French twist, but even that looked out of place among all the big, poufy hair worn by the servants.

"Do you know where this Zauberwald place is?" I asked, panting as we ran down a side corridor.

"No, but I have only been here for three years. Old Ted might know—he's been with the baron for many years."

"Old Ted—that's the guy who takes care of the horses?"

"Aye." She flung open a door, and dashed inside. I followed, avoiding the inky shapes of furniture as best I could. I ran into something hard, a chair I think, and swore under my breath as I half ran, half hopped, rubbing my shin. Elizabet threw open a pair of French doors and ran outside, turning to the right and heading out into the neat, orderly hedges I had seen from an upper window.

"Wait, I've got a stitch in my side and a possibly broken shinbone. Ow. Ow, ow, ow." I hobbled after her, telling myself the pain was of minor importance when it came to Nikola.

I don't know how she could see in the dark as well as she could—even with the moonlight, it was still awfully black out—but in next to no time we were at the stables, me completely out of breath, and Elizabet barely winded.

"I . . . have . . . got to . . . get to the gym . . . again . . ." I gasped, doubled over as Elizabet called for Ted.

"Aye, then, I'm here, lass, what is it you be needin'?" An old man appeared at the stable door, his back twisted, but a cheerful look on his face. His gaze moved from Elizabet over to me, his eyes widening in surprise. "Oy! It's the trollop! What you be doin' with a woman the likes of her?"

"I am really getting tired of being referred to as a slut," I said, trying to stand up straight and give the man a look that should tell him a thing or two, but I was still out of breath, and my side and shin hurt something fierce. "I need a horse. One with a regular saddle."

"His lordship didn't say nothing about—"

"Nikola is in danger, grave danger, and the longer you stand there and argue with me, the more likely it is he'll be dead by the time I find him, so please, for the love of all that is holy, get me a horse!"

"The master is in danger?" the old man asked, his eyes narrowing.

"Yes!" I threw my hands up in a gesture of disgust. "Horse! Now!"

"The master went out riding not half an hour ago," Ted said cannily. "How be he in danger?"

"This is like a freaking nightmare! Listen to me, you obstinate old codger!" I grabbed his lapels and shook him, infirmity or no infirmity. "Nikola is going to be killed if you don't get me a horse, and show me where the Zauberforest is."

"Zauberwald," Elizabet corrected.

He eyed me for a few seconds, and I was just about to shove him aside and go find a horse for myself when he nodded his head, pushing me off him before hobbling back into the stable. "I'll have to tell you where to find the Zauberwald, since I can't ride anymore, and my boy is off seeing his girl."

My shoulders slumped a little in relief at his words, although that relief soon turned to impatience as he saddled up the familiar Thor. I was relieved to see that he put a regular saddle on the horse, and tried to ignore the fact that the last time I tried to ride away from the castle, I ended up on the ground far more times than I liked.

"Halfway down the mountain, small trail leading off the left when the road doubles back for the third time, take the fork to the left after that, clearing is past a bunch of trees," I repeated some minutes later as I got settled in the saddle, my dress hiked up around my knees. "Gotcha. Now let's just hope I'm not too late."

That was the refrain that repeated through my head like a chant: *I hope I'm not too late, I hope I'm not too late. . . .*

I don't know whether Thor the horse was used to my method of riding, or the proper saddle kept me upright and in place on his back, but whatever the reason, I was pathetically grateful that I didn't fall as I urged Thor into a canter. We headed down the road in a flurry of dust, the wind whistling past us while I chanted under my breath. Luckily, there was enough light to see by, and Thor seemed tolerably familiar with the road, so it wasn't long before I saw the third bend ahead, and the faintest marks in the shadows of trees where Ted had indicated a game trail led to the heart of the Zauber-wald.

I turned off the road and onto the path, ducking low over Thor's neck as we entered the stand of trees, my heart racing, and my breath seeming to catch in my throat.

Instantly, the blackness closed around us, and I was left trying to guide the horse by the glimpses I had of the waning moon. The trees here weren't tightly grown together, but their fir branches obscured the sky enough to leave it slow going. The scent of pine filled the night air, Thor's hoofbeats now deadened by the dense carpet of dropped needles. Only a dull thud was audible, and that was mostly drowned out by the sound of the wind in the trees, occasional calls of animals and birds, and once or twice, I thought I heard snatches of conversation.

I sent up a little prayer that I wasn't too late, and directed Thor to what I imagined was the center of the wood.

Luckily for me, he had more sense than I did, for after about five minutes of my praying, muttering to myself, and desperately trying to listen for sounds of two men killing their vampire brother, Thor suddenly tossed his head, gave a soft, snorting whinny, and turned sharply to the left.

"What the hell, horse?" I whispered, and tried to steer him back on the path that I thought I could still make out.

Thor was adamant, though, and after two more minutes of me trying to get him to go in the right direction, he stopped and dropped his head as if he was going to graze.

"Fine, I'll do this without you," I snarled under my breath, and slid my way out of the saddle.

I took one step and stumbled over something large and warm. I knew it was warm because I fell on it, recoiling instinctively until a familiar scent hit my nose.

"Nikola?" I whispered, patting the shape until I recognized it for one of his legs. Fear froze me for a second, until I realized that if he was still warm, he couldn't be dead.

I quelled the horrible part of my mind that pointed out he could be freshly dead, and I could be, at that moment, lying across a dead man.

Instead, I patted my way up his body until I reached his chest, which I was intensely relieved to feel rising and falling under my questing hands. "Thank god I'm not too late. Are you poisoned, too?"

"I don't like it, not one bit, I don't," a male voice said fairly close by, accompanied by the sound of a large body brushing tree branches aside. "The master, he's been good to me da and me, and I don't see no reason to play a trick like this on him."

"But that is why we approached you to help us, Ted. It is of the baron that we are thinking," a gruff German voice answered. "He is our brother! Do you think we would want harm to come to him? Imogen told us that this woman who has taken up residence has bewitched his mind. You must help us save him from her."

Imogen said that? I was stung by her betrayal. I thought we'd bonded! But what a fool I had been to believe her tale. At what point had I talked myself into believing she was on my side? Just because she was concerned about her father? I shook my head at my own stupidity. She'd told me more than once that she'd do anything to save him . . . obviously, that anything included using me.

"She'd been *poisoned*," I muttered to myself. Oh, I just bet she had. There was no coincidence in the fact that she'd been conveniently poisoned and thus been unable to go after Nikola. She was obviously working with her uncles to . . . to what? That stumped me. I didn't have time to work it out, though. What I had to do was to get Nikola away from there, and fast.

"That has to be one of your odious brothers," I murmured to Nikola even as I felt for his head. There was a huge lump behind one of his ears, leaving my fingers wet and sticky with blood. "Great. No wonder you're unconscious."

"You must fetch the strumpet and bring her to us," a second German voice said. "So that we might end the enchantment, and free our dear brother from her unholy plans."

"I am really getting tired of everyone in the eighteenth century believing I'm some sort of satanic slut,"

I grumbled softly to Nikola's unconscious body, wiping my hands on his jacket before gently pulling him toward me. "Nikola, wake up, we have to go."

"I suppose that would be all right," the man named Ted (assumedly the stable dude's son who was supposed to be out seeing his girlfriend) said slowly. "But I think I should ask me da about it first."

"We have no time, my friend. You see how the moon is high in the sky? We must act now to take the enchantment off the baron. Quickly, you will return to the castle and fetch the whore, and return here as soon as you may. We will perform the sacrifice then, and save our brother."

Sacrifice?

I clasped Nikola's head in my hands and shook it gently. "Nikola! Wake up! They're going to sacrifice something, and I have a horrible feeling it's going to be me. Oh, for heaven's sake, now what do I do?"

I didn't have time to come up with a suitably Mac-Gyver-esque plan; it was obvious that as soon as Nikola's evil brothers got rid of the groom's son, they would come back to check on Nikola, which meant I had to get him out of there pronto.

"OK, let's get you onto the horse, and maybe I can hide you in the forest until you come to." Thor, who was busily snuffling Nikola's feet, looked on with interest as I half dragged, half carried Nikola the few steps to his side. Unfortunately, there's a big difference between dragging a full-grown, solidly built man a few feet and lifting him up onto the back of a horse, and it quickly became apparent that I'd have to find another way to move him.

Sounds of voices speaking in German, growing louder along with the snapping of branches, spurred me into instant action.

"Sorry about this, but it's the only option," I whispered to Nikola as I wrestled his coat off his torso, and wrapped it around his head, tying the sleeves around it to provide a buffering cocoon. I ripped off his neck-cloth, a thick swath of linen about eight inches wide and a yard long, and tied it around one of his ankles, tying the other end to the stirrup. With another murmured apology, I grabbed Thor's bridle and turned him so Nikola lay behind him. Light flashed in the trees, the golden light of a lantern as it shone through the branches.

I flinched as I hauled the resisting horse forward, aware that the thumping sounds of the first couple of hesitant steps forward were made by Nikola's body being dragged across lumps of sod, wood, and rocks, but after the horse shied in protest of the awkward burden he hauled, he walked forward docilely enough.

We'd just made it past a couple of fir trees that seemed to have twined around each other as they grew when there was an angry shout behind us.

"Crap!" I swore, and, grabbing the bridle firmly, bolted forward, praying that I had wrapped Nikola's head well enough to keep it from being damaged any further.

The yelling was now accompanied by the sound of men running after us. I dodged around another big fir, trying frantically to think of a way to lose them. I couldn't drag Nikola much farther without risking harming him, and, without help, couldn't get him onto the horse. As I rounded the tree, moonlight spilled onto the ground in front of me. My heart leaped at the sight of the faintly visible swirling mass of light that seemed to hang in the air in the center of the clearing. "My swirly thing!"

"You! Trollop! Stop!"

I glanced over my shoulder to see the thinner of Nikola's brothers dashing around trees, a sword in his hand. He was about thirty feet behind us, and I could see, even in the flickering shadow of the trees, the man's lips pulled back to reveal a horrible grimace of sheer evil.

I ran for the swirly thing, stopping just at the edge of it, and threw myself down at Nikola's feet, desperately trying to wrench free the cloth I'd tied around his ankle. The weight of his body had tightened the knot, however, making it impossible for me to undo.

"I hope to god our lizard overlords understand why I had to do this," I told Nikola as I leaped back to my feet and, grabbing the horse by his bridle, ran straight into the middle of the swirling light.

The Incredible Adventures of Iolanthe Tennyson

July 15

The noise was what woke me up. It was a horrible, strangled sort of noise, one that suddenly became very loud and annoying, and disrupted my happy little sleep.

I frowned when the noise increased to a volume that irritated my nerves, frowning even more when the lovely warmth that surrounded me suddenly darkened. I opened one eye and looked up into the disheveled face of a man.

A very handsome man with black hair, and the most gorgeous eyes the color of a pale blue topaz.

A man who looked familiar.

"I bloody well should look familiar, since you were riding me just a few hours ago. Why the devil did you try to asphyxiate me with my own coat? Is it because I insisted that you be the one to seduce me? Or was that your way of starting some very curious form of love-making? If it is the latter, I must inform you that I will not have it. I am a fair man, a generous man, a man who is willing to let his woman seduce him if that is her desire, but I do not find having my vision and breathing obstructed in any manner titillating. Henceforth, you will leave off the rough lovemaking, and return to the sort where you apply your naked flesh to mine in a more congenial manner."

"Nikola?" I asked, as slowly the shadowed recesses of my brain brightened with dawning enlightenment. I opened the other eye and for a few seconds wondered what the hell had happened. I went ahead and asked him. "Why do you look like you've been dragged through a hedge backward? Why is your face all red?"

"Why did you bind my head and tie me to Thor?" he countered.

"Huh?" I sat up, and immediately the world spun around me. Nikola grabbed my arms and held me for the few seconds it took for everything to resume its proper place. "Oh, man, what was I drinking last night? I have the hangover to end all hangovers."

"You have not been hung, although I believe I would be within my rights to throttle you. Are you well?"

This last was said with much more concern than the former, and after a minute of letting my brain get back to the business of running my body, I nodded. "Just a bit woozy, although I don't quite understand what you're talking about."

"This," he said, gesturing toward his boot. The remnants of a piece of white cloth fluttered from his ankle. "And that."

I looked at where he pointed, and saw a big horse

happily grazing a few yards from us, another white cloth dangling from one stirrup.

"That's . . . that's . . ." I closed my eyes for a moment to try to remember the horse's name.

"Thor."

"Thor! That's right. Oh, holy Jesus!" With the mention of the name, the full memory of the terrifying flight through the woods returned to me. I got to my knees, holding on to Nikola's arm as I quickly looked around us, half expecting to see one of his horrible brothers lurking in the shadows of the trees.

Although we were in the shade of the trees, the sun was high in the sky, casting its rays down on earth and human and horse alike . . . and the swirly thing that crested the slight hill about twenty feet away. "The swirly thing is still there, although"—I bit my lower lip as I got to my feet—"it looks different. It looks dimmer, if that makes sense."

Nikola nodded, winced at the gesture, and put his hand to the back of his head before saying, "It would look different, given its use. I take it that is the object you mentioned seeing before you were transported to me?"

"Yes, and what do you mean—oh, your head! How does it feel?" Gently, I touched his head, finding a small bump where a larger one had been earlier.

"Sore. Someone hit me on the back of it. Yes, that's the spot. It's healing now, but when I woke up, I felt as if Alexander had marched his entire army over it."

My hands dropped, and my gaze skittered away for a few seconds while I fought the guilty thought that I'd made it worse. I cleared my throat. "I'm pretty sure it was one of your brothers who knocked you out. Um. How does the rest of you feel?"

"A bit battered, but improving with every passing minute. I appear to have some ability that allows me to heal at an accelerated rate. I made a few notes about that before you woke up." He shook out his jacket, and put it on before pulling a small knife from his boot to cut the cloth from first his ankle and then the stirrup. "Why did you tie me to a horse and drag me here?"

"That's going to take some explaining. The super-short version is that once I saw the swirly thing, I knew I'd have to risk it."

"Risk what?" he asked, frowning as he bent to put away the knife.

"Bring you through it to my time."

He stood up and gave me a long look. "You did what?"

"Welcome to 2012," I said with a smile, spreading my hands. "I think you're going to like it."

"I may well like it, but that's not something we're bound to find out. We did not travel through time, Io. You simply stumbled over a root or rock and became insensible."

"You don't think we came through the swirly thing?" I looked around the clearing, but there was nothing there to offer a clue as to the year. "Why not? You know I came through it to your time."

"It is impossible because that"—he gestured toward the object in question—"is clearly a portal, and you said yourself it has diminished."

"Yeah, it does look a lot fainter, but I don't see what that has to do with anything."

"You drew upon its energy to arrive here. It faded in response. There is not enough energy left in it to transport two people and a horse."

"Or it sent us back, and what you see is what it looks like after it did so."

He frowned at that line of reasoning, and was about to argue when I stopped him with a question of my own. "How did you know it was a portal? Did you know this was here all along? I told you that I came through a swirly light thing—why didn't you tell me this is where it was located?"

"I did not know this was the object that you used to reach me," he said, giving a little head shake that had a swift flash of pain crossing his face. "I have never seen this phenomenon before, but I know it is a portal because that is the exact location that a demon lord named Magoth used when he laid the curse upon me. He appeared out of nothing; thus, he must have used some sort of a portal from a different place to this one. It is only logical to assume that what one man might do, so might another."

"A demon cursed you?" I asked, my skin crawling at the thought.

"A *demon lord*," he said with emphasis. "He told me that he was commissioned to destroy me, but that the method was not specified, so he chose the most heinous punishment he could think of, and cursed me to be a Dark One."

"Holy freak-out," I said, unable to imagine how horrible that had been.

"He also took my soul, but I have learned to cope

without that," Nikola added in an offhand manner, just as if the loss of a soul were a minor inconvenience.

"You have got to be kidding. . . . No, you're not, are you? You don't have a soul?"

"No." He took a look around us, then, putting both hands on my waist, hoisted me up and onto the saddle. "I thought you would have noticed."

I was a bit taken aback by that statement. "Well, shoot, Nikola, it's not like I go around checking everyone I meet to see if a devil has taken their soul. But . . . is that why you're all angsty inside?"

"Angsty?" He patted his coat and pulled out a familiar notebook. "I do not know the meaning of this word, but assuming you are referring to the emptiness that fills me, then yes, that is due to the loss of my soul."

"I wondered about that." I grabbed the horse's mane when Nikola took hold of Thor's bridle and turned him, walking back toward the way I'd come through the trees. "I thought maybe it was something I was imagining. What exactly is a demon lord? And why did someone hire him to curse you?"

He was silent for a minute, finding a path for us through the trees, keeping to the shade and holding branches back for me whenever possible. For some reason that, and the knowledge that he really and truly was cursed into being a vampire, tugged at my heartstrings.

"I've never been able to find out who damned me to this curse, although I have my suspicions. A demon lord is one of the princes of Abaddon."

"And what's—"

"Hell. At least, that's what I assume, since no one has ever told me differently. When I was cursed, I did some research into the phenomenon of Dark Ones," he said very matter-of-factly.

I bit back a giggle. Of course he researched the subject—I didn't expect anything different from Mr. Scientific Reason.

"There isn't much documented about them, but what I did find reassured me that although Dark Ones are not commonly found, there are others, many of whom are from my native Moravia. I wrote to the society to inform them that I was newly made a member of their group, and received in return an offer of assistance should I have any questions."

"Vampires have their own society?" I asked, a bit flabbergasted at that. "Do they have local chapters? A newsletter? A Facebook page?"

He stopped, glared at me, and pulled out his notebook again.

I giggled.

"Yes, there is a society for Dark Ones," he said after tucking away the notebook, and taking Thor's bridle again. He marched on through the trees. "They did not send me any other letters containing news or otherwise. Years later, after Benedikt was born, I thought of contacting them to discuss his weaning, but my wife discovered that if she gave him a piece of raw meat, he would gain sustenance from that. As he grew older, he commenced to taking blood from living animals, and later to people. It was a most interesting experience, and one I documented fully. Someday, I shall publish my findings."

"I bet that would make fascinating reading."

He glanced over his shoulder to me, suspicion evident in his eyes.

"I mean it. I never really thought about what baby vampires eat. I guess I thought they just, you know, ate off their moms."

"They do. They nurse until they are weaned and then they consume blood. At least, that is what Benedikt did. Imogen was different, but I attribute that to the fact that she very much resembles her mother, whereas Benedikt favors me."

"That's really interesting. Do you ever eat stuff that isn't blood?"

"Not now." He frowned, and pushed back the low-hanging branch of a giant fir tree. "I tried to at first, but it made me violently ill. I decided that something was not agreeing with me, and systematically began to eliminate those items of food that I could not stomach. After two years, I realized that it was food itself that my body had difficulty with. It would seem that Dark Ones do not digest food the same way as others."

"Huh. That's really weird. So you just went on a blood diet?"

"Yes."

"Then why did Elizabet say that you liked maggoty pheasant?"

He sighed, and avoided a pool of sunlight, skirting it as we continued through the trees. "The servants would have commented if they saw that I did not take any nourishment, so I developed a method of pretending to consume food. Mostly, I had meals in my study. When that was unavoidable, I made sure one of my dogs was in the room with me, and simply slipped the food off my plate to whatever beast was handy. It saved me from attracting attention I prefer to do without, kept the dogs well fed, and made my cook happy."

"You're one smart cookie, you know that?" I asked, a warm glow of happiness spreading through me as I watched the back of his head.

"Cookie. Hmm. Cookie. A sweet biscuit?"

"Yup, you got that one."

"I have a question for you, if it is my turn to ask."

"Shoot. Er . . . that means go ahead."

He stopped in the middle of reaching for his note-book, and asked instead, "I have had the short explanation—if you can call it that—of what actions you took, and now I would like a more detailed version. Why did you tie me to Thor and wrap my head in my coat?"

I sighed. "I had a feeling you weren't going to let me get away without explaining fully. The truth is that your brothers—how do I say this so it doesn't sound really circumstantial?—your brothers were planning on killing you."

"I am immortal," he said after a few seconds of digesting that thought. I found it interesting—and telling—that he didn't at all question the idea of his brothers wanting to do him in.

"But you can be killed. You said so yourself."

"Yes, I can, but it is not an easy task to accomplish." He was silent again for another minute. "How do you know that they have planned to see that harm befalls me?"

"Imogen told me."

He shot me a startled look, but kept walking.

"The Imogen in my time, that is. She was very upset, if that makes it better. Extremely so. She refused to even come up to this forest to take pictures because she said it has so many bad memories for her. Oh, holy cow, Imogen! We just left her!"

"We will be home shortly."

"No, we won't. Nikola, whether or not you want to admit it, I dragged you through that wormhole or portal or whatever the hell it is, smack-dab into the twenty-first century. It's 2012 now, and although Imogen is still alive—at least I hope she is . . . oh, man, if the fact that I saved you messed things up, I'm going to be so pissed—anyway, assuming the lizards haven't taken over and she's here, then she's just fine and dandy. And she did tell me to do whatever it took to save you. She was really insistent about that, so I guess I really shouldn't worry, although now I feel terribly guilty over leaving her alone in the eighteenth century. That worry is retracted, however, if it turns out she was in with your brothers. Which I don't think she would be, because honestly, what would she gain?"

"My daughter would never betray me in such a fashion," Nikola said stiffly. "I make no such claim about my brothers; they have long resented the fact that my mother left her fortune to them in a trust that I administer, and I can readily believe that they would wish to see me gone so they can take over the control of their fortunes. However, to suggest that the same might be applied to my daughter is unreasonable."

"Maybe. Although they did tell that kid named Ted

that Imogen was in on the whole thing, but I can see where that might be a red herring."

He sighed and pulled out his notebook.

"Again, though, I don't see what she'd benefit from it. If you were to die, your son would get the castle, wouldn't he?"

"Yes."

"So that's out, unless Imogen plans to knock him off, too. 'Knock him off' means murder, by the way."

"Thank you, I gathered the meaning of the phrase from the context," he murmured politely.

"I just hope she'll be OK with no one to look after her but that crazy woman who sees smut everywhere."

"Imogen is a woman grown, and capable of taking care of herself in all matters but that of men, and I have placed my trust in Frau Leiven to guard against Imogen being allowed undesired contact with such individuals. My word, as you have no doubt seen for yourself, is absolute. Frau Leiven will guard her from danger on *that* source."

I didn't miss the emphasis.

"I swear to god, if you call me a trollop or strumpet or whore, I'll deck you," I growled, waving one fist at him.

He didn't even look at me. "As for your other statement, I see that I shall have to show to you that based on the state of that portal, what you suggest is just not possible. I don't suppose you would care to make a wager on the subject?"

"What subject?" I asked, confused.

"Whether or not it would be possible to take two

people and a horse through the portal at the center of the Zauberwald."

"I suppose. What did you have in mind to wager? I wouldn't have minded one of those da Vinci drawings, but I suppose those are long gone."

"Whoever wins the wager will seduce the other person."

I burst into laughter, but a quick glance at his face made it absolutely clear that he was quite serious. "Right, so if I lose the bet, you get to seduce me, and if I win the bet, I'm the one doing the seducing? I may be a bit thick in the head what with all those falls I took yesterday, but I don't see any motivation in this wager for ensuring a win. I mean, we both benefit whether we win or lose."

He flashed a roguish, very wolflike smile back at me, and was about to reply when we suddenly stopped. Sunlight shone ahead, signaling the end of the forested area. Nikola had been forced to make a circuitous path through the trees to stay in the shade, and when we reached the ragged edge of the tree line, he paused, looking out at the road.

It was paved.

I cracked my knuckles, and smiled as I drawled, "Excellent. I believe I shall introduce some fun things into the next seduction. Have you ever heard of massage oil that heats when you blow on it?"

"What is that?" he asked, pointing toward the road. "It looks too smooth to be cobblestones."

"It's called blacktop, or asphalt. It does have stones in it, actually, just all ground up and blended with some other things, and then heated up to a really high temperature, which makes it viscous. It's poured on roads while it's hot, and then kind of smoothed out, so cars can drive on it."

He took a deep breath as he pulled out his notebook. "I cannot believe I miscalculated so greatly with regards to that portal. It *looked* depleted. I'm going to need a second journal if this keeps up."

"There's bound to be a learning curve, but that's to be expected. After all, I had to have someone explain to me how to use the closet stool thing that's really a camping toilet."

"Closestool."

"Yeah, yeah, my point is that it's your turn to not know how everything works, but don't worry, I'll be happy to explain stuff as we come upon it. Let's go down to town, and I'll find a phone and call my cousin to pick us up."

He took a deep breath, his fingers twitching a little.

I smiled. "How much of that sentence did you understand?"

"Everything to the point where you mentioned a phone."

I leaned down and patted his arm. "It'll make sense in a while. Town's that way, to the left."

He gave the road a considering look, then turned the horse to the right, staying in the shadow of the trees as he led Thor uphill, rather than down. "No. I refuse to accept that the portal was anything but depleted. Therefore, we will go home, and then I will show you that despite the miracle of the smooth cobblestoned road, we have not done the impossible and used a spent portal."

"Your castle isn't there any longer, Nikola. I'm sorry, I know it's going to be upsetting to realize that neither of your kids maintained it after you were killed, but I'm afraid that's the truth. The castle is a ruin now, some of it having been destroyed in a war during the nineteen hundreds, according to what my cousin told me, and the rest of it falling into decay afterward."

Nikola said nothing, just set his jaw, and grimly led Thor and me up the winding road. Hidden as we were by the stand of forest that covered the slopes of the mountain, it wasn't until we came to the end of the tree line that Nikola stopped and stared, his head tilted back.

The ruins of a castle were clearly visible atop the mountainside.

"I'm sorry," I said again, sliding off the horse to put my hand on Nikola's arm. His face wore a stricken look, as if some vital part of his being had been severed. "I'm really, really sorry."

"For the fact that my home is destroyed," he asked, his eyes still on the remains of the castle, "or for the disillusionment I feel in realizing that I don't after all know how the world functions?"

"For your castle," I said, giving in to the urge that had been tormenting me. I wrapped my arms around him and hugged him. His scent teased me until I buried my face in his neck, breathing deeply, and fighting the almost desperate need I had to bite him.

It still shocked me, this sudden urge to bite him, but since it didn't seem to discombobulate Nikola, I was willing to cope with it without becoming obnoxiously paranoid that I was going to turn into a vampire, too.

His arms came around me, pulling me tight against his body. My inner bits gave a cheer of happiness.

I told you that Dark Ones do not work that way.

"I know, but how else do you explain the fact that I want to bite you? I've never bitten any other sexual partner. It's totally unlike me. And don't tell me that I also said I don't sleep with guys I haven't known for a long time, because I'm well aware that I've totally gone out of character on that front, as well."

"I wasn't going to say anything about that." He donned a noble expression.

I shook my finger at the expression, and bit his chin. "Maybe not, but you were thinking it."

"Perhaps." His hands slid down from my waist to my behind. *What you feel is not your desire to bite me, but my need to feed on you, sweetling.*

I giggled at the endearment, and wriggled against him. *A bit peckish, are you?*

I begin to suspect that I shall always be so around you. Cease squirming in that distracting manner; I am attempting to conduct a thorough scientific study of the area.

You are? I pushed back from where I had, in fact, been brazenly rubbing myself on him. "How are you doing that?"

"I am examining my surroundings in a comprehensive manner."

I watched him for a minute or two. He stood with one arm still around me, his eyes slowly scanning across the area in front of us.

"You're just looking," I said, a bit confused (it was becoming an all too familiar state).

"Yes. It is the scientific way. I shall be happy to explain it to you at a later time."

"But that's hardly a thorough scientific study. I mean, if you wanted to do that, you should make a grid of the area, and then examine each square of the grid for clues or evidence or whatever it is you do when you want to know every little thing about that spot. You'll probably need those little number cards to mark stuff of interest, and of course latex gloves and those bootie things that keep you from leaving footprints. I wonder if it would be possible to get an infrared camera? I've always wanted one of those. Hmm."

He stopped scanning and frowned at me. "What are you babbling about?"

"A thorough scientific study." I shook my head. "Those cameras are probably too expensive, and besides, I heard they're best used at night, and who in their right mind is going to try to examine the ground at night?"

He started to reach for his notebook, gave me an odd look, and let his hand drop. "I refuse to be a slave to your determination to make me insane with curiosity. I do not care what bootie things are, or why an infrared camera is too expensive, let alone what it is, and why you would need gloves made of latacks."

"Latex, and that's fine, punkin," I said, patting his arm in a supportive manner. "You have plenty of time to learn about the twenty-first century; you don't have to do it all at once."

"No, but I wish to learn as much as I can so that when we return home, I will have ample notes to study at leisure."

I stared at him, little goose bumps crawling up my arms. "When we return home?"

"Yes. Once we have explored what there is here, of course. I will not rush you, although I hesitate to leave Imogen alone for more than a few weeks."

"But . . . uh . . . Nikola, we are home."

He turned to face me, a frown pulling down his brows. "We are in the future."

"Which is my home, yes."

"It is not, however, mine."

"But it's the future! It's better than what you left!" I said, frustration building inside me. "The technology alone is going to blow your mind."

"I do not wish for my mind to be blown," he said, his frown growing. "Are you saying that you do not wish to return with me to my home?"

I opened and closed my mouth a couple of times before I could finally put words into action. "No, I'm not saying that, but, Nikola, we don't even know that it's possible to return back to your time. You said yourself that the portal looked like it was almost wiped out."

"And with time, it may strengthen. It might not, but that will be an issue we can address should that happen. Until then, I intend to explore your world, and when the portal is once again usable, return home." His gaze pinned me back. "I had assumed you would return with me."

"I . . . I think that you need to give the present a chance before you make plans to return to the past," I said carefully.

He studied me. "You did not like my home and my time."

"I didn't say that. I just said that I think you need to try out my time before you—before *we* make a decision. OK?"

He was silent a few minutes. "Very well. You were at my home for a few days; I can do the same for you."

I bit back the comment that such a short time wasn't going to be nearly enough to show him what the present was like, knowing full well that the same could be said to me of the past. This wasn't an argument that was going to be settled quickly or easily.

I changed the subject. "Exactly how hungry are you? Should I give in to my biteyness so that you can fill up, or can it wait until we can find somewhere more private than the side of the road next to a haunted forest?"

He sighed. "The Zauberwald is not haunted; it is simply . . . different."

I wrapped my arms around him, and gently bit the tendon in his neck.

"Your attempt to seduce me into making love to you is not at all appropriate at this time," he said sternly a few seconds before his mouth took over mine, his tongue going all bossy in a way that had me melting against him. "It is daylight, and should I give in to your wanton and wholly inappropriate demands, I would end up with severe burns along my back and buttocks."

"There's always the forest," I pointed out with a coyness that took me by surprise. I was never coy! "And I could be on top in case any pesky sunlight sneaked through the branches."

He thought for a moment, his gaze flickering over to the line of trees. I could feel him considering it, weighing the desire and hunger that he kept so severely reined in with an excited curiosity about this new environment. "That would result with pine needles finding their way into parts of me that would prefer not to entertain them."

I smiled, and gave him a swift kiss before turning to where Thor was cropping the grass. I let Nikola stand in the shade while I led the horse over to him. "Later it is. If you put my shawl over your head, do you think you could ride?"

"I am an expert horseman. I can ride with or without a shawl with equal ease."

"Smart-ass. You know what I mean."

He picked me up and heaved me into the saddle. "I do, but the question is moot. Thor would not be happy with two riders." He took the bridle again, and began to lead the horse along the edge of the tree line, staying in the shade as much as possible.

"I'm sure he wouldn't be, but it would be faster, and it would alleviate my guilt at riding when you have to walk. Oh, man, your face is turning red. Here, let me drape the shawl over your head. That might protect you a bit."

He tried to wave the shawl away, but after a few minutes of arguing, he gave in and let me drape it over his head.

We walked along in silence for a few minutes, the only sounds audible the sharp, high calls of birds, and the occasional low drone of noise that I had no problem picking out as belonging to a car.

"So, how old were you when you were vamped?"

Nikola glanced back at me, his pale blue eyes filled with curiosity. "I was seven and twenty. My mother died about a year later. She was taken by typhoid fever. My brothers had it, as well, but they survived."

"I'm sorry. That must have been really hard on you. And you had no friendly neighborhood vamp to show you the ropes?"

"What rope?"

I waved it away. "It's just an expression. What did your family think about what happened to you?"

Thor's muffled hoofbeats filled in the silence for a minute. "My mother was dead, as was her second husband. My brothers were two and three years younger than me."

He didn't say anything more, but I sensed some strong emotion in him, an unhappy emotion, one that I wanted to explore, but with a mental oath at myself, I kept my lips (and mental microphone) quiet. Of course he felt a strong emotion; he was remembering how his world had changed at the hands of a demon lord. I wanted to ask who he believed had damned him in that way, but a swift glance at the rigid set of his shoulders and the tense line of his jaw told me my questions would not be welcome.

Instead, I spent the next forty minutes chatting about the town, and what differences he'd find once we reached there. I explained about cars, and cell phones, and airplanes, and was just broaching the subject of computers when we made the last turn of the twisty road that led into town. Below us, in the smooth pastureland that was the valley floor, the GothFaire still sat in its U shape of brightly colored tents, with equally colorful travel trailers arranged in a neat formation on the far side of the fairway.

"They're still here?" I asked aloud, my eyes on a distant figure of a man as he wandered through the fair. "Well, that's a stroke of luck. Look, Nikola, the fair is still here."

He glanced over at it, his brows rising a little under the shadow cast by the shawl over his head. "Ah. Are there conjurers? I've always had an interest in conjurers. When I was very young, I wished to become one, but my mother said that no baron had ever been a conjurer, and she refused to get a tutor for me so that I might learn the art. I studied it on my own, naturally, but I believe that I would have been an excellent conjurer if only I had been apprenticed accordingly."

"You are seriously the strangest man I've ever met," I told him, sliding off Thor. "Fascinating, but strange."

"You also find me arousing," he said with a smug, very male expression on his handsome face. "Even now you wish to wrestle me to the verge, and ride my manly parts."

"Look, it's bad enough that you know I'm thinking these smutty things about you, but you don't have to tell me that you know I'm thinking them!"

"Why?"

"Why? What do you mean, why? Isn't it obvious?"

"If it was obvious, I wouldn't have asked. I'm not the sort of man who talks just to hear himself speak. I do, however, have a curiosity about such things, which I believe I've mentioned in the past. So if I ask why, it is because I do not understand how acknowledging the fact that you spend an inordinate amount of time dwelling on the subject of riding me, not to mention reliving those moments earlier in the previous evening when you did, in fact, do just that, is repugnant to you. You wish to ride me, and I have no objection to such a desire, so we are of one mind regarding that subject. Why would you not wish to admit it?"

"For someone who doesn't talk just to hear himself, you sure do go on and on," I said somewhat tartly. The fact that he was absolutely right was neither here nor there, but I was determined to rise above such things and move on. "And as long as we're being strictly factual, I may want to ride you like a ten-cent pony, but I don't wish to do so on the side of the road. Come on, let's get into town so all that riding can commence. Er . . . not in public, but in private. In my room. Assuming Gretl doesn't have a hissy over you, which I don't think she will, but you never know. GothFaire doesn't open until nighttime, so we have plenty of time for all those things you are thinking about doing to me—oh yes, don't look so innocent. I'm completely aware of your determination to try some kinky position you read about in a naughty French pamphlet you have hidden behind some boring books in your study—what was I saying? Oh, the GothFaire doesn't open until later, so we can visit it then, and you can see Imogen and your son and his wife."

He stopped and stared at me, his eyes wide beneath the folds of my shawl wrapped around his head. "Benedikt has married? He's too young!"

"He's over three hundred years," I reminded him.

He grumbled at that, but allowed me to take the lead and hustle him toward town.

The Incredible Adventures of Iolanthe Tennyson

July 15, Part 2 (there's a lot to write about)

I had to stop writing about the stuff that happened when we came back to the present day because all hell broke loose, but I don't want to ruin anything by doing that foreshadowing crap, so I won't say anything other than man alive! Just when you think everything is peachy keen.

Nikola coped with things much better than I expected, certainly much better than I had dealt with the eighteenth century. Mind you, he didn't have to undergo the hell that was finding a camping toilet all done up to look spiffy and stuff inside a house (but let's face facts—it was still a camping toilet).

When we walked into town, Nikola was all big eyes and curiosity about everything—cars and people and buildings—but he took it all in stride and simply made copious notes about what he wanted explained.

The people in town were equally cool about the fact that we led a horse into town, but given the pastureland around it, I gathered it wasn't an unknown thing to see someone ride around the more urban areas. By the time I begged a woman who was outside gardening to use her phone, and called Gretl (and submitted to her screams of joy, and later a tirade about disappearing without a word to her), Nikola had removed the shawl I'd tossed over his head to protect his face from the sun, and begun to conduct what he thought of as a scientific examination of the people of the twenty-first century.

"I know, I know, I have tons of explaining to do, and I'll gladly do it, but if you could bring me some clothes and my passport and the credit cards that're tucked into my suitcase, and meet me in town at the hotel, I'll tell you what happened. Although you probably should be braced for a really weird tale," I told her after she had run out of steam. "I don't suppose anyone found my purse and camera, did they?"

"Did you lose them?"

"They were . . . well . . . yeah, not sure. I assume they were stolen when I went through the . . . um . . . yeah. They were probably stolen. Never mind, I just wondered if anyone found them and brought them to the police or something."

"Io, you aren't making any sense at all. Why must I meet you at the hotel? Why will you not come home? And how were your things stolen?"

"I want you to come here because I've got a friend with me, and after some thought, I decided that it wasn't fair to foist him on you, too. He's a bit . . . uh . . . different. And I'll explain how I lost my things later. Please grab some of my things and stuff them in the duffel bag for me, and I'll see you in half an hour at the hotel, OK?"

"Io, what is going—"

"Gotta run. Nikola just found a FedEx woman, and I think he's grilling her about the truck. See you in a little while!"

I hung up before she could continue, hurried past the gardening woman with scattered thanks, and grabbed Nikola's arm just as the woman was about to urge him into her truck.

The hussy.

"There you are, munchkin," I said loudly, baring my teeth at the skinny blond woman. She had her hand on Nikola's arm, and was urging him to climb up into the truck in a syrupy voice that made the hairs on the back of my neck stand on end. I grabbed Thor's reins from where they'd been looped around the mailbox, and hauled him over next to Nikola, covertly shoving the horse until he sidestepped toward the woman. "I told you I wouldn't be long. No, Thor! Bad horsie! You shouldn't step on people's feet; they don't like it."

Nikola gave me a long look.

I smiled even broader at the woman as she swore in German, holding up one foot and hopping around in pain. "Sorry. You done here, Nikola? Excellent. Let's go on up to the hotel and see if there's somewhere we can park Thor."

He frowned at me, then looked back at the truck. "This woman has offered to show me the inside of her carriage. It appears to be run on that engine you mentioned, and I wish to see it. If I am to explore your world, then I must understand how things function, and that includes how a—" He glanced at the side of the truck. "—how a FedEx works."

"Oh, honey," I said, taking him by the arm and gently pulling him away from the temptress. "She wants to show you much more than just how she delivers packages."

Io, I wish to see inside this carriage.

I know you do, but honestly, that woman doesn't give a hoot about you looking around at how the truck is built. She just wants to jump your bones.

He looked faintly puzzled. *Why would she want to kill me and assault my bones? I have done nothing to her.*

Nikola, you're what, sixty-some years old? Well, you don't look more than thirty, an extremely handsome thirty, what with your gorgeous eyes, and that black hair, and of course your face, not to mention your chest and legs and naughty parts, and that woman—really, could she be any more blatant? I'm standing right here with my hand on you and she's still yammering away in German. What's she saying? I bet she's whispering mechanical sweet nothings in your ear, isn't she? Anyway, she just wants to do all those things to you that I want to do, and since I don't share, she's not going to have the chance to do them in the back of her smutmobile.

He gave me another long look as he pulled out his notebook. *I understand now. You are jealous.*

So not true.

The woman tried to tug Nikola toward the truck.

I saw red. "Look, babe, you may do things differently here in Austria, and I'm all for being a good American abroad and stuff like that, but if you do that one more time, I'm going to deck you. He's not up for grabs, *capisce*?"

The woman snarled something rude at me in German. Nikola laughed, and answered her in the same language before taking Thor's reins, and slipping his other arm around me, urging me forward toward the center of town.

"All right, Mr. Urbane, what did she say that made you laugh? And what did you say back to her that made her look so shocked?"

"She asked if I could get rid of my mother so that she might answer all my questions about her carriage."

I gasped. "Your *mother*! That bitch!"

He gave my waist a little squeeze. "I told her that you were my woman, and that although I appreciated the fact that she wanted to bone me, only you were allowed to do that."

"Uh . . . Nikola, we're going to have to have a chat about colloquialisms in the very near future," I said, wondering how on earth I was going to explain to him the intricacies of modern slang. "But seriously, your mother? OK, I look older than you, but still. I only look a little older than you, just a smidgen older, but that's because you look so frigging young."

He shrugged. "If you like, I will change myself to appear older, although you do not look ancient, as you are thinking. You look . . . mature."

I opened my eyes really wide and looked at him. "You do *not* tell a woman she looks mature. That's tantamount to saying she's an old hag."

"Ah? How about ripe?"

I took a deep breath. "Look, I may not be as buffed

and toned as Miss Austrian Hussypants back there, but I am *not* mature, and I am *not* ripe. I'm thirty-nine if you want to be absolutely specific, and my friends, my *friends* say that I look much younger. Much, much younger! OK, so forty is just two months away, but that doesn't mean squat, because everyone knows that women just get better after thirty, whereas men have already peaked and are declining. So you can stuff that up your . . . hey. What do you mean you will change yourself to appear older?"

"If it bothers you that I appear to be younger, I will modify my appearance."

I stared at him in amazement. "You mean dye your hair or something?"

"No. I did this for my wife, when she aged. She, too, disliked the fact that I looked much younger than her." His brows pulled together a little. "I assume that is a trait particular to women, although Imogen does not yet display such leanings."

"You mean you can actually change how you look?" I waved a hand around in a vague gesture. "Like, magically? Can you turn into a bat, too? Or a wolf?"

He looked at me as if I were the one being out of the ordinary. "Of course not. And yes, I discovered soon after Benedikt was born that I could alter my appearance to show age if I so chose. When my wife died, it changed back without me being aware of it until one day Imogen pointed out that I looked younger."

"Why did you get younger?"

He gave a little shrug. "It wasn't something I consciously controlled. I assume it was just how I was comfortable appearing to others."

"Wow. That's . . . wow. I guess it must be so you guys don't stand out in a crowd," I said, musing on the idea. "I mean, a person who never ages would attract attention. But what did your servants think when you started to go back to Nikola Prime?"

"We were living in Vienna when she died. Following that, I went back to England for a few years, then returned here with the servants, and opened up Andras Castle again."

"Clever. So, can you do it right now?"

He looked startled. "Do what?"

"Change so you look older? I wouldn't make such a big fuss about it, but my cousin is going to bring my things to the hotel, and I don't want her thinking I'm cradle robbing."

He stopped in the middle of one of the little squares that were satellites to the center of town. His eyes narrowed in concentration as he looked at me, the irises darkening to sapphire. I watched him closely, holding my breath, not knowing what to expect.

His face shifted slightly, blurring a little, then sharpening until faint lines fanned out from his eyes. A few strands of silver appeared at his temples, barely visible, but there if you looked close enough.

"That's amazing! How do you do that?"

He smiled, his new laugh lines crinkling in a way that made my knees want to melt. Nikola looking like he was thirty was utterly gorgeous. Nikola looking fifteen years older was mind-numbingly irresistible. I just wanted to rip off his clothes and molest him. "It's a matter of shifting my mental age."

"Huh?"

We resumed walking. "I did some thinking about this when my wife complained that I would continue to look young while she aged—and the day that she noticed I no longer looked as young—and came to the conclusion that I could alter my appearance if I felt older or younger. I call it a mental age. It is the age that I feel I am, despite the number of years that I carry."

"Well, if that's the case, then I'm mentally twenty-five, which is a really scary thought, since I was a mess at twenty-five. Nikola . . ." I stopped him with a hand on his chest. "I'm sorry. I shouldn't have bitched at you and made you change how you look. That wasn't fair of me. I honestly liked you the way you were, even if I will be letting myself in for some cradle-robbing jokes. Go back to the way you are comfortable looking."

"If you insist," he said, pulling me forward into a kiss despite the fact that we were clearly visible by everyone walking or driving through the square. His mouth was as hot as sin, and twice as delicious, and I came seriously close to just throwing caution to the wind and tackling him right then and there, but luckily, Nikola had more presence of mind than me, and managed to break off the kiss before I did so.

Not more presence of mind, sweetling. I've just had longer to learn to control my desires. Although if we do not find a private place in the next hour, that control will be severely tested, and I will not answer for my actions.

Don't worry, we'll have a hotel room to . . . er . . . feed you. Um. I hate to tell you this, Nikola, but you didn't change back. You still have laugh lines and a tiny bit of silver in your hair.

"You told me to appear as I was comfortable. I have

done so," he said blithely, his hand on my back as we continued through the square.

"To the left," I said, pointing and looking at him from the corner of my eye. I wanted to protest that he didn't need to stay looking older than me just to make me happy, but damn. He really was beyond sexy like this.

He smiled, and I damned my inability to keep my thoughts to myself.

"Why are we going to a hotel to meet your cousin? You said earlier that we would stay with her."

"Yes, well ..." I coughed. "The bed in the room where I'm staying squeaks, and I thought we'd be more comfortable at a hotel."

"It squeaks?" His eyes widened, turning to pale blue that shimmered with heat. "Just so. A hotel would be better."

I ignored the fact that I was blushing like crazy, and concentrated instead on walking the next three blocks without once thinking about licking Nikola.

Or touching him.

Or rubbing myself against his naked flesh.

Sweetling, if you do not cease thinking about those things, I will bed you right here in the street, and there is not even a verge in which we might disport ourselves.

Sorry. I'll try not to think about how much I want to touch your chest, and stomach, and legs, and ... and ... dear god, Nikola! Stop thinking about that! It's too much! Wait ... with a strap?

Yes. It holds you up at the correct angle. I'm told that the sensation of such an angle is quite pleasing for the female.

My legs felt like rubber as his erotic thoughts—and they were far, far more erotic than my own musings—filled my brain, but we made it to the hotel without either of us embarrassing ourselves.

I left Nikola in the shade of a bookstore while I ran across the street to the hotel, and inquired of the woman at the desk if she knew of somewhere we could stable Thor.

"A horse?" she asked without batting so much as one eyelash. "There is a small stable to the rear of the building that my husband uses for a car he is rebuilding, but if you like, your horse could stay in one of the empty stalls."

"That would be perfect. I'm happy to pay for his board, if you know of someone who can feed him and clean out his stall, and that sort of thing. I'm sure my friend will make more permanent arrangements as soon as he can, but that might take a couple of days."

The middle-aged woman smiled. "Do not distress yourself with worry. It unbalances your aura."

"Um. OK. Can we take Thor back to the stable now?"

"If you like. I will show you the way."

The woman accompanied us around the side of the hotel (thankfully the side that had shade), to a small outbuilding that was mercifully shaded by a giant chestnut tree. She hauled open the large door to reveal four stalls, two of which were taken up by a car that was in pieces, while a third held a number of wooden crates. The fourth stall also held a couple of crates, which we moved out before settling Thor into the stall's confines.

"I will call a friend at a local riding stable," the hotel

woman said as she pulled out a cell phone. "She will bring hay and grain for your horse."

"Some brushes and currycombs would be welcome," Nikola told her. "He will need grooming, and I am loath to leave him unbrushed."

The woman nodded, and waved us back toward the hotel as she spoke rapidly in German.

The hotel lobby was small and what travel agents would call "eclectic." The owners, Gretl had told me when she was showing me around town, were aging hippies who had moved to Austria from Canada, and were heavily active in the arts and crafts community. I stood next to a zebra-striped love seat, eyeing a tall lamp topped with a yellow satin fringed lampshade, while Nikola stood considering a red and pink heart-print sofa. I was in full agreement with Gretl's assessment that the hotel was an acquired taste.

"This furniture," Nikola said, his gaze moving over to a spotted green beanbag chair. He checked himself. "It is furniture, is it not?"

"Yes." I glanced over my shoulder to make sure that the hotel owner wasn't within earshot. "Very odd furniture, but it's meant to be sat on."

"It is quite unique. I like the colors on that chest."

A purple, green, and teal standing chest of drawers in the corner had been painted with various African animals. The squat legs of the chest were done in purple and white stripes.

"It's . . . special. Thank god, there's Gretl."

I ran to the (yellow polka-dot) door to hug Gretl when she came in hauling my duffel bag. "Gretl! Oh my god, you don't know how happy I am to see you again!"

She dropped the bag and hugged me back, immediately going into full scold mode. "Where have you been? Why did you not call me if you decided to go somewhere on your own? Do you know how worried I've been? The police, they said they could not find proof that you traveled anywhere, but I was sure that you had been abducted, and they would not do anything. Oh, Io! I have been so worried!"

It took a good five minutes to calm her down to the point where she listened to my repeated apologies, and the (admittedly flimsy) story I made up about falling asleep in the forest and waking up to find my things stolen, followed by a brief spate of mental confusion (which she had no trouble believing, drat her) that led me to wander the area until I was given succor by a kindly individual in the person of Nikola.

She took one look at Nikola, and the objections to the likeliness of my spending a few days with a stranger evaporated on her lips. After considering him for a few seconds, she spoke to him in German.

He answered in English. "I have family who live in this area, and was visiting them when I found Io lost. She seemed rather dazed and confused about where she was—"

I like the fact that you're telling the absolute truth, and yet it's coming out in a way that won't have her calling the police.

It is a gift, he said modestly.

"—so naturally, I did what I could to provide a safe haven for her."

After insisting I was a prostitute.

It seemed likely that you were, given your ensemble

and the circumstances. I will point out that I have apologized for that mistaken belief a number of times.

Once. You apologized once. Once does not a number of times make. And don't you dare tell me that I'm nitpicking, because I know I am. I just felt it was important to mention that you thought I was a hooker long before I molested you.

Why would I wish to pick a nit? he asked, genuinely confused.

We'll have that colloquial chat soon, I promised, and turned my attention back to Gretl, who was now saying polite things about him taking me in, while gently chastising me for not calling.

"I'm sorry, I forgot your phone number, and I didn't have my cell phone," I lied, thanking heaven that her number was unlisted. "Nikola brought me back here as soon as possible, and by then, I had remembered what your phone number was, and so here we are."

"Yes," she said slowly, her gaze shifting from Nikola to me. I don't think she believed my story, but luckily, she was distracted by him, and didn't grill me further about the missing things. "You are going to stay here?"

The unspoken question was whether Nikola was going to stay with me.

I smiled, and tried to not look like the sort of a woman who hooks up with a man after a few hours' acquaintanceship. "Yes, Nikola thought he'd like to see the fair while it's still here, and he's happy to show me around the area, so I thought we'd stay at the hotel so as not to disturb you if we come in late at night."

"How very thoughtful of you," she said, her lips

twitching a little. She glanced back at Nikola, a faint line between her brows. "Have we met before? You seem familiar to me, but I can't quite remember where it was we met."

Nikola made a courtly bow that made my stomach go all wobbly. "I cannot say that I've had the honor."

"Um . . . as it happens, Nikola is related to Imogen."

"He is?" Gretl looked delighted. Nikola looked surprised. "Imogen is a very old friend of mine. How are you related to her?"

"He's her . . . er . . . cousin."

I most certainly am not.

No, but there's no way in hell I'm going to try to explain that you are Imogen's dad when you look younger than Gretl does. You're just going to have to be Imogen's cousin to the folks who don't understand about vampires and immortality.

"He looks like Imogen's brother, so that's probably where you see the resemblance."

"Benedikt resembles *me*," Nikola said firmly, with a pointed look at me.

I smiled, and took my things from Gretl, tucking away my passport and credit cards. "Shall we meet for dinner? I'm going to get a room and go take a proper bath . . . er . . . take a bath, but if you'd like to meet for dinner, that would be great."

She demurred, her eyes on Nikola before giving me a look that let me know she wanted to say something in private.

"I'll walk you out to your car," I said, dropping the duffel bag at Nikola's feet. "Be right back."

"I'm not going to tell you to be careful," Gretl said as soon as we were out of earshot. "Because you are old enough to know what you are doing."

"Thank you. I realize this is a bit unexpected and certainly out of character for me, but Nikola is a very nice guy, and he . . . uh . . . I promised to help him with a little research problem, so I'm going to be busy with that for some time."

"Research problem? He is a scientist?"

"In a manner of speaking. More freelance than official," I said, hedging wildly, but luckily, Gretl didn't seem to notice.

"I would have thought he was an actor. Why is he in period costume if he is not?"

"Reenactors," I said quickly. "He belongs to a reenactor group that . . . uh . . . reenacts." I winced at just how stupid I sounded.

"I do not know of any historical reenactment groups in this area," she said, her brow furrowed in thought. "Is he perhaps from Vienna?"

"Yes, that's it. You don't mind if I stay with him, do you? I wouldn't want to hurt your feelings, especially after you invited me to come and stay with you for the summer—"

She patted my hand and stopped my pathetic apology. "My dear, if you have found a man with whom you have a future to share, then I am very happy for you. It is my fondest wish, you know. No, I am not hurt, and I do not mind that you should wish to stay with him, although I do warn you to be careful. We know nothing about him, about who he is, what he has done in the past."

I smiled, a wry little smile to be sure, but still a smile. "His past isn't as murky as you might think. I'll call you tomorrow just to let you know I'm still alive and kicking, all right?"

"Take care, Io," she said, giving me another hug before getting into her car.

I returned to the hotel lobby, nodding when Nikola asked me if my cousin was safely dispatched.

Yes. She's worried that you might have an unsavory past, and could possibly turn out to be a deranged ax murderer or something like that.

She is a wise woman, he answered, startling me. *It is the truth that you do not know me. I could indeed be a murderer.*

I looked at him as I tried to take back my duffel bag. *I may not have known you for long, Nikola, but I think I'd feel if you were so twisted inside that you could murder people. You're actually just the opposite.*

What is the opposite of a murderer? One who gives life?

Not so much literally, but yes, you do give life. Or rather, you make lives better. You don't think I didn't notice that every servant you have is in some way askew from normal? I bet it wouldn't have been easy for your crippled groom to have found work anywhere else, or for Elizabet to have gainful employment with one working arm, or even for that flaming footman to have a job where he wasn't abused for his sexual proclivities.

Given some of the noblemen in Austria, he might have gone far, Nikola replied with wry humor.

Even your horses are, for lack of a better word, runts of the litter. Thor has one eye and is missing an ear. The horse you rode has scars all up and down her chest and front legs. I read Black Beauty *as a child, you know. I'm well aware that in your time appearance was everything, and there you were riding around on horses that any other man of consequence would have sent to the knacker.*

It was merely a matter of convenience, nothing more, he objected. *I couldn't be bothered to replace something so trivial as a horse or a servant. I had important, weighty matters on my mind. That is all.*

Uh-huh. I touched his hand. *You've got an emptiness inside you, but it's not evil. And if you'd just let go of my bag, I could get us a room and then show you just how much I appreciate the fact that you're not going to kill me in my sleep and chop me up into little bits.*

I will carry your bag.

I sighed, and marched over to the registration desk (lavender with green tree frogs painted on the top). There was a brief tussle when Nikola wished to do the registering for a room.

You may think I'm old-fashioned as often as you like—although I should point out that I was born in 1637, so technically, I am old-fashioned—but I have yet to be accused of not knowing what's proper and what's not, and allowing a woman to register a hotel room for me, as well as pay for it, is not proper. Cease offering that woman the small item you insist she needs. My money is perfectly good.

It's called a credit card, and your money is made of gold, three-hundred-year-old gold. Just one of those coins you tried to give her could rent a room here for a year. Nikola, please put your money away. I will allow you to pay me for the room if you like, but let me put it on my credit card—otherwise we'll stand out, and I don't think we need any more attention than you are already getting being dressed as you are.

He looked down at himself, then out the window to where people were strolling down the street, enjoying the sunny afternoon. Some men were in jeans or other types of pants, but most wore knee-length shorts and T-shirts.

"I see that the fashion for breeches remains, but do not men wear stockings in your time?" he asked a few minutes later as we walked up two flights of stairs to our room. "Or waistcoats?"

"The guys in shorts weren't wearing breeches. They're actually walking shorts, and their shirts were T-shirts. So no, no stockings and fancy breeches, or heavily embroidered waistcoats, or even the fancy coat you're wearing over all of it. They do wear ties, although they're not as big as your neckcloth. We'll have to go shopping after I've had a bath in a real bathtub."

It was fascinating to watch Nikola be introduced to new things. I explained briefly about the telephone, radio, and TV that sat in the room, then stood back and watched him approach them in what he considered a scientific method. He asked questions about each item—almost all of which I couldn't answer—then proceeded to make little sketches of them in his notebook, as well as copious notes.

"Let me show you how to use the toilet," I said, going into the small attached bathroom.

"I don't have to use the toilet," he protested, following me into the room.

"No, but you might at some point."

He shook his head. "That will not happen."

"Of course it will. Are you embarrassed because my toilets are nicer than your toilets?"

"Not in the least. I'm simply saying that I do not need to use one."

"What, you mean never?" I gawked at him. "Vampires don't pee?"

"We have no need to do so, no."

My level of gawking increased. "But . . . but how does your body get rid of waste?"

He shrugged. "It no longer creates waste. Thus the functions associated with that are dormant."

"Well, that's really handy. I wish I could do the same thing. Boy, the savings on toilet paper alone must be staggering. All right, so no toilet. Now, this is the shower. You do take showers, right? I mean, you were taking a bath last night when I walked in on you."

"Yes, we bathe," he said with a look that told me he was this close to rolling his eyes. "We also cleanse our teeth, comb our hair, and shave our whiskers."

I showed him how to turn on the shower, and then, feeling somewhat itchy, said, "I feel like I've got three hundred years of dirt on me, so I'm going to take a shower. Why don't you watch TV for a bit while I'm doing so, and when I'm done, I'll feed you, and most likely seduce you like you've never been seduced before."

He looked interested at that suggestion, and went into the other room while I disrobed and got into the shower. I was just sighing with happiness as I used a tiny sample bottle of shampoo when Nikola asked, *What is it you're doing that gives you so much pleasure?*

Just enjoying the amenities of modern life. Did you turn the TV on?

Yes. It is interesting, like a lantern show, but with much more detail. I approve of it. You will explain how it works to me later.

Um. Yeah. We'll consult Wikipedia. I took up the body shampoo and sea sponge, soaping myself up in a businesslike manner that suddenly ceased when I felt Nikola's stunned interest. *Is anything the matter?*

No. The word came out strangled. *Continue cleansing your body.*

I slid my hands, soapy and wet, down my breasts. *If you insist.*

My hands went even lower, swirling little soapy circles on my stomach before sliding onward to more personal parts.

He moaned into my head. *Oh, yes, right there, sweetling. Touch yourself there again.*

I did, thrilled not by the touch of my own fingers, but by the incredible arousal that Nikola felt at my doing so.

I shifted, swirling long, soapy curlicues down the fronts of my legs, then up the backs to my behind.

He moaned again.

Do your belly once more, he demanded, panting a little into my mind.

I looked critically at the shower, decided that although it wasn't any too large, I wasn't going to kick up a fuss at being too cramped.

I'd rather, I said, soaping my breasts again, *that you be the one to wash my belly. And whatever else might strike your fancy.*

The words had barely left my mind before he was there, naked, the door to the shower flung open, allowing cooler air to swirl around me for a second or two. "I am your servant, madame."

I giggled as he took the sponge from me, about to turn around to face him, but unable to do so when he pulled me backward against his body, his hands busily possessing themselves of my breasts and stomach and pubic areas. "A less servile man I have never met, Nikola. Oh, merciful heavens, do that again!"

His fingers dipped and swirled and teased sensitive flesh, sending me immediately soaring. "If you bend forward, I will be able to make love to you," he murmured in my ear as I rocked my pelvis against his magic fingers.

"There isn't enough room for me to bend forward," I pointed out, my body tightening in anticipation. "How about if I turn around, and you hoist me up and we do it that way?"

"You are too slippery for me to hold safely," he said, the hardness of his penis rubbing along my behind. "Put your hands on the floor. There is enough room for you to double over in that manner."

"I'm likely to drown in that position. Or at least get water up my nose, which isn't at all pleasant. How about if we turn sideways, I wrap one leg around you, while supporting myself on the other?"

He bit my shoulder, just a little love bite, but the hunger swept over him in an overpowering, consuming wave of need and want. *You are not tall enough that I would be able to accommodate you.*

I'm perfectly normal in height, thank you.

Wrap one of your legs around me, and brace the other against the wall. That will allow me to support you without letting you slip.

You mean like this? Ow! Ow ow ow! Leg cramp! Wait a sec, let's try this: You squish me against the wall and I can brace both legs against the opposite wall, with you in between.

That sounds most awkward. If we turn so that my back is to the water, and you stand on your hands, you can wrap your legs around my waist, and—

"Oh, screw this," I said, driven half-mad with need just by his emotions alone. I spun the shower knob to turn off the water, threw open the shower door, and pulled Nikola out to the bedroom.

We didn't make it to the bed.

Floor! I demanded.

This is much easier, he agreed when I tumbled to the soft carpet, my hands everywhere as I tried to touch and taste all of him at once. I nipped his hip, I bit his thigh, I nibbled on his ribs all the while that he was nipping, biting, and nibbling on me. At one point, I was trying to bite his ear just as he was about to do the same, and I cracked my head on his, biting a bit harder than I intended.

He jerked back, and to my horror, I saw a drop of blood on the curve of his ear. "Oh, Nikola! I'm so sorry. You moved just as I was going to nibble—"

"Do it again!" he commanded, burying his face in my neck.

I will, but not so hard this time, I answered as I kissed his ear, intending to brush away the drop of blood. Some deep-seated need had me licking it off, though, part of my mind recoiling at the thought that I might pick up some horrible disease from him, the other part savoring the sweetly spicy taste of his blood.

By the time I was in a frenzy of lust, he stretched over me, his eyes blazing a dark topaz blue. *I will not ask if you are ready for me, because I can feel that you—*

"Too much talking! Not enough action!" I grabbed his butt and wrapped my legs around his hips, urging him with mind and body to send me flying into the wonderful Land of Orgasm.

You are the most irreverent, brazen, delectably delicious woman I have ever known, he murmured into my mind, groaning out loud when he slid into my body. I swear my eyes just about crossed at the sensation, but it wasn't until I felt his breath on my neck, followed by the graze of his teeth, that I gave myself up to the pleasure that only he could bring me. The sharp, hot pain of his bite was followed instantly by the soul-deep satisfaction that he felt as our bodies were joined together, my life flowing to him even as he allowed himself his own moment of pure rapture.

"And you are the most amazing lover I've ever had. That was indescribable, Nikola," I said some five minutes later, when I managed to get my brain working again. "I keep thinking you can't possibly get any better, and yet you do. You're going to kill me with sex one of these days, you know that, don't you?"

"I can but try," he said, rolling off me to lie on the floor, his chest damp with exertion.

"Hey!" I reached a languid hand over to pinch him. "It's rude to tell the person you just pleasured to the moon and back that you want her dead."

He didn't smile and make a joke, as I expected him to. Instead he opened his eyes and gave me a curious look. "How attached are you to your soul?"

"What?" I sat up and turned to look at him. He lay before me like a statue of one of those Greek gods come to life, all lines of thick muscles, and sculpted expanses of flesh that, even sated as I was, made my mouth water. "What the hell sort of question is that?"

"A straightforward one. How attached are you to the idea of having a soul?"

"I . . . I . . . I don't know how to answer that. I don't think I've ever thought about my soul. In fact, I didn't really think it existed until you said you lost yours when—hey! You don't mean—"

He nodded. "If you would not miss it, I could locate a demon lord, and arrange it so that you, too, could become a Dark One."

"You want me to become a vampire?" I was shocked by that statement, shocked and horrified, and for a second terrified.

"I want you to stay with me." The words were spoken with simple honesty, which in itself might have given me pause, but it was the emotion behind the words that kept me from recoiling from him. "If you were as I am, then you would not die, and we would never be separated."

"Are you . . . Nikola, are you saying you're in love with me?"

He looked thoughtful, one hand absently scratching his chest. "I came to the conclusion many years ago that I do not know how to love a woman. I love my daughter, of course, but she is my child. I tried to love my wife, since she was due that honor, but . . . there was something lacking in me. I enjoy being with you, Io. I enjoy your mind, and the times when our bodies join together. It pleases me that you enjoy me, as well, and I wish for you to remain at my side for as many years as I can envision being granted to me, but I am a Dark One. I will not die of old age, and you will. I do not wish for you to do so. I would that you were like Imogen, immortal, and able to accompany me through the path of life. If that is love, then yes, I am capable of love for you."

I sat silent for a few minutes, trying to work through everything he said.

"What of you?" he asked, suddenly looking very vulnerable and unsure.

I leaned down to kiss him, allowing my lips to linger on his warm, so very sweet mouth. "I don't know what I feel, either, Nikola. I like you a lot, more than any other man I've ever known. I want to be with you, too, and I think that it would probably be very easy for me to fall in love with you, but I don't want to become a vampire. I just . . . I just don't think that's for me."

His expression grew shuttered, and he started to roll away from me, the hurt so deep in him that it made tears sting my eyes. "No, wait," I said, grabbing his arm and forcing him to turn back toward me. "It doesn't mean I don't want to spend my life with you. I think I do, I really think I do. But not at the cost of my soul. If there was a way I could become like Imogen, but keep my soul—"

"Imogen has her soul," he interrupted.

I stared down at him, his eyes once again a pale

frosty blue. "She does? But I thought she's a vamp, too?"

"She is a Moravian, but she has her soul. My son does not, but she does." His eyes narrowed in thought. "I have wondered if it was due to her gender that she was allowed to retain her soul, while Benedikt was not. I have long meant to contact the Moravian Society to inquire about that, but more important studies always seemed to claim my time. However, I shall make the time to contact the society when we return home."

I let that subject go in favor of one more important. "So you think maybe there's a way I can be like Imogen? Because I would do that. So long as I could keep my soul, I would do that. It would hurt to see the few family members I have, like Gretl, grow old and eventually die, but that can happen at any time, and . . . and . . . well, to be honest, I can see myself spending a long, long time with you."

"Then we are in agreement," he said, one hand sliding down my back to my behind. "We will find a way for you to become a Moravian like Imogen—without sacrificing your soul—and you will return with me to my home."

"Nice try to slip that last bit in while distracting me with a butt grope," I said, leaning down to kiss him again.

He pulled me across his body, his legs capturing mine, erotic thoughts dancing once again in his brain. I let him fulfill all his smutty thoughts, content that, at least for the moment, we were of one mind.

16 July 2012

"Hey, Mr. Sleepyhead, wake up or we're going to miss the fair, and it's the last night for it, so we really should go so you can see Imogen and Ben."

The voice that woke Nikola was filled with warmth and happiness, and made him think of pleasurable afternoons spent in bedsport. "I'm sleeping. You have exhausted me with your demands for sensual delights, and I, being a mere man, have used up all my strength ensuring the fulfillment of your many needs."

"You're a vampire, and everyone knows vampires don't take naps. Besides, you've slept for three hours, and if Mr. Pokey down there is any indicator, you're more than rarin' to go again."

"I may be a Dark One, you insatiably sassy wench, but I am also a man, and thus I need copious amounts of sleep after pleasuring my woman to the tips of her toes. What is that?" He squinted at a large yellow glossy object she set next to him on the edge of the bed.

"It's a present."

"For me?" He sat up, anticipation driving away the need to sleep. He had a secret love of receiving unexpected presents, something he'd never before told another person, but here was Io handing him some sort of slippery yellow paper that evidently contained a present. He was extraordinarily pleased.

"You haven't even opened it," Io laughed, pushing the object toward him. "I don't know why you look so happy about it when you haven't seen what I got you. I had to guess your size, and you may not like them, but if we want to go out and about, you need something a little more conventional to wear."

"Garments?" he asked, pulling out of the slippery yellow substance an item that was clearly meant to be a shirt, although it lacked attributes with which he was familiar. It was followed by a clear slippery package that contained other objects, some sort of abbreviated black stockings that looked as if they'd barely go over his ankles, a somewhat worn pair of blue breeches, and an odd pair of shoes that had no laces whatsoever.

He loved them all. They were presents that she had picked out just for him, not for any other man, but for him. She had put much thought into them, considered what he might like, and chosen items that she knew would satisfy his needs and desires and wants.

She had brought him presents, surprise presents, presents he wasn't in the least bit anticipating. He wanted to touch all the presents, wanted to lay her out on the bed and show them to her before stripping her naked and licking every inch of her supple, silky body.

He was, in fact, trying to work out a way to combine the special joy of both touching his presents and engaging in lovemaking with her when she asked, in a hesitant voice, "Do you like them?"

"They are tolerable," he said, going for a lofty, disinterested tone, as befitted a man of his stature.

"Man of your stature, my shiny pink butt," she said, smacking him on the arm, her smile belying the words. "Do you like the color of the shirt? I wanted to get a red one, because red silk is just so yummy, but then I saw this blue one that matches your eyes, and I couldn't resist it. And it goes nicely with the jeans."

"The jeans are perfect," he said, holding up the shoes to examine them.

"Those are the loafers, silly. These are the jeans." She held up the long breeches. "They're stonewashed, which I don't particularly care for, but they were all the store had that I thought would fit you. Oh, there's a belt, too."

She handed him a slim black leather belt.

"There are castles on it," he said, examining the embossing on the leather.

"Yeah, kind of touristy, but I figured no one would look too closely at it, so you wouldn't mind—Nikola, what's wrong?"

His throat tightened painfully. He had to swallow three times before he could finally get out, "Nothing is wrong. I am simply admiring the castles on the belt that you have given me."

She watched him for a moment, her eyes concerned; then to his surprise she took the belt and shoes from his hands, pushed him onto his back, and leaned down, taking his face in her hands. "You are the sweetest man I know. I can't believe you're all *verklempt* because I bought you a few things to wear. Surely you must have received presents in the past?"

"Imogen embroidered handkerchiefs for me each Twelfth Night," he admitted. "My wife would sometimes make me stockings."

"And that's it? Socks and hankies? No one ever gave you anything else?"

"My wife gave me children."

"That doesn't count. Oh, my poor, sweet darling—" He allowed her to kiss his face and chest, enjoying greatly the little murmurs she made as she did so.

He was ready and willing to make love to her right then and there, but Io had other ideas.

"Later, punkin, later. Right now, we need to get you dressed so you can take me out and feed me, because I'm so famished I could just about eat your belt."

He quickly snatched the item in question out of her reach, just in case she wasn't joking. After a short bit of explanation as to what the mysterious slithery material was (he made note of the word "plastic," since Io used it a lot), he donned the male undergarments she said were commonplace, not at all displeased with how the silken material caressed his nether parts. By the time he had clad himself in the shirt, long breeches, and shoes, he felt very much like an adventurer about to step onto unknown shores.

"Well, it is kind of an adventure," Io agreed as they left the hotel. "I know I felt that way once I figured out I had traveled back in time. Oooh, a burger place, just what I want. You aren't going to mind if I eat in front of you? I hate to be rude, but I'm starving, and I know you can't eat."

"I can if I have to, but I see no need to do so. I am quite satisfied after dining earlier," he said, unable to keep from pinching her adorable bottom.

She squealed, and, with a promise to be right back, hurried across the road to a small building that bore pictures of odd-looking food products on its walls. He contented himself with watching her, frowning when a man nearby turned to look at her as she walked past, automatically reaching for the saber he wore at his side.

Dammit, Io had made him leave it back at the hotel room, claiming that a weapon like that would attract attention from the local magistrates.

"*I* am the law at my home," he said under his breath as he waited for Io. "No one would dare look at my woman in such a manner. No one would tell me I cannot defend what is mine. I dislike being incommoded in this fashion—"

His grumbling stopped abruptly when he caught sight of a familiar shape suddenly made visible as a wave of local villagers, strolling around the shops and businesses, parted briefly. Although the man had his back to Nikola, he could have sworn that it was his brother Rolf.

Had Rolf produced descendants after all? Ones who resembled him? He moved through the crowd intent on seeing the man better, but he disappeared into the crowd by the time Nikola had reached the spot where he had stood.

Nikola glanced around him, but was unable to find anyone who resembled the man he sought. He did, however, notice a shop behind him that had the words WE BUY GOLD on the window. He was reminded of Io's explanation of how money worked in her century, and accordingly stepped into the shop, a few of his coins in his hand.

When he emerged a few minutes later, having sold only one coin, the shop owner saw him to the door saying, "I wish I could buy your entire collection, but as I told the other gentleman who offered me some silver coins, I cannot buy more than one without some form of identification. It is the law, you understand. If you bring me your passport, then I will be able to purchase more coins from you."

"I will discuss your offer with my woman. She knows more about these things than me," Nikola said politely, carefully putting into his pocket the paper money the man had given him. He had to admit that even though he wasn't used to wearing long breeches, the ones that Io had given him were quite comfortable, and had handy pockets that he would make sure were included in all his breeches from that moment forward.

"Er . . . all right." The man waved him off, and as Nikola returned to the shop where Io had gone to find food, he felt much more in control. He had clothing that would allow him to blend in, and now he had currency that would allow him to purchase anything he might need.

He was planning on buying some sort of present for Io when she hurried up to him with a small bag in one hand, while jamming some sort of long strips of food into her mouth with the other. "Sorry to take so long. You sure you don't want anything? I got two burgers, and a jumbo fries in case you wanted to try modern food. You know, the kind without maggots all over it."

He sniffed at her food, but it held no appeal to him. It certainly couldn't come close to the scent of her that perpetually teased his nose and left him halfway aroused just being near her. "I do not require food other than you, thank you."

She sighed blissfully as she ate another handful of the strips, sliding one arm through his and directing them to the main street that led out of town. "I'll eat as we walk to the fair, if you don't mind. It's not a long walk, and although I could rent a car, I think we'll have to ease you into the complexities of modern vehicles."

"You wouldn't have to do so if you had allowed me to examine the FedEx," he pointed out, turning to stare at a woman who emerged from a shop clad in small scraps of clothing that barely hid her breasts and woman's parts.

"Oh, that lady would have loved—what's wrong? Oh." Io smothered a laugh as his gaze went from the nearly naked woman to her. "That's a bikini. It's what some women who don't have any body fat wear when they go swimming or, in that woman's case, to a tanning salon."

"I begin to see that there may be some merits to your century," Nikola said with a little smile.

She punched him in the arm, just as he knew she would do.

"Dawg. Did you people watch while I was in the fast-food place?"

"I exchanged one of my coins for your currency. Look." He stopped and pulled out the wad of paper money, showing it to her. "Did I negotiate an adequate amount for one coin? The man was quite excited about my coins, and wished only to give me ten paper monies for one, but I told him I must have more. He did not like that, but I know merchants well, and knew he would not offer me a fair price at first. After bargaining for a few minutes, he gave in and gave me these many monies, and I felt that it was a fair exchange. He also wished to purchase the rest of my coins, but said I must have identification in order for him to do so. I do not have a passport."

"No, but I have one. Maybe I could—" Io's eyes widened at the sight of the money, and glancing around quickly, she shoved his hand toward his pocket. "Put that away! I don't know that there are pickpockets around here, but fairs usually have them, so I wouldn't be surprised. And yes, that's a metric butt ton of money, so you did very well."

"Good." He was pleased that he had such success in her world with his first attempt. He must be sure to make notes about it later, so as to document how well he did here. "Now *I* will pay for our lodgings."

"Just one of those bills will pay for a whole week," Io said, unwrapping some food and taking a bite. "Not to change the subject, but I think we should discuss what you're going to say when you see Imogen and your son."

"What I'm going to say?"

"So you don't freak them out by suddenly appearing from the past. Imogen said you had died, remember."

"I find it difficult to forget something like my own death," he said drily.

"Although oddly enough, Ben said you were alive and well and living in South America ogling nubile young girls." She gave him a long look. "Obviously, given the fact that your brothers were trying to kill you, he was lying about your death, but I'm curious as to why he'd do that. I don't suppose you have any insight into that?"

"If Benedikt felt it necessary to speak falsely about me, I'm sure he had a very good reason," he answered with serenity. There might be many unknowns in his life—and certainly more so now that he found himself in a world that was full of oddities—but in one thing he was confident: the integrity of his children. "I cannot anticipate what that might be, but I am sure that Benedikt will explain himself. I admit that I will be pleased to see them. I was just returning home from leaving Benedikt at the university in Heidelberg when you ran into my horse. I assume they have done well for themselves over the centuries?"

"I guess so," she answered rather indistinctly around a mouthful of food. "I told you that Ben had a wife now. She seemed nice enough, although . . ." Io wadded up her bag and tossed it into a round receptacle that was placed on the street. "At the time, I thought she was as bonkers as Ben, because she said she had some ghosts visiting her. But I guess now that I'm dating a vampire, and have traveled through time twice, I should just stop fighting it and go with the flow. Your daughter-in-law has Viking ghosts, Nikola. Ones that seem to think she's some sort of goddess."

"Fascinating," he said, and pulled out his notebook to make a note about interviewing the ghosts. He wished to stop and make more comprehensive notes, but Io insisted that they stop by a bank so that he could get smaller denominations of currency.

"No one would be able to make change for the sort of bills you're hauling around," she told him as they emerged into the dusky twilight that enveloped the valley.

He had been careful to keep to the shadows earlier, but now with the sun setting, he was able to join the throng of people who were streaming out of town, on foot and in the metal carriages that Io had described earlier—and about which he badly wanted to make a scientific study—all headed to the field outside of the town where he could see colorful tents and small oblong buildings.

"Remember, we're going to tell everyone that you're Imogen and Ben's cousin," Io warned him as they stood in front of a wooden structure bearing the legend "Ticket Booth." Io pointed out which notes he would need for the tickets to the fair. "And yes, I know that irks you, but there's just no way we can explain your appearance otherwise."

"I look older now," he pointed out.

"A tiny bit, yes. Enough that I don't feel like I'm robbing the cradle, but certainly not old enough to have kids who are Imogen's and Ben's ages. Hi, two adults, please."

He followed after Io as she led him onto the fairgrounds, his quick gaze taking in many things. "I know what a tattoo is, but what purpose does piercing offer?" he asked, stopping in front of one of the booths.

Io pulled him away from the front of the intriguing images. "You truly do not want to know."

He dug in his heels and refused to budge. "On the contrary, I do. I am a scientist, and more, an adventurer. You yourself said so. Thus, I must record my adventures, and I cannot do that if you tug me away from interesting ones."

She stopped trying to pull him away from the booth, gesturing toward the flap that hid the inside of the tent while saying, "By all means, go ahead and see for yourself. I wouldn't want to deprive you of an adventure, or the pursuit of knowledge."

You are smiling, he said as he entered the close confines of the tent. Inside, there was some sort of odd reclining chair, several tables, and a woman with heavily drawn black around her eyes who looked up from a journal she was reading. *I suspect you know something you are not telling me. What is it?*

No, no, I wouldn't want to ruin your scientific studies of piercings and modern society. You just go on and find out for yourself.

"May I help sir?" the woman asked, getting to her feet. She appeared to have small bits of metal stuck to her nose, eyebrows, and lower lip. He stared at those for a few moments before recognizing the look she was giving him.

"My woman is outside," he told her. "I do not wish to have sexual congress with you."

She paused for a moment, then pursed her lips. "Your loss. Do you wish for a tattoo? Piercing?" She brazenly eyed the front of his breeches. "Would sir be interested in a Prince Albert, perhaps?"

"I am a baron, not a prince, and my name is Nikola, not Albert," he corrected her.

The woman smiled. "A Prince Albert is a piercing, Baron. A small circular barbell is inserted in your cock. It will give much pleasure to your partner, I assure you. If you would remove your jeans, I will assess you for what size barbell would be best to start with."

He stared at the woman for a few seconds, then turned on his heel and exited the tent. Io stifled a laugh when she saw his face.

He ignored it, saying simply, "The creation of the bikini aside, I must question the sanity of your times, Io."

She laughed out loud. "Where piercings are concerned, I totally agree. The woman who runs that place wanted me to get my nipples tattooed. I shudder to think of what she offered to do to you."

"You don't want to know."

"Moving along, then . . . if you're done exploring the subject of body enhancements, Imogen's booth is on the right, at the end. Now, be gentle with her, Nikola. She's not expecting you to suddenly come back to life, and we wouldn't want to give her a heart attack or some—well, hell. She's not there."

He looked where Io pointed to a booth covered in black canvas with gold runes painted on it. "My daughter is a soothsayer?"

"She reads rune stones, yes." Io bit her delicious lower lip, instantly causing him to want to do the same. "I wonder where she went? This is all sorts of anticlimactic, Nikola. I was ready for a happy reunion. I brought tissues and everything, in case Imogen cried buckets at seeing her beloved daddy risen from the grave—hey!"

Io rammed into him, half turning as she did so to glare back at the person who had shoved her.

Nikola turned to deal with the rude person, but at that moment, the crowd of fairgoers went berserk as a sense of pandemonium gripped them. Women screamed, men shouted, children shrieked in fear, and all of them turned as one body and stampeded past Nikola and Io to the open end of the fair, and safety.

"What on earth—" Io started to say.

Nikola thrust her into the space between his daughter's booth and the one next to it, standing protectively in front of her so that she wouldn't be trampled.

"What's going on?" Io said, nudging his back and trying to peer over his shoulder.

The crowd streaming past them began to thin, and he could see at the far end three men who were stalking down the center aisle, sweeping bloodied scythes before them. "It would appear the grim reaper is here. And he is a triplet."

"Who? And what?"

Io pushed him so she could see, but he stood solid, his gaze narrowed on the three men as they approached. "Perhaps it isn't the grim reaper—there are three men, and other than the blood-splattered scythes they are all holding, they appear perfectly ordinary."

"Liches!" a woman with short red hair yelled as she bolted past them, following on the heels of the crowd. "For the love of the goddess, everyone take shelter! Liches are here!"

"I stand corrected," Nikola said, watching the men. "They are evidently liches."

"What's a lich?" Io asked, holding his shoulder and craning her head to see them.

"I have no idea. Assumedly someone who slaughters others with iron farm implements. No, remain behind me, there is no time for me to find a place for you to seek shelter as that woman advised. I will keep you safe from harm."

"OK, one, that he-man crap doesn't pull a lot of weight with me. Well, a little, because I appreciate the fact that you're standing there thinking about ways of disarming them should they come after us, and I flunked out of my self-defense class because I get squeamish about hitting people, and yes, I know that's not the right attitude to have when defending oneself— lord knows, my instructor kept telling me that self-defense wasn't about anything but keeping yourself safe—but regardless, I do appreciate it, and at the same time, I don't. If you know what I mean. Which I can see that you don't by the fact that you're looking at me like I'm one antler short of a reindeer."

Your conversations never fail to interest me, sweetling, but now is not the time for blethering.

I was not blethering! she said, mentally bristling. *I never blether! I am not a bletherer! What's blethering? Wait, it's like babbling, isn't it? Well, Mr. My Words Are Like Pearls from a Swine's Ear—*

Sow.

I beg your pardon?

It's pearls from a sow's ear, not swine's ear. "What the devil?"

A small group of people ran past them from the opposite direction, a man and two women, one of whom had familiar long, blond hair.

"Oh, look, there's Imogen," Io said helpfully, clutching his shoulders as she peered around his head. "And I think that's your son. Hell's teeth! That's one heck of a big sword Ben's carrying!"

Two other men approached, clearly following on the heels of the threesome. Nikola noted the two swords held by one of the men, and the large ax held by the other.

"Stay here," he said, and, reaching out, snatched one of the swords from the closest of the two men.

"What? Nikola! Dammit, man! I will not be left—holy deranged ax murderers!"

Io followed him, much to his irritation. *I asked you to stay back, Io, and I expect you to honor that request.*

It wasn't a request, it was an order. An annoying and unrealistic order. One that I'd have to be an idiot to follow, so you can just stop thinking about tying me to the booth, and instead pay attention to the dude with the beard, because he doesn't look any too happy about you taking his sword, and I think he's going to—look out!

Io screamed just as the man whom he had de-sworded swung at him. Everything seemed to happen at once: He slammed the hilt of the sword against the head of the man, sending him reeling backward, then on the backswing, parried a thrust by the man holding the ax, tripping him so he, too, fell over backward, crashing heavily against one of the booths. The sounds of breaking wood, tearing canvas, and the tinkle of shattered glass were followed by some profane oaths. In front of him, the man and two women stopped to look back just as the three scythe holders shouted, and ran forward toward them.

"Papa?" he heard the blond woman ask, her voice filled with incredulity.

"Nikola, wait," Io yelled, leaping over the prone form of the man with the ax, stopping to kick out his leg from under him when he tried to rise and disentangle himself from the booth.

When we return home, I will make sure to find the time to explain to you why it is that you must attend to me when I give orders, he told Io sternly as she ran up behind him, clutching the back of his shirt. *Do not block my arms, sweetling. I must be able to swing the sword, and I can't do that if you are clinging to me.*

Oh, sorry. She let go, her concern for him warming him to the tips of his toes. She truly cared about what happened to him, and was honestly worried that he would be harmed. He cherished that sentiment almost as much as he cherished the silk undergarments that made wearing tight breeches extremely comfortable.

Seriously? You're fawning over your undies now? I can understand some of that, because you look really hot in them, and I just want to fondle . . . but no, now is not the time. Pay attention, Nikola. There are baddies in front and behind you. We can discuss your underwear later, in the hotel room.

I am a Dark One, he reminded her, striding forward past where Imogen was standing and staring at him with an open mouth. *You will cease worrying. It is extremely difficult to kill me.* "Imogen, you will catch flies if your mouth hangs open like that. Benedikt, stand back. I will attend to these ruffians."

"Who the hockey pucks is that?" the tall woman next to his son asked, giving him a less-than-friendly look.

Benedikt looked older than when he had last seen him, but Nikola felt a swell of pride that his son had grown to be a man of prepossessing appearance. "Your mother would be pleased," he told his son before swinging his sword, catching the nearest of the scythe wielders on the shoulder, neatly severing his arm.

The man stopped dead in his tracks, looking in blank astonishment at the sight of his arm—still holding the bloody scythe—lying on the ground in front of him. "Oy!"

The man nearest him also stopped, but his attention was on Benedikt, his black eyes narrowed until they were veritable slits. "There's the Dark One! Kill the women and take him!"

"That's my arm!" the first man said, looking from the blood spurting from his shoulder down to the arm on the ground. "Oy!"

"Over my dead body," Benedikt growled, focused now on the threatening man. He swung a large two-handed sword that Nikola instantly coveted.

"Hell's teeth, you just cut off that guy's arm!" Io gasped. "You just . . . it's . . . it's right there on the ground. An arm. On the ground. Not attached or anything. Are you OK?"

The man she was addressing looked from his arm to Io. "He's had me arm off!"

"I know, I can see it. It's right there in front of you."

"Oy," the man said a third time before nudging the arm with the toe of his shoe.

"The master says we has to bring you in alive," the

middle scythe man snarled, spittle flying from his mouth, his lips pulled back in a sneer that Nikola felt he'd tolerated long enough.

"Imogen, stand next to Io. You, too, woman," he told the auburn-haired woman who frowned at him. "I will take care of these swine."

"Sow," came a soft voice from behind him.

Now is not the time to be witty, he told Io. "Benedikt, can you disable the smaller man? I will take care of this nasty piece of business."

"Your *father*?" the woman asked, her voice filled with surprise. "I thought you said your dad was a jerk who was in South America hitting on all sorts of scantily clad women?"

"It's me arm," the one-handed scyther said, picking up the object in question. He tried to push it back onto his shoulder, but the arm just fell to the ground again. "Now what am I supposed to do?"

"If you had a decent bone in your body, you'd die," Nikola told him, his sword flashing in the air when the middle scythe man, his eyes widening when he got a good look at who was attacking him, snarled an obscenity that would have made a sinner blush.

"Yes, it's my father," Benedikt said, giving him an odd look before rushing at the third man, who had leaped forward toward the women.

"Hi, Fran. That South America stuff was just something Imogen told Ben, probably to keep him from being devastated that his dad was killed by his brothers. Nikola's brothers, not Ben's brothers. I don't think Ben has any brothers." *Nikola, you don't have any other children, do you?*

Now is not the time, woman! Nikola panted, alternately parrying and thrusting to disable, disarm, or smite down the man who clearly had nefarious designs against his son and daughter. *It might have escaped your attention, busy as you are discussing arms and such with the potential murderer who is even now attempting to tie his severed arm onto his body using his belt — which I cannot help notice does not possess a fine embossing of castles, as my present does — but I am conducting some business that requires my full attention, and thus I will be able to engage in trivial conversation with you later, after I have dispatched these rogues.*

Oh, sure, when you blather, it's just fine, but when I do, I'm distracting you? Men! Io winced in sympathy when the edge of the scythe slashed against his upper arm. *Are you OK? That looks deep.*

Not enough to hinder me. Just stay back.

"Imogen said what?" Fran asked, shaking her head before she hefted a large mallet that had been used to pound in a stake, and took a swing at the nearest man.

"Io, why are you here with my father?" Imogen asked her, then spun around and shouted, "Finnvid! What are you and Eirik doing back there? Why are you playing with the aura photo booth? Come and help us kill the liches!"

It didn't take Nikola long to disable and destroy the middle lich — scythes being a notoriously awkward weapon to wield in close combat — after which he turned his attention to the third ruffian, but Benedikt had just knocked that man's scythe away, and was about to skewer the man with his broadsword when the woman stopped him.

"No, Ben, don't!"

"They killed four innocent mortals!" Ben snarled, raising the sword.

The woman grabbed his arm. "I know, but killing them isn't the answer. Besides, if we let them live—"

Nikola twirled his sword, and neatly beheaded the lich.

"—we can find out what they know about David. Oh." The woman turned angry eyes to him. "Well, thank you very much, Ben's dad! That guy might have given us just the clue we needed to find David!"

"I'll not tell you anything," the lich's head spat out, his fierce expression made somewhat less effective by the fact that there was no body attached. "Not if you tortured me!"

"What the—hell's toenails!" Io clutched his arm and stared at the animated head. "That guy's head is still talking!"

"How very curious," Nikola said, studying the head for a moment before handing Io the sword and pulling out his notebook. "Evidently liches can't be destroyed by a simple decapitation."

"You're going to pay for this, mate," the armless lich yelled, shaking his arm at Nikola. "It'll cost me a packet to get this reattached, and I'm not going to pay for it meself!"

Nikola eyed the man, then reached for the sword.

"No," Io said, turning away. "One decapitation is enough for me today, even if the head . . . wow, he really does know a lot of curse words, doesn't he?"

"He's quite the potty mouth," Benedikt's woman agreed.

"I feel woozy," the one-armed lich said, and staggered to the side, collapsing next to a tent. "Someone fetch a healer!"

The head continued to hurl abuse, alternating with some choice threats that Nikola took down carefully.

Benedikt's woman sighed. "Imogen, maybe we could use your scarf to gag him."

"I'm so glad I chose this one to wear, and not one of the good silk ones," Imogen said, handing over a blue and purple strip of fabric. She turned to him and gazed with wide, blue eyes that reminded him of her mother. "Papa, what are you doing here?"

"Io brought me," he said simply, still making notes as Benedikt helped his woman tie a gag around the lich's mouth. It tried to bite them, but eventually they got the scarf bound around the head a few times.

"Oh!" Io stopped reading over his shoulder and went to Imogen, putting an arm around her. "I'm so sorry! We meant to do this much differently. We wanted to break it to you gently that your father was still alive, and not killed by your uncles as you've believed all these years, but then those men attacked—exactly what is a lich? And why did they have scythes, of all things? And then there you were, and of course, there was no time to explain everything. I hope we haven't given you some sort of a trauma by having Nikola come back from the dead like that, but . . . um . . . well, here he is!"

Benedikt turned to face them, his face stony. "And I wish to hell he'd go back to wherever it is he crawled from."

The Incredible Adventures of Iolanthe Tennyson

July 16

"I hope you realize just how incredibly lucky you are that at this moment I don't have a blunt object at hand," I told Ben, moving to stand in front of Nikola. I'm not normally an aggressive person, but I couldn't believe what a bastard Ben was being to his father. Of all the nerve, telling him he wanted him gone!

"Are you threatening him?" Fran asked, an expression of utter incredulity chasing amusement across her face.

"Yes, yes, I am," I said, lifting my chin and just daring either Ben or her to laugh at me. "Your father was excited and happy to see you again, and for you to say such hurtful and cruel things to him after what he's been through—well, you seriously have a smack upside the head coming, that's all I'll say!"

Nikola sighed and put away his notebook. "Io, do not upset yourself. You told me that Benedikt was not told the truth about my death. He is obviously reacting to whatever falsehood Imogen saw fit to tell him."

"I didn't tell him a falsehood of any sort," Imogen said slowly, her expression suddenly wary.

"Of course you did. You told Ben that his dad was alive and kicking in Rio or somewhere, obviously because you wanted to save him the horror of knowing Nikola was killed by your uncles. I don't blame you, although I would have thought, at seventeen, Ben could have handled the news, but you clearly felt otherwise—"

"No, Io, I didn't," Imogen interrupted, moving over to stand next to Ben. "I didn't lie to Benedikt. . . . I lied to you. When I said my father died that night more than three hundred years ago, I was speaking more figuratively than literally."

I gawked at her. *What the hell?*

I don't know. Nikola tucked away his notebook and frowned at Imogen. *Obviously, something has occurred about which we know nothing.*

"Dammit, I knew if I brought you back with me, something horrible would happen to the future."

"What are you talking about—there you are." Imogen turned to face the two men whom Nikola had disabled earlier. Both men looked like they wanted to pick a fight with him.

They're welcome to try, Nikola said with some amusement.

"What were you doing back there?" Imogen asked one of them, the one who was clutching the ax and glaring at Nikola. "You were supposed to help us. As it is, my father took care of the liches."

"Your father?" the man asked, his frown fading. "The one who ogles women in Brazil?"

"Well, it's better than lizards taking over," I told Nikola. "Although really, it's not very nice to know *everyone* thinks you're a smutmonger."

"Smut—" Nikola pulled his notebook out and made another note.

"Yes, that's him. And this is Io. She's the cousin of a friend of mine. And . . . erm . . . somehow knows my father."

A little blush crept up my chest. I coughed. "We . . . uh . . ."

"Io is my lover," Nikola said, sliding an arm around me. "She does a great many things to me that bring me much pleasure, and which I have not enjoyed since your mother died. I will not discuss them further, however, because you are yet an innocent maiden, and it is not suitable that you should know such things. However, I wish to put your mind to rest, since I know you are worried that I am lonely. Io has agreed to spend her life with me. We are in pursuit of a method by which we can make her Moravian without losing her soul. She does not wish to be soulless. I have told her it isn't that bad, but she is adamant, and I must honor her wishes in this regard."

The others stared at us like we were both buck naked and dancing the cancan.

To my complete surprise, Ben leaned forward and sniffed the air, an indefinable expression crossing his face.

"She's what?" Fran said almost in a shriek.

"It's faint, but it's there," Ben said, giving me an odd look. "Evidently she's his Beloved."

"Look, I realize that Nikola could have broken the news about our relationship in a more fitting manner, but really, what we do behind closed doors is our business," I told Ben, feeling irritable for some reason. "I'm sorry if it upsets you that your dad has found someone, but—"

"I'm not upset that he's found his Beloved," Ben interrupted. "I'm furious that he chose now to inflict himself on us. We don't have time for this."

"Right, something is going on, and I think I can explain part of what's causing it. See, there's this paradox when you time travel that if you change something in the past, even something really minor, things in the future can be affected, and what we changed wasn't minor at all—" I was interrupted yet again, this time by a woman speaking from behind me.

"Are the liches gone? Ah, yes, I see they are dead. All but the one passed out on Miranda's booth."

"We have one of their heads," Fran said, holding up the still-living head by the scarf wrapped around it. "We hope to question it about David."

"Just so." The woman, who was probably in her sixties, had one of those ageless complexions, and black hair that bore a thick white streak. She considered first Nikola, then me, her eyes widening a little when they got to me. "Another Dark One. And a weaver. One doesn't see many of you about," she told me. "Are you here to help Fran and Ben? If so, I would warn against it. Such tactics never turn out as one expects."

"I can't knit, let alone weave," I answered, feeling even more irritated. *I just knew something like this would happen, Nikola.*

No, you said lizards would have become our over-lords. This is different.

Pfft. That's just a matter of semantics. Now what are we going to do?

"Not a textile weaver," the woman said, frowning slightly. "You are a weaver of time. Benedikt, I believe you should dispose of those bodies before the public returns. Where are Hans and Karl?"

"In the main tent, guarding the audience there." Ben made an annoyed click of his tongue when his gaze settled on Nikola. "So long as you've shoved yourself in where you're not wanted, you can help clean up the mess you caused."

"Hey!" I gave Ben a little shove. "I realize that the paradox has messed stuff up, and for some reason you feel that you can be rude as hell to your father, but I'm not going to stand for it."

"Io, you do not need to defend me," Nikola said in a deceptively calm voice. I knew full well he was just as annoyed with his son as I was.

Yes, but I realize that a situation out of our control has caused him to have such animosity toward me, and thus he's not responsible for his behavior.

Like hell he isn't.

"And I will thank you to stop shoving Ben around," Fran said, pushing forward toward me. "*He* hasn't done anything wrong."

"Francesca," Ben said in a warning tone.

"Are you implying that Nikola *has* done something wrong?" I asked, bristling with indignation at the slur.

It is only a slur if you allow it to be one.

Hush. I'm defending your honor.

I was not aware it needed defending, he answered, but once again, I felt a sense of astonished gratitude from him that just made me want to simultaneously cry and molest him.

I prefer the molesting.

"From what Ben and Imogen have told me, yes, he is very much in the wrong. He treated them horribly. Ben has every right to—"

"Ben can just stick his attitude up his behind," I interrupted. It felt good to be the one doing it for a change.

Imogen gasped. "Io!"

"I'm sorry to be rude, but he started it, and to his father yet, a man who was looking forward to seeing how his children had changed since he died. Almost died. Would have died if we hadn't come through the swirly thing. So you can just stick that in your holier-than-thou pipe and smoke it!"

Ben blinked at me in surprise. Fran looked like she was thinking about decking me. The two guys who got in Nikola's way moved around to stand behind Fran, one of them saying, "Would you like us to put a scold's bridle on that female, Goddess Fran? The Dark One might be a bit more difficult, but if Finnvid and I were to summon some of my men, we would be able to take him."

"You lay one finger on Io"—suddenly, Nikola was in front of me, blocking me from the two other men— "and you will not live to see the sun rise again."

"We're ghosts," the man said with a cocky grin. "We're already dead."

Nikola's sword flashed, and the man suddenly froze,

a look of horror on his face. The sword tip was at his crotch, the tip of the blade slipping easily through the fabric of his pants. "Then you will be a gelded ghost."

"Don't you dare hurt Eirik!" Fran said, trying to push past the two ghosts—who, I had to say, looked awfully solid and not at all how one imagines a ghost— but Ben pulled her back against him.

"It's all right, Francesca. He won't hurt your ghosts."

"This is your woman?" Nikola asked Ben, nodding toward Fran.

"My Beloved, yes."

"And his wife. We were married three weeks ago. My mother insisted." Fran still looked like she wanted to deck me, but at least she stopped looking daggers at Nikola, too.

"Ah," Nikola said, blinking a couple of times. "I have a daughter-by-marriage." He turned to me. "My son has married, Io. I suppose he is old enough, although I would have preferred that he discuss the matter with me, first."

"You were dead, punkin," I said, patting his arm. "That's got to limit the amount of father-son communication possible."

"There is that," Nikola agreed, and turned back to the group in front of us. He gave the ghost a look that probably would have killed a lesser man. "You will cease making threats against my woman. I will not geld you at this time, but should you think to harm her, you will have me to answer to."

To my complete surprise, the ghost smiled, and nodded. The other one nodded, as well. "I did not realize that the female was yours," the ghost said when Nikola dropped the tip of the sword. "The mother-by-marriage of the Goddess Fran must be honored."

I gawked. "Wait . . . what? No, we're not married—"

"I hesitate to interrupt this fascinating conversation, but the mundane police should be arriving shortly if those sirens are anything to go by, and I would advise you to clean up the mess and begin the process of convincing everyone the attack by the liches was part of the show," the dark-haired woman said, giving me another odd look. "Sir Edward wishes for me to speak with you, child. You will come with me."

"You know, I think I'm just going to stick with Nikola," I said, taking his hand. My stomach tightened with pleasure when his fingers wrapped around mine. "Given how rude people are to him, I think it's best that we stay together."

"He may join us. In fact, I believe you all should. There is a mystery here that Sir Edward insists must be unraveled," the woman said, and, turning on her heel, strode to the other end of the fair.

"That is Tallulah," Imogen said, her expression now bland as she looked from me to Nikola. "She is very wise."

"What do you think, Nikola?" I asked, nodding toward the receding figure of the woman.

He looked thoughtful. "It is quite evident that something is amiss with your time. If that lady can help clarify what we might do to correct things, then yes, I believe we should accompany her."

"Benedikt?" Imogen nodded toward the retreating Tallulah, obviously asking him what they should do.

"We'll clear up the bodies first," Ben said, stooping

to collect the headless corpse in front of him. The ghosts picked up the second body, and the now-unconscious armless man. "We'll put them in Miranda's trailer. Imogen, go with ... *them.*"

"You needn't say the word 'them' like we're giant ants about to devour the town," I said, sniffing loudly, but moving when Nikola tugged on my hand. "Although if I was, I know who'd I'd squash flat first."

Ahem.

Not literally, of course. Just kind of ... er ... never mind.

Ten minutes later we were seated around and near a table in a travel trailer that was evidently Tallulah's home. She sat opposite Nikola and me, while Imogen, Ben, and Fran sat across from us on a cocoa-colored suede couch. The two ghosts—who informed me candidly they were the pride of Valhalla sent to help Fran with some project—lurked at the far end of the trailer in two spinning chairs, which they seemed greatly to enjoy.

"The police are here, but Peter has it under control. Peter is one of the owners of the GothFaire," Fran explained when she and Ben sat down. "Kurt and Karl got dressed up like the liches and told the police they were part of the show, so I think everything will return to normal. Or as normal as it gets around here. Oh, I guess we should do introductions." Fran gestured toward the two ghosts. "That's Eirik Redblood, and his friend Finnvid. They're Viking ghosts that I inadvertently resurrected in Sweden. The rest of Eirik's men are in Valhalla. You met Ben and me a few days ago, and this is Tallulah, who is known for her scrying and crystal-reading abilities. Sir Edward is her ... er ..."

"Boyfriend," Tallulah said with complacency. Before her, she held a small black mirrored glass bowl, into which she poured a dash of water. "Sir Edward died some two hundred years ago, but we have not allowed that to alter our relationship. He resides in the beyond."

"Beyond what?" I couldn't help but ask. *Don't you think I'm doing really well at not even blinking at the idea of people who have ghosts as boyfriends?*

If I died, would you wish to continue a relationship with me? Nikola asked.

Beneath the cover of the table, I took his hand and squeezed it. *Yes.*

"The beyond is the name for that form of reality that lies between this and the next," Tallulah answered, which didn't really help me at all, but I decided that it probably wasn't the best moment to make a fuss about just what exactly she meant.

Nikola, of course, pulled out his notebook and made a few notes.

Imogen made a sound that I could've sworn was a giggle, but when I glanced at her, her face was impassive.

"OK. So your ghost friend thinks there's a mystery surrounding us? Does it have something to do with the swirly time-travel thing, or why Ben is being such a giant ball of snot to his father?"

"That is totally uncalled for," Fran said loudly.

"Swirly time-travel thing?" Tallulah looked up from her bowl. "Do you mean a portal?"

"That's what Nikola called it, but I just think of it as the swirly thing. It was almost gone by the time we came through it."

Her eyes seemed to strip away all my layers of defense, and peer straight into my soul. "I believe before we go any further that we would all benefit from a recap of your experiences with the portal."

"Sure, but don't expect us to have many answers. It took me forever to figure out what exactly happened, although Nikola seemed to have coped better with the whole thing. Except the part where he was convinced I was a prostitute."

"It was understandable given the situation," he said mildly, squeezing my fingers where they rested on his thigh.

"Several days ago I came to visit the fair with my cousin Gretl." I settled back and gave a succinct accounting of high points from the last few days, skipping over much of the craziness where I thought I was insane, and focusing on the nefarious plan by Nikola's brothers to destroy him. When I finished with us arriving back in the present, there was a profound silence for a good minute.

"I don't know what to think. I knew that my uncles had something to do with Papa severing ties with us, but to plan a scheme to physically harm him . . . it just seems so wrong." Imogen finally broke the silence, her gaze moving from Nikola to Ben. "Are you sure about this, Io?"

"Absolutely. Just as I'm sure that in the present before I went through the swirly portal, you told me that your father was dead, and Ben told me he was in South America. It's clear that although lizards didn't take over the world because we altered the past, something did change, because you guys are so hostile and mean to Nikola."

"No," Imogen said, shaking her head briefly. "Your recollection of that day meshes with mine. Nothing has changed."

"Then why did you tell Io that I was murdered?" Nikola asked her.

She pleated the material of her dress while she thought for a few seconds. "I—that night when you left the castle, something happened to you. But you weren't killed. At least, your body wasn't. But Rolf and Arnulf came to me the next day and said that you had ordered me from the house, and that I wasn't to return. Ever."

I looked at Nikola. *I hate to keep repeating myself, but what the hell?*

He shook his head. *This does not make sense.* "And you believed them?"

"Not at first. I tried for several days to see you, but you had locked yourself away in your study and refused to see me. At last you had to emerge from your study, and then . . ." She rubbed her arms. "Then it was like you had died inside. You were cold and cruel and said that Ben and I had betrayed you, and destroyed your heart, and that you would not tolerate vipers in your nest. You cast me out of the house, and cut off funds to Benedikt so that he had to leave university. In vain we protested that we had done nothing to betray you. You would not listen."

Emotion was so thick in her voice it was impossible not to feel empathy. I turned to Nikola and smacked him on the arm. "What the hell was the matter with you? Your own kids!"

"That cannot be," he said, frowning. "I would never spurn my children in such a manner."

"Destroyed your heart," I repeated, scooting a little closer to him. The pain he felt at Imogen's words more than exceeded hers. "What does that mean?"

"Papa never said," Imogen answered sadly. "He did not explain, nor did he answer my pleas to tell me what I had done to harm him."

"Do you think it meant your late wife?" I asked Nikola. "But she was dead for seven years when we met, and—"

"When we met," Nikola said slowly, looking at me with speculation. "Tell me, Imogen, in this past that you remember, was Io in it?"

"Io?" She considered me with a slight pucker between her brows. "No, I don't think so. It was a very long time ago, but I do not remember Io being the woman with whom you were smitten."

"But there was one?" Nikola pounced on her words. "There was a woman present at the time?"

"I think so." She turned to Ben. "You have a better memory than me—do you remember the woman who Papa kept before that horrible day?"

"No. I was away from home." Ben looked thoughtful. "Although I do remember you writing to me and telling me that you were most pleased because he was interested in a woman again. I don't remember her name, though."

"It is possible that there are two planes of time," Nikola said, sketching something in his notebook. "One is the past that Imogen and Benedikt remember, where I severed relations with them—something I find difficult to believe, but might be explained if for some reason I thought they had destroyed a woman I loved—and the second plane of time, which I remember, and which Io has participated in. It is not beyond reason that the two planes touch at several points, and it is at one of those points that we moved from one time to the other."

"So you're saying, what, that in Ben and Imogen's past, your brothers killed me, or some other woman"—*and buster, it had better not be another woman, because then I really will feel like a tramp*—"and in the past we lived through, they tried to kill you, instead?"

"It is possible, given that my brothers had the desire and ability to kill anyone." He tapped the end of the pencil against his chin, which just made me want to bite it. His chin, not the pencil.

Something struck me, other than the desire to molest Nikola. I turned to Imogen. "You told me that your uncles had killed your father. Why did you say that if, in your version of the past, Nikola severed ties with you himself?"

She exchanged a glance with Ben. "My uncles and Papa have never been very close. And yet, at the time of his . . . derangement . . . they were not only present, but in his confidence where I was not. That was most unusual, and Benedikt and I suspected later that they had done something to Papa, cast some spell upon him, or corrupted his love for us. We had no proof, but it could not be a coincidence that they were present to poison his mind."

"I do not recall any such thing," Nikola said, his gaze blind as he sorted through his memories. "They made me an unwelcome visit the day that Io insisted I accompany her through the portal, but we did not spend enough time together for either of them to have any effect on me."

"That's because I got you away from them so fast," I said with a sense of pride that I felt was wholly warranted. "Why did they come to visit you in the first place?"

He shrugged. "I couldn't make any sense of out either of them. Rolf babbled about how someone near me meant ill for me, and Arnulf simply groveled in his usual manner, and echoed Rolf."

"Whatever it was, you can bet it was part of their plan to knock you off."

"Possibly." Nikola looked somewhat pensive. "From my experiences with them, however, I would find it difficult to believe that they had the drive to conduct such a heinous act."

I let that supposition go, knowing Nikola well enough to understand that I wasn't going to convince him of his brothers' betrayal without solid proof. "OK, so it seems like it's pretty clear that both pasts were real, but since you're here now, that means your past is the right past, so the one where you were a jerk to your kids didn't happen, and thus, they can stop being pissed at you and can be grateful you're alive and well and here to be a daddy to them again." I sniffled a little with happiness. "It's like a deranged Hallmark movie. Oh my god, Nikola!"

"No, I am not a god, although if it pleases you to think so about me—"

"No, silly." I whumped him on the arm. "What if there's another you? The one that Ben and Imogen know? What if there's a second you who is living in Brazil hitting on all the tanned, bikini-clad women?"

"That would be impossible," he said, putting away his notebook.

"No, impossible is traveling back in time three centuries and falling for a vampire."

"The Nikola who spurned his children did so at the loss of his heart. My heart is very much in place, as are you. Therefore, that is the past that is negated, and my past is, as you point out, the valid one."

"But we don't know for certain what else we might have affected," I said.

"The only thing that changed concerned my existence, and if that was devoted solely to the pursuit of pleasure and nothing else, then it was trivial at best. I doubt if the shift of trivial to nonexistent—in that context, at least—would affect any great changes on the future."

"I suppose that's true," I said slowly.

Imogen gave a stifled sort of sob, then flung herself on Nikola, murmuring, "Papa! Oh, Papa, how I've missed you."

It was, as I said, very much a Hallmark moment, and although Ben seemed to harbor some less than Precious Moments feelings, he did at least let Nikola hug him, and answered his father's questions about his life readily enough.

"Once again I find myself in a position of interrupting," Tallulah said in a neutral voice that nonetheless had everyone retaking their seats. "But this is only part of the mystery of which Sir Edward speaks."

I'm so glad we got that straightened out, I told Nikola, leaning into his side and enjoying the feeling of his hand on my thigh. *I hated the way they were treating you. What do you think of how they turned out?*

They are intelligent and charming, as I knew they would be, he said with lofty disregard of the fact that a few minutes before he was distressed by their behavior. *My wife always said that they took after me.*

Man, what an ego. If I didn't think you were smart and sexy as hell, I'd be all over you for that.

I know you wish to seduce me, he said with what was meant to be a rebuke, but plainly wasn't in that he was at that exact moment thinking of the most erotic things that could be done to the human body with a tongue and two hands, *but I feel compelled to listen to this woman. She appears to have interesting insights.*

"It's not something to do with David, is it?" Fran asked, trying to see into the bowl of water. "You said last week that you couldn't see anything about how he was or even where he was. Has something changed with that?"

"No," Tallulah said, somewhat hesitantly. She held her gaze on the bowl as she tipped and rotated it slowly, making the water lap lazily from side to side. "At least, not in the sense you mean. Sir Edward claims that Nikola's presence here foretells violence to come, and that it might spill over to your concerns if left unchecked."

"In what way?" Nikola asked, his curiosity temporarily overriding his smutty thoughts.

"And what sort of violence?" I asked, worried that, by bringing him to the present, we'd set in motion a horrible war or something similar.

"It is an unbalance." Tallulah set down her bowl and gave us both a frown. "The shifting of the balance will cause great pain for many if it is not redressed. You are a weaver, Iolanthe Tennyson. Time that you should have woven together to form a barrier has been unmade. Beyond that, I cannot see."

"What?" I said in a voice that was more a horrified squeak than anything else. "You're saying that this unbalanced violence is my fault? Is it because I went through the swirly portal?"

"You are a weaver," she repeated, just like that was supposed to make things clearer. "You can summon and dismiss portals in time. You have stated that you traveled through a portal you summoned, but you did not state whether or not you closed it so that no others could use it as you did."

"But—but—" I stopped, turning to Nikola as his mind was suddenly filled with speculation and worry.

"Do you mean to say that someone else has used the portal that we used?" Nikola asked, his muscles tense.

"Has already, or may in the future, yes," Tallulah answered, her eyes grave as they watched me. "Did you close the portal?"

"No! That is, I don't know. Maybe I did. I didn't even know there were such people as weavers, not that I'm sure I am one."

"I have never seen a portal in the Zauberwald except when the demon lord cursed me," Nikola said, his fingers stroking along the top of my hand. "I had no idea such people existed, either, but it would explain why the portal was present when you were there, but missing when you were not."

"Did you close it?" Ben asked me, but looking at his father.

"I have no idea. I guess not, if something has to be

done to close it. It was really faded when we last saw it. Nikola thought it was depleted. Is that the same thing?"

"No," Tallulah said. "A portal is just that, an access point to somewhere or some other time. It has no power itself, but draws on those who master it. There are few beings who can do so—demon lords, as Nikola mentioned, Guardians, and of course weavers. If you have little experience controlling it, then it is likely that it would have run out of power after you used it, and thus you would require a period of rest before you could use it again."

"Kind of like charging up its batteries?" I asked, trying to get a grip on the whole idea that I was a magic-door-in-time wrangler.

"If you like, although as I said, the portal itself does not have the power; you do. Do I take it that you suspect someone other than you has used the portal?"

That last question was addressed to Nikola, who answered in an equally somber voice, "I believe so."

"And do you know who that person might be?"

"Yes." He looked at me, and I felt a sudden spike of fear in my gut when I felt the distress that gripped him. "I thought I saw one of my brothers earlier while we were in town."

The fear grew until I felt sick. "No! Oh, for the love of the four and twenty virgins, if they saw us use the swirly portal—but how could they use it, as well, if we ran it out of juice? Or rather, I ran out of portal-using juice?"

"Perhaps it hadn't yet run out of energy," Nikola said, his fingers drawing random symbols on the table. "If they saw us disappear into it—or even if they concluded what happened by our absence and the presence of the portal—then they might have used it before we resumed our awareness here in your time."

"That's right, we were out for a bit. It was nighttime when we went through, and afternoon when we came to here. Holy hairy pickles, Batman, your murderous half brothers are running around the present doing who knows what horrible things. What if they still want to kill you?"

"Or you," he said, pulling me closer. "Since evidently they did that in the alternate past."

I looked at him, speechless with horror.

What on earth had I done?

The Incredible Adventures of Iolanthe Tennyson

July 16 (still, yes)

"We don't know for certain that my uncles used the portal after you," Ben pointed out. "But at least you can keep them from killing Io easily enough. You just have to complete the Joining, and then Io will be a proper Beloved."

"I told you we've already hooked up." I gave Ben a look that should have told him that I wasn't up to hearing snide comments about my relationship with Nikola. "You don't have to belabor the point."

"Belabor?" Nikola looked puzzled.

"The word 'Beloved,' it's not what you think," Fran told me with a tight little smile. "The vampires—"

"Dark Ones," Ben and Nikola said in chorus.

"—have a special relationship with one woman, who they call their Beloved. That's a capital *B* Beloved. It's like a title. Anyway, Beloveds are special because they can redeem the soul of the vamp—Dark Ones, but to do that, they have to go through seven steps called

Joining. I don't really remember exactly what the steps are, because Ben and I did part of them several years ago, when I was only sixteen—"

"We don't need to bore them with that," Ben said quickly, giving her a look that made her laugh.

"Sixteen?" Nikola's eyebrows rose. "That is too young. Women of sixteen do not yet know their own minds. I taught you to respect women better than that, Benedikt."

To my great enjoyment, Ben looked abashed. "It wasn't like that—yes, Francesca was only sixteen when we met, but we spent several years apart before we— before we decided to—"

"You dug yourself into that hole," Fran said with another laugh. "And no, I'm not going to help you get out of it."

"It was not until a few months ago that the Former Virgin Goddess Fran allowed the Dark One to engage in bedsport," the ghost named Eirik said helpfully. "We guarded her most diligently until she insisted that we allow her to enjoy his manroot. She sought much advice from us on how to please him, however, and what to do should he decide he preferred sheep to her."

Fran sighed heavily. "Just an FYI—don't ever ask them for advice. But we've strayed from the point. Imogen, do you remember what the steps are?"

"Of course. The first step is a marking, followed by protection from afar, an exchange of . . . er . . . fluids, usually a kiss. Then the Dark One entrusts the Beloved with his life, by giving her a means to destroy him, which then leads to . . . well, an intimate situation . . .

A TALE OF TWO VAMPIRES

273

after which the Beloved helps him overcome his darker self, and that leads to a blood exchange. The last step isn't really a step, it's more of a coup de grâce, and that's where she sacrifices herself to save him."

"You have got to be kidding!" I said, aghast.

"No." She shrugged. "Those are the seven steps. If Benedikt says you smell like a Beloved, then you must have completed the majority of them. And yet not all, because Papa does not have his soul back."

"A sacrifice? What sort of sacrifice? Like death sort of sacrifice?" I pointed at Fran. "She's still alive. How can you sacrifice yourself and live? I don't want to be a sacrifice! I just want to live with Nikola and do all the things he's almost constantly thinking about doing, and several that I have thought up which I haven't yet let him see, and I can't possibly do that if I'm dead. Besides, the whole point is to let me live as long as he does."

"Calm down, it's not as dire as it sounds," Fran said, giving me a genuine smile this time. "The sacrifice part is very open to interpretation. From what the other Beloveds said when we met up while we were in Vienna last week, it depends on the couple. It could be something as simple as giving up your job and family and life at home to live with your vampire, or something with a bit more oomph to it."

"Like what?" I asked. *I don't mind giving up my job, because I don't have one. And I don't have close family, so that wouldn't be an issue, either.*

"Well . . . one of the Beloveds threw herself in front of her vampire when someone was about to stake him, and she got stabbed instead. Another one got her throat cut, but that was a really special circumstance because I heard that she got turned, and lost her soul. But then she got it back, so it ended up OK."

"Eek," I said faintly, clutching Nikola's arm. *I'm sorry if this is going to sound selfish and uncaring, but I don't want to be stabbed or have my throat cut. Or lose my soul!*

"How do you know this?" Nikola asked Ben, looking up from where he was—naturally—taking notes. "This is not something I taught you."

"No. Actually . . ." Ben cleared his throat. "I learned it after you severed ties with us. I turned to the Moravian Council for help, and they gave me quite a bit more information than you ever did. I used to think you deliberately withheld the information from us in an attempt to put us at a disadvantage, but with this new insight into the past, I'm willing to admit that you didn't intend that to be the result."

"I have never heard of this Beloved business, or the Joining needed to create one." He looked at me. "Hindsight leads me to believe that I should have contacted the Moravian Society earlier, Io. I should not have let the fact that they knew things I had not yet determined for myself sway me from contacting them. I have nothing but my pride to blame."

"You didn't know better," I reassured him, leaning in to give him a quick kiss. "No one told you how to be a vampire after the demon lord made you one, so you couldn't have known all the rules."

"I should have contacted them," he repeated. "I may prefer to discover knowledge for myself, but I should have made an exception in this situation. However, that is now moot. This Beloved that you speak of, she has her soul, yes?"

"Yes," Fran said, smiling at Ben. "I have to say, it's kind of romantic that your dad had to come into the future to find his one true love."

"Oh, we're not in love," I said quickly, a little embarrassed that everyone should think we were a madly romantic couple. "I mean, I'm very fond of Nikola, and we enjoy being together, and yes, I did say that I wouldn't mind spending however long with him because he's really fascinating, but we're not *in love*. Just kind of . . . in fond. Right, Nikola?"

"I shall draft a letter to the council immediately, demanding that they tell me everything that they told my son," Nikola said to himself as he made another note.

"See?" I waved toward Nikola.

Fran turned to her husband. "Didn't you tell me that all vamps are madly in love with their Beloveds?"

"Yes, but—"

"And Io smells like a Beloved?"

I straightened up. "I beg your pardon!"

"Then that means he has to be in love with her," Fran said, gesturing toward me. "So why isn't your dad getting with the program?"

"He's always been a little . . . different," Ben said with obvious apology.

"Hey! There's nothing wrong with your dad. He just likes to keep track of important stuff and things he's curious about. Nikola, tell your kid that you're not weird just because you're not in love with me."

"And perhaps I'll conduct some research into the phenomenon of losing and regaining a soul—hmm? Why are you pinching me?"

"Ben thinks you're defective or something because you're not in love with me."

"He does?" Nikola eyed his son. "I tried to love your mother, but was unable to do so despite the fact that she was quite worthy of that emotion. It is no surprise that I am unable to do likewise for Io."

"Mama was not your Beloved," Imogen said, giving me a long look. "Evidently Io is."

"And that should make a difference?" Nikola asked them.

"Yes," Fran answered.

"Ah." He considered me. *Would you like me to be in love with you, sweetling?*

No! Of course not! No, unless . . . you know . . . you wanted to be. I don't want you to feel like you have to pretend you're in love with me, because that's not the sort of relationship we have.

Exactly what do we have? In reference to our relationship, that is?

Well . . . we like each other a lot.

Yes, we do.

And of course, the sex is spectacular.

Most gratifyingly so, yes.

And we want to spend time together. I mean, I like being with you, and you said you like being with me, so that's what we have.

With no love?

No. Er . . . not unless you wanted it. Do you?

I don't know. Do you?

Everyone is staring at us. I cleared my throat. *I think this is going to be one of those discussions that we'll have to have another time.*

As you like. He turned back to the others. "Io is thinking over whether or not she wishes for us to be in love. Until she makes up her mind, we should go on with what advice this kind lady has for us."

"I wondered if anyone was going to remember me," Tallulah said with a private smile. "It is Sir Edward who offers the advice, and that is this: Find the man who has used the portal. Find him as quickly as you can, and do what you must to restore balance where you have brought unbalance. For if you do not . . ."

Her voice trailed off dramatically, leaving me with a shiver down my back and arms. Once again, I leaned into Nikola for comfort.

"If we do not?" he asked her.

Her gaze moved along each of us, ending on me. "If you do not, countless lives will be sacrificed."

It wasn't until almost an hour later that we were able to gather—"we" being Imogen, Ben, Fran, and Nikola and me—in Imogen's trailer. She had insisted that we meet Peter Sauber, who was one of the two owners of the fair, and explained to him that Nikola was her long-lost father.

"Cousin!" I had said quickly, flashing a very toothy smile to Imogen before turning it on the balding, slightly worried-looking man. "Nikola is Imogen's cousin. He couldn't be her father because he barely looks ten years older than her. He's her cousin."

"It's all right, Io," Imogen said, patting my hand. "Peter knows about Ben and me. What we are, I mean."

"Oh." I pursed my lips as I examined the man in question. "Sorry. Are you a vamp, too?"

"No," he said, his forehead wrinkling a little. "I'm a magician. It's a pleasure to meet you, Baron. I understood that you were in South America recently."

"No, that was the wrong past," I corrected him, smiling at Nikola just because he was so incredibly handsome, it took every ounce of strength I possessed to keep from flinging myself on him.

You are more than welcome to—

Stop right there, or I will have no resistance whatsoever.

Nikola laughed in my head.

"The wrong . . . no, don't tell me. There's enough going on without trying to figure that out."

After meeting a few more people, we finally ended up in Imogen's pretty trailer, the inside of which was done in shades of olive and taupe.

Imogen, Fran, and I sat together on a gently curved taupe and olive polka-dot sofa, while Ben and his father stood at the far end of the trailer, their heads together as they discussed something. It made my heart happy to see Nikola reunited with his son, especially since it was obvious they were having such an emotionally intense conversation.

"Io, I think I owe you an apology," Fran said, drawing my attention back.

"About being so mean to Nikola? I suppose it's understandable, although really, even if Nikola had been from the past you remembered, he's still Ben's daddy, and thus due a little respect—"

"No," Fran said, holding up a hand to stop me. "I

meant about mentioning you guys being in love. I didn't realize that it was possible for a vamp and his Beloved not to be in love, and I think I made you very uncomfortable. I'm very sorry if I did."

"Ah, that." I waved a hand like it didn't mean anything. "I think it's because Nikola and I are so much more matu—er—settled in our ways. We're not young, like you and Ben are. Or rather just you. Not that you're an infant, but . . . oh, you know what I mean."

"Yes, I do." She laughed. "I'm glad I didn't offend you. And I'm really glad that you found Nikola, no matter how it came about, or what form the relationship takes. It's just nice to see another Dark One who's found his other half."

I couldn't help but look at Nikola, my gaze caressing him in a manner that I knew was going to spell trouble if I let it continue. I swear, my mouth started watering just from looking at him with his head next to Ben's as they talked quietly.

"Isn't that cute?" I said softly, nodding toward them. "Seeing them together like that, I feel like the Grinch when his heart grows so many sizes."

"What do you think they're talking about?" Fran asked Imogen.

She smiled, her eyes a bit bright with tears of happiness. "I don't know, and I don't care. I'm just so pleased to have Papa back, the Papa I remember from my youth. He was always such a loving man . . . until that day."

"Which didn't happen anymore," I pointed out, feeling my own eyes getting misty, as well. "I bet they're talking about something deep and important. I bet

Nikola's telling Ben how proud he is of him, and how much he's missed him, and maybe even is offering fatherly advice."

"Oh, yes," Imogen said, sniffling happily.

What are you talking to Ben about? I couldn't help but ask. *Something sweet and tender and touching?*

Yes. Nikola glanced my way. *I asked Benedikt if he often caught his pubic hair on the fastening device of these breeches. He said that is what Jockeys are for. What is a Jockey? I do not wish to appear ignorant in front of my son. Is it something you stuff down the front of the breeches to protect your genitals?*

I burst into laughter, unable to keep the mirth contained. "Oh, yes, they're having a deep and important conversation."

The two men, evidently through with said discussion, sat down opposite us. "You said you wished to help us locate Rolf?" Nikola asked, shooting me a look that let me know he could read my thoughts of just how I'd protect his pubic hair from undue zipper pinching.

"We would be happy to help you, but there's a situation that has been growing steadily worse, culminating in the attack you saw earlier," Ben answered, leaning back in one of Imogen's curved easy chairs. "The liches were sent by an Ilargi, a lichmaster who is also working with a group experimenting on therions and now Dark Ones. The man who is the father of Francesca's half sister, Petra, is responsible for the kidnapping of my blood brother David."

"You have a blood brother?" Nikola asked, a little startled.

"Yes." Ben's eyes were dark with anger. "He is a therion, a leo of his pride, and he was helping me when he was taken. We've tried for three months to locate where de Marco—the lichmaster—has taken him, but every time we get close to finding where they're holding David, they move him. Fran's ghosts have assisted us, as well as those therions who haven't gone into hiding to protect themselves, but we don't have much information to go on."

What's a therion?

I don't know. He thought for a moment. *The word means dangerous animal in Greek. Perhaps . . . yes, I believe he's speaking about a man who has an animal spirit. I read of such things, but I did not know if it was the wild imaginings of the author or a genuine being.*

"So, there are animal spirit dudes who this lich guy is experimenting on?" I asked, not minding if I was the one who looked ignorant.

"Animal spirit . . . ah. Therions are shape-shifters," Ben explained. "David's animal form is that of an Asiatic lion. His pride, the group of therions that he leads, are all also lion shifters. The lichmaster is intent on building an army of therions he can control." His gaze shifted to Nikola. "And lately, he's wanted to try to control Dark Ones, as well, hence his interest in capturing me."

"Which is not going to happen," Fran said, moving over to sit on the arm of his chair, one hand tangled in his hair as she leaned into him.

Nikola watched them with interest for a few seconds before looking at me, one eyebrow cocked. *I'm not as young as she is,* I pointed out. *I don't perch on arms of chairs well. Not to mention that it's undignified.*

I do not think so.

Well, I do. Also, I'm not a young thing who can't keep her hands off of you. I am, as you so obnoxiously pointed out, mature. I can sit in the same room with you without feeling the need to maul you, or touch your hair, or kiss you.

All of that sounds rather nice, actually.

Well, it can just sound nice. I'm not going to pretend I'm a giddy twenty-something madly in love with you. Besides, my behind is bigger than hers and needs a more substantial platform.

Your bottom is lovely, and just the size it should be. It gives me great pleasure. I enjoy looking at it and stroking it. I also wish to bite it, but I suspect you might find that objectionable, so I am content to keep that desire to myself until such time as you will let me do so.

"Oh, screw it," I said, and took three steps to plop myself down on Nikola's lap, wrapping one arm around him, and glaring at Imogen when she giggled. "Right, so those scythe guys were trying to grab you for their lich boss?"

"Yes. He's made an attempt to kidnap Ben before, right after we were married." Fran looked worried. "We were close to finding the whereabouts of David, and several of the therions de Marco has turned feral, for lack of a better word, caught us, and we had to run for our lives."

"Tallulah said that Uncle Rolf might be tied in with the David situation," Imogen said, her expression turning serious. "But I do not see how that can be. He is mortal, not a therion, and not a Dark One. Surely the lichmaster would have no interest in him, or vice versa."

"I can see no reason why this lichmaster would have an interest in Rolf," Nikola agreed, mentally considering and discarding various possibilities.

"Maybe you can't, but I can," I said, suddenly feeling chilled. I put my other arm around him, my stomach sick at the thought.

I can't breathe if you clutch my head to your breasts like this.

You don't need to breathe. You're a vampire. And I want to keep you safe.

Once again, gratitude and astonishment filled him as he gently pried my arms from around his head. *As do I with you, sweetling, but we have nothing to fear from Rolf. I am immortal, and it seems we are close to making you so, as well.*

"What do you mean?" Imogen asked, stark white stress lines appearing around her mouth as she tightened her lips.

"I mean what if Rolf decided he needed some help getting rid of Nikola? He wanted him dead in the past; who's to say he doesn't want him dead now, too? Maybe that's why he followed us here. Maybe he is seeing this as a way of settling a score, or satisfying a need to destroy, or who knows what? If he wanted Nikola dead, then who better to go to than a vampire-torturing lichmaster with a bunch of rabid werewolves at his command?"

"Therions, not werewolves," Ben corrected automatically, but I saw the way he glanced at Fran. He suddenly looked just as worried as I felt.

"I don't see how Rolf would know about de Marco, though," Fran said slowly.

"But is it likely that he would be able to find information about this lich dude? That's the only issue I see. I mean, he's not a vampire like you are, Nikola."

"No, but he discovered what happened to me shortly after I was cursed," Nikola mused. "He's very good at uncovering secrets, and although I still do not understand why he would be anxious to see me dead, I will admit that he possesses the skills and intelligence to ferret out any assistance there is to be had. It is logical to conclude that he will strive to do so. We must prepare for the worst, and hope that our expectations of Rolf's resourcefulness are inflated."

"I'm confused," Imogen said, looking exactly that. "It would be horrible for de Marco to kidnap Papa, just as it would be horrible if he were to get Ben, or any Dark One for that matter. But how is that unbalancing the present, as Tallulah said? How will this mean the deaths of many people?"

Nikola stilled as he read my thoughts, shaking his head in disbelief.

"You don't think it's possible?" I asked him.

"Unfortunately, I do think he could do that. I was simply appalled because of the realization that the son of my mother could do something so heinous. She would have died of shame had she known what a man he turned out to be."

"Both of them. Remember your other brother was in on the plan to kill you."

"What's possible?" Fran asked, but before we could answer, the door was thrown open and the two ghosts came in.

"Goddess Fran," the one named Eirik said, bowing

to Fran. "Dark One. Dark One. Mother-by-marriage of the Goddess Fran. Imogen."

"Father of Imogen," the second ghost said, bowing even lower to Nikola. "I am Finnvid, warrior of Valhalla, beloved of ale wenches, slaughterer of many Huns and Visigoths. Your daughter, Imogen, and I have spent many nights swiving. She is very good at it, and I, as a warrior and one who is beloved by the ale wenches I mentioned earlier, bring her much pleasure in bedsport. For that reason, and because I do not wish to return to Valhalla and be left to swive the ale wenches who seek my bed so frequently, I seek permission from you to wed Imogen, and provide her with countless nights of enjoyment beneath me. We will name our first son in your honor, and he will be strong and ready to fight for you should you need his sword arm. Our daughters will be comely and make excellent wives. We will name one of them after Imogen's mother, and if you like, one after your woman, although I do not understand how a name can have only vowels and no consonants. We will put some consonants in the daughter's name."

Finnvid bowed again, then waited, clearly leaving the conversational ball in Nikola's court.

"Oh, Finnvid," Imogen said in a little exasperation. "I told you that we'd wait a bit to talk to Papa."

"I waited," Finnvid protested.

"You wish to wed a ghost?" Nikola finally asked, looking hard at Imogen.

"Well . . ." She made a vague gesture. "I'm not getting any younger, and . . . er . . . he's right, we do hit it off quite well, although I don't think he needed to mention the ale wenches quite so much. So, yes, I think I'd like to marry him, and that way, I won't be *de trop* when Benedikt and Fran are around, and now, of course, you and Io. You don't mind, do you?"

"I have consonants in my name," I protested. "I just don't use them very much."

"You do not use them at all," Nikola corrected. "I spoke to you about that, but you took offense and struck me."

"I did not hit you! I barely touched you. And besides, you deserved it, you were being obnoxious about my name, not to mention you kept sneaking peeks at my boobs." I stopped, and cleared my throat. "But that's not here or there. You go right ahead and do your fatherly thing."

"What fatherly thing?"

"Whatever it is fathers do when a Viking ghost asks to marry their daughter." Nikola just stared blankly at me. I slapped my hands on my thighs. "Well, how do I know what that is? I'm not a father!"

"They wish to name a child after you. I believe that involves you in the marriage negotiations," he countered.

"Oh, no, you don't. You're not getting me involved in whatever bizarro historical thing dads did in your day. Dowries, wasn't that it? Didn't you dower your daughters when they got married?"

"No."

"No?" I looked at him in surprise.

"I only have one daughter, and she's never been married, so no, I have not dowered my daughters."

I smacked him on the arm. "You know what I meant, Mr. Literal."

He examined Finnvid, who straightened up and clearly tried to look like suitable marriage material. "Two sons," Nikola finally said.

Imogen sighed, and rose, moving over to a counter to plug in an electric teakettle.

"Two?" Finnvid asked.

"You will name one son after me, and one after my father. The naming of daughters I leave to Imogen, although it would please me to see one named after Io. With more consonants in the name, obviously."

"You are beyond obnoxious," I told Nikola, getting off his lap and going toward the back of the trailer. "Imogen, I take it you have a bathroom?"

"Yes, it's just before the door to my bedroom."

I tended a little business, and returned to find Imogen pouring out cups of tea for herself, Fran, and me. The gentlemen had disappeared.

Is everything all right? I asked Nikola, worried at his absence.

Yes. The ghosts insist we celebrate the betrothal of Imogen with ale, which Benedikt says can be found in something called a food truck. What is a food truck?

It's a truck with food. I thought we were going to tackle the issue of your brother?

We will shortly, but first I must negotiate the terms of the marriage settlement with the Viking.

Are you really OK with the idea of having a ghost for a son-in-law? I mean, can they even have children?

I am promised two grandsons and as many grand-daughters, so I assume the answer is yes.

"Congratulations," I told Imogen, toasting her with my cup of tea. "I hope you both will be very happy.

And...er...don't pay any attention to that stuff about naming children after your dad or me. Although obviously, if you wanted to name a kid after your father, that's fine. I didn't know—well, it's not like I even knew ghosts existed, let alone could be tangible and stuff like that—but I didn't know that ghosts could *have* children."

"It depends on the ghost, evidently," Fran said, sipping her tea. "Mine were raised by means of the *Vikingahärta*, an amulet which belongs to Loki, a big pain-in-the-patootie Norse god, so those ghosts are more substantial than your run-of-the-mill spirits, or so I gather. They can stay corporeal indefinitely."

I set down my cup. "I just don't know that I'm going to get used to this sort of thing."

"It's OK. I know just how you feel," Fran said, patting my hand. She still wore her gloves, I noticed. She saw me looking at them, and grimaced. "I'm a psychometrist. I feel emotions and things like that by touching objects."

"Really? That's kind of neat."

"It is if you're not the one who has to deal with it," she said with another grimace. "It's not nearly as handy as someone who can summon a time-traveling portal. You don't happen to have a screwdriver, do you?"

"A screwdriver?" I shook my head.

"Yeah, you know, like the Doctor?" She laughed when I continued to stare at her. "Never mind, it was just a little joke. I've been watching too much of the BBC. Did you really freak out when you met Ben's dad?"

I sighed heavily. "Mostly. And a lot of it was his fault.

I thought I was going crazy because I could hear his thoughts."

"I imagine that was quite unnerving if you didn't realize you were being marked," Imogen said. "How exactly did you meet Papa?"

I settled back and went over the last few days in more details than I had at Tallulah's trailer, glossing over the parts where I couldn't keep my hands off Nikola. By the time I'd gotten to the smutty FedEx woman, the men returned, looking extremely pleased with themselves. The Vikings smelled of ale and staggered in after Nikola and Ben, who just looked dark, dangerous, and oh-so-sexy. At least Nikola did.

"So what's the game plan?" I asked when everyone was settled again. Nikola and I had possession of Imogen's couch, which allowed me to surreptitiously press my leg against his in a way that made me very happy. Ben took up his spot on the chair, with Fran perched next to him. Imogen sat on a small ottoman next to Finnvid, and the other ghost, Eirik, murmured something about needing to stretch his back, so he lay down in the aisle and promptly fell asleep.

"As I see it, we have two problems," Fran said, combing her fingers through Ben's hair. "The first is the situation with David, but I don't expect that to be solved immediately unless we get a whole lot luckier than we have been in the last three months. The second is to find Ben's wicked uncle Rafe."

"Ralph," I said, frowning a little and wondering how we were going to find him.

"Rolf," Nikola corrected.

"And stop him from meeting with your lichmaster,

and thus destroying every vampire he can find in a three-hundred-year span," I said.

"What?" Fran shrieked, making Ben jerk away and give her a pained look. "Sorry, Ben, didn't mean to shout in your ear. What did you mean destroy every vampire in three hundred years? How can Ben's uncle do that?"

"If he could use the portal to zip around time and capture vampires, he could do an unimaginable amount of damage," I explained.

"Sweet mother of reason," Fran said, looking horrified. "Is that what you were about to mention earlier? I can't believe — it couldn't be possible — no, surely Rolf wouldn't go in for wholesale genocide. Would he?"

She asked the question of Nikola, but it was Ben who answered. "He might well do exactly that." His gaze turned to his father. "I've always wanted to ask you this, but given the circumstances . . . well, that's all changed now. Who do you think engaged the demon lord who turned you?"

Nikola was silent for a moment or two, his mind whirring with speculation about the question. "I've never known for certain," he said slowly. "I've had a suspicion, but the demon lord refused to tell me, and I was in no fit state to challenge him on the question. You appear to be implying that my brothers had something to do with it. Do you have any proof?"

"No," Ben admitted. "But it seems to me that they are the ones who stood to benefit."

"From Nikola being made a Dark One?" I patted Nikola's leg. "Why? It just makes him immortal. If they wanted his position or inheritance, then they wouldn't have wanted him living forever."

"We have long tried to understand our uncles' reasoning, but we can't. It just doesn't make any sense," Imogen said. "Ben says it is because we don't know all the truth of what happened at that time, that there were unseen forces at work, but he has always been a little prone to conspiracy theories."

"I have not!" Ben snorted, outraged.

Imogen smiled a tolerant smile.

"It doesn't make sense at all. My brothers couldn't inherit Andras Castle," Nikola said thoughtfully. "They were not sons of my father, and thus they had no claim on the castle. That will pass to Benedikt when I die."

"They can't? Well, crap." I kicked my toe at nothing. "There goes my brilliant explanation."

"But Imogen and I weren't born when you were changed into a Dark One. Perhaps they thought they could take control of the castle and your fortune if you were dead?"

"Not the castle," Nikola repeated, his mind still going over all the possibilities. "But my fortune ... yes, that I could see them gaining if I had no descendants. It is, however, merely speculation."

"I suppose we can't damn them based on just the fact that it makes perfect sense." I sighed sadly. "Oh well. Maybe we can beat the truth out of them once we catch them."

Nikola looked at me as if he'd never seen me. "*Beat* it out of them? You expect me to beat my own brothers?"

"Well, not torture them, obviously, but surely a little arm-twisting to admit the truth wouldn't be out of the question. Or wait, can you just, you know, do a mind thing on them to make them admit the truth?"

"Mind thing?"

I giggled at the expression on Nikola's face.

"Unfortunately, Io, they can't do that," Fran said. "I should know, I've asked Ben to do it often enough, but he insists they can't."

"No, we can't," Ben said firmly, giving her a stern look that just made her kiss his forehead.

You really seem to have gotten cheated. You can't turn into a bat or a wolf, you can't do the brain thing on people and make them your unwilling slaves, and you can't seduce women with your eyes.

Who said I can't?

He gave me a come-hither look that just about had me pouncing on him. *All right, I take it back, you can seduce with your eyes. But you'd better not be trying that on anyone else, or you'll find yourself with one pissed-off almost-Beloved on your hands.*

You are a very violent woman. I didn't not realize this at first.

I am not! I'm a pacifist! I don't believe in guns, or the death penalty, or wars, or stuff like that.

You are many things, sweetling, but you are not a pacifist.

"The question is," Imogen said, leaning against her ghost while I glared at her father. "How are we to find Uncle Rolf?"

"As to that, I believe I have an idea," Nikola said, pulling out his notebook.

Approximately an hour and a half later, I emerged from a small shop, a triumphant—if somewhat dazed—smile on my face.

"Did he buy the coins?" Nikola asked as I got into the small minivan that we'd rented a short while before. "Was your passport enough documentation?"

"Did he mention Uncle Rolf?" Imogen asked.

"Yes to all three. Here, put this away somewhere safe. You're now officially the richest person I know," I said, handing Nikola a check. "You're also the only baron I know, but that's probably beside the point. The coin dude wanted me to wait until morning so he could give me cash, but I said we were going to be leaving town tonight, and that we'd trust him for a check."

"What did he say?" Fran asked from where she sat next to Ben. The minivan was full to the gills with Viking ghosts, Nikola's children, and Fran. "Is he going to do it?"

"No." I shook my head, my gaze on Nikola where he sat in the front passenger seat. "He refused to play along and call up the mysterious man who offered him the silver coins. He said it was unethical, or some such crap."

"Did you threaten to beat him?" Nikola inquired politely.

"I am a pacifist, dammit! Of course I didn't threaten to beat him up!"

Nikola raised one eyebrow.

"OK, maybe I said I had friends who wouldn't take kindly to him not doing as I asked, but that's entirely different from saying I was going to punch him in the gooch if he didn't do what I wanted."

"What's a gooch?" I heard Imogen ask from the back row of seats.

"You don't want to know; it's very rude," I said quickly, glaring at Nikola.

"In what form, then, will his help take?" Nikola asked.

I thinned my lips. "How on earth do you know that he's helping us?"

"You are not angry. You are not swearing. Therefore, you are not upset with him, which you would be if you were unable to get any information from him. What form did it take?"

"An address." I started the car, and pulled out of my pocket a slip of paper. "Evidently you weren't the only one who had the bright idea of using a shill with ID to sell coins. Herr Kenner was so kind as to give me the address of a person who sold him several thousands of dollars' worth of silver coins when I told him I'd sell your coins to his competitor. Turns out he's an avid collector of old Austrian money, and he was just about drooling when I let him have them."

"Do we go there now? It's getting pretty late," Fran pointed out.

I looked at the clock in the van. "I suppose midnight is a bit too late to be showing up on someone's doorstep. Do you think it would be safe to wait until morning?" I asked Nikola.

"With regards to Rolf, do you mean? I do not see that a slight delay will endanger us, no."

You just want to go back to the hotel and do wicked things to me, don't you?

Oh, yes.

And I want you to do each and every one of them. Multiple times. However, right now, I think our time would be better spent tackling the issue of your brother.

Better spent? He let me feel just how badly he wanted to feed on me.

Feast, sweetling, feast, not feed. Anyone can feed me, but only you offer me a feast of endless delights.

"Right, that is going to get you bonus points," I told him, and pulled out into the sparse traffic.

"What is?" Imogen asked, giggling when her ghost nibbled on her neck.

"I said that Io offered me—"

"Ahem! No kissing and telling."

He frowned. "We weren't kissing."

"It's a phrase. File it away for colloquial night. Right now, I think it is more important that we tackle Rolf than to give in to some people's lustful thoughts, no matter how tantalizing they are, especially the ones involving some sort of swing of such erotic complexity that it would be wholly at home in a high-end sex shop."

Ben and Fran laughed aloud.

They have shops that sell sexual favors?

No. Well, I'm sure they do, but that's not what I meant. And stop distracting me with smutty thoughts. I have to concentrate on making this GPS unit speak English so it can tell us where we're going.

Nikola glanced at the electronic device I indicated, pulling out his notebook. *Colloquial night had better be soon, because I am fast filling up this journal.*

The address that Herr Kenner had given me turned out to be about twenty-five minutes out of town, in a large, ranch-style house that sat on the other side of the valley, with an outstanding view of not only St. Andras but the ruins of the castle, as well.

"I don't know how your uncle found this place," Fran told Ben as we silently marched up the long flagstone walkway to a Gothic-reproduction door. "But he has very good taste. This house is gorgeous."

"Very pretty," Imogen agreed. "The view is outstanding."

"I think maybe just Nikola and I should be the ones to approach his brother," I said, looking over the group of people with a somewhat critical eye. "We're kind of a large group."

"There's safety in numbers," Fran pointed out.

"Aye, and in swords," Finnvid answered, pulling his from a scabbard strapped across his back.

"She has a point," Ben said, taking Fran by the arm. He gestured to the flowering shrubs lining the opposite side of the walkway. "Imogen, you and Finnvid hide behind that big plant. Francesca and I will be on the other side of the lawn, behind that hedge. We'll be nearby if you need us."

We waited until everyone had taken their places before Nikola pressed the button beneath an intercom, looking askance at it when a disembodied voice said something in German.

Nikola answered in kind. *The voice asked what I wanted. I told it that I wished to speak with Rolf.*

Huh. You'd have thought they would have something to say to that.

Nikola tensed, tugging me to the side until I was partially hidden by his body. *There is someone behind the door. I can hear breathing.*

The door clicked, and was open by a slim, elegant-looking young man with large gray eyes, dark, carefully tousled hair, and wearing a tight-fitting, expensive suit made of some shiny navy blue material that would have been right at home on the set of one of the *Queer Eye* TV shows. "Yes? To whom did you wish to speak?"

The man spoke with a slight German accent, and a hint of a lisp that seemed more affected than authentic.

Nikola made him a very slight bow. "I understand that my brother Rolf is here. Rolf von Linden. We wish to see him."

"Oh. You must be the bawon." The man eyed first Nikola—and I noticed that his visual examination seemed to take an inordinate amount of time—then me before sighing and stepping back, gesturing us into the house. "Vewy well, but you cannot stay long. Heww von Linden is assisting me with a little pwoject, and we weally cannot take much time fwom it."

I stared at him for a few seconds, wondering why he felt it necessary to exaggerate his speech impediment to such a point where it was almost a parody, but decided that it wasn't important.

Nikola led the way into the house, telling me as he did so, *Stay close to me, Io. Until we speak to Rolf, I do not trust him.*

Me, either. For one, I'd like to sic a few gay friends on him. And for another, he just seems too slick to be true. He didn't even bat an eyelash when you asked for Rolf.

The door closed behind me with a finality that sent

a little shiver down my back. I turned back when the man at the door made a slight noise of satisfaction. *Then there's the matter of that.*

What? Nikola turned, frowning a little at the object held in the man's hand. *What is that?*

It's called a Taser, and I suspect we're going to—

The world exploded in a burst of blue, red, and purple pain that swirled around and in me, sucking me down into its murky depths.

17 July

The voices seemed to ebb and flow like the water Nikola had seen on a beach in the south of France—with soft, gentle little laps at his awareness that allowed him to drift aimlessly on a sea of insensibility.

If only the voices would stop nudging him, he could relax fully. But that wasn't really true, was it? He couldn't relax, not when danger hung overhead, danger for—"Io!" he gasped aloud, and leaped to his feet without being aware that he had been lying on a cold stone floor. *Sweetling, where are you?*

There was no answering voice in his head, no sense of her presence, of her warmth, of everything about her that seemed so natural to him, it was no more than an extension of his being. *Io? Are you well?*

He snarled wordlessly at the silence that was his only answer, quickly taking in his surroundings. He was in some sort of a monk's cell, a narrow room with a sliver of a window high on the wall. The room was bare of furniture, possessing only the window and a door.

He rushed to the door, intending on jerking it open, but it was locked, and remained steadfastly closed despite his attempt to force it otherwise.

The memory of the strange, lisping man holding an oddly shaped pistol on himself and Io tormented him, mostly because he was convinced that some ill had befallen her, an ill he should have prevented. *Do not fear, my love, I will find you. And should you be harmed, I will see to it that the whoreson who touched you will die a prolonged and painful death.*

He rattled the door a few more times, paced the length of the cell for approximately a quarter of an hour, and was about to give in to the urge to swear loudly and profanely at his stupidity in allowing Io to be placed in harm's way when the analytical side of his mind, that which regularly held debates with the more frivolous part, urged him to look again at the door.

It was hewn of a solid wood, oak most likely, bound in iron. He narrowed his eyes at the lock and the round, circular door pull that served as a handle.

It looked familiar. It looked very familiar. It looked, in fact, just like those found in the row of rooms in the murky depths of his own castle, rooms that were stuffed with odds and ends, broken furniture, cast-off items of everyday usage, and a wine cellar that had been his father's pride.

A slow smile curled his lips. *Bless you, Io, for giving me presents.* He pulled from his pocket the small flat object that Io had slipped into his hand when they left the hotel earlier that day, saying she'd picked it up at the men's shop where she'd bought his clothes. "It's some sort of a survival gadget. It has a tiny little knife, and a screwdriver, and tweezers, and a bunch of other little things that are supposed to come in handy. I thought it looked kind of scientific, so you'd like it."

I do indeed like it, he told her, even if she couldn't hear him. He examined the flat object, about half the size of his palm, before eventually extracting a long, thin tool. Seven minutes later, he'd taken apart the ancient lock, and pulled open the door to his cell. Like the cellar back home, the room he emerged into was dimly lit, this time, by a globe overhead.

"Bulb, not globe," he corrected himself, remembering that Io had called the object that made light out of nothing a bulb. This bulb was hung somewhat haphazardly on a cord that wove drunkenly down the ceiling, disappearing into the wall at the far end.

He glanced around, noting the narrow passage lined with numerous doors. There was no one in sight, and unable to resist the desire to know what was in the nearest room, he tried the door. It was locked. As was the one next to it, and on down the passage. Nikola walked to the end where his own cell had been, pulled out the tiny screwdriver, and went to work on the lock of nearest door. It was a bit more rusted than his had been, but after a few minutes' work, he was able to open the door.

The air that swirled out to cover him was fetid, rank with the odor of unwashed bodies, and blood. His nose wrinkled with the scent of rotting animal flesh at the same moment that whatever was within the cell realized he was at the door. An inhuman howl of rage rent the air, and another swish of air warned of the swift movement within. Nikola just had time to see a pair of burning black eyes beneath a matted, filthy mass of hair before he slammed the door shut again, hastily twisting the lock so that it caught into the teeth of the mechanism. A second howl followed the slam of a large body against the solid door. Nikola quickly screwed the faceplate back onto the lock, the memory of those insane, burning eyes giving him pause.

"If they captured me, they must have done likewise to Io," he said softly, and went to the next door, carefully stripping the lock down to where he could open it. He cracked the door just enough to catch a whiff of the air contained within, found it just as abominable as the last one, and had the door closed and locked before the occupant even knew he was there.

Three more such rooms followed before he came to one that didn't bear the odor of animalistic, violent humans.

He peered cautiously into it, opening the door a little wider when the air smelled nothing worse than a little musty. A figure lay curled up in the corner, but it wasn't the figure of a man. It was a large, cinnamon-colored lion, and it stood up slowly, its eyes wary as Nikola glanced around its cell.

"You wouldn't happen to be named David, would you?" he asked.

The lion blinked at him for a few seconds; then its entire body seemed to shudder and ripple before changing into that of a nude man. "It's Daffyd, actually, but everyone calls me David. Are you one of de Marco's men?"

"Do you have clothing? Your nudity does not disturb me, but I would not like Io to be exposed to it."

"Er . . ." The man stepped back to where a pile of clothing sat in the corner. "Io?"

"Yes. She is my woman. She is highly sensitive, and would not care to see you without clothing. In your human form, that is. I believe she would greatly enjoy seeing your lion form. It is true she has stated that she takes much pleasure in seeing me without clothing, but I cannot believe that to see others would be at all pleasing to her. You must be a therion. My son mentioned you to me. He did not, however, say that you would be sans clothing. Ah. That is better. Do you know where Io is?"

"No, I don't." David had a slight Welsh accent.

Nikola studied him, this man his son had chosen for a blood brother. He was still somewhat disturbed that Benedikt and Imogen could believe him capable of severing all ties with them, his beloved children, and he felt instinctively that Benedikt, for whatever reason, had felt the loss of a father more than Imogen. He badly wanted to know what sort of a man his son had turned out to be, so logically, he must look to the people with whom he had surrounded himself.

But that could wait until he found Io and reassured himself that she was not harmed. "I must find her. You may accompany me if you desire. I realize that my son seeks your freedom, but Io's safety must come first."

"Yes, if she is your woman, then I imagine it must," David replied with a little amusement in his eyes. "I will accompany you, although I don't quite understand just who you are."

"I am Nikola Czerny." He turned on his heel and left the cell, moving to the last three doors.

"Czerny? Are you related to Benedikt?"

"He is my son." The next cell smelled worse than a privy. Nikola hastily closed the door and turned to the second-to-last door.

"Ferals. What a tragedy. They are long past saving. I thought you were dead," David said, peering over Nikola's shoulder as he unbolted the lock. "Ben said something once about you not being around anymore."

"That was the incorrect past, according to Io." He exhaled in relief when a familiar scent caught his nose as he opened the door a crack. The air smelled of warm, sleepy woman, his warm, sleepy woman, one who was lying on her side with her back to the door. "Io! Are you injured?"

She didn't appear to be. He rushed to her side, quickly making an examination of her body parts. Arms and legs appeared to be untouched, as was her face. In fact, she appeared to be doing nothing more sinister than taking a nap.

"Sweetling, wake up."

She didn't seem to want to. He scooped her up and rose, a need to get her to safety overriding his curiosity about where they had been taken, and who was behind their abduction.

"Is she all right?" David asked, following when he strode back down the long, narrow corridor.

"I assume so, since there are no markings."

"Did de Marco capture you, too?"

"I am not sure. There was a man with a slight lisp and some sort of bulky firearm that Io said was a

Teaser, but we were tracking my brother when we found him, so it not clear to me who is responsible for—can you hold her for me, please?"

David looked surprised as Nikola thrust Io's warm, supple body into his arms. Nikola hesitated a moment, giving the younger man a good, stern look. "You will not enjoy the warmth of her body against yours. You will not admire her satiny freckled skin. You will not desire to touch her breasts and thighs and other parts. She is *my* woman."

The therion had the cheek to grin. "You really have it bad. Like father, like son, eh?"

"Io is not like my daughter-by-marriage. She does not perch on the side of my chair and ruffle her hand through my hair. She does, however, sit on my lap, which pleases me more. If you would stand a little out of the light of the bulb, I will disassemble this lock and we shall free ourselves."

The lock of the door to the corridor was just as old as the cell doors, and it was only a matter of a minute before he reclaimed the still sleeping Io, and followed David up a narrow flight of wooden stairs.

Right into a room containing two surprised-looking people seated around a long table dotted with food and drink.

Nikola took one look at the occupants of the room, and gave David Io's delicious form again. "Would you mind holding her once more?"

"Actually, I would. I have a score to settle with that man," David said, handing her back, his voice rough with emotion and his eyes glittering with an unholy light.

"What the deuce are you doing up here?" Rolf, who had been stuffing his face with a turkey leg, sputtered bits of greasy turkey skin and flesh as he shoved back his chair and leaped to his feet. "How did you get out of the cell? Damn me, man, you told me he wouldn't be able to get out!"

The lisping man who had incapacitated them rose to his feet, as well, but it was David he was staring in horror at, not Rolf. David's body did that rippling, shifting motion that resulted in him stalking forward in lion form.

"Did you see that, sweetling?" Nikola asked Io, shaking her slightly in case she was on the verge of waking up. "It's fascinating. I must make a comprehensive study of how it's done. You can assist me."

"Dammit, Nikola, I demand to know how you got free!" Rolf set down his turkey leg and advanced, his narrow eyes now only little slits in a face that Nikola was shocked to realize was filled with malice.

He looked for somewhere safe where he could set down Io, but at that moment, she stirred.

"Hrang?" she asked, blinking her eyes and frowning as she tried to focus on him. She lifted a hand and poked him in the cheek. "Nia?"

"Yes, sweetling, it's me. Sit here while I deal with my brother." He placed her in a chair and turned to Rolf, who had snatched up a long carving knife and was advancing upon him.

A soft, slithering noise behind him had him whirling back to Io just in time to see her fall off the chair and land face-first onto the floor. She lifted her head slightly, and said in a voice thick with befuddlement, "Ow. Nikla?"

"Stay there, my love," he commanded, turning back to face his brother. "Rolf, I am disappointed in you. If Mother were alive, you would have broken her heart."

Rolf froze, fury overtaking his expression of malice. "How dare you mention her!"

A scream echoed from the far end of the room where David the lion had pounced on the lisping man.

"Do not kill him yet," Nikola called to David as the lion began savaging the man now crawling on the floor and babbling for mercy. "He conducted an act of Teasing against Io, and thus I must exact my revenge on him, as well."

"Taser," Io said thickly. "That was it. That precious guy had a Taser. Gonna whack him on the kneecaps with it."

"You were the one who brought her endless grief," Rolf yelled, gesturing with the knife. "If you had died like you were supposed to do, she would have gotten over it. But no, you had to bargain with that demon lord to make you immortal, and she worried herself into her grave over what happened to you."

Nikola stared in stark surprise at his brother, ignoring the sounds behind him of muttered swearing and a chair scraping as if someone was using it to pull her still-dazed self to her feet. *Do not harm yourself, sweetling. I will be able to assist you just as soon as I've dealt with Rolf.*

I'm OK, she answered, her thoughts still a bit confused and somewhat scattered. *I love you, Nikola.*

He shot a startled glance over his shoulder.

Whoops. Did you hear that?

Yes.

Frak. Can you pretend you didn't?

No.

An adorably indignant look crossed over her face. She made an effort to straighten up and glare at him. *Well, I think you could if you put your mind to it.*

We will talk about this later, Io. Right now I must ascertain just what Rolf meant by his statement.

What statement? Rolf is here? She squinted past him. *Oh, yeah, he is here. Can I break his kneecaps?*

He shook his head, turning back to Rolf. *It is not seemly for me to stand by and do nothing while you mete out revenge. No, I must be the one to break his kneecaps. I am nothing if not generous, however, and for that reason, I will allow you to box his ears.*

I have no idea what's involved with ear boxing, and frankly, I don't think I'm going to want to know, so you can just get off your he-man high horse, and let me have a shot at the kneecapping—Nikola!

Io screamed in his head just as Rolf lunged at him, the knife held high. Nikola, long a devotee of esoteric manuscripts from the Far East, lashed out with his foot and knocked the knife out of Rolf's hand.

Rolf screamed in a perfect echo of the lisping man, who was now blocked from view by the large body of an extremely annoyed lion. "You've broken my hand! My own brother has broken my hand!"

"No," Nikola said coolly, picking up the knife and gesturing with it. "But I will do so if you attempt to harm Io or me again. How did you know about the demon lord who cursed me? I never told you how it happened."

"Who do you think arranged for him to kill you?" Rolf said sullenly, clutching his hand to his chest as he slumped into a chair, defeat visible in his posture.

"I knew it," Io said, limping forward.

Did he harm your leg?

No, I whacked it on the chair trying to stand up. Did you hear him? He as much as admitted that he was the one responsible for hiring the demon lord to off you. Io snatched up a broom and continued on toward Rolf.

"Keep your whore away from me," Rolf said with a curl to his lip, leaning to the side just as if she were polluting the very air with her presence.

Gee thanks.

Pardon?

For thinking that bit about me polluting the air.

I didn't say you were, I was merely noting to myself what Rolf did, so that I might record it in my notes at a later time. No, my love, do not try to beat him with that broom. For one, you aren't strong enough, and for another, he is not the one responsible for my curse.

He just said he was! Do you need to clean your ears or something?

Another scream from the man David was attacking diverted his attention for a moment. "David?"

With reluctance, the lion backed up a few steps, shimmered in that unique way he had, and resumed the shape of a man.

"Holy naked man!" Io's eyes widened as she stared at David.

"Er . . . hello. You must be Io."

"I am. And you're ... you were ... were you just a lion a second ago?"

"Yes. I am a therion." David made a little bow to her that had her jaw dropping a smidgen.

"Avert your eyes, sweetling," Nikola told her. "I know how distressing it must be for you to view another man without his clothing on."

"Oh, yeah, it's terribly distressing," Io said, continuing to stare as David picked up his clothing and once again began to don it. "I'm feeling traumatized. Wow, he really has a nice—"

Nikola scowled. Io bit off the sentence and gave him a weak smile. "Sorry, punkin. It just took me by surprise. Carry on."

"Thank you." He turned back to Rolf, who was now moodily watching the lisping man weakly flail around on the floor. "Rolf, tell me how you know about the demon lord."

"Which one? The one who cursed you, or the one who helped me find Lemuel?"

"Who is Lemuel?"

"Him." Rolf nodded toward the man writhing and moaning on the floor.

"Just so. You have met with a demon lord recently?"

"What business is it of yours?" Rolf snapped in reply.

"It most certainly is my business if you arrange for Io and me to be kidnapped and taken to a lichmaster who evidently has an interest in torturing Dark Ones."

Rolf shrugged. "I don't know about a lichmaster, but I did talk to Ashtaroth, a demon lord who put me in contact with Lemuel. He said his master would reward

me greatly once he found out about the portal in Zauberwald."

"Ashtaroth," Nikola said slowly. David, now fully
clothed, moved around to stand slightly behind them.
Io gave him a long look before returning her attention
to where it should be.

That's the guy who Ben and Fran were looking for.

*Yes. He has a lion form, as you saw. Later, we might
make a study of how he shifts form.*

We *might make a study?*

*I thought that you might wish to assist me in my
studies.*

She smiled, and warmth flooded through his loins,
spreading out to his limbs. *You'd let me help?*

*Of course. You, too, have a scientific mind, and like to
learn new things. You will be of a great help to me.*

*Nikola, I think that's just about the nicest thing any-
one has ever said to me. Is Ashtaroth the demon lord
who made you a vamp?*

No. That demon lord's name was Magoth. "How did
you know to contact a demon lord?"

Rolf's expression was sulky and somewhat petulant.
"I suppose you're going to push and poke until you
have all the answers, aren't you? You always were like
that. You just had to know the answers to everything.
That trait has always irritated me, do you know that?
You don't care, do you? You never did. Well, brother
mine, let me assuage that annoying curiosity of yours—
I knew how to contact Ashtaroth because I read my
father's letters."

"Your father was the one who summoned Magoth,"
Nikola said, nodding. It fit with what he knew of his

brothers—they might be aggravating, and whiny, and constantly demanding more money from him, but they were not the murderous whoresons that Benedikt had hinted.

Your stepdad had you made into a vampire? Io asked in disbelief. *Why?*

"Io wishes to know why your father summoned Magoth," Nikola told Rolf. "She did not know him as we did. She does not realize that he hated me, and resented the fact that I was the firstborn."

"You think you know everything, don't you?" Rolf's upper lip curled. "Well, you don't. How's that feel, brother? Don't like it, do you? I can see by the look on your face that you're not going to let it rest until you hear it all, and since my head hurts and I want to go to bed and get some sleep, I'll tell you what my father did. Yes, he summoned Magoth, but he paid the demon lord to destroy you in the most heinous fashion he could manage. The stupid demon lord double-crossed my father, though, by making you a bloodsucker instead of tormenting you to death."

"That is just about the most obscene thing I've ever heard," Io said, clutching her broom tightly. Nikola put an arm around her to keep her from rushing his brother. "I've heard of some asshat stepparents before, but none of them were so jealous of their stepkids that they actually hunted down a demon lord! OK, so I didn't know there were such things as demon lords until Nikola told me, but still, my point stands."

"My father didn't give a snap for Nikola being the firstborn," Rolf said, his shoulders slumping. He looked, Nikola thought, every one of his more than three hundred years.

"Did he want Nikola's castle, then?" Io asked, pressed close, her warmth seeping into all the dark places inside him. He wanted to scoop her up in his arms and locate the nearest bed, whereupon he would allow her to seduce him for several days. Nonstop.

"*Pfft.* Have you seen it? It's a ruins," Rolf said dismissively. "He didn't want the castle. He wanted the money, money that should have gone to my mother rather than Nikola, and thus to us."

"You were right," Io said with a look of admiration that warmed him to his toenails. "They didn't want your castle. This was all about money. But I don't understand why this demon lord dude turned you into a vamp instead of torturing you to death."

David laughed as Nikola gave her an outraged look.

"Sorry, punkin, that came out wrong. But you know what I mean."

"The demon lord was deranged, that's why," Rolf said, reaching for the pitcher of ale. "Papa paid him to destroy you, but Magoth thought it would be funny to make you into a bloodsucker instead. Papa was furious, of course, but there wasn't anything he could do about it because he had an apoplectic fit and died two days later."

"Well," Io said, setting aside her broom. "I can't say that I'm sorry to hear that. What a poop." She glanced toward Nikola. "So now what?"

"Now we get you out of this place, and contact Benedikt to let him and Imogen know where we are."

"I don't think you'll have to do that," David said with a sudden smile, strolling across the kitchen to open a door that allowed sunlight to flood the room.

Voices that were barely audible from outside grew louder, and before Nikola could so much as pull out his notebook to record the pertinent events of the last half hour, a group of eight people rushed into the room, voices high with excitement.

Benedikt and his soon-to-be ghost-by-marriage were at the front, with several other men following, and Imogen and Francesca bringing up the rear.

"David!" Benedikt shouted upon sighting his friend. The two men embraced as Francesca pushed forward.

"Nikola! Io! Oh, I'm so glad you're all right. Ben, look, your dad found David."

Much confusion followed in the subsequent quarter hour, but it was Io who put an end to it by the method of standing on the long table, and placing her fingers in her mouth to perform an earsplitting whistle that froze everyone in their tracks.

"Right! Let's all simmer down so we can figure out who is who. Ben, are those dudes werewolves like David?" Io asked, pointing at the four other men who were in a circle around David, all of whom were talking at the same time.

"Sorry, yes, those are members of his pride. We called them in when it became apparent that you and my father had been taken. The lich whose head we finally convinced to talk told us about this place. No one else was close enough to help, and we had some hope that if we found you here, we'd be able to gain information about where David was being held, as well. We had no idea that we'd find you all together." Ben clapped his friend on the back, his smile of such happiness that Nikola was well pleased.

My son is generous and free with his affection, he told Io, unable to keep the pride from her.

She slid an arm around his waist. *He is. I like him now that he's done being a jerk to you. I like Fran, too.*

And Imogen? You will have no problems dealing with her? I have brought her up to be a modest, gentle maiden, but she always had her mother's will, and sometimes would not yield to my desires the way she should.

Io laughed into his head. *I'm sure she had you wrapped around her little finger. Yes, of course I like her. She's very nice, and I think she's very much in love with that Viking ghost. Him, I'm not so sure of, but he seems to be crazy about her, too, so I guess all is well.*

Yes, all is well. We can return home knowing that my children are as happy in their lives as we are in ours.

Io shot him a look, but said nothing.

The Incredible Adventures of Iolanthe Tennyson

July 23

Boy, I can't tell you how good it is to be typing this up on a laptop, rather than writing with that horrible goose feather, or even writing it all out longhand on a spiral notebook from the St. Andras drugstore.

Nikola, of course, is fascinated by the laptop . . . but I'm jumping ahead, and I swore I wasn't going to do that.

We got back to St. Andras about dinnertime a couple of nights ago. That was the same day that we found ourselves in Innsbruck (where the over-the-top lisping guy, whose name turned out to be Lemuel, had taken us), the day when I came out of my Taser-induced stupor to find Nikola being all brave and heroic and smart, and figuring out the truth behind his brothers and the whole deal with being made a vampire.

"It's all very well and fine you knowing this," I said quietly to him a couple of hours later while Ben drove us in our rental van back to St. Andras. It was even more cramped in the van because now we had Rolf with us, as well, but obviously we couldn't leave him behind to sell out other vampires to the lichmaster dude. "But what are we going to do with *him*?"

Nikola instantly knew whom I was talking about. *We will have to take him back with us, naturally. And I will see to it that he does not abuse the portal.*

I bit my lip, a little queasy at the thought that Nikola was so calmly sure I would be going back to the past with him. I glanced around, but no one appeared to be paying attention to us as we drove through the mountains toward St. Andras. *I thought we were going to stay here for a bit, so you could see how things worked, and appreciate all the technology and stuff that this century has.*

We have stayed, he said with a little surprise. *I have seen many things.*

Yeah, but we haven't been here for very long. Certainly not long enough to see everything.

He considered me, his icy blue eyes not so icy when you knew what lay behind them. *You wish to stay longer? We have Rolf. We have protected the Dark Ones of this time, and found David for Benedikt. There is nothing more to keep us here, unless you are worried that Rolf and Arnulf will attempt to murder me again. I have told you that I will take care of that situation, too.*

Yeah, by giving them more money.

He shrugged. *I have more than I need, and they have not many years left to them. It cannot hurt me to give up a little more wealth to them.*

I'm sure they had enough to begin with, but that's not the point.

Then what is?

I made a vague sort of gesture. *I just thought you'd want to stay here for a bit. There are so many wonders to be seen here.*

But if I learn them all, what will I have left to study?

He had me there. I was left to gnaw my lower lip and keep my dark, unhappy thoughts to myself as we drove back into town.

It was dusk when we arrived at the fairgrounds.

"I thought David was following us?" Fran said as she got out of the van.

I took the hand Nikola offered, and got out, as well, stretching from the long ride.

"He will be along later. He needed some time with his pride before he rejoins us and we can go over all that happened, and what we'll do next about de Marco," Ben answered.

"I do not understand why you insisted on bringing me back here," Rolf groused as he emerged from the van. "I do not wish to be here. It is not nearly as exciting as Innsbruck. I wish to return to Innsbruck. I wish to be paid the amount of money that is owed to me for the capture of my brother."

"You're going to be paid a knuckle sandwich and a two-by-four across the knees if you don't knock it off," I mumbled, evidently not soft enough to escape Nikola's ears.

Woman, you are not helping matters.

Bah. He's being a pain in the ass and you know it.

Yes, and you are inflaming his anger. I do not wish to have to separate you while we are here in your time, but I will if I must.

I couldn't help but giggle at his stern-dad voice. *You're so cute when you're fatherly.*

I assure you, Io, at this moment I feel anything but fatherly toward you.

Oooh, someone's hungry, I said, slinking toward him with a look in my eyes that should let him know just how much I wanted to sate his desires. All of them.

He started toward me at the same moment, but unfortunately, life or fate or whoever it is who dictates when things get messed up chose that moment to put a halt to what I hoped would be one hell of an evening.

It will be one hell of an evening, sweetling. Just one that is delayed for a short while.

"Imogen! Benedikt! You are back so soon?" Tallulah emerged from between two tents, holding a squirming pug puppy in her arms. "Have you run into trouble?"

"Just the opposite," Fran said, smiling. "We found David with Nikola and Io. And there were only two guys guarding them, one of which was Ben's uncle, and—"

Tallulah held up her hand, glancing over at a group of tourists that were waiting for the ticket stand to open. "Perhaps we should continue this elsewhere? There is half an hour before the fair is to commence."

We all followed her into her trailer, some of us more reluctantly than others.

"I hate to be a party pooper, or appear ungrateful that you guys came to save us, and now want to rehash the experience—not that we haven't done that during the three-hour ride here—but Nikola's hungry, I'm hungry, and we still have to figure out what we're going to do with *him*."

"Nikola, your woman is being rude to me," Rolf said, sniffing when he was forced to take a seat next to Finnvid.

"In what manner is she being rude?" Nikola asked, smiling into my mind when I sat on his lap.

"Chairs are in demand," I told Eirik the ghost when he raised his eyebrows.

He grinned.

"She keeps referring to me as *him*. With an emphasis on the word that is not at all pleasant, or even respectful." Rolf sniffed again, and told Finnvid, "My father may not have been a baron, but he was very wellborn, and I will not be looked down upon by a whore."

Finnvid looked at me in openmouthed amazement. "The Goddess Fran's mother-by-marriage, soon-to-be my mother-by-marriage, is a whore?"

"OK, the next person who says that word is getting a punch on the schnoz," I said, waving a fist in the air.

And you do not think you are bloodthirsty.

No, I'm not. You are, because you're always thirsty for my blood. But me? I'm a pacifist through and through. I'm just not going to stand for your nasty little brother to keep saying I'm a slut.

I've explained to you that he heard that from Frau Leiven when we were all mistaken about you—

I know, I know, but he can just get with the program and realize that it was simply a matter of difference of apparel between centuries. Oh, hell, now Tallulah's been talking and I haven't listened to a word. Hush so I can listen.

Nikola gave a mental eye roll (it's not as awkward as it sounds), and pulled me tighter against him.

"I don't understand," Imogen was in the middle of saying. "You told us that we needed to find Rolf to save people from being killed, and we have done so. Why is the world still unbalanced and in peril?"

Tallulah, who had given Imogen the puppy to hold in order to take up her bowl of water, consulted it. I leaned forward to see what it was that the bowl held, but all I saw was an inky blackness. "The balance of time is still skewed because the threat still remains."

I looked at Rolf with mean eyes.

"Nikola!" he said, pointing at me.

"I'm not doing anything!" I protested.

"You mean Ben's uncle?" Fran asked from where she was (once again, drat her young self) draped on the arm of Ben's chair.

"He is part of it, but he is not the whole," Tallulah intoned, staring at her bowl. "The means by which the deaths of countless souls can be made still exists, and will continue to exist until it is no more."

"The swirly thing?" I asked, my stomach turning over. Oh, I wanted the portal closed, all right, with Nikola and me on this side of it, but I also knew just how much he wanted to go home. But this was my home, not his, my time, not one with which he was familiar.

"The portal that you summoned must be closed. It is known to too many people now."

"The only guys who know about it are us, Rolf, and that Lemuel guy, and David has him, so I don't imagine he's going to have any opportunity to do anything but be mauled by a bunch of angry lions," I pointed out.

"That is not true, sweetling," Nikola said, looking past me to Rolf. "Is it?"

Rolf started, guilt chasing fear across his face. "Er ... what?"

"Who else did you tell about the portal?" Nikola asked, his voice deceptively calm. I knew better, however. Beneath the surface, his anger was as hot as the hunger that he held at bay. "Who else did you give the means to destroy Dark Ones?"

"No one! I told no one! Er ... I might have hinted at something like a portal to the demon lord Ashtaroth, but—"

Nikola gave a mental groan.

That's bad, yes?

Very bad.

I glared at Rolf. "You bastard."

"My parents were properly wed!" he snapped back, but the fire had gone out in him. He slumped back, his arms across his chest, and glared at us all.

Io—

I know, I know. I cleared my throat, not wanting to say what had to be said, but seeing no other way around it. "I have to close the swirly thing. I don't know how to do that, though."

"You will find the way," Tallulah said, pushing back the bowl. I was uncomfortably aware of her gaze on me.

"I'm glad someone has faith in me, because I have to admit that right now I don't." I took a deep breath and glanced at Nikola. "I don't suppose you know how to lock up a portal?"

"Lock up? No." Tallulah rose to her feet, her hands flat on the table as she leaned toward me. "You cannot simply close the portal, Io. You must destroy it for good so that no one may ever use it again. That is the only way to bring back balance, and to ensure it remains."

I felt literally sick to my stomach with the knowledge of what this would mean to Nikola. I looked at him, taking in those bright pale blue eyes ringed with impossibly thick black lashes, his long, straight aquiline nose, that chin that I loved biting so much, and felt a few tears burn behind my own eyes. *I'm sorry, punkin. I'm so sorry.*

He gave me a supportive squeeze. *I know you are, and I will do what I can to make your life a happy one.*

"You will . . . huh?"

"I will do everything in my power to make sure that you do not regret the choice to stay with me," he answered, filling my head with all sorts of erotic promises.

"You think I'm going to go back with you before I destroy the swirly portal?" I asked, knowing the answer even as the words left my lips. Of course he expected that—he always intended on returning back to his time, and assumed I'd be going back with him. "But . . . we're here now. Couldn't we just stay here?"

"Uh-oh," Fran murmured, getting up and pulling Ben up after her. "I think this is where we make ourselves scarce."

"I believe that would be wise," Tallulah said, glancing at her watch. "You may make use of my trailer as long as you need it. I will be in my booth, should you wish to consult with me again."

"Where are you taking me?" Rolf said in an outraged voice when Finnvid, after a whisper from Imogen, yanked him to his feet and shoved him along the aisle. "Unhand me, you deranged spirit!"

"Come with me, Uncle Rolf," Imogen said in her soothing voice. "Papa and Io need a few minutes alone."

"I don't care what they need, I will not be treated in this manner—"

In a matter of seconds, the trailer was cleared of everyone, the puppy included. I stroked a hand along Nikola's cheek, relishing the emotions that rolled through me when he turned his head to kiss my palm.

"You do not wish to return with me."

It was a statement, not a question, and behind it was an entire world of pain.

"I want to be with you. I want to spend my life with you. Dammit, I already told you that I was in love with you, and I don't have any idea how or when that happened, because everything was just fine with us being fond of each other, and now I just want to cry because I do love you, Nikola. I love you so much I want to stand on top of this trailer and yell it out to everyone."

"But you do not wish to return with me to my home."

"It's not that. I liked your castle. But you haven't spent as much time here as I spent in your time. There's so much more to see, Nikola. So many cool gadgets and scientific crap and advances that you can't even dream of, and you'll never know about them if we go back to your time. We'll never have a microwave, or a laptop, or even a hair dryer, and let me tell you, I miss my hair dryer almost more than I do modern underwear and toilet paper. Well, OK, not more than toilet paper. That really is something that is missed once it's gone."

"And what of Andras Castle?"

"Well . . . we can rebuild it, and live there."

"What of the servants? How will they go on without me to provide for them?"

"They've been dead three hundred years, Nikola."

"But they were alive when we left. It's not that I care about them, you understand. I simply do not like shirking my duties."

I shook my head at him, warmed at the genuine concern for others that he felt. "Oh, come on. I think we both know that you are Mr. Pushover when it comes to any misfit you run across. Why else would you have that motley collection of servants? But honestly, I'm sure they got along just fine before they met you, as they did after you went through the portal."

He looked at me, just looked at me for a few minutes, keeping his thoughts closed off so I couldn't hear what it was he was thinking. But I felt his emotions. I felt the pain, and the doubt, and the need to protect. I felt his innate nobility of character, and I knew what he was going to say before he said it.

"Then we will stay here, in your time. We will take up our lives here, and begin again."

"Nikola—"

"No." He laid a finger across my lips. I bit it. "I did not think I was capable of it, but somehow, it has overtaken me, as well. You are my life now, Io. You are my heart and being and I cannot think of existing without you. You say you love me so much you wish to yell out your feelings—I love you so much that I am willing to do whatever it takes to make you happy. We will remain here, in your time, and you will spend endless

nights making up to me the sacrifice I have made because I love you so greatly."

I laughed and kissed him, tears spilling over my eyelashes as I let him feel the depth of my emotions for
him. *And I love you so much that I'm going to let you
get away with that wholly and utterly outrageous statement. Come on, lover boy, let's go back to the hotel so I
can feed you. Then we'll go do a bit of shopping.*

"Shopping?" he asked, allowing me to escape his
lap. "More presents?"

"More presents. But this time, I think, we'll get me
some. And I need to call my cousin. But mostly, I want
to shop."

He said nothing, but gave me a long look as I left the
trailer.

"I don't know why, but I feel kind of sad," Fran said
softly as, several hours later, we stood before the swirly
portal.

"He made his choice," Ben told her, giving her a
squeeze.

"Yes, but it seems kind of sad that he's going to give
up his home just to stay here. I mean, I totally understand, because now is much nicer than three hundred
years ago, and of course, he has Io and you and Imogen
and everything, but it still seems kind of a shame."

I set down the large carrier bag that held a bit of
shopping we'd done before the shops all closed. We'd
come straight to the clearing from my shopping spree,
stopping only long enough to pick up Nikola's children
and brother before heading for the portal.

I stared at the swirling smoke as it twirled and

twined around on itself, marveling once again that such an ethereal thing could work such miracles.

And be the tool of unspeakable horrors.

"This portal is going to be destroyed," I said loudly, my eyes on Rolf. He was extremely grumpy, having been woken up from where he was sleeping in Imogen's trailer, Finnvid having remained behind to guard him. "Your demon lord buddy won't be able to use it to do squat."

"You woke me up for this?" he asked, his voice shrill in the night air. "You dragged me out of a warm bed to be shown this portal? I have already seen it, woman!"

"I just want to make sure that you understand that it's not going to be functioning anymore. No one will be able to go through it. You got that?"

He said something in German that I suspected was very rude. Nikola gave a start, and answered back in a manner that had Rolf sniffing to himself and wrapping the blanket he held tightly around him.

So you think all I have to do is focus on this portal, and will it destroyed?

I believe if you focus all your attention on that, yes, you will be able to seal it forever.

I looked deeply into his eyes. *I love you, Baron Nikola. I'm going to expect you to marry me.*

So you can be a baroness?

So I can be your baroness.

We will do so immediately, then. "Imogen, Io has proposed marriage to me, and I have accepted. You will enjoy witnessing our marriage ceremony."

I laughed out loud. "You aren't supposed to tell people I proposed to you, you big oaf." I moved around the portal to hug Imogen, who was offering her congratulations. "I was wrong about your father. I am madly in love with him, even though I just know he's going to tell everyone that I proposed to him. Despite that, I will make him very, very happy. I promise."

"I think that you already do," she said, giving me a kiss on the cheek.

I hugged Fran, as well, since she was standing next to Imogen. "And I forgive you for being mean to my future husband."

"Mean? Me?" She giggled. "I would never!"

I laughed with her, passing Ben and the two Vikings, stopping at Finnvid, who stood with one hand on Rolf. "My name is Iolanthe," I told the former, giving him a little hug, too. "Note the consonants in it. Just don't name a girl Yolanda, OK? Rolf. You know, I can't think of a life more annoying than having it filled with you. So I think I'm going to take pity on everyone."

I smiled at the startled look on his face, and ignored the warning voice in my head. *Io, what are you about?*

Before Rolf could do more than sputter a profanity, I grabbed him by his shirt and, using the one move I could remember from my self-defense class, spun him around, directly at the portal. He gave a shriek, his arms cartwheeling wildly, and then all was quiet.

"Sweetling," Nikola said, shaking his head as he strolled over to me. "I know you disliked him, but now we will not be able to keep an eye on him."

I licked the tip of his nose before wrapping my arms around his waist. "I want you to be happy, too, you know. It matters more to me than anything. More even than showing you just how fabulous the future can be.

I love you so much, I'm willing to sacrifice even my need for toilet paper."

He didn't expect it, not at all, and for that, I was grateful. Because if he knew in advance that I was going to flip him over my hip, right into the portal, and follow him through a second later, he would have made a big deal about it.

"And it's not a big deal," I told him half a day later, when we woke up to find ourselves lying in the afternoon shade of the trees. "I knew that, in the end, I wasn't going to be happy unless you were happy, and besides, I did come prepared this time."

"If you're going to continue to make sheep's eyes at him, I shall leave," Rolf said. He'd been bitching ever since we'd woken up about ten minutes before, complaining nonstop that I had ruined his life. He had watched with acid comments when I—with Nikola's advice—managed to disperse the swirly portal until nothing more remained of it but a memory. "It's enough to make my stomach sour. Nikola, I shall be raiding your cellar, and expect to hear no chastisement later."

"You are welcome to whatever you can drink," Nikola said as Rolf staggered off into the woods, still complaining about his ill-treatment.

Nikola shook his head, and looked at the carrier bag I'd grabbed before throwing myself through the portal. "Did you bring your presents?"

"Yes. A laptop for us to play on." I pulled out a small black laptop. "You're going to have to rig up some way to recharge the battery, but I figure that'll be a good project to keep you busy for a while. And the same goes for powering my hair dryer."

He looked at the pink dryer I laid on top of the laptop. "You will need to explain electricity in more detail, then."

"I'll do my best. I got an encyclopedia on DVD for the laptop, so that should help with the parts I don't know. And then there's—"

"Toilet paper," he said, nodding at the large package I set to the side. "I understand it is important to you, but, Io, I did not mean for you to sacrifice your happiness for mine. I was content to stay in your time and learn all that there was to learn."

"Silly man," I told him, leaning over to kiss him. "Content isn't good enough. I want you ecstatically happy."

He fell backward, pulling me down on top of him, his hands busily sliding up my skirt so that he could stroke my thighs. "I am always ecstatic where you are concerned. As Rolf has gone, and the portal is no more, I will allow you to seduce me here in the Zauberwald, but then we will discuss your heedless actions, and how you must learn that I am master in my home, and your place therein."

"Oooh, getting all bossy with me, are you?" I murmured, kissing a line down his chest as I unbuttoned his shirt, my fingers and mouth going wild on all the exposed flesh.

"Yes. I am a dominant man, Iolanthe. You may not have noticed this about me—arms up, please; thank you—but I am, and I expect that since you made your choice to live with me at my home, a choice that I would have preferred we discuss before you made such a large sacrifice, but as you have made that choice, then I expect you will abide by my rules."

Too many words, I said, wriggling as he peeled off my shirt and bra, his fingers gently stroking my bare breasts. I paused for a moment, looking down at him, noting the deep sapphire blue of his eyes. "I made a sacrifice. Did you—"

"Yes," he said, pulling me down so my breast was at his mouth. *I have my soul back. And for that, my love, as for everything else about you, I will be eternally grateful.*

I do so love it when you get mushy on me, I said, squirming with happiness as he laved his tongue along a very sensitive nipple.

"Then I shall mush for you any time you like. Would you remove my breeches, please? But be careful, they are the only ones I have, and I wish to preserve the silken undergarment that keeps my testicles safe from the toothed apparatus."

"It's called a zipper, and I have good news." I pulled off his shoes and socks, and helped him out of his jeans and underwear before grabbing the carrier bag. "When you were with Ben and Finnvid trying to calm Rolf down, I picked up a few more undies for you. See? All sorts of colors."

He looked at the rainbow of silk material I splayed across his belly, his penis happily waving at me as he touched first one, then another of the underwear. "Presents?"

"Yes, my darling, presents. For you. I bet if we're careful, we can make them last a very long time. And then when they wear out, we'll make a pattern from one, and have some more made up for—Nikola!"

He didn't give me any warning, just pulled me over his body, and impaled me, the silk underwear beneath my thighs as his fingers dug into my hips, urging me on.

It didn't take long for me to give in to the pleasure that I knew I'd always find with him. He murmured words of love that filled me with so much joy, it threatened to spill out over me, drowning us both. And when he pulled me tighter, his mouth finding the sensitive flesh of my neck, I braced myself for that fraction of a second when he bit deeply, taking what only I could give him, and returning it with love.

It was heaven. And no matter how much I might miss the conveniences of my former life, I knew that this new one would be infinitely better.

Subject: Um . . .
From: Ihaveconsonants@andrascastle.com
To: Benedikt.Czerny@gothfaire.com
CC: Imogen@gothfaire.com
CC: Francesca.Czerny@gothfaire.com

Hey guys, guess what? We found another portal!

"And I said to her, Look, you don't own me, okay? Yes, we have incredibly hot sex, but there's more to a relationship than just that. And she said that she just wanted to be with me, and couldn't live without me, and all sorts of things like that. Don't get me wrong. It's nice to have your girlfriend want you and all, but there's such a thing as stifling someone! There are times when I think you're so lucky, Fran. You have no idea what it's like to be in a relationship that's doomed from the very start."

I stared blankly at the sidewalk, my heart contracting at Geoff's words. She was a remarkably pretty girl despite her masculine name (she said her parents didn't believe in conforming to traditional gender roles), with shoulder-length black hair and cute freckles. Although we'd been roomies for almost a year, I was still a bit startled by her lack of awareness.

"You tell your boyfriend you want some space, and poof! He gives you space. You see him, what, once a year? And the rest of the time he leaves you alone to do whatever you want. Now that's a mature relationship. Do you have a couple of bucks I can borrow? I don't get paid until Friday."

"He's not really my boyfriend." I reached into my jeans pocket for my Starbucks card, handing it to her as she stopped at the walk-up latte window and ordered a latte and an Americano.

"Thanks, Fran. You're a doll. What were we talking about? Oh, your boyfriend. You're so lucky with him."

"He's just a guy I know. Used to know."

"Your setup is perfect," Geoff said with blithe disregard. "He's in Europe, and you're here, doing your own thing. No one on your back all the time, telling you what to do. No one demanding that you stop what you're doing to pay attention to her. No one pressuring you with drama queen scenes, saying she will die if you're not right there for her. I envy you, Fran. I really do."

I accepted the latte she handed me, following as she led the way down the street toward the old redbrick building where we shared a third-floor apartment, each step causing my soul to cry a little more. I ached to tell her the truth, but had decided when I first met her that she would never understand. Her feet were too firmly planted in the everyday world. How could I explain that my former boyfriend was a vampire?

"I told Carmen that I needed a little space, too, but you know what she did? Started cutting herself." Geoff's cell phone burbled. She pulled it out as she continued to talk. "Like I don't have enough of my own emotional issues that I have to deal with hers, too? Do you have any idea what a stress it is to be bisexual these days? My therapist says I'm just asking for trouble, but what does she know? Oh, great, it's the drama queen again. This is like the fiftieth time she's texted me today. I had to turn off my phone in surgery because she wouldn't stop sending me messages, and Dr. Abbot said she was going to end up pulling some poor dog's tooth instead of cleaning it if my phone made her jump just one more time."

I murmured something noncommittal.

We stopped in front of the residents' door at the side of the building. The first floor was taken up by a bookstore, one of my favorite places to spend time. "My hands are full, Fran. Can you get your keys?"

I set my latte on the large metal mailbox that was attached to the building and hunted through the backpack I used as a bag for my keys, my fingers groping blindly in its depths.

"I tell you, if I could, I'd trade Carmen for your Brent any day."

"Ben," I corrected, his name bringing another little zap of pain to my chest. "He's not mine. You can have him."

"He's like the ideal man, leaving you alone except for when you want him. If I was into guys as much as girls—and I'm not because some men are okay, but most of them have way too many issues for me—then I'd definitely give you a run for your money with him. But I'm not, so you don't have to worry."

"That's reassuring," I murmured, the tiniest of smiles making an appearance as I pulled out a couple of paperbacks in order to grope around the bottom of my backpack. If there was one thing I knew about Ben, it was that he wasn't looking for another woman.

At least I didn't think he was. I frowned, thinking about the last time I'd spoken to him. It was the last and biggest in a series of arguments, and he'd sounded so distant and cold. . . .

"I'm loyal that way. It's one of the reasons why we're

such good roomies. Because seriously, there are some weirdos out there you can get stuck with. And you're just as normal as they come." She glanced toward my hands. "Well, almost as normal as they come. But you know, hey, everyone has their little quirks, right? And I can definitely put up with you being a tiny bit paranoid about germs and insisting on wearing latex gloves all the time. It doesn't bother me at all. It's probably good, actually, given all the colds and flus that go around nowadays, and if you want to look like a goth by wearing black lace gloves over the latex ones ... Well, that's no big deal, either. My last roomie was into that Lolita crap, and you looking a bit gothy is a big improvement on that, let me tell you! Although you don't really look goth anymore since you cut your hair and dyed it auburn—"

I frowned harder into the blackness of my bag, still not finding my keys, so frustrated by that fact, it took me a few seconds to realize that Geoff wasn't talking anymore. I looked around, my eyes opening in surprise as a large man in black overalls shoved Geoff into a van.

"Goddess!" I yelled, dropping my backpack to run toward them. "Stop that! Help! Someone help! My friend is being kidnapped!"

"Mmrph!" Geoff said, the man's hand over her mouth. Her eyes were filled with panic as she struggled. A second man was in the back of the van, grabbing her legs as she tried to kick the first guy.

"Help!" I screamed again, but the street, normally filled with shoppers, was strangely devoid of anyone else. It was up to me to save Geoff. Without thinking, I leaped forward as the driver of the van gunned the engine, throwing myself into the back of the van on top of Geoff and the first man, who was in the process of slamming shut the door.

"Let go of her," I growled, curling my fingers into a

fist the way Ben had showed me all those years ago. "Or you're going to be really, really sorry!"

"You'll be the one who is sorry," the man said in a heavy Scandinavian accent, his eyes holding a red light that warned me he wasn't a common, average kidnapper. "The master seeks this one. Begone."

Before I could land the punch I was about to make, the man threw his weight against me, sending me flying backward. Frantic to keep from falling, I grabbed at him, but it did little good. All I got was a necklace the man had been wearing before I tumbled out of the van, hitting the street hard enough to knock me silly for a few seconds. When I looked up, trying desperately to clear my vision, the street was empty.

"The master," I repeated, getting painfully to my feet and hobbling over to the sidewalk. I'd heard someone refer to the master five years ago. "Oh, no, it couldn't be him. What on earth does he want with Geoff? It's me he swore to get revenge against!"

I looked down at the necklace in my hand. Because of my gloves, I couldn't feel anything other than the weight of the gold chain. I should have called the police and reported an abduction. I should have screamed until someone came to help me. I should have let someone with power get Geoff back. I should have ...

"Bloody boiling bullfrogs!" I snarled, ripping off one of my black lace gloves and the thin latex glove beneath it, taking a deep breath. If it really was who I thought it was behind the kidnapping, the police wouldn't be able to help at all, which meant it was up to me to find out who was behind the abduction of Geoff.

The second my bare hand touched the chain, my head was filled with images, a variety of faces that I didn't recognize, a confusing jumble of women in old-fashioned outfits with bodices and long skirts, of men riding horses across a coastline, waving swords and yelling at the top of their lungs, and of a big structure burning while screams ripped into the night.

"And if that doesn't say Loki at work a millennium ago, then I don't know what does," I growled a minute later, stuffing the necklace into my pocket as I pulled on my gloves again, hurrying down the road to a busy cross street. I hesitated at the bus stop, knowing time was of the essence. If the emotions I'd felt on the kidnapper's necklace were right—and I had no reason to doubt my psychometric abilities—then he and his buddies were planning on hustling Geoff to the airport in a few hours. I had little time to make it to the warehouse they were using before she was out of my reach.

"This situation calls for a little splurging. After all, if you can't spend a little mad money when your roomie is kidnapped, when can you?" I muttered to myself as I hunted down a cab. I finally found one and gave the driver instructions on where to go. "I don't know the address, but I do know it's on Knowles Street. Big warehouse with the picture of a penguin painted on the side."

"Sounds like the old Icy Treats place," she said, punching in a couple of buttons on her laptop before pulling out into traffic. "Shouldn't take us long to get there."

Fifteen minutes later we pulled up a half block away. I looked at the warehouse, worried that we were too late, but no, there was the nose of a black van just barely visible from behind an industrial-sized trash bin. I glanced back at the cab, gnawing on my lower lip for a second. "Um . . . how much would it cost for you to wait here for me?"

"How long will you be?" the driver asked me. She had bright yellow hair—not blond, actual yellow—and so many piercings on her head I couldn't count them all.

"I don't know. Maybe ten minutes?"

She named a figure. "But you'll have to pay me what you owe me now. I'm not allowed to let customers leave without paying."

I flinched at the amount she mentioned, but gave a mental shrug as I pulled out some cash, thrusting it toward her. "Wait for me. I'll be as quick as I can."

"Ten minutes. After that, I leave," she said, getting out of her cab to lean a hip against it. "I need a smoke anyway."

I nodded and hurried behind the trash bin, peering around it in the very best James Bond "sneaking up on kidnappers" manner. No one was in the van, and although the warehouse had windows, they were boarded up. I prayed they had no sort of high-tech security system as I dashed to a small door along the wall, pausing to snatch up a big piece of metal pipe that was lying near the trash bin. I weighed it for a couple of seconds, trying to decide if I could actually bring myself to use it, but the memory of the stark horror in Geoff's eyes had me clutching it tight. "You are going to be one sorry god if she's hurt," I snarled under my breath.

The door creaked a little when I opened it a few inches, making me flinch and hold my breath, but no sound emerged from the warehouse, and nothing met my gaze as I peeked in. Sending a little prayer to the god and goddess my mother always swore would always protect me, I slid inside, braced for an outcry or attack.

The warehouse was mostly empty, a huge old building filled with a whole lot of black, and a few faint rustling noises that I took to be rodents. I wasn't particularly afraid of rats and mice, finding the two-legged variety much more worrisome. But the relative quiet of the warehouse worried me. Was I too late? Had the men taken Geoff off in another car?

The faintest murmur of male voices had me stiffening as I turned to the right, where the vaguely black shape of a staircase loomed. I gripped my piece of pipe and started up the stairs, blindly feeling my way up each step, moving slowly and carefully so as not to alert anyone to my presence.

By the time I neared the top of the stairs, the sounds of voices were much clearer. I flattened myself against the steps and eased up my head to see how many of them there were. In a small oval pool of bluish white light, three men stood around another person, who had been tied to a chair.

Three against one. Not very good odds. But I wasn't about to let Loki take my roomie. With another deep breath, I lifted my pipe and flung myself up the last couple of stairs, yelling a one-word spell of protection that my mother had insisted I learn. *"Salvatio!"*

The first man dropped before I even realized that I had swung my pipe at his head.

"Oh my god!" Geoff screamed as I stood stunned for a second, staring down at the man lying at my feet. "That was awesome!"

The two other men clearly couldn't believe it, either, because they stared at their fallen buddy for a couple of seconds before turning identical expressions of surprise on me.

That didn't last long. The one who had shoved me out of the van yelled something in a Nordic language and ran for me.

"I can't believe I'm doing this," I told him as I swung my pipe and sidestepped him, the pipe connecting with the back of his head with a metallic clang that made my stomach turn over. "I'm not at all a brave person. I don't beat people up. Ever. Well, okay, maybe a demon or two, but they aren't real people."

"The master will have your life for this," the third guy said as he slammed me up against a wall.

"Get him! Smash him! Beat his brains in!" Geoff chanted from her chair, the scrape of wood against the floor audible as she chair-hopped over to us.

"Eep," I managed to squeak out, trying to crack the man on the head with my pipe, but he had wised up after watching his two buddies drop and held my arm straight out at my side. His fingers started to tighten around my neck, causing black splotches to dance in front of my face. "Tell your master that he can't have Geoff. If he wants to get tough, he'll have to face me, and the last time he did that, it didn't end well for him."

The man stopped strangling me for a second, a look of confusion filling his eyes. "Who are you?" he asked.

The chair screeched against the floor.

I twisted my body, bringing my knee up to nail the guy in the noogies, biting his arm at the same time. He cursed profanely, dropping to his knees as I raised my pipe high over my head. "My name is Francesca Ghetti, the keeper of the Vikingahärta, and Loki's worst nightmare!"

"You go, Fran!" Geoff cheered as I stood over the kidnapper.

Her words brought some sanity back to me. I was panting, the blood rushing in my ears, my heart beating wildly. I looked down on the man for a second, toying with the thought of braining him, too, but instead I just stomped on his foot hard enough to make him yelp, and jumped over his halfhearted attempt to grab me.

"There's an X-Acto knife over there," Geoff said, nodding toward a rickety table half hidden by shadows. "I've been watching it for the last ten minutes, trying to figure out how I could get to it. Oh no, you don't, Buster Brown."

As I snatched up the knife, Geoff kicked at the kidnapper, who was just getting to his feet. He howled as she hit him dead center in his groin.

"Oh, that has to hurt," I murmured as I bent over

her, cutting through the nylon cord that bound her to the chair. "Poor guy isn't going to have kids after this."

"Poor guy? Are you insane? He's a kidnapper! You sure you don't want to smash his brains in?" Geoff asked when her bonds fell to the ground. She rubbed her wrists, glaring down at the writhing man. One of the others started to moan and move his arms and legs.

"I'm sure. Let's get out of here before the other two wake up."

"Okay, but you know, no one would blame you for roughing them up a little. . . ."

We made it outside before the groin man started down the stairs (hunched over quite a bit). I didn't stop to explain to Geoff, just grabbed her arm and hauled her after me to where the cabby was just getting back in her car. "Take us to 1021 Woodline Avenue," I told the cabby, shoving Geoff in the car. I glanced back at the warehouse, adding, "And hurry, please."

The door to the warehouse was flung open, and two men staggered out. I was relieved to see that I hadn't done any permanent damage to them, and hoped the third wasn't seriously hurt. The cabby eyed them for a moment, then met my gaze in the rearview mirror. "You in some sort of trouble?"

"No. Someone else is going to be, though," I said grimly.

"Gotcha." She gunned the engine and pulled a very illegal U-turn, the shouts of the guys faintly following us as we zipped down the road.

I leaned back against the seat, letting go of my breath.

"You want to tell me what all that was about?" Geoff asked, examining her wrists.

"Er . . . not really."

"They thought I was you, you know," she said, eyeing me carefully.

"They what?"

She nodded. "They called me Francesca. I guess it's because I copied your haircut before you cut yours. They said the master wanted to see you, and they were going to take me to him. What the hell is going on, Fran? Who were those goons? And why would they want to kidnap you to take you to some bondage dude? Or wait—*was* it a kidnapping?"

"Bondage dude?" I asked, confused how she leaped from Loki to that.

"Master, remember? What else is that if not bondage?" She eyed me again. "You know, I had no idea you were into that sort of thing. I'm not, myself, but I have friends who run a little club in town—"

I held up my hand to stop her. "I'm not into bondage. The master in this instance isn't into bondage, either. At least I don't think he is. He's an old man. A really old man." Like a couple of thousand years, at least. "He's . . . uh . . ."

She raised an eyebrow as I thought frantically of what to tell her. Almost a year of living with her had made me very well aware that she freaked out at anything even remotely supernatural. There was no way she wouldn't do the same if I told her the old Norse gods were alive and well and after revenge.

At least one of them was.

"He's what?" she asked, prodding me.

"He's . . ." My shoulders slumped. "He's into bondage."

"I knew it! I knew there was more to you than just a germ fetish! So this was what, a fantasy setup? Wow, that's really wild. I'll give you Mistress Dominica's number later, if you like, although if you have your own connection, you probably won't care too much. Are you a bottom or a top?"

I blinked at her. "Eh . . ."

"Bottom. I knew it. I'm a top, myself, but as I told you when I moved in, you don't have to worry that I'm going to try to seduce you." She smiled at the cabdriver's startled glance in the mirror. "I have to give it to you guys—that was a hell of a kidnapping fantasy. I guess I won't be siccing Daddy's lawyers on the guys if they were your friends, although I have to say I thought they were a bit rough, especially when that one guy slammed you up against the wall. Unless, of course, you like that." She gave me a considering look.

I smiled feebly, and spent the remainder of the ride wondering why the vengeful Norse god Loki would pick now to pop back up in my life.